'Readers will be highly amused, very satisfied, and eager
for the next Argeneau tale'
Booklist

'With its whip-smart dialogue and sassy characters,
Love Bites . . . is a great romantic comedy worth tasting'
Romance Reviews Today

SINGLE WHITE VAMPIRE

'A cheeky, madcap tale . . . vampire lovers will find
themselves laughing throughout'
Publishers Weekly

'*Single White Vampire* is a wonderfully funny, fast-moving
story that's an absolute delight to read . . . Fans of humorous
romance won't want to miss this one, even if vampires aren't
their cup of tea'
Romantic Times BOOKreviews

TALL, DARK & HUNGRY

'Delightful and full of interesting characters and romance'
Romantic Times BOOKreviews

'*Tall, Dark & Hungry* takes us on an heartwarming journey of
healing hearts and sizzling attraction as Bastien and Terri race
through New York and around the world in search of love'
A Romance Review

The Argeneau Vampire series by Lynsay Sands:

Love Bites

Single White Vampire

Tall, Dark & Hungry

A Quick Bite

A Bite to Remember

Bite Me if you Can

The Accidental Vampire

Vampires Are Forever

Vampire Interrupted

The Rogue Hunter

The Immortal Hunter

The Renegade Hunter

Tall, Dark and Hungry

LYNSAY SANDS

First published in Great Britain in 2010 by
Gollancz
An imprint of the Orion Publishing Group
Orion House, 5 Upper St Martin's Lane, London WC2H 9EA
An Hachette UK Company

5 7 9 10 8 6 4

A CIP catalogue record for this book is available
from the British Library

ISBN 978 0 575 09384 3

Typeset by carrstudio.co.uk

Printed in Great Britain by
Clays Ltd, St Ives plc

www.lynsaysands.net

www.orionbooks.co.uk

The Orion Publishing Group's policy is to use papers that are
natural, renewable and recyclable products and made from wood
grown in sustainable forests. The logging and manufacturing
processes are expected to conform to the environmental regulations
of the country of origin.

Tall, Dark and Hungry

For David

Chapter One

"The chicken's very good."

Bastien watched with amusement as Kate C. Leever scraped up a forkful of the *Poulet au Citron* she'd ordered and held it to his brother Lucern's lips. He was even more amused when his brother opened his mouth to accept the bite of food, murmured in appreciation, then chewed and swallowed.

He hadn't seen Lucern do more than pretend to eat in his whole life. By the time Bastien was born, his brother—already two hundred plus years old—had tired of even gourmet fare. The taste of food began to pall after a hundred or so years of feasting on whatever you wanted. Now, having passed his four hundredth birthday, Bastien himself found eating to be nothing more than a nuisance, something he forced himself to do occasionally at board meetings or dinner parties to prevent discovery of his true nature.

"It really is good," Lucern announced. "Everything's a little new and different nowadays."

"No," Bastien disagreed. "It probably tastes much the same as it always did. It's *love* that's reawakened your taste buds and rejuvenated your desire for food."

Lucern shrugged. He seemed not at all upset by the teasing emphasis Bastien put on the word, and he had no trouble admitting his deep and abiding feelings for the woman seated beside him. "Perhaps. Everything does seem more vibrant and interesting now. I find myself seeing things anew, seeing them as Kate must see them, rather than with the jaundiced eye I've cast over everything for ages. It makes a nice change."

Bastien said nothing, merely lifted his glass of wine. But as he took a sip, Lucern's words caused something of a twinge inside him. Were he to examine it, he might have likened it to envy. But Bastien wasn't prepared to examine it. There was no time for love or even loneliness in his life; he had too many responsibilities. Bastien had always been responsible. When his father died, it had been Bastien who stepped up to take over the duties of the family business. It was in his nature. Bastien's life was made up of taking care of each individual crisis that came along, whether in business or within the family. If there was a problem, Bastien was the man everyone looked to for the solution, and that was how it had been even before his father's death. Bastien had often run the business and made decisions in his father's stead over the last several hundred years since Jean-Claude Argeneau had developed the drinking problem that saw him burn to death: one of the very few ways their kind could die.

"So, Bastien."

His eyes narrowed at Kate's tone. He had known her long enough to recognize the *we're-about-to-tackle-something-unpleasant, but-it-needs-to-be-done* voice. He'd heard it often enough, but always directed at Lucern. It was unusual to hear with his own name in the mix.

"We invited you out to lunch for a reason."

Bastien raised his eyebrows. He'd suspected as much when Lucern called and invited him to meet here at La Bonne Soupe for this meal. His brother knew he wasn't much into eating anymore. That being the case, Bastien had suspected this sudden invitation might have something to do with the couple's upcoming nuptials, but he wasn't sure what specifically his brother could want.

The wedding was in exactly two weeks. It was here in New York, which had seemed the most likely choice for the ceremony as Kate, and now Lucern too, lived and worked here. The oldest Argeneau son had made the move to Manhattan six months earlier to be closer to his fiancée, who also happened to be his editor. It had seemed a good idea for him to be near while she made the necessary adjustments to her *turning*. Aside from the physical changes, becoming one of their kind meant learning a whole new range of habits and skills, so Lucern had made the move to New York to help her with those, as well as to help with the wedding arrangements. Fortunately, being a successful author allowed him the freedom to make such a move with little difficulty.

Bastien had to admit that New York was the best place to hold the ceremony and celebration. While neither family lived here—the Argeneaus were based in Toronto, and the Leevers, Kate's family, lived in Michigan—all her friends and coworkers were in New York. And, as this was where Kate—as well as Lucern now—lived and worked, it made it easier for them to make the necessary arrangements for the wedding.

Luc had originally intended on occupying the penthouse suite above the New York offices of Argeneau Enterprises until the wedding, but after moving his things into the apartment that first night, he had gone to visit Kate and simply stayed. By the time Bastien fled Toronto—and his mother's matchmaking efforts there—to work out of the Manhattan offices, Lucern had already moved most of his things into Kate's tiny apartment, and Bastien had the penthouse to himself. As usual. He rather preferred it that way, and wasn't looking forward to the temporary invasion of guests and family that the wedding would bring. However, he consoled himself that it would only be for a weekend; then he would have his blessed peace again, and no interference from his mother.

He shook his head at the thought of Marguerite's latest antics. She had always been involved in her children's lives, eager to see them happy, but her latest stunt had shocked even him. Bastien was the last of her children to remain single, and the woman was determined to see him settled in a loving relationship like his brothers and sister. That was understandable, he supposed, but her way of getting it done was madness. His sister Lissianna and her psychologist husband, Greg, had worked out so well, Marguerite had decided to round up a female psychologist for Bastien in the hope that he would fall in love with her. The silly woman had made appointments with every female psychologist in Toronto, ferreted out the single ones, chosen those she liked best and thought he might like, then had announced she was a vampire and put the thought into their heads that they should request to speak to a family member about her "delusions." Bastien had spent weeks running around Toronto, going from psychologist to psychologist, clearing memories and ensuring that no damage resulted from her stunt. Then he'd escaped to New York to avoid getting caught in any more of her madcap schemes.

Yes, his mother was going off her rocker with nothing to occupy herself. He hoped Lissianna's recently announced pregnancy would prove a distraction. Bastien didn't mind the idea of settling down and having someone to share his life with, like his siblings had, but he wasn't holding his breath waiting for it to happen. He'd been alone so long, he began to wonder if it would ever be otherwise. Perhaps Josephine had been his one hope at happiness.

Unwilling to contemplate the memory of the human woman he had loved and lost, Bastien glanced between Lucern and Kate. "So, what is this favor you want?"

The couple exchanged a glance, then Lucern said, "You should have ordered something to eat, brother. It's on me."

Bastien was vaguely amused at the stalling tactic. Much like himself, his brother hated to ask for anything. "It must be a big favor if you're willing to spring for lunch," he teased.

"You make me sound cheap," Lucern said with a scowl.

"You are. Or were," he allowed. "Though you appear to have improved since Kate's arrival in your life. She's managed to make you loosen the purse strings somewhat. There was a time you wouldn't even consider living in a city as expensive as New York."

Luc shrugged. "She's here," he said simply.

"Actually, I'm the one who needs the favor," Kate announced.

"Oh?" Bastien turned to her with interest. He liked his soon-to-be sister-in-law. She was perfect for Luc. His brother was lucky to have found her.

"Yes. My best friend, Terri—well, she's my cousin, really. Well, she's both, cousin and best friend, but—"

"This would be your maid of honor?" Bastien interrupted patiently.

"Yes!" She beamed at him, apparently pleased that he recognized the name. But it shouldn't have surprised her; Bastien was good with details. Besides, the woman was the maid of honor and he was best man. As such, they would be paired off and stuck together for the whole of the upcoming wedding. Of course he recalled!

"What about her?" he asked as Kate continued to smile in silence. When she hesitated, he prodded, "Is she arriving at the same time as everyone else, or a day or two early?"

"Actually, she's coming *two weeks* early," Kate admitted. "She had vacation time coming to her and took it all in one large lump to fly over here and help with the wedding."

"It's a good thing, too," Lucern muttered, then admitted, "We can use all the help we can get. You wouldn't believe how complicated weddings are, Bastien. First the date has to be picked, the hall reserved, and the invitations chosen and sent. Then there is the caterer to be chosen, the meals decided on, what wine to serve, the flowers to use and in what arrangements, the music in the church, whether you'll have a band or a d.j. at the reception, and what music to play there. The colors have to be picked and coordinated so that the decorations, flowers, tuxedos, and dresses can be chosen and so on." He shook his head. "It's a wonder couples survive all of that and make it to the wedding still together. Take my advice: If you ever find a mate, skip the wedding nonsense and fly to Vegas."

"Skip the wedding nonsense and fly to Vegas?" Kate echoed in disbelief.

"Oh, now, Kate, honey, you know I didn't mean—," Luc began backpedaling in earnest.

"I gather weddings are a pain to arrange, but surely the worst of it is out of the way?" Bastien queried, trying to save his brother from the wrath filling his fiancée's face.

A relieved Lucern eagerly grasped at the change of subject. "Well, yes. Most of the arrangements are made and set, but there always seems to be something cropping up that needs doing. Last week, it was making toilet paper flowers. Who knows what it will be next week?"

"Toilet-paper flowers?" Bastien asked in surprise.

"Kleenex flowers," Kate corrected, sounding irritable. "We made them out of Kleenex facial tissues."

"Yes," Lucern said agreeably, then turned to explain to Bastien: "She had me folding and tying all these bloody toilet tissues, then fanning them into flowers to put on the cars for the wedding party. I told her we should have someone else do them, or just buy them, but she insisted that making them was tradition in her family. Bought flowers wouldn't do, so I spent hours and hours last week just folding and tying and fanning out toilet paper."

"Kleenex," Kate snapped.

"Some of them are toilet tissues," Lucern informed her.

"What?" She looked at him with horror.

"Well, I ran out of Kleenex, and you insisted on so many for the cars, I started using toilet tissue. I don't think it will make much difference. Tissue is tissue, right? Besides, you weren't there to ask. You were working late as usual." He turned to Bastien and explained, "She's been working late a lot lately, trying to do Chris's work as well as her own."

Bastien raised an eyebrow, but Kate just made a face. "I'm not doing C.K.'s work. Chris is editing his own writers, and I'm editing mine. It's just that he's going away to the California writers conference today, and I'll be fielding any emergencies that arise while he's gone. I've been trying to get ahead on my editing so that I don't fall behind if anything crops up, if you see what I mean."

Bastien nodded in understanding, then returned the conversation to the subject it had started on. "So your maid of honor is coming two weeks early. She should be arriving soon, then. Where is she staying?"

"Ah." Kate looked uncomfortable, then blew out a breath on a sigh. "Actually, that's the favor I wanted to ask," she admitted. "You see, I considered having her stay with me, but my apartment is really small. A tiny little one-bedroom is the best I can afford in Manhattan on my salary, and with Lucern there it's already quite crowded. I considered putting Terri up in a hotel. Luc even offered to pay for it, but I know she would refuse and insist on paying for herself. And what with all the expense she's already going to as my maid of honor, I didn't want to burden her any more than necessary. She really can't afford this, but she wouldn't say so."

"Proud?" Bastien guessed.

"Yes. Very. Her mother was a single parent, and Terri has been taking care of herself since Aunt Maggie died when she was nineteen. She's stubborn and has trouble asking for, or accepting, help."

Bastien nodded. He understood pride. He had a good deal of it himself. Too much, perhaps, at times. "You want me to put her up in the penthouse," he guessed.

"Yes. If you wouldn't mind," Kate admitted, looking hopeful.

Bastien smiled indulgently. His brother's fiancée made the request as if it were a huge imposition. Which it wasn't. The penthouse had five bedrooms and was huge. He also wasn't there very much, and would probably never even see the girl. He'd leave Terri in the housekeeper's capable hands; she wouldn't be any bother to him at all.

9

"That isn't a problem, Kate. She's welcome to one of the rooms in the penthouse. When is she arriving? Sometime this weekend, I should imagine, if she's coming two weeks early."

"Yes." Kate exchanged another glance with Lucern before admitting, "She arrives today, actually."

"Today?" Bastien didn't bother hiding his surprise.

"I know. It's very short notice, and I'm sorry. I would have asked sooner if I'd known. Originally, she was supposed to come the day before the wedding like everyone else. But Terri decided to surprise me and took the time off. I only found out an hour ago, because it apparently occurred to her that she'd better be sure I was home and she wouldn't be left sitting on my doorstep for a couple of days or something, so she called me from the plane."

"Well, it's a good thing she did," Bastien commented, then noticed another exchange of glances between the pair, and narrowed his eyes. It was obvious there was more to this favor than Kate's maid of honor staying with him. It suddenly struck him: "I suppose she needs a lift from the airport?"

"Well, she was going to take a taxi, but you know how expensive that is, and she really—"

"Can't afford it, but is too proud to say so, and you know she wouldn't take the money from you if you offered it, so you insisted you'd have someone pick her up," Bastien finished for her.

Katie narrowed her eyes. "Are you reading my mind?"

"No," he assured her. "Just a lucky guess."

10

"Oh." She relaxed. "You guessed right. Would it be too much bother?"

Bastien's gaze slid to his brother, and Kate added, "Lucern can go with you, of course. He offered to do it himself, but he doesn't know the highways as well as you do, or the airports or where to go. I would have gone myself, but I'm so swamped at work right now, I—"

"Luc and I will collect her," Bastien assured her, smiling at Kate's diplomatic excuse. Lucern didn't need to know the roads; he could have taken one of the family's company cars, with a driver. The truth was, Lucern was still somewhat antisocial. He wasn't as bad as he used to be, but he was still a touch awkward in social situations, and Bastien suspected Kate was afraid that he would greet her cousin and best friend with a grunt of "Follow me," then remain silent all the way into town. Bastien, on the other hand, dealt with humans all the time and was a little more social. He also—luckily enough for Kate, and for the as yet unseen Terri—happened to have a light afternoon at the office. It wouldn't be a problem taking time off.

"Great," Lucern said dryly. "Has it occurred to you, Katie my love, that you are sending two men, who haven't a clue what your cousin and best friend in the whole world looks like, to collect her? How will we spot her?"

"You can make up a sign with her name on it," Kate suggested brightly. "And between the two of you, I *know* you'll find and deliver her safely."

Bastien took in his brother's doubtful expression with amusement. There had been a definite warning to Kate's words: *Bring her back safe, or else.*

"Darn, I have to go. We have a production meeting this afternoon. That's why I couldn't get out of work to pick her up myself," Kate explained, getting to her feet. She bent to kiss Lucern, started to straighten, then bent to press another kiss to his lips. It ended with a sighed "I love you, Luc."

"And I love you, Kate," Lucern replied. His tongue slid out to lick quickly across her lower lip, and in the next moment, the two lovers were kissing again.

Bastien sighed and directed his gaze to the diners around them. He knew from experience that there would now be several more moments of soft sighs and kisses before Kate would tear herself away. The pair was pathetic. He only hoped this honeymoon phase they were enjoying passed soon. He feared not, however. It had been nearly a year since his brother Etienne had married Rachel, and two years since Lissianna and Greg's marriage; yet neither couple appeared to be passing out of this same lusty, loving phase. His whole damned family seemed to be rather slow at moving out of it. They were all equally pathetic. He was the only member of the family, aside from his mother, who didn't spend ridiculous amounts of time making out in public, private, or anywhere they found themselves. But, then, neither he nor his mother had anyone to make out with.

Bastien ignored the twinge of envy that ate at him as he heard another soft sigh from Kate, followed by a faint moan. In the next moment, his head whipped around in surprise when Kate spoke in suddenly businesslike tones.

"This might help." Kate had straightened and was digging a photo out of her purse. "It's a relatively new picture. Terri e-mailed it to me last month. Now, I have to go. *Be nice to her.*" She set the photo onto the table between them, then turned and began easing her way through the tables toward the exit of the tiny, crowded restaurant.

"God, she's wonderful," Lucern sighed as he watched Kate pause and step to the side to make room for someone entering the small eatery.

Bastien rolled his eyes, not missing the fact that his brother's gaze was fixed firmly on his fiancée's derriere. Suddenly aware that his own gaze had followed Lucern's, he gave his head a shake and turned his attention to the photo on the table. It was a picture of a woman in her late twenties. She had full lips curved in an impish smile; and large, soft eyes.

"A beauty," he commented, noting that Kate's cousin appeared to be Kate's opposite. She was brunette to Kate's blonde, and buxom and curvy in a way that made him think of ripe fruit, as opposed to Kate's slender figure. But she was stunning in her own way.

"Is she?" Lucern asked with disinterest, his gaze still following his soon-to-be wife.

"If you'd stop ogling Kate and take a look, you could see for yourself," Bastien pointed out.

Lucern turned an amused glance his way, then looked at the picture and shrugged with disinterest. "She's all right. Not as beautiful as Katie, though."

Bastien snorted. "No one is as beautiful as Katie, in your eyes."

"You're right," Lucern agreed, lifting his glass to take a swallow of whiskey before adding, "Kate's perfect in my eyes. No one comes close to her in anything."

"Forgive me, brother. But I believe the modern expression is 'You got it bad.'" Bastien gave an amused shake of his head. He liked Kate well enough, but she wasn't perfect. Damned near, perhaps, but not quite. "So? What time does this Terri person's plane get in?"

Lucern glanced at his wristwatch, shrugging. "In about an hour."

"What?" Bastien squawked.

"What, what?" Lucern asked.

"You're joking! She doesn't get in in an hour."

"Yes, she does."

Bastien stared at him blankly, then asked, "Which airport?"

"JFK."

"Dear God."

"What?" Lucern asked. He looked concerned as Bastien began scanning the tiny restaurant in search of their waitress. Of course she'd disappeared right when they wanted her, probably into the kitchen.

"You could have mentioned this before, damn it," Bastien growled. "Hell, why didn't Kate mention it? She knows it takes an hour to get to JFK. Where the hell is that waitress?"

"She probably didn't realize how late it was," Lucern

excused Kate. "Besides, she's a little distracted right now."

"Yeah? Well, it will be her fault if we're late."

"We'll make it," Lucern said soothingly as the waitress walked back out of the kitchen. Gesturing her over, he added, "Terri has to collect her luggage and go through customs anyway."

Bastien shook his head in disgust. Lucern rarely worried about anything anymore, but a couple hundred years in the business world had made him a details man. "She may have to get through customs, but we still have to get the car and drive there. Let's just hope traffic isn't particularly slow today."

Leaving Lucern to deal with the bill, Bastien took out his cellphone and called his driver. While he drove himself or took taxis at night, when he traveled during daylight Bastien always had a driver. Aside from saving the trouble of finding parking, it prevented his being out in sunlight any longer than necessary—he simply had to jog from the car to the entrance of wherever he needed to go. Not that he couldn't have stood walking a few minutes in sunlight, or even longer than that really, but it meant he would need to ingest more blood, which could be pretty inconvenient at times.

Once assured that the car was on its way, Bastien snapped the phone closed and slid it back into his pocket, then began to consider how best to handle this situation. While he used a chauffeured limo when necessary, his usual driver was on vacation and Bastien really didn't want to spend the hour-long

15

drive out to the airport watching everything he said around the replacement driver. They would have to ride back to the office to collect his car. He'd also pack some blood in a cooler to take with them in case of an emergency, Bastien decided. All of his cars had special window treatments to prevent UV rays from getting in to do any damage, but should the car break down or get a flat tire and they be forced to fix it or walk any distance in sunlight, things could get uncomfortable, or even dangerous.

All of this would take time, of course, and increase the chances that they weren't going to be on time to collect Terri, but if luck was with them and traffic wasn't slow . . .

"Traffic's slow," Lucern said a short time later.

Bastien gave a short laugh. "Of course it is. Murphy's law, right?"

Lucern grunted.

"Reach in the backseat and grab my briefcase. You'll have to make the sign."

"Won't we recognize Terri from the picture?" Lucern retrieved the case and set it on his lap.

"Maybe. But I don't want to count on that. If we miss her, Kate will kill us both."

Luc gave another grunt. He had never been big on talking. Bastien supposed that was why Kate had wanted someone else along to collect her cousin. The only time Luc seemed to talk was when she was around. It was also the only time he smiled. She brought something out of him no one else could, and which apparently retreated or dropped dead the moment she was out of sight. When Kate wasn't around, it was difficult to get more than a couple of words out of Lucern; a grunt was his response of choice.

"What do you want on it?"

Bastien glanced to the side. Not only had Lucern managed to string more than two words together, he'd pulled a large notepad and pen from the briefcase and was ready to write. "Just put her name on it."

"Right." Lucern scrawled the name Terri across the paper, then paused. "What's her last name?"

"You're asking *me*? She's *your* fiancée's cousin, not mine."

"Yeah," Luc agreed, pursing his lips thoughtfully. "Didn't Kate mention it at lunch?"

"No. Not that I recall." Bastien glanced at him. "You really don't know?"

"I can't remember."

"Well, Kate must have mentioned it a time or two over the last few months."

"Yeah." Luc was silent for a moment, then bent his head to write on the page again.

Relieved that his brother remembered, Bastien turned his attention back to traffic, then spared a glance at his watch. "If her flight isn't early and customs takes twenty minutes or so, we might just get there before she gives up and hops in a taxi. Where will she go if she doesn't find anyone waiting for her?"

"Probably Kate's office."

"Yeah. That would thrill Kate. Let's hope the flight isn't early."

It wasn't.

"Two hours late," Lucern grunted as they made

their way into the arrivals terminal. "All that rushing to get here on time, and we end up cooling our heels for two hours."

Bastien smiled faintly at his brother's disgust. They had arrived at the airport only to discover Kate's cousin's flight had made an unscheduled stop in Detroit for "mechanical difficulties," and had stayed there while something was fixed. It was due to arrive two hours late. Bastien had been concerned by the news until he had approached the airline desk to inquire and learned that the problem was with one of the bathrooms on the plane. Not that the clerk had told him that; Bastien had slipped briefly into her mind to find out. It wasn't something the airline wanted to advertise, and the mysterious "mechanical difficulties" sounded better to them than admitting one of their toilets had gone screwy. They didn't want the motto "Fly the crappy skies."

With two hours to kill until Terri's flight arrived, Bastien and Lucern had retired to a bar, having to make their way into the nearest departure terminal to find one. Now they were returning to the arrival area to await Terri, hoping as they did so that she wouldn't be held up too long at customs. Both were rather weary of waiting, and eager to get out of the airport, what with its buzz of stressed-out travelers and anxious friends and family.

"Here they come," Bastien announced. The first weary travelers began to appear beyond the blocked off area. "Where's the sign you made?"

"Oh, yes." Lucern pulled the piece of paper from his pocket. The moment it was unfolded enough for

18

Bastien to read, he snatched it incredulously out of his brother's hand.

" 'Terri, Kate's cousin and best friend?' " he read with disbelief.

"I couldn't remember her name," Lucern said with a shrug. "She'll know who it's for. Hurry and hold it up, a whole load of them are coming out and she might be one of them."

Bastien glanced toward the arch where travelers were appearing in clusters of three or four. It would seem that customs wasn't holding them up at all. "They must have worked double time to get the luggage out so fast. And customs must have extra people on."

"Hmm," was all Lucern said. Bastien raised the makeshift sign over his head to be easily seen. "They're probably rushing them through to try to make up for the delay."

The two men were silent as several dozen people arrived, were met by happy relatives or friends and departed the arrivals area. Bastien would guess that a good fifty people came and went before he spotted a woman making a beeline for them. He might not have recognized her if she weren't walking toward them with a tired smile of greeting on her face. Without realizing it, his arms relaxed, allowing his sign to lower.

The woman was just as curvy and ripe-looking as she had been in her photo, but her hairstyle had changed. It had been up in a ponytail in the photo; now, it was down and flowing around her shoulders in soft chestnut waves. She still wore jeans, Bastien noted with interest. Tight white jeans, a white University of Leeds T-shirt, and white running shoes made up her outfit. She had obviously dressed for comfort.

"Lucern!" She beamed at Bastien, pausing before him and, after the briefest hesitation, giving him a warm welcoming hug. "Kate's told me loads about you. It's a pleasure to meet the man who's made her so happy."

Bastien stared down at the top of the woman's head in surprise, his arms dropping automatically to embrace her. Lucern watched with amusement. Catching the grin on his brother's face, Bastien cleared his throat as Kate's cousin released him and stepped back. "Terri, I presume?"

She laughed at his stiff tones. "Yes, of course." Then she paused and tilted her head to examine him. "Kate was right. You must be the most handsome man in New York. She said that's how I'd recognize you," she confided with a grin.

Bastien found himself grinning back, ridiculously pleased at the compliment, until Lucern got tired of being ignored and announced, "That would be me, then. *I'm* Lucern, the most handsome man in New York. The man you just hugged is my brother Bastien.

Terri Simpson turned a startled gaze to the man who had just spoken. Perhaps an inch shorter than the man she'd just hugged, the speaker eyed her with amusement. Terri was surprised she hadn't noticed this fellow, but while he was almost a twin to the man he'd just called Bastien, he wasn't an exact copy. They had the same nose, but his lower lip wasn't quite as full as Bastien's, who also had a more defined jawline. There was also something different about the eyes. Both had large silvery blue irises, but Bastien's were deeper and filled with an indefinable emotion that called out to her.

Actually, Terri was almost relieved that the man she'd hugged wasn't Lucern. Deciding not to dwell on why, she stepped forward to hug Kate's fiancé. "My apologies, Lucern. I just spotted the sign and assumed . . ." She let the sentence trail off as she briefly embraced him, then stepped back. "You two must have been waiting here for hours. Sorry about that."

"There was nothing you could do about it," Bastien remarked, "so there is nothing to apologize for. Can I take that for you?"

Terri found herself relieved of her luggage as Bastien took the handle of her suitcase while Lucern slipped the strap of her carryon off her shoulder; then the two men ushered her out of the building. Moments later, she found herself in the front seat of a Mercedes on the highway.

"You must be exhausted after your flight."

Terri flashed a smile at the man seated beside her. Bastien. She liked the name. She liked the look of the man too. She didn't usually go for business types, but he cut a sharp figure in the no doubt designer suit he was wearing. She glanced over her shoulder at Kate's fiancé, who now sat silent in the backseat. He had a notepad out, resting on his knee, and was scribbling away on it. For the first time, she noted he wore cords

21

and a sweater. He was a writer. No need for a business suit.

"Actually, I caught a bit of a nap on the plane," she answered finally, settling back in her seat. It seemed obvious that Lucern wasn't going to do much talking. Kate had warned her that he wasn't very sociable, which was why she'd sworn to try to get his brother to accompany him to the airport. Kate hadn't mentioned that the brother was better looking, however. Terri decided she'd have to talk to Kate about leaving out such details. A little mental preparation would have been a good thing. At the moment, she felt as if she'd been kicked in the stomach. Butterflies were definitely taking wing in her tummy. "I'm more hungry than tired. I slept a little on the plane, but with the delay and everything it's been a while since the flight meal was served."

"We'll take care of that as soon as we get you to the penthouse," Bastien said, his gaze finding her briefly before returning to the highway traffic. "My housekeeper is an excellent cook, and will no doubt be grateful for the chance to prove it."

"I take it you don't eat in much?" she asked.

"What makes you say that?"

Terri raised her eyebrows at his sharp tone, then merely shrugged. "If you ate in a lot, and had lots of dinner parties and such, your housekeeper wouldn't be grateful for the chance to cook for someone."

"Oh, yes. Of course." His frown became a wry smile.

"Am I waiting for Kate at your place, then?" Terri

asked. She was made curious by the surprise that covered Bastien's face. When he glanced in the rearview mirror, Terri turned to peer at the other passenger in the car, but Lucern apparently wasn't listening; he was still scribbling busily away in his notepad. She turned back in time to see Bastien scowl, then he glanced at her and sighed.

"Kate didn't tell you?"

"Tell me what?"

"You'll be staying at the penthouse. Her apartment is too small for the three of you."

"Three of us?" she asked in surprise.

"You, Kate, and Lucern."

"Oh, of course!" It hadn't occurred to her that Lucern might have moved right in with her, but if the two were as in love as Kate said, Terri supposed it was to be expected. He would hardly want to stay in Toronto while she was here in New York, and fortunately his work allowed him to move as he liked. Of course he would be staying with Kate. No doubt they would move somewhere larger than her one-bedroom soon, but Terri knew her cousin well enough to know she'd stay in her little apartment and support herself until the wedding. Which left Terri apparently staying with Kate's brother-in-law to be.

Discomfort nipped at her at the idea of his having to put her up for the next two weeks. She didn't like to trouble people. "Perhaps I should rent a hotel room. I don't want to put you out."

"That isn't necessary," Bastien Argeneau assured her firmly. "The penthouse has five bedrooms and a housekeeper, as I mentioned. And I'm quite busy at the moment, so you probably won't see much of me. You can come and go as you like. You are most welcome in my home."

Chapter Two

"Get out!"

Terri stared at her host's panic-stricken face. She could hardly believe that he'd suddenly turned on her, shouting those words, now that they'd finally reached his home.

The ride here had taken the better part of an hour. She and Bastien had chatted most of the way, and Terri had spent a portion of that time trying to place his accent. Spending the past several years in Europe had given her something of an ear for them. Bastien had a hint of one, which she couldn't place. It was most unusual. He spoke at times with the formality of a time gone by, but used modern terminology just as often. Terri thought she heard a touch of London in his accent, but she wasn't certain.

When she hadn't been able to figure it out by listening to him speak, she had tried to place his ethnic origins by examining his features—but that hadn't really helped, either. His dark good looks could have been almost Mediterranean, but his pale skin tone didn't bear that out. As for his name: Bastien Argeneau was definitely French. Kate had mentioned that the family was from Canada, but they resided in Toronto, which Terri knew was in Ontario. Still, she supposed the family could be French Canadian. And perhaps what she thought was a hint of an English accent was simply Canadian. She'd met a couple of Canadians in her life, but hadn't really paid much attention to their accents.

Finally admitting that she couldn't figure out his accent, Terri had determined to ask Kate later, and had given up the matter to concentrate on their conversation. For the most part, they'd touched on topics that were relatively neutral, like the weather and the wedding: safe topics that revealed nothing personal, and that Terri knew were geared to make her feel comfortable and at ease with this relative stranger with whom she would be staying. He took pains several times to reassure her that she was welcome in his home, following that up with assurances that he was terribly busy, not likely to be around much and so wouldn't make a nuisance of himself.

Terri had felt pretty relaxed about the whole deal by the time they pulled into the underground parking garage of the Argeneau building. They had still been chatting lightly and laughing as they gathered her luggage. Lucern had even put away his scribbling and joined the conversation as he took her carry-on again and followed Bastien into the secured elevator to the penthouse. They'd all been smiling at Bastien's gentle teasing of his brother for being "blinded by love," when the elevator doors slid open and he'd started to lead the way into his home. Then he'd stopped dead so that Terri had bumped into his back, whirled around with a panicked expression and shouted "Get out!"

So much for being welcome in his home.

"Bastien?" There was a question in Lucern's voice as he set down Terri's case and moved past her. "What . . ."

The way his voice trailed off as he looked into the room beyond—a room Terri couldn't see into, because Bastien's broad shoulders blocked the way— told her there was something of great interest inside.

"Vincent!" Lucern barked. "Let Bastien's housekeeper go!"

Well, that was too much for Terri. Stepping around Bastien, she peered into the living room and at the couple there. At first glance, it appeared that they had interrupted a passionate embrace, but that was only for the first second. Then Terri noted that the man— Vincent, she presumed—was wearing a black cape. And what she saw wasn't so much an amorous act but the classic vampire embrace. It looked like the fellow was biting the old woman's neck.

Terri felt her eyebrows fly up, even as hands settled heavily on her shoulders. They were Bastien's hands, she guessed, since Lucern was in front of her, but she hardly noticed before Lucern was barking again.

"Damn it, Vinny! Let go of that woman."

"You know I hate being called Vinny, Luc. Call me Vincent. Or better yet, call me Dracul," the caped fellow corrected in a very bad Transylvanian accent. He straightened from the older woman and turned to them. His eyes held irritation for a moment, then his gaze landed on Terri. His expression gave way to a seductive smile.

Leaving the maid swaying on her feet, Vincent glided across the room to stand before Terri. His smile was a sexy curve of the mouth, his irises were silver blue and held a hungry look that captured her attention. He enveloped one of her small hands in his, and raised it to his lips.

"Enchanté," he growled.

Terri opened her mouth to respond, but paused in surprise when the man turned her hand over and pressed his lips to her wrist.

"Stop that!" Bastien stepped to the side, tugging Terri away from the man with a hand on her elbow even as he used the other to slap Vincent in the back of the head. If the fact that all three men sported those unique silver-blue eyes and dark good looks hadn't told her, that gesture—one only an irritated relative would use—told Terri this man was obviously an Argeneau. "What the hell are you doing here, Vincent?"

"Dracul," he insisted with a sniff, then turned and walked to the nearest chair. Grasping his cape, he held it out slightly so that it swirled around him as he turned. Then he dropped dramatically to sit. "I have the lead role in *Dracula*. The musical."

"*Dracula* the musical?" Bastien echoed in disbelief.

Vincent grinned. "Yeah. Cool, huh? The *lead*." He nodded. "I'm a stage presence."

"Dear God," Terri heard Bastien breathe. He seemed horrified by the whole ordeal, but she was fascinated. She volunteered a lot of time to the local community theater, and she loved this kind of stuff. Pulling away from her host's light hold, she moved to the couch and perched on the end of it to ask, "Are you a method actor?"

"Why, yes!" He beamed at her. "How did you know?"

"Well, the scene we walked into suggested you were. Er . . ." Terri's words became a surprised silence as a glance across the room showed the housekeeper was no longer swaying on her feet. In fact, she'd fainted dead away. Lucern was lifting her into his arms.

"Where is her room, Bastien?" he asked as the two men now turned to notice his predicament.

"Oh. I'll show—" Bastien stopped abruptly and turned an uncertain gaze back to Terri, as if he were reluctant to leave her alone with Vincent.

His brother solved the problem by saying, "Just tell me, and I'll go put her in bed."

"*That* hall, the last room on the right," Bastien indicated, gesturing to one of the two corridors that led off the large living room.

Terri shook her head and watched Lucern carry the woman out. The housekeeper really hadn't taken Vincent's playacting at all well. She was overreacting, and obviously fainthearted. Terri turned back to the actor. "As I was saying, the scene we walked in on said as much. So, you have to live your roles to make them feel real to you. You have to act them out?"

"Yeah." Vincent grinned. "I always live out my role. If I'm playing a bartender, I tend bar for a while. If I'm a salesman I get a job selling cars. Whatever. Fortunately, with this role I don't have to act mu—"

"Vinny!" Bastien's tone made both Terri and Vincent glance his way. His expression was forbidding, so much so that the actor didn't even bother to correct the name. In fact, he seemed to read more into the look than Terri, because after a moment of silence he arched his eyebrows.

"She's not one of us?"

"No." Bastien's expression was icy. Terri was a little startled by the transformation. He had seemed attractive and friendly and not the least threatening until now, but this expression made him seem just a bit dangerous. In a good way, she decided, as her gaze slid over his broad shoulders and the cut of his slacks. He was a good-looking, well-built—

"You haven't answered my question. What are you doing here?"

Bastien's cold query drew Terri from her itemization of his good points and back to the men.

Vincent answered, "I told you, I have the lead—"

"Fine," Bastien interrupted. "That explains why you're in New York. Now, why are you here? In my home?"

"Oh." Vincent gave a laugh. "You mean Aunt Marguerite's home, don't you? She said I could stay here until we see if the play is going to last any length of time, until I know if I need my own apartment in the city or not."

Bastien closed his eyes briefly and silently cursed

his mother. She was such a tenderhearted person. Unfortunately, Vincent had it right. This really was her apartment. His father had purchased the building years ago and set up offices here. He'd designed this penthouse above, allowing a room for each of his children should they wish to visit. On his father's death, Bastien had taken to staying here when in New York, and had come to think of it as his own because he was the only one who usually did stay here. But, in truth, it was still his mother's apartment, and she had every right to allow whoever she wanted to stay here.

To be fair, Marguerite probably hadn't thought it would be a problem. It was a huge apartment and, with Vincent acting at night and Bastien working during the day, in the normal course of events it wouldn't have been a problem. He doubted the two of them would even have run into each other very often. But that was in the normal course of events. Today, nothing was normal. And Terri's presence caused something of a dilemma, because Vincent was a biter.

No, Vincent wasn't doing his normal method acting when they'd walked in—or perhaps he was, since he didn't usually walk around in a cape—but if so, it was only incidental to the fact that he had been feeding. And off the bloody housekeeper!

Bastien scowled at his cousin. Vincent, and his father before him, couldn't survive on bagged blood. They needed a specific enzyme that died several moments after blood left the human body. It was a problem Bastien had his lab working on, but until they discovered how to fix the problem, Vincent, like his father, had to feed off the living. Still, the man knew better than to feed in Bastien's home. He'd been taught better than that.

"Sorry," Vincent said with a chagrined shrug, not even pretending he hadn't been reading Bastien's thoughts. "It was a long flight and I was hungry. No harm done, though."

Bastien sighed and ran a hand through his hair. Fortunately, it appeared Vincent was right; there was no harm done. Terri assumed the man was a method actor, playacting. Which reminded Bastien of something Kate had once said when mentioning her maid of honor. Terri was a professor at the University of Leeds. She taught something to do with the media, but she spent a lot of time volunteering in community theater. Thank God for small favors. It had saved coming up with an explanation for what they had walked in on. Knowledgeable on plays and acting in general, she'd made the obvious assumption. At least, it was an assumption more obvious than thinking the truth; that Vincent—that all of them—were vampires.

"Your housekeeper is resting quietly," Lucern announced, returning to the living room.

Bastien nodded. "Thanks, Luc." He glanced at their cousin. "So, what's this about a lead role in a musical?"

"*Dracula*." Vincent nodded. "I landed the role last week. We start rehearsals soon." He grinned gleefully. "It's perfectly atrocious. Rotten campy music, ridiculous lines—and they want me to use this horrid Transylvanian accent. I think it will be a hit. I predict a long run."

Terri burst out laughing, and Bastien found a smile curving his lips at the musical sound. She was lovely when she smiled and irresistible when she laughed.

Got the hots for Kate's cousin?

Bastien gave a start as Vincent's thought intruded on his own. Vincent was still reading his mind. He scowled, then stiffened as the intercom buzzed behind him. Someone was in the elevator and waiting to come up. Without a key like the one Bastien always carried, the elevator had to be unlocked from upstairs to work. No doubt Mrs. Houlihan, the housekeeper, had unlocked it for Vincent to come up. Either that or Bastien's mother had given Vinny her key.

"That might be Kate," Lucern said, showing a noticeable increase in animation at the very idea. It was always amazing to see the difference that came over Luc when his fianceé was around. It was as if a switch were flipped and he came fully to life. Bastien often wondered what it must be like to truly enjoy life again as Lucern seemed to be doing.

It was something he might never know, Bastien realized without rancor. He moved to the wall unit and flipped a switch, bringing up an image of the interior of the elevator on a small monitor. Sure enough, Kate was in the elevator. She wasn't alone.

"Who's that with her?"

Lucern moved closer to look. "It's C.K."

"C.K.?" Bastien asked.

Lucern nodded. Now it was Terri who stood and came to peer curiously at the stranger. "He's a co-worker of Kate's. Another editor. Isn't he?" She looked to Lucern for verification and he nodded again.

Bastien pushed the button to allow the elevator to climb up to the penthouse suite. "Why would she be bringing him here?"

Lucern merely shrugged and made his way to the elevator, though Bastien knew it wasn't curiosity that moved him. He doubted his brother cared at all why the other editor was there; Luc was just eager to see Kate. He was *always* eager to see Kate.

"So. I'm Vincent Argeneau. And you are?"

Bastien turned to see that his cousin had taken Terri's hand again. He had every intention of interrupting the cozy little scene . . . just as soon as Terri gave her full name. Bastien still didn't have a clue what it was.

"Terri. Terri Lea Simpson."

"And are you a thespian, too? You must have something to do with acting to know about method actors and such. You're certainly lovely enough to be an actress."

"No." Terri laughed at the compliment and shook her head. "I've always been interested in the theater, unfortunately I have no ability in that area. I teach scriptwriting, actually, and volunteer in community theater."

That was all Bastien wanted to hear. He started forward at once, intending to bring an end to his cousin's flirting, but the elevator doors opened just as he did. His attention was drawn to the trio in the entry as he heard Kate's distressed, "Oh, Lucern! You'll never guess what's happened!"

After the briefest of hesitations—a hesitation that ended only when Terri moved past him to join the three people in the entry—Bastien followed her to find out what the dilemma was. It did seem to be the day for problems.

"We had the production meeting, then Chris went home to finish packing and collect his things for the California conference. He forgot his briefcase at the office, his flight was at five, and he didn't have time to come back for it, so I said I'd leave early and run it out to him. And thank goodness I did!"

"Er . . . Kate? Do you think we could move into the living room so I can put my foot up?" the other editor asked. "My leg's killing me."

"Oh. Of course, Chris. He's supposed to keep his leg elevated," Kate explained to the rest of them. She took his arm to help him into the living room. "It's broken."

Bastien merely raised an eyebrow. That fact was rather obvious from the ungainly cast on the man's right leg.

"How did he break it?" Terri asked. She seemed to be the only person who cared.

"Oh! Terri." Releasing Chris, Kate turned to her cousin and hugged her in greeting. "They found you. I'm so glad. How was your flight? I hope you don't mind staying here, but my apartment's so small and, now that I have to fly out of town, I wouldn't want you to be there all by yourself and—"

Bastien had been grinning at the way that Kate's abandoning him had left the injured editor flailing about, trying to find his balance, but as her words registered, he turned his attention fully on his soon-to-be sister-in-law. "Fly out of town?"

Terri and Lucern spoke the words at the exact same moment, bringing an end to the hug the two women had been enjoying.

"Yes, I—"

"Kate!" It was a panicked cry from the male editor, who was losing his battle to stay upright.

"Oh, Chris!" She whirled just in time to catch his arm and keep him on his feet, then helped him the rest of the way to the couch. She fussed briefly over setting his casted leg on Bastien's mahogany coffee table, then placed a couple of the black accent pillows from the blue-gray couch beneath to raise it higher and save the surface of the wood. Then she straightened with a sigh. "Where was I?"

"Explaining why you have to fly out of town," Lucern growled, moving closer in a way another woman might find threatening, but that Kate merely took as an opportunity to cuddle with her man. She slid an arm around him and leaned close with a sigh that might have been pleasure or relief.

"Yes, well, as I was saying, I had to run C.K.'s briefcase over to him. But there was no answer when I buzzed his apartment, and I knew he was waiting for it, so I finally buzzed his landlady and had her come up with me. She unlocked the door and we went in, calling for him. I heard him shout from the bathroom, and you won't believe it!"

"What?" Terri asked.

"The toilet from the apartment above had fallen through the floor and landed smack on top of him."

"It wasn't just the toilet," Chris inserted, looking

36

slightly embarrassed. "A good portion of the ceiling came with it."

"Yes. And he was trapped underneath. And the pipes had broken and water was pouring down on him."

"Fresh water," Chris clarified quickly.

"Yes. And, well, the landlady rushed out to call for paramedics and a plumber, and I got the toilet off of him."

"It wasn't just a toilet, Kate," he repeated, looking more upset.

"And . . ." She paused and sighed. "Well, I went to the hospital with him, of course."

"Of course you did," Lucern crooned. "You're such a good person, my love."

She smiled at the compliment and kissed him.

"But what has that got to do with you flying out of town?" Terri asked.

Kate broke the kiss and turned back to continue. "Well, I had to call the office and explain that a toilet had felled Chris."

"It was a good portion of the ceiling too, Kate!" The man was sounding a tad testy, but Bastien managed not to laugh. He supposed he'd be testy, too, if a toilet had fallen on him.

"And the minute they heard what had happened, they started fretting over what to do about the conference in California."

"They want you to go in his place," Lucern guessed unhappily.

"Yes." Kate didn't sound too pleased, either. She

rubbed a hand lightly over Lucern's chest. "This is a five-day conference, but I'm flying in the day before and not returning until the morning after, so it's a week. I'm going to miss you, my love."

"No, you won't." Lucern pressed a firm kiss to her forehead. "I'm coming with you."

"You are?" Her face lit up like the sky on the Fourth of July. "Oh, Lucern!"

The couple immediately indulged in another kiss. Bastien was expecting another of their marathon kissing sessions, but much to his surprise, Kate broke the kiss after only a moment. She headed for the elevator, dragging Lucern behind her. "We haven't a minute to lose. We need to pack and book another seat on the flight for you, and—"

"Er . . . Kate?" Bastien called, halting the pair as they arrived at the elevator and pressed the button. "Aren't you forgetting something?"

Kate turned back with a questioning expression as the elevator doors opened. Her gaze slid over the inhabitants of the room, then landed on Terri. "Oh, Terri!" She rushed back to clasp her cousin's hands. "I'm terribly sorry about all this. I know you flew over here to help with things, but there's no one else who can go, and really there's nothing to do for the wedding anyway—everything's taken care of. Just enjoy yourself, relax and tour New York. Have a good time. Please don't hate me."

"Of course I don't hate you," Terri laughed, giving her a hug. "Of course you have to go. Besides, I rather dumped myself on you without warning. It's okay, go on. I'll be fine."

"Er, Kate?" Bastien said as the two women broke apart. When his soon-to-be sister-in-law glanced toward him, he gestured to the couch where her coworker sat, leg elevated. He hadn't meant Terri was whom she'd forgotten; it hadn't occurred to him that some apology or explanation should be made to the woman. Work was work. It was C.K. he thought Kate had forgotten about.

"Oh!" Her eyes widened on Chris. "I'm sorry. I forgot to ask."

"Ask what?" Bastien queried, afraid he already knew.

"Chris can't go back to his apartment until it's repaired, and he has nowhere to stay. You have Mrs. Houlihan to look after him and . . . well, I was hoping he could stay here. If you didn't mind," she added.

"Of course he doesn't mind." Lucern moved forward to take his fiancée's hand and lead her back to the elevator as he said, "Bastien can always be counted on in a pinch. He'll take care of everything on this end, and he'll even send the things we'll need once we're there."

Bastien frowned, oddly displeased by those words despite their truth. He *was* the one everyone always turned to. They did all count on him. And, in this instance, he would certainly send the "things" they would need in California. Namely, blood. But while he usually had no problem being the one everyone counted on, for some reason Lucern's assuming that as usual he would take care of things, was rather annoying.

"We'll call when we get to California," Lucern assured him, pressing a button on the elevator panel.

Bastien stared as the metal elevator doors slid closed, then turned slowly to survey his guests. Terri was standing beside him, looking a little lost. He didn't blame her. She had taken the last of her vacation time and flown all the way here from England to help with her cousin's wedding, but Kate wasn't going to be around.

Chris was shifting uncomfortably on the couch, looking as if he'd rather be uninjured and on a plane to California. Who wouldn't?

And Vincent was standing by the editor, glancing from him to Terri as if trying to decide who would make the tastier snack. Bastien wasn't surprised when his gaze settled on Terri.

"Bastien, I could use a bite," his cousin announced as if on cue. "It was a long flight."

"You will eat out, thank you," Bastien said firmly.

"Okay," Vinny agreed easily—too easily, Bastien thought. And he wasn't surprised when his cousin turned to Terri and asked, "You wouldn't happen to be hungry, would you? Care to step out for a bite?"

"Actually—"

"Mrs. Houlihan will make you something," Bastien interrupted quickly, moving closer to Terri in a protective manner. He'd be damned if his cousin was going to sink his teeth into her. She was—well, she wasn't on the menu.

"Do you think she could make something for me, too?" Chris Keyes asked tentatively from the sofa. "I could do with something to eat as well."

"She'll make something for both of you," Bastien

agreed, then glanced at his cousin. "You'll have to find your own food."

"Oh, surely Mrs. Houlihan could make enough for him to join us," Terri said.

"Vincent has a . . . digestive condition. He needs a very particular diet, and I'm afraid I haven't anything here he can have." Bastien spoke carefully, knowing his cousin would get the message. Everyone in this household was under his protection and off-limits. Well, Terri and Mrs Houlihan definitely were. Bastien didn't know Chris and didn't much care if Vincent bit him, except that, were he to do so, one of the women might witness the act. No, Vincent would have to prowl the streets for his food. It shouldn't be that difficult a task.

"I'll go see if Mrs. Houlihan has recovered sufficiently to see to a meal. In the meantime, Vincent, behave." Bastien started to exit the room, then thought better of it and turned back. He was glad he had, for he noted Vincent had moved closer to Terri, his eyes on her lovely neck. "Terri, perhaps I should show you to your room on the way. You can get settled while the meal is being prepared."

Sardonic amusement flashed across Vincent's face, but he remained silent.

"Oh, that would be nice." Terri picked up her carry-on and moved toward her suitcase, but Bastien beat her to it.

"This way," he said, and led her to the guest rooms. He gave her the one Lissianna usually used. It was the more feminine of the chambers, and it also happened to be right next to the master bedroom, which he was now occupying. Close enough for him to keep a protective eye on her, he assured himself as he led her inside and glanced around the rose-and-blue-hued room.

"Mrs. Houlihan keeps all the rooms ready in case family or friends drop in, so you should be all set," he said as he set her suitcase down at the foot of the bed. "But if there is anything you need, don't hesitate to ask."

"Thank you, it's lovely." Terri set her carry-on down on the bed and unzipped it, commenting, "It's a shame about Kate's friend having the toilet fall on him. What a freak accident. And this is the worst time for it."

Bastien knew she was thinking that now she had absolutely no reason to be there burdening him, but her words also made him realize that while he had removed Terri from Vincent's grasp, he had left Kate's coworker firmly in it. Alone. "She'll be grateful for your presence now more than ever," he assured her. "In fact, you may find yourself doing more than you ever intended in preparation for the wedding."

Terri looked a little more chipper at the thought. "I hadn't thought of that."

"Yes. Well, it's true. Kate will be grateful for your help. In fact, you may be sorry you came. She and Lucern have both been going a little squirrelly trying to arrange it all, and fix last-minute problems. Now it will be you dealing with it. You and me."

"Oh yes, you're the best man," she remembered with a smile. Then she added, "Actually, Kate said that your mother was very helpful, so I wasn't too sure if she really needed me. But I'd already booked the flight, so I came anyway."

"Mother has been as helpful as always," Bastien allowed. "But Lissianna's pregnant, and Mother's been rather busy lately helping set up a nursery and such."

"Lissianna? That's your sister, right?" Terri asked. "Kate mentioned her."

"Yes." He hesitated, then admitted, "Kate hasn't spoken much about you to me. Apparently she told Lucern about you, but I don't see him as often as all that. I've been bouncing between Canada and Europe for most of the last six months, and only shifted to New York recently," he explained, so she wouldn't be offended that Kate hadn't told him about her. "I notice you don't have much of a British accent. You weren't born there. Did you move to England because your husband is from there, or—"

"I'm not married," Terri said quietly.

"Oh." Bastien nodded, unable to stop the smile that spread across his lips. He was glad she wasn't married, though he wasn't prepared to examine why too closely. "Well. Take your time about settling in. I'll call you when Mrs. Houlihan has finished making—"

He stopped speaking as a sudden shriek sounded from the living room.

Chapter Three

Bastien cursed under his breath and hurried out of the guestroom. He was very aware, as he ran back up the hall, that Terri was on his heels. He'd rather she wasn't; the Lord alone knew what they were about to find. Well, actually, with Vincent in the penthouse it was an easy guess. He might have tried to bite Mrs. Houlihan again and failed to control her mind, but that was doubtful. Vincent was as old as Bastien, and found it easy to manipulate the minds of his victims. Which meant that Mrs. Houlihan had probably walked in on him biting Kate's coworker.

That was exactly what had happened, Bastien saw as he skidded into the living room. Vincent must have been serious when he'd said he was hungry. The man was still bent over the back of the couch, his teeth fastened on C.K.'s neck. He hadn't stopped feeding at Mrs. Houlihan's interruption, but had merely speared the housekeeper with hard eyes. No doubt he was trying to control the woman's thoughts as he fed, but he hadn't succeeded by the time Bastien arrived on the scene.

Terri was on Bastien's heels, and he felt alarm course through him at the thought of her witnessing this, but even as she flew into the room behind him, Vincent retracted his teeth and straightened.

Just beginning to relax, Bastien noted the horrified stare of his housekeeper and followed her gaze to Chris Keyes's neck. He immediately grimaced upon spotting the two red dots there, one with a teardrop of blood sliding down the skin beneath. Bastien gave Vincent a look that made his cousin glance down. Sighting the problem, Vinny nonchalantly reached down and turned his dazed victim's head enough to hide the mark from Terri's view.

Fortunately, she didn't appear to have noticed. Her focus was on the housekeeper. "It's okay," she said soothingly, moving to the woman's side. "Mrs. Houlihan, is it?"

The housekeeper wasn't in the mood to be soothed. She jerked away from Terri's gentle hold as if the younger woman were tainted.

"It's not all right," she snapped, then turned on Bastien in fury. "Mr. Argeneau, sir, you've been a good employer. You have. And this has been an easy job, and I'll not deny it. You're hardly here, there's no cooking involved and little more than dusting. I spend most days watching my soap operas. But now you've brought these . . . these . . . monsters here." She included everyone in her sweeping look. "I'm no one's dinner. I quit."

"Mrs. Houlihan." Bastien moved to follow as the woman whirled to storm out of the room, pausing when Terri caught his arm.

"Perhaps you should let her go," Terri suggested quietly. "The woman's obviously high-strung. I mean, she can't really believe Vincent is a vampire. That's just silly. I'm thinking she's just upset that she'll actually have to start working."

"I'm sure that's it," Vincent agreed, but his innocent expression was unable to fool Bastien for a moment. His cousin was silently laughing his head off at the situation. He'd always had a slightly twisted sense of humor.

"Yes, I'm sure it is," Bastien agreed, just for simplicity's sake "But I still need to talk to her."

He needed to clear the woman's memory. Keeping her on was impossible now, so long as Vincent and the others were around, but he had to at least wipe her memory before she went blabbing about what she had seen.

Bastien strode out into the entry and paused in shock. It was empty. He'd expected to find Mrs. Houlihan collecting her coat from the closet or something, but she was gone. The elevator doors were closed and the room empty. The only exit was the elevator or the archway he'd just come through. She couldn't have left so quickly. What about her things? All her clothes in her room? Her coat?

Turning on his heel, he strode back into the living room and straight to the wall unit holding the monitor with a view of the interior of the elevator. It was still on, and right there, live and in black-and-white,

46

was his very upset housekeeper. She was riding down to the main floor with arms folded defensively across her chest and one foot tapping as she anxiously watched the lit floor numbers mark her journey downward.

The woman had left, just like that. She'd lived here for some ten years and had just walked out, leaving everything she owned behind. Bastien could hardly believe it. Dear God, he had to catch up to her and repair this somehow—not just clear it from her memory, but make reparation. Where would she go, for heaven's sake?

He turned back to the others, mouth opening to excuse himself from the room, but paused. Terri was eyeing him sympathetically, apparently thinking he was upset at losing a maid. Vincent was grinning unabashed, not at all concerned that he had just thrown Bastien's life into turmoil. And Chris Keyes was shifting uncomfortably on the couch, apparently having recovered from the momentary daze Vincent had induced while feeding off him.

"Er . . ."

Bastien glanced toward the editor, and the fellow grimaced. "Would it be too much trouble to ask for a glass of water? They gave me painkillers at the hospital, but those are wearing off and I could really use more."

"Water? Yes," Bastien said, relieved to find that Vincent had at least managed to veil the editor's mind while feeding. He glanced to Terri. He had to see her fed, too. But he'd promised Mrs Houlihan would make the meal. And Vincent—he had to deal with Vincent.

That was when Bastien realized that fate had just turned everything upside down. His orderly life was gone, and at that moment he really wasn't sure if he'd ever get it back. At least not before Lucern and Kate's wedding. How long was that? Oh, yes. Two weeks. Fourteen days of hell before his life might get back to normal.

How had this happened, he wondered with a combination of dismay and confusion. Things like this simply didn't happen to him. He was the details man—he didn't *have* problems, he solved them for everyone else.

He had a problem now. Three of them, in fact. Terri, Vinny, and the editor. Actually, he had four problems, because he really had to catch up to Mrs. Houlihan and clear her memory before she told anyone about Vinny. He supposed he could wipe her mind clean and convince her to return too, but the chances of the memory wipe sticking weren't good if she stayed in the penthouse: there was a good chance that some situation, something said, or just seeing Vinny prancing around in his cape and teeth would bring the memory back. In effect, he and his kind were able to bury memories, not really eliminate them. Still, he had to bury that memory, and quickly, to avoid future trouble. But first he had to see everyone situated here and give Vincent a good talking-to. Otherwise Terri might soon be sporting her own puncture marks.

Speaking of the editor, Bastien decided to put him in one of the guest rooms. The man would be safer there. That seemed a sound decision. It also gave

Bastien a purpose and made him feel more in charge again, despite the chaos reigning around him.

"Right." He clapped his hands together. "Let's get organized. You need a room . . . er . . ." He stared at the editor, trying to recall the fellow's name. He'd remembered it earlier. C-something, he thought, but the name just wouldn't come. He didn't bother to try to hide his irritation as he asked, "What's your name again?"

"Chris," the slender editor answered. "Chris Keyes. Kate probably calls me C.K. when she mentions me, though."

"Oh, yeah." Bastien didn't really care; he had more important things on his mind at the moment. His glance slid to Vincent. "Which room did you take?"

"Lucern's."

"Fine. The editor can have Etienne's room," Bastien decided. It put the blond man between Vincent and Terri. Hopefully, if Vinny got hungry, he would go to the nearest source of nourishment and leave Terri alone. Bastien really didn't want to kick his cousin's ass in front of these two. Well, not in front of Terri at any rate. He didn't much care what the editor thought of him. *Christopher*, he reminded himself, going naturally for the long version of the name and bypassing nicknames altogether.

"Can you walk?" he asked the editor.

"Not without help," the fellow admitted apologetically.

Bastien grimaced. It looked like he'd have to cart him around like a baby. Which wasn't a problem, he could lift and carry the man easily enough. It just seemed a bother.

"You aren't going to take him to his room already, are you?" Kate's cousin asked as Bastien moved toward the editor. "He hasn't eaten yet. And do you know, I didn't notice Kate carrying any kind of luggage or overnight bag for him when they came in." She eyed the invalid with concern. "Didn't you two stop at your apartment to collect some clothes from your apartment?"

"There wasn't time," C.K. admitted, looking not at all pleased. "Kate called the airport from the hospital once she knew that she would be taking my place, then raced here to drop me off. There was only one plane headed for California tonight that had two seats left on it, and that didn't leave much time to spare. She had to collect Luc and get going if she wanted to make it."

Bastien wasn't at all surprised to hear that Kate had expected that Luc would accompany her to California. The two had been inseparable ever since Luc had turned her.

"He'll need clothes," Terri pointed out almost apologetically.

"Yes," Bastien agreed. Another problem for him to attend to.

Terri patted his arm sympathetically. "It doesn't appear to be your day."

Bastien almost assured her that everything would be fine, that he was used to dealing with crises, but he very much feared that doing so would bring an end to the soothing way Terri was touching him; and he found he quite liked her touch. So, for the first time in his life, Bastien kept his mouth shut, shook his head, and went for the sympathy play. "No, it doesn't."

"Umm."

"What?" He cast a scowl down at Chris Keyes, irritated with the editor's interruption of the brief interlude.

"Do you think it would be possible to get me that glass of water?" the editor asked. "Those painkillers from the hospital—I could really use one about now."

"Get him a drink, Vinny."

"Vincent," Bastien's cousin corrected firmly. "And get it yourself, I'm not your housekeeper."

"No, you're the reason I no longer *have* a housekeeper," Bastien growled. "Get the drink."

"I'll get it." Terri rushed off before Bastien could protest. It wasn't until she was out of the room that he remembered she wouldn't have a clue where the kitchen was. Fortunately, she took the right hallway. She'd find her way, Bastien assured himself, then rubbed one hand wearily across his forehead as he considered the tasks ahead and what order to accomplish them in.

First, he had to deal with Vincent. It would be best to get his cousin out of the apartment and on his way to feeding; that was the only way to keep him from nibbling on the guests. Then Bastien would go after Mrs. Houlihan and wipe her memory, swing by Keyes's apartment to collect him some clothes, pick up some food for Chris and Terri, then stick the editor in a room for the night, leaving himself free to entertain Kate's cousin. He was smiling over this idea when he realized his cousin would be back by then, and no doubt do his level best to charm the pants right off Terri. Literally. His smile died as he acknowledged that his life had become a sort of hell.

"Bastien?"

"Hmm?" His gloomy thoughts vanished as he turned to Terri. She had returned to the room, handed the editor a cup of what presumably was water, and now moved to Bastien's side. He smiled. She was a lovely woman—a lovely, thoughtful woman who had taken a good chunk of her vacation to fly 2,320 miles to help her cousin and best friend out with wedding preparations, only to find herself dumped at his door like some stray puppy while her cousin and Lucern wandered the earth attending romance writer conventions, making love in hotels, and no doubt kissing every two steps of the way, like the brainless lovesick duo they were.

"While I was in the kitchen getting Chris the glass of water, I had a quick look around and I noticed you have no food."

"Oh?" Bastien asked vaguely, thinking that perhaps describing her as being "dumped on him like a stray puppy" was unkind. There was nothing doglike about this woman. She was more a cat-type—sleek and graceful.

"No food at all," she added significantly.

"I see." Bastien's eyes dropped down her figure. All those curves weren't really very sleek or catlike, which is why he supposed he hadn't made the association at first. But she had those large green eyes like a cat. Which were rather similar to Kate's, he noticed now. They must be a family trait, he decided, his gaze

52

briefly drifting back up to her eyes before returning to her figure. She really had a gorgeous body, and her University of Leeds T-shirt and tight white jeans showed it to advantage. She definitely wasn't a puppy.

"Or dishes even," Terri continued. "There was one cup that I presume Mrs Houlihan used for her tea, a teapot, some tea bags, but that was it. In the whole kitchen, that was it. Hello? Bastien? Can you hear me?"

Bastien blinked as the sudden concern and touch of impatience in Terri's tone made it through his distracted state. It took him a minute to grasp what she'd been trying to tell him as he'd ogled her body, but after a moment the key words popped to the fore of his mind. "No food. Or dishes. Right. We'll go shopping tomorrow. In the meantime . . ." He turned to survey the room, his gaze skating over the still wincing and shifting editor, his amused cousin, and the room at large. It stopped at the bar. "There are glasses in the bar," he announced, feeling rather triumphant. "And I'll . . . er . . ." What was it humans did when they were hungry but didn't want to cook? Oh, yes! They–

"Order in?" Vincent suggested.

"I knew that," Bastien snapped. Family could be so bloody annoying at times. Sighing, he turned back to Terri and forced a smile, completely ignoring her bewildered expression. "We'll order in tonight and go shopping tomorrow."

"Uh-huh." She nodded slowly, then tilted her head. "Have you lived here long?"

"About twenty years in this building, but over a

hundred in the city," Bastien answered. Then he blinked and corrected himself: "My *family* has had the penthouse that long, I mean. None of us really lives here at all. I just use it when I'm in New York conducting business. Other family members drop in from time to time when they're in town," he added, with a glance at his cousin.

"I see." Terri smiled slightly, then shook her head and dug into her back pocket. She pulled out a wad of American bills. "Well, I can contribute to the takeout. What are we ordering?"

"Whatever you like, but there's no need to contribute. You're my guest."

"But—"

"No buts. You're my guest," he said firmly. He turned away to bring an end to the discussion, and his gaze landed grimly on Keyes. Bastien immediately pulled out the small notepad and pen he always carried around in his pocket for just such occasions and handed them over. "Write down your address and give me your keys, and I'll pick you up some clothes while Vincent and I are out collecting dinner." It wasn't a request.

"You!" He turned on his cousin as C.K. set to work. "Vincent, get that damned cape off and get ready to go out.

"And you—" His attention shifted to Terri, but one glimpse of her soft eyes and even softer-looking lips made his businesslike attitude disappear. A smile curved his lips again, and his voice was noticably gentler as he said, "Just sit down and relax, Terri. I'll be back soon with dinner."

Then he took the notepad, pen, and keys the editor was holding out, grabbed his now capeless cousin by the arm, and escorted him determinedly to the elevator.

"I think he likes you."

Terri glanced toward Chris Keyes as the elevator doors closed on her host and his cousin. "What?" she asked in surprise.

"Well, he certainly treats you nicer than the rest of us."

Terri ignored the comment. The man was shifting about on the couch again, looking pained. "Is there something I can do to make you more comfortable?" she asked.

"No. Well, if you wouldn't mind? Another pillow under my leg might help until the painkillers kick in. Thanks for the water, by the way."

"No problem." Terri grabbed another cushion off the couch and set it under his cast on the coffee table. "Better?"

"Not really, but it will have to do."

She bit her lip at the surly comment. Men were such babies when sick or injured. "I'm just going to go to my room to start unpacking," she announced, turning toward the hall. "Shout if you need me."

"Do you think they have a television in this place?"

Terri paused at the hall and turned slowly, her gaze moving around the room. She didn't see a television. But there was a remote control on the coffee table by C.K.'s cast-encased foot. Walking back to him, she picked it up and looked it over with mounting confusion. There were more buttons on the thing than there were keys on a computer keyboard, and all of them with incomprehensible short forms and symbols. Two of them said TV, but with differing symbols beneath. Terri chose the first, and glanced around with a start as a soft whirring issued from the opposite wall. Her eyebrows rose as she watched a portion of wall slide upward to reveal a large television.

"Voila," she said, with more relief than cheer. She hit the second button, and the television clicked on. Glad to have solved the problem, Terri handed the remote to C.K. and turned to leave the room, grateful when she managed to escape without being called back again.

She found her room without difficulty, and closed the door behind her with a small sigh. None of this was going as she'd expected. Terri had imagined spending this first night on the couch in Kate's cozy little apartment, sharing a bowl of popcorn as the two of them laughed and giggled over past events and planned out the wedding. In fact, she'd rather looked forward to it. Terri had also expected to live out of her suitcase for two weeks, sleeping on Kate's lumpy old couch, and spending her time running around doing last-minute errands in her cousin's stead.

Instead, here she was in this huge, gorgeous bedroom in the Argeneau penthouse suite, with drawers for her clothes, her own bathroom, a huge TV, and nothing to do. Terri supposed it was almost shameful to complain, but she'd rather looked forward to the way she'd imagined the trip.

Shaking her head, she grabbed her carry-on and walked to the door Bastien had said led to the bathroom. Terri opened it and stepped inside. It was as lovely as the bedroom, of course—large, luxurious, and all hers. Her gaze drifted over the tub, the shower, the potted plants, the wicker chair, the double sink, then to the door opposite the one she'd entered. Curious, she set her bag on a corner of the large vanity and walked over to open it.

Terri's eyebrows lifted at the sight before her. She'd thought her room large and gorgeous? This bedroom had to be the master suite. There was a huge king-size bed, antique by her guess, with four corner posts, an overhead awning, and heavy dark drapes that could be pulled closed around it. All the other furniture looked antique too, drawers, armoires, table and chairs, sofa and stuffed chairs. The room was bigger than her entire cottage back in Huddersfield, England.

After hesitating on the threshold, Terri braved entering, feeling like a thief. It was possible that this was Marguerite Argeneau's room. After all, Vincent had said it was actually Bastien's mother's apartment. If it was her room, then it was unoccupied at the moment, which would ease some of Terri's guilt about allowing her curiosity such free rein.

There were three doors leading off the master bedroom. Curious to know where they went, Terri moved to the first and opened it. The hallway. She closed it quickly and moved to the next door, which revealed a huge walk-in closet. Every stitch of clothing inside was male. There were suits mostly, with a couple of more casual clothes to break up the monotony. Chinos, cords, casual tops and sweaters. There were no jeans though, she noticed.

It was Bastien's room, then. Terri started to pull the closet door closed, only to pause as her gaze landed on a tall metal stand in the far back corner.

Terri's deceased husband, Ian, had spent a lot of time in the hospital during the battle against Hodgkin's disease that eventually claimed him. But he'd also spent a lot of time at home. At first, Terri had thought it important to keep him home to keep his spirits high and help him fight the illness. Once she'd finally gotten through the denial phase, and accepted that he wouldn't survive, she'd been determined to make his life as happy, normal and comfortable as possible. He'd died at home, with herself, his brother Dave and Dave's wife, Sandi, in attendance. Terri was very familiar with medical paraphernalia thanks to that period of her life. She recognized an IV stand when she saw one. And there was no reason on earth that she could think of for Bastien to have one here.

Then she recalled that this was really his mother's room, and that his father was dead. Kate had never said how the senior Argeneau had passed on. Now Terri suspected it may have been in a manner similar to her own mother's death, and Ian's, which had been slow, lingering, and painful. It was an unpleasant thing to think about, and none of Terri's business—until and unless Bastien told her. But then, this room wasn't any of her business either. She was being snoopy.

Terri pulled the door closed and hesitated, torn between stopping and leaving or continuing her snooping. The fact that there was only one door left to look behind decided it: She'd gone this far, she might as well just peek through the last door before going back to her own room.

A gasp of amazement slid from her lips as she did. Beyond lay a bathroom bigger even than the bedroom she'd been given. "Luxurious" did not describe it; even "opulent" was a poor description. Toilet, bidet, sinks, shower, and Jacuzzi—all were done in white, with gold accessories. And the gold looked real to Terri. The floor was a rich black marble with gold and white shot through, and mirrors were everywhere. The room was positively decadent. And it raised possibilities in her mind that were even more wicked.

Terri pulled the door closed and made a beeline back into her own bathroom. It was only once she had that door safely closed behind her that she wondered why, since the master suite had its own bathroom, there was a connecting door to hers. It didn't bother her that the rooms were connected; she wasn't going to lock the door or anything. Her cousin would hardly leave her where she wasn't safe. She was just curious as to the reason for the connecting door.

Shrugging the question aside, Terri moved to the vanity and opened her case to begin unpacking.

"I don't know what the big deal is."

"You cannot feed on my guests. Period," Bastien

said firmly. He'd been lecturing his cousin since the elevator doors had closed.

"You're so squeamish, Bastien." Vincent laughed. "I'd like to see you have to hunt your food the old-fashioned way like I do. It gets a bit tiring, you know. Constantly prowling around, looking for dinner."

"Yes. I know. I did have to do it myself, if you'll recall," Bastien said. "And I know it can be a bother, but still—no feeding on my guests. Now, be a good cousin and go find a snack to tide you over for the night. *Not* the people in my apartment."

"Oh, fine," Vincent agreed. He arched an eyebrow. "But first maybe I should help you order some takeout."

"I can manage on my own, thank you," Bastien replied. In his more than four hundred years of life, no one had ever before suggested that there was something he couldn't do. He'd been competent practically from birth.

"No?" Vincent asked lightly. "I bet you've never ordered takeout before. I doubt you've ever even had to deal with it. The closest you've probably ever gotten is asking your secretary to arrange catering for a business meeting."

Vincent was right on the money, but Bastien kept his mouth shut, refusing to acknowledge it.

"Will you do McDonald's, Chinese, pizza, or subs?"

"What are subs?" Bastien was surprised into asking.

"Oh ho! You don't even know," Vinny crowed.

"Oh, all right. I've never done takeout before," Bastien admitted. He was more the wine and caviar

60

type when it came to dating. Of course, they hadn't had takeout the last time he'd dated. "Now, what are subs?"

"Submarine sandwiches. They're large buns, like French bread, sort of, with meat, cheese, lettuce, and things inside."

Bastien made a face. "They sound absolutely disgusting."

"They do rather, don't they?" Vincent agreed. "I don't suppose you asked Terri and Chris what they'd like?"

"No," he admitted, and was irritated with himself for not doing so, but he rarely asked anyone what they wanted. He was the decision-making guy; he usually decided what was in the best interests of everyone else and did it, or else arranged to have it done. He would do the same now, he decided. "Which is the healthiest choice?"

Vincent considered. "Probably submarines. At least, if the commercials are true. They have all the nutrition a growing human needs . . . and you can lose a hundred pounds eating them."

"What?" Bastien asked.

"Seriously," Vincent said with a laugh. "Some guy ate them every day for every meal and lost a ton of weight." He paused and pursed his lips thoughtfully. "Mind you, he also apparently walked to the sub shop to get them, so maybe that's why he really lost the weight."

"Vincent," Bastien said with exasperation, "which takeout foods are healthiest?"

"Subs," Vincent insisted. "It's got your four basic

61

food groups. Or is it five?" Raising a hand, he began to count off fingers. "Dairy, bread, meat, vegetables . . . I think there are four for humans."

"Whatever. I'll get subs."

"I'll come along and help you," Vincent offered. The elevator doors opened onto the parking garage.

Bastien shook his head. "Thanks, but I'll be fine. Besides, I have to take care of a couple of matters first."

"Chris's clothes?"

"That's one thing, yes," Bastien admitted as he led the way through the nearly empty parking garage. It was past working hours on a Friday night, and most of the employees had left for home already.

"And the other?"

"I also have to track down Mrs. Houlihan and wipe her memory."

"Why bother? No one will believe the old bird. They'll think she's batty."

"And what if they don't?" Bastien snapped, then paused and turned a narrowed gaze on his cousin. "Please tell me you generally erase the memories of your meals, that you don't leave them wandering around shrieking, 'I was bitten by a vampire.' Surely you have that much sense?" It wasn't really sense Bastien was worried about. It was the adrenaline rush Vincent seemed to enjoy. Risk-taking was like a drug to him.

"Of course, I do," his cousin replied.

Relieved, Bastien began to walk again. Vincent went on, "I would have wiped the old bird's memory, but you guys walked in. I managed to veil the editor's memory though, and I'd have taken care of the housekeeper too, but you and Sleeping Beauty came rushing in."

"Sleeping Beauty?" Bastien glanced curiously at his cousin.

"The name suits her," Vincent said with a grin. "Just looking at her, you can see she's got passions waiting to be woken."

"You can?"

"Sure. She's like ripe fruit, ready to burst out of her skin."

Bastien gave a start. That description, the term ripe fruit, had come to mind when he'd first seen her. Apparently it had entered Vincent's head as well. "Why do you say that?"

"The way she walks, dresses, talks." Vinny shrugged. "All of the above."

"Yes, but—"

"So, where does this Mrs. Houlihan live?" Vincent interrupted, and Bastien's mind shifted gears to the most important problem at hand: His housekeeper. His ex-housekeeper. And her whereabouts.

Irritation returned to him, and it focused directly on the man walking beside him. He said, "She lives, or did live, in the penthouse."

Vincent whistled through his teeth. "And she left everything behind when she went? I don't think she even stopped for a coat! Not a good sign." He shook his head as he contemplated, then got over it and asked, "So, where do you think she went? Her son's? A daughter's?"

"She has a son and daughter?" Bastien asked. He was so surprised that he stopped walking again.

"How the hell am I supposed to know? I was just guessing," Vincent said with a laugh. His gaze sharpened. "Don't *you* know?"

"I haven't any idea if she even has family in New York," Bastien admitted with an unhappy sigh.

"Dear God, Bastien! She worked for you, and you haven't a clue if she has kids or family? Man! You're a piece of work. You get all squeamish about me feeding off humans, but you're the one who treats them like cattle."

"I do not," Bastien protested.

"No? What's her first name then?"

"Whose?" he muttered

"Your housekeeper's."

Bastien grimaced and turned to his car. He had stopped behind it, and ignoring his cousin, he retrieved his keys from his pocket and pushed the button on the remote to unlock the doors. He felt some relief upon getting inside. Until his cousin slid into the passenger seat.

"It's Gladys," Vincent announced with more than a little satisfaction.

Bastien ignored him. He inserted the keys and turned the engine over.

"I always find out my donors' names before I feed," his cousin continued in prim tones as Bastien backed out of the parking spot and drove toward the exit. "I don't like to treat them like cattle. Hey!" he cried out, grabbing at the dashboard to prevent flying through the windshield. Bastien had slammed on the brakes half inside the parking garage, half out on the edge of the street.

"That's why they make seat belts," Bastien said with grim satisfaction. He leaned past his cousin to open the passenger door. "Out."

Vincent peered at him in surprise, then grinned his very irritating, very knowing grin. "Okay. Deal with the matter on your own, if you like. But it's true, you know. You may not feed on humans anymore, but you still treat them like cows."

"And you don't, of course," Bastien sniped as the other vampire slid out of the car.

Vincent straightened on the pavement, turned, and bent to peer back in. "No, I don't. Some of my best friends are human." He waited a moment to be sure that sank in, then asked, "Can you say the same?" He straightened and slammed the door, leaving Bastien staring after him as he walked off down the sidewalk.

Chapter Four

"Damn," Bastien muttered, hitting the button to lock all the doors as he sat back in the driver's seat. Galling as it was to contemplate, Vincent might have a point. Bastien didn't have a single, solitary friend who was not of his own kind. He had human business acquaintances, but only out of necessity; and he kept them at a distance as much as possible, dealing with them only to the degree that business required.

And no, he hadn't taken the trouble to learn Mrs. Houlihan's first name, or anything else about the housekeeper. Why bother? She'd just die eventually anyway and have to be replaced like the last one. And the one before her. And the one before her. As all humans died.

Did he treat mortals like cattle, despite the fact that he no longer needed to feed off them directly? Bastien hated to admit it, but perhaps he did.

"Damn." He let his breath out on a slow sigh, then gave a start when a tap sounded on his window. Turning, he peered out at Vincent, who was gesturing for him to roll it down. Bastien hit the button to do so.

"I just thought I should mention, you might want to check with Sleeping Beauty and be sure she isn't vegetarian. She looks the type." On that note, Vincent straightened and started back off down the street.

Bastien hit the button to roll the window back up, then reached grimly for his cell phone. He punched in the number to the apartment, not at all sure that either Terri or Chris would answer a phone that wasn't theirs. Fortunately, Terri did, picking up the phone on the third ring and saying politely, "Hello, Argeneau residence."

"Hi, Terri, this is Bastien Argeneau." He paused and grimaced at the pompous ring that had. The Argeneau part hadn't really been necessary, had it? He plowed on: "I was thinking of picking up some subs for supper. Is that all right? You aren't a vegetarian, are you?"

"That sounds great!" Terri said. "No, I'm not a vegetarian. Can you pick up some chips and pop with that, too? Barbecue chips, Dr Pepper, and make my sub an assorted, please. Everything on it, including hot peppers."

"Er . . . yes. Assorted. Everything. Hot peppers," Bastien repeated, tugging out his small notepad and pen to scribble down her order under Chris Keyes's address. "Barbecue chips and Dr. Who?"

"Pepper. Dr Pepper," she repeated. "Shall I check with Chris and see what he wants?"

"Er, yes. Sure. That would be good," he agreed, then winced as she set the phone down, apparently on a table, because the *clack* in his ear was almost painful. Several moments passed as he waited; then she was back.

"Hello?"

"Yes, I'm here."

"Chris wants a meatball sub, plain chips, and Canada Dry ginger ale."

"Meatball, plain chips, Canada Dry," Bastien muttered, then stilled. "A meatball sub? Like what they put in spaghetti Bolognese?"

"Yes."

"Oh. Okay." Silence reigned between them briefly; then he cleared his throat. "Is everything okay up there?"

"Fine. Chris is watching television, and I'm unpacking," she said. "Where are you? You can't have gone far. You didn't leave long ago."

"No, I'm downstairs in the parking garage, just leaving actually," he admitted. "I just thought I should check and be sure you weren't a vegetarian or anything. I wouldn't want to bring home a sub and find you couldn't eat it."

"Nope. Not vegetarian. I love meat."

Bastien smiled at her enthusiasm. At least there was *something* Vincent had got wrong.

"Are *you* a vegetarian?" she asked curiously, then gave a laugh. "Well, I guess not, or you wouldn't be suggesting subs. Well, I suppose you could be," she corrected herself. "You could like vegetarian subs. But you just don't seem the veggie type to me."

"Don't I?" he asked with a grin. "What kind of guy do I seem to you?"

"A steak man. Rare," she said firmly. Then, "Am I right? You like your steak rare?"

"Very rare," he said solemnly. She responded with a tinkle of laughter that helped ease some of the tension he had been feeling since talking to Vincent. As Bastien listened to the sound, he was suddenly aware of a distinct reluctance to hang up the phone. He'd rather sit and talk to her than take care of business. Mind you, he'd rather talk to her in person, where he could watch the way her eyes danced with humor when she spoke, and the way her face became expressive and animated, and how her hands flew about like two birds as she described things. He'd found her charming and quite distracting on the way home from the airport.

"Well, give us a call if you have trouble finding Chris's apartment, and I'll put him on the phone to give you directions."

Bastien nodded. She was telling him to get off the phone and get moving. It felt almost like a rejection. It seemed she wasn't as eager to sit there talking as he. He cleared his throat and said, "Yes, I'll do that. Bye."

He disengaged the phone before she could respond, embarrassed and a touch angry at his eagerness to talk to her. She was only a human, he reminded himself—not really worth wasting time on. She'd be around for another thirty to fifty years, then drop dead, be put in the ground, and turn to dust as Josephine had.

Bastien swallowed hard at the memory of the one love he'd had in his life. He'd been young at the time, only eighty-eight, and had spent his life until then sewing his wild oats but not caring very deeply for the women he'd sown them with. Until Josephine. He'd fallen for her hard. So hard, in fact, that he'd ignored that he could read her mind: a sure sign, his mother always said, that a couple would make bad life mates. He had revealed himself to her, begging her to join him in eternal night—or what he had thought was eternal night back then; they'd had no clue in those days that they would eventually be allowed to walk in sunlight thanks to the advent of blood banks and the safety they offered.

"Josephine." The name was a whisper on his lips as he put the cell phone away. The great love of his existence. He'd offered her eternal life and all his riches, which was no small sum. But, repelled by what he claimed to be, she'd turned him down cold. Josephine had believed him soulless. She'd been so terrified of him, she'd dropped to her knees and begged God for immediate deliverance. She'd feared jeopardizing her own soul by even knowing him. Bastien had been forced to wipe her memory and give her up. He'd stood by and watched her fall in love with a human, marry him, bear his children, age, and die. It had broken his heart.

A sudden honk from behind made Bastien stiffen, then glance in the rearview mirror. Someone was leaving work late and wanted out. He was blocking the way.

Forcing himself to move, Bastien shifted the car

into drive and eased out onto the street, turning right to avoid having to wait for the traffic to clear. He drove up several streets without really thinking, then decided he'd better soon figure out what he was doing or he could end up driving around all night.

His first priority was Mrs. Houlihan, but he didn't have a clue where to start looking. As Vincent had made him realize, he didn't even know her first name, let alone if she had family to go to. He presumed she did. The woman would hardly be walking the streets, homeless and hungry and cold just to escape him. Would she?

Bastien grimaced to himself. For all he knew, she would. He didn't know a thing about his ex-housekeeper. Which meant the woman was not a matter he could deal with at the moment. He'd have to leave her for now and put his secretary on the matter tomorrow. Meredith had several dealings with Mrs. Houlihan, and might know more than he. If not, she could find out who had hired the woman and what was known about her. Bastien couldn't even recall how long the woman had been working for him. She'd been just another faceless employee until today.

With that issue on hold, Bastien decided to head to . . . What the hell was that editor's name again?

"Chris!" He spoke the same triumphantly as his memory kicked in. Christopher. Keyes. He'd see to getting the man some clothes from his apartment, pick up some subs from . . . whereever they sold subs, and head back to the penthouse where he could relax and figure out what to do with his houseguests until he had a new housekeeper to take care of them.

Even with his efficient secretary on the job, finding a replacement for Mrs. Houlihan could take days, even weeks. Because of what the family were, employees for any job with the Argeneaus had to be vetted very carefully.

"Hmmm. Weeks without a housekeeper," he murmured thoughtfully as he glanced at the address on his notepad. He turned the next corner to head in the right general direction. Weeks while he would be responsible for his guests. At least for Terri. The editor wasn't *really* his responsibility. He hadn't actually agreed to the man's presence in the penthouse; he was just suffering it at present. But Terri—he had agreed to take her in. In his book, that made her safety and well-being his responsibility. Which included keeping her out of Vincent's clutches.

Perhaps he'd take some time off work for the next little while and stick around the apartment to keep an eye on her. Yet the idea of taking time off was so alien to Bastien, the mere fact that he considered it was startling.

Time off work. He contemplated the matter seriously, and it did seem to be the best move if he was to keep Terri safe. Bastien was sure Kate would never forgive him if he allowed Vincent to bite her. He himself certainly wouldn't be happy about it. The very thought of his cousin's lips and teeth on the tender flesh of Terri's neck—or anything else—was repugnant! Yes. He'd take time off work and—well, sitting around the apartment would be boring. He couldn't see himself doing that. He'd never sat about

72

in his life. He was constantly on the go, his life constantly busy.

He stepped on the brake as the light ahead turned red, then glanced idly about until his attention was caught by a large sign in what appeared to be an empty lot, advertising the hours of a flea market. Bastien stared at it with interest. It was the weekend, and spring had arrived, which meant flea markets and street fairs would be springing up all over the city. He wondered if Terri might enjoy attending a couple of those while she was in New York. Then he spotted a taxi driving by with a Metropolitan Museum of Art sign set on its yellow top.

She might like to go there, too. Bastien hadn't been to the Met since its grand opening in Central Park back in . . . 1880, he thought it was. Had it been that long? He frowned over the date, but was pretty sure he was right. He'd always intended to go back, but had never really been able to find the time.

Dear God, it had been over 120-some years since he'd managed a couple of hours out to visit a museum? Well, it was about damned time he did, Bastien decided. He'd take Terri there. That's what he'd do. She'd enjoy it. But he wouldn't want to take her there on the weekend. The museum would be terribly crowded then. Perhaps Monday was a better day for a trip like that. He considered as the light changed, and he eased his foot from the brake to the gas pedal. Yes, he'd take her around the flea markets and street fairs this weekend, then take her to the museum on Monday. After that? Well, there were tons of places to take her and things to see in New York. Plays for instance. He hadn't seen one of those in—

Bastien's mind shied away from the calculation. He was pretty sure it had been longer than since he'd been to a museum. The idea of going just hadn't seemed all that interesting before now; but with Terri to entertain, and imagining it through her eyes, it did.

The thought reminded him of Lucern's words earlier that day. *"Everything seems more vibrant and interesting now. I find myself seeing things anew, seeing them as Kate must see them, rather than with the jaundiced eye I've cast over everything for ages. It makes a nice change."*

Bastien slammed his foot down on the brakes and sat frozen in the driver's seat, ignoring the sudden rush of honking behind him. He was causing a traffic jam, but he just didn't care. His mind was racing. Everything seemed more interesting when he considered showing it to Terri. He had an unusual concern for her well-being, and was distracted with the idea of keeping her and Vincent apart that—in truth—had nothing to do with what Kate might think or say. He doubted she'd be pleased if the editor got bit either, but that didn't really bother him. No. He wanted to keep Terri away from Vincent because the very idea of his cousin wooing her under his nose made him sick, because . . . *he was interested in her himself*.

A banging on the window drew his distracted gaze. A driver had gotten out of his vehicle and was now yelling and pounding on Bastien's door. He couldn't hear what the man was shouting—the honking from behind was too loud—but Bastien gathered the fellow wasn't happy with the holdup. He watched the man's mouth move for several minutes, then put the suggestion in his head to shut up and get back into his car. The moment the fellow did, Bastien eased his foot down on the gas pedal and set his Mercedes moving again.

The incident set his mind going in another direction. He had put the suggestion in the angry driver's mind without any effort. Could he control and read Terri's mind? If he could, she wasn't for him. It he couldn't . . . He'd have to wait till he got back to the penthouse to see.

Eager to get home, Bastien put on some speed, cursing the fact that Chris Keyes lived in Morningside Heights in the Upper West Side, far from his own expensive area of town.

When he got there, Bastien found he didn't need the keys C.K. had given him. The door to the apartment was wide open. An old lady stood inside, hands on hips as she nattered at a pair of workers carting out chunks of plaster and wood—clearing away the rubble from the fallen ceiling, was Bastien's guess. He entered and approached the woman, presuming she was the landlady. Wasting a good deal of time, he tried to explain to her that he was there on Chris's behalf; then he got tired of reassuring her and slipped into her mind to suggest she not notice his presence at all. Bastien then had to do so with the two workmen as well before being free to move into the bedroom.

He should have done so in the first place, Bastien thought with irritation as he slipped out of the apartment several minutes later. He had a haphazard collection of clothes stuffed into a gym bag he'd found on the bedroom floor. Tossing the bag on the passenger seat of his car, he started the engine, then paused. The next stop on his list was to collect subs, but he had no idea where those would be sold. Bastien almost got out of the car to ask the nearest passerby where he could find a shop that sold subs, then changed his mind. He'd wait till he was closer to home to ask directions. If the subs were usually heated, which he suspected a meatball sub would be—and for all he knew Terri's assorted sub might be too—he didn't want them to be cold by the time he returned. They sounded disgusting enough without being presented cold.

Unfortunately, it appeared that sub shops were scarce in the elite section of the city that housed Argeneau Enterprises; and the directions Bastien eventually got made him backtrack quite a fair distance to find what he was looking for. It also appeared that such shops were quite popular, because the line inside was atrocious. Bastien was tempted to leap into people's minds to cut to the front of the line, but forced himself to be patient and wait like everyone else. This wasn't an emergency. He had no excuse for such manipulation.

Half an hour later, and well over two hours after he had set out, Bastien rode up the elevator to the penthouse suite, carrying the gym bag with the editor's clothes, and a paper bag holding three subs, plain chips, two bags of barbecue chips, two Dr Peppers, and a Canada Dry ginger ale. He'd double ordered

Terri's selections, to give himself something to pick at so she wouldn't wonder why he wasn't eating.

"The conquering hero returns," Vincent said as Bastien strode into the living room.

Bastien ignored him and focused his attention on his two charges instead, then gaped. "They're asleep!"

"Well, what did you expect?" his cousin asked in amusement. "You took forever. I've been back for an hour—and I was on foot and actually had to hunt down my meal, not pick it up from the corner sub shop."

Bastien turned a suspicious glance his way. "You *did* feed outside? You didn't—?"

"No, I didn't bite your houseguests," Vincent assured him, then gestured to the editor who was sound asleep in a sitting position, his head bobbing on his chest. "That one's sleeping thanks to his painkillers, I think. And Terri's had a terribly long day. And it *is* late."

Bastien's gaze narrowed at the way Vincent's expression and voice softened. "It's only"—he lifted his watch to check—"nine."

"Nine here, two in the morning in England," Vinny pointed out.

"Oh yes." Bastien glanced from the sleeping woman to the bag of food in his hand. Despite how disgusting it sounded, the subs actually smelled good. "Do you think I should wake her up to eat?"

"No." His cousin shook his head. "She's been up since four A.M. England time."

"Four A.M.?" Bastien asked in dismay. He set the bags down on the coffee table.

"Her flight left at ten. She had to check in three hours before that, and Huddersfield is more than an hour's drive from Manchester Airport. Between all of that and the seven-hour flight turning into a nine-hour one thanks to the delay in Detroit—not to mention the long drive into town—she's had a terribly long, wearying day. Best to let her sleep."

"Hmmm." Bastien nodded in agreement, then scowled at Vincent. The man had obviously been talking to Terri before she'd drifted off. That annoyed him. "How long ago did she fall asleep?"

"About half an hour."

He nodded. If Vincent had taken an hour finding his dinner, that meant he'd got to talk to Terri for around half an hour. Bastien couldn't decide if he was annoyed that the man had got to talk to her for that time, or pleased that his conversation hadn't been invigorating enough to keep her awake. Deciding that it didn't matter, he moved around the coffee table and carefully scooped the woman up in his arms.

"Going to tuck her in?" Vincent teased.

"She'll get a crick in her neck sleeping out here," Bastien answered in a murmur. He carried her out of the room and down the hall. He managed to get the guest room door open, carry her inside, and set her on the bed without waking her up. Then he went to the master bedroom and tugged the comforter off the bed there to cover her with, rather than possibly wake her by trying to pull the duvet on her own bed out from under her. Once she was tucked in, he straightened and stared for a moment.

When awake, Terri Simpson seemed a curious

78

bundle of contradictions: funny, kind, unconsciously sexy, yet with a wickedly mischievous sense of humor. Asleep she was pure innocence, her face soft and sweet. She appeared to be a lovely human being, both inside and out. It was rare for him to think so highly of a mortal, or anyone for that matter. Most people he met seemed greedy and grasping. He had learned over time that everyone has an agenda; the trick was discovering what it was.

But Bastien didn't see that in this woman. She had flown thousands of miles and given up her vacation to help Kate with the upcoming wedding. He hadn't known her long, but from what he had seen, Terri was happiest giving and she didn't expect or feel comfortable taking anything from others. Most people would have delighted in having these luxurious accommodations rather than Kate's lumpy old couch, yet this woman had been uncomfortable at the idea of staying here. And she hadn't been happy that Bastien wouldn't let her contribute to the pittance for the dinner she now wasn't going to eat. He would learn more in the days to come, but at the moment, it appeared that Bastien had finally met a woman he could like and respect—and not feel that she was out to get something from him.

Terri sighed and shifted on the bed, and Bastien smiled; then he blinked in surprise as a loud snore ripped through the room. He stared at her aghast, covering his mouth to stifle the laughter that threatened to spill out. He backed quickly out of the room.

Well, Bastien thought as he pulled the door closed, no one was perfect. Chuckling openly, he walked back to the living room and took Terri's spot on the couch. It was still warm from her body, and he enjoyed the sensation before reaching for the food bag.

"What about *him?*" Vincent gestured to the sleeping editor as Bastien peered curiously into the bag of Subs.

"What about him?" Bastien pulled out one of the packages of barbecue chips and struggled with it briefly before managing to get it open.

"He'll get a crick in his neck, too, if you don't put him to bed," Vincent pointed out.

Bastien shrugged. Peering inside the bag, he saw thin slices of cooked potato with a sprinkling of red seasoning. "So, he gets a crick. He should have taken himself to bed."

Vincent chuckled, then gaped as Bastien took one chip out and bit cautiously into it. "What are you doing?"

"Trying the potato chips," he stated as he chewed the brittle delectation and pushed it around inside his mouth so that he could get the full flavor. It wasn't bad. Not bad at all. He didn't remember there being anything like this the last time he'd bothered with food.

"Dear God," his cousin breathed.

"What?" Bastien peered over in question.

"You're eating." Vincent stared in amazement, then added, "Food. You must be in love."

Bastien swallowed, and gave a bark of laughter. "Being in love isn't like being pregnant, Vincent. We don't eat when we're in love."

"Every one of us I know that has fallen in love has started eating again," his cousin said grimly.

Bastien considered as he swallowed, then popped another chip into his mouth. Lissianna had eaten. He wasn't sure about Etienne, but he knew Lucern was eating again. His chewing slowed, but then he shook his head and forced himself to relax. He'd only met the woman today. He couldn't be in love. Deeply in like, maybe, but not in love. And two chips did not really translate to "eating"—at least, not in his book.

"Speaking of food, when is the last time you *really* fed?"

There was no hiding his start of surprise at the question. Bastien knew Vincent wasn't referring to hunting, but simply to ingesting blood. And much to his amazement, Bastien suddenly realized that he hadn't done so since early that morning. He'd started to feel the need for blood while waiting at the airport for Terri's plane to arrive, but he hadn't thought of it since she hugged him. He'd been too distracted by everything else that was going on. Bastien refused to even think that his distraction was solely due to Terri's arrival. A lot had happened since then: Vincent's being here, the housekeeper quitting, Kate's arrival with her coworker, then leaving with Lucern. Lots, he assured himself.

Unfortunately that didn't explain why, now that things had settled down, he still wasn't feeling any particular desire for blood. Perhaps he just needed to see or actually smell the substance to stir his appetite. No doubt, once he went to his room and retrieved a bag of blood from the refrigerator built into his bed, he'd have his hunger back.

Bastien closed the chip bag, stuck it back with the rest of the food, and stood to carry it all to the kitchen. It was as he put the bag in the empty fridge that he recalled Terri stating the kitchen was empty of anything but a teapot, one cup, and tea bags. He closed the fridge door and opened a cupboard or two. Mrs. Houlihan had had her own small apartment in the back of the penthouse with a kitchen and everything, and he didn't doubt for a minute that those cupboards were full of food and dishes and whatever else outfitted a good kitchen. This one, however, was completely bare.

He should really see that it was filled up, Bastien decided. As it was, there was nothing to give Terri in the morning but tea. And cold subs, he supposed, closing the kitchen cupboards and tugging his notepad from his pocket.

He made a notation as he left the room and started up the hall to the master suite. He would put his secretary on to this task, too—when he called the office on Monday about Mrs. Houlihan, and about his taking some time off. She'd hire whoever was necessary and see that his cupboards and fridge were well stocked by the time they got back from the museum that day. In the meantime, he'd just have to take Terri out to eat. It wouldn't be a problem, as there were tons of restaurants in New York.

"Whistling and smiling too. Also signs of a man in love."

Bastien glanced around and found Vincent leaning nonchalantly against the door to Lucern's room. His cousin stood, legs crossed at the ankles, arms crossed over his chest, watching him with taunting amusement.

"I wasn't whistling."

"Yes, you were."

Bastien didn't bother denying it again. In truth, he *might* have been whistling as he walked up the hall; he wasn't sure. If so, it had been an unconscious act. He kind of thought he might have been smiling. It *was* possible. He had been feeling happy, after all; but he couldn't have been doing both. "Nobody can smile and whistle at the same time," he argued.

"You started up the hall smiling, then began to whistle about halfway along. You were also jingling the change in your pocket," Vincent informed him. "A classic happy-go-lucky, man-in-love action."

"How the hell would you know?" Bastien asked with irritation.

"I'm an actor," Vincent said with a shrug. "Knowing the outward signs of emotion is my business. I can't act like a man in love if I don't know what a man in love acts like. And you, my dear cousin, are showing all the classic first signs of a man falling in love."

"I just met her today," Bastien protested.

"Hmm. Love's a funny thing and often hits hard and fast. As you well know," Vincent said solemnly. "Besides, I said falling in love—not already there."

On that note, he turned and entered Lucern's bedroom, leaving Bastien alone in the hall. He'd been referring to Josephine when he said "As you well know." Vincent and Bastien had been close friends at the time he'd met and fallen in love with her. Vinny had witnessed Bastien's pain as Josephine had rejected him and called him a monster. Until then, Bastien had enjoyed the social whirl and the wild times the human world had to offer. It was after she broke his heart that he'd lost interest in it all and immersed himself in the family business. He had worked hard at accumulating money ever since. Money was the cornerstone of life; it never let you down or judged you; and money never said no.

Unfortunately, his close friendship with Vincent had been one of the things Bastien had let fall by the wayside in his determined drive to bury himself in the demands of business. He hadn't really noticed its absence until this evening. His cousin's teasing and cajolery tonight had reminded him of what he had been missing these last three hundred years or so. He'd been missing a lot. It was time to make up for it, but cautiously. Bastien had no desire to get his heart broken again.

Chapter Five

"Isn't it a beautiful day?" Terri asked, sucking in a deep breath of the fetid New York air as if it were an elixir.

Bastien nodded in agreement, even managing not to grimace. "Beautiful."

"The sun is shining. Birds are singing. I love springtime."

She sounded like a Disney character, he thought with irritation. Next she'd break out in song. An ode to the sun.

"Sun." Bastien muttered the word as if it were a curse. How could he have forgotten about the sun? He was a bloody vampire! And yet he'd made plans and invited Terri on an outing where he would spend the day wandering outside. And sunlight was in huge supply. It was a beautiful spring day, an uncharacteristically hot and *sunny* spring day. Bastien wouldn't even be surprised to hear that there were people sun-bathing all over the city, their skin being eaten alive by the sun's rays. As was his. The only difference was that his body was working in overdrive to continu-ously repair and replenish itself. Were he like others, his skin would just be aging by the minute. Instead, his body was dehydrating by the second.

On top of that, while Bastien had intended on packing a cooler full of blood to bring with him on this trip, he, the details man, had forgotten to do so. Not that this really made much difference, he sup-posed. He could hardly have walked around, bag of blood in hand as casually as others carried bottled water. Bastien had imagined he would just slip away every once in a while to replenish the much-needed liquid he was using at such an accelerated rate, but now that he was here, he saw how difficult that would be. He would have been reluctant to leave Terri alone in the neighborhood they were presently in.

"Bastien?" Terri asked, calling him back from his thoughts. "Are you going to stand at this table all day?"

He grimaced. This table at this particular flea mar-ket had a canvas awning, and he had been standing under it for several minutes. It was the only booth that did have one, but he couldn't stand here forever. He'd have to brave the sun again sooner or later, if only to go home. And he supposed that would be the smartest thing to do, but he really, really didn't want to end this outing so prematurely.

Bastien had woken up at six o'clock this morning and hopped eagerly in the shower, his mind on the

day ahead. He'd found himself whistling as he showered and dressed, then made his way out to the living
room to find Chris Keyes still on the couch, but
awake and looking rumpled and miserable. It seemed
the editor had suffered a fitful night on the sofa, waking and dozing off, then waking again, unable to do
anything else since he didn't know which room he
was supposed to have and would have had trouble
getting there on his own anyway.

Bastien had listened with little interest to the man
ramble about his rough night, until he heard mention
that Terri was fetching a glass of water from the
kitchen so that he might take another painkiller.
Leaving the editor alone in the living room, he'd immediately headed to the kitchen. There Terri was
rinsing out the cup she'd fetched water in the night
before. While she'd run fresh water into it, Bastien
had asked her about attending a couple of flea markets with him, surprised at how nervous he felt. It
wasn't until she'd turned bright, interested eyes on
him and told him she'd love to go that he'd felt himself relax.

Assuring her that he'd take her out to breakfast before they went anywhere, Bastien excused himself.
He rode the elevator down to the floor holding the
Argeneau offices, and quickly wrote up a list of instructions for his secretary to find when she arrived
on Monday. He hadn't wanted to forget to have her
take care of finding out if there were any relatives
that Mrs. Houlihan might have gone to in the city, or
to arrange for his kitchen to be stocked, and to have
her cancel any business meetings scheduled for the

next week. After setting the note on her desk, he'd returned to the penthouse to be informed by a sighing Chris Keyes that Terri had gone to her room to shower and change.

Bastien had been in such a good mood as he contemplated the day ahead, he'd taken pity on the editor and helped him to the room between the one Vincent was occupying and the one Terri was in. He'd even seen the man into the bathroom, waited patiently outside while he saw to his needs, then helped him out and onto the bed. He'd handed Chris the remote control to the television on the console against the wall opposite the bed, and promised he'd have someone deliver him a meal. Then Bastien fetched the gym bag full of clothes he'd gotten the night before and set it on the bed beside him, where it was within easy reach if the editor needed it.

Having done all that he could for Chris at the moment—or all he was willing to do—he'd gone out to the living room and found Terri dressed and ready to go. All other thoughts had been wiped from his mind at the sight of her happy excited face; and when she'd asked if they were taking a real New York cab and if they were, if she could flag it down like she'd seen done on TV, Bastien had said yes. Her excitement and pleasure as they had headed out and ridden downtown in the taxi she flagged had carried him along right up until they'd stepped out of the cab and he'd become aware of the sun beating cheerfully down on him. It was then Bastien had realized he'd forgotten the blood. He could not believe that he had been so remiss. He was an idiot! And that idiocy was about to see him ruin the day. He could not continue to walk around in this heat with the sun killing him.

Perhaps it would help if he bought a big floppy hat and a long-sleeved shirt from one of the booths or something. Bastien grimaced. He might as well buy a clown nose and floppy shoes, too. This day wasn't going at all as he'd hoped.

"Bastien?" Terri was suddenly at his side, concern on her face. "You look a bit . . . ill. Are you feeling all right?"

"Yes, I—It's just the heat and sun," he said finally. He wasn't surprised he looked sick. They had been outside for two hours, and he was really starting to feel it.

"I think I could use a break," he admitted, and sighed inwardly at the concern on her face. Now she'd think he was some pitifully weak guy who couldn't handle a little walking.

"If you like." She frowned. "You really aren't feeling well, are you?"

"No, I just—" He sighed. "I forgot about the sun. I have a bit of an allergy to it."

"Oh!" She looked relieved. "Well, why didn't you just say so?"

"I forgot," Bastien said. Then he realized how stupid that sounded. He'd hardly forget he was allergic to the sun. Then inspiration struck, and he added, "It's not really a regular thing for me. I'm just on some medication that makes me photosensitive."

"Oh." Something flickered in Terri's expression before her gaze slid over him with concern. "My husband was on medication that did that to him."

89

"It's nothing serious," Bastien assured her. "But the medication does make me react to sunlight, and I didn't think of that until I got out here and— What are you doing?" he interrupted himself to ask as she pulled him from the shade and started to drag him along the street.

"We're getting you out of the sun. You should have said you had an allergy. I'd have understood." Pausing on the corner, she glanced at the through traffic, spotted an approaching taxi, and stepped off the curb. Waving one hand like a pro, as if she'd lived in New York all her life, Terri stepped back up onto the curb as the taxi put its blinker on to pull over and slid to a stop in front of them.

"Where to?" the driver asked once they were in.

Terri glanced at Bastien. "I don't know your address."

Bastien hesitated. He really didn't want to bring their outing to an end. He just wanted to move indoors.

"Care to go to Macy's?" he asked. "It's not as cheap as the flea market, but still cheaper than England."

"Sure." She grinned.

"Some people just don't know how to behave," Terri muttered. She watched in disgust as an older female customer shrieked at the hapless cashier who had made the unfortunate mistake of trying to help her. The customer wanted to return a toaster, but didn't have a sales slip or even the box the toaster came in. When the cashier apologetically explained that she couldn't put through the return as it was, that it was company policy, the woman had gone off, and was still doing so. Did she look like a thief? she shrieked. She'd purchased the item in good faith and expected to be treated better than this at Macy's, and so on. Terri was finding it almost painful to watch. The cashier didn't deserve such abuse, and sickened by the scene, Terri turned to see Bastien watching with a frown.

"I wonder where the washrooms are," she murmured, glancing around the busy store.

Bastien peered down at her. "I know," he announced. "This way."

He gestured the way they had come, and Terri fell into step beside him. Bastien led her to the escalator. They rode up a floor, then turned right and walked a little distance.

"Up that hall," he said, helpfully. "I'll be waiting right here when you come out."

Nodding, Terri followed his directions. The door to the ladies' room was open, and Terri stepped inside and almost groaned aloud at the sight of the long line of shoppers waiting their turn at the stalls. The size of the line was daunting, and really rather incomprehensible to Terri, until she spotted the signs and realized that half the bathroom had been closed off for cleaning.

Wasn't that just her luck? she thought. Her timing had always been bad. Well, there was nothing for it but to wait. She just hoped Bastien was a patient man.

Outside, Bastien leaned against the wall, crossed his arms over his chest, his feet at the ankles, and prepared to wait. Women always took forever in the washroom. He'd learned that a long time ago. Three-hundred-plus-years ago, actually. It was one thing that hadn't changed over the ages, and a fact that still bewildered him. What did they do in there for all that time? He'd asked his mother and Lissianna the question many times over the centuries, but they'd never given him a satisfactory answer.

Perhaps Terri would be the exception to the rule. Not that he minded waiting. While it was a relief to be out of the sun, a good deal of damage had already been done, and he felt horrid. A bag or two of blood would be a welcome relief. His head was pounding and his body cramping from the exposure.

Two women turned the corner and walked past him, chattering happily as they headed toward the ladies' room. And that was another thing. Women often visited the bathroom in pairs. What was that all about?

The *tap-tap* of shoes drew his gaze to the left as the customer who had been haranguing the poor salesclerk downstairs came around the corner into view. She was grim-faced and mean-looking, a bitter old pill. She was the type of person Bastien had always preferred biting in the past—back when feeding off living humans was necessary. Bastien had always tended toward biting people he didn't like. It just caused less guilt than feasting on someone sweet and nice and unsuspecting. He'd often chosen people who were criminals, or the selfish, but the mean-spirited were always his favorite. Bastien had taken great delight in leaving the crusty old nasties feeling weak and confused.

He smiled pleasantly as this crusty old biddy came

abreast of him, and received a sneer for his trouble. Oh, yes—she was the sort he would have delighted in taking down a peg. In the past, while taking their blood, he'd often taken the opportunity to put the thought in these nasty people's heads that they should be kinder to those around them, which had always left him with a sense of satisfaction. It had felt almost like he was doing the world a favor by feeding on them.

Bastien stilled as she moved past him and he caught a whiff of her. Blood—sweet and heady. He felt his cramps intensify, and tried to ignore them by pondering the woman's blood type. She was a diabetic, he recognized from her scent. And she was a diabetic who either didn't know she was, or who didn't take care of the problem. He was guessing the latter. He was also guessing that she had an open cut somewhere, or the scent wouldn't be so strong.

He watched her walk down the hall and disappear through the bathroom door. A moment later however, she came marching back out. And march was the only word for it; the woman was obviously on the warpath

"If you're waiting for someone, you can expect a long wait," she informed him with almost gleeful anger. "They've got half the stalls closed for cleanup, leaving a ridiculous line. Idiot women! They should be complaining, like I plan on doing. Service used to be important."

Some people just weren't happy unless they had something to bitch about, Bastien thought with a sigh. He would definitely have done the world a favor by biting her, if he was still a biter.

A whiff of the sweet scent of blood hit him again as she passed. This time, it was stronger, which could only mean the open cut was on this side of her. The concentrated scent this time caused concentrated pain, and Bastien half doubled over with it. He really needed blood. He should have stayed out of the sun. He was an idiot, and one who he very much feared was about to ruin not just the trip around the flea market, but the entire day. He was going to have to return to the penthouse early just so he could feed. The task would take only a matter of minutes, but their outing would certainly be ruined.

"What's the matter with you?"

Bastien glanced up to see the biddy staring at him with disgust.

"What are you, one of those drug addicts?" she asked, and again there was a hint of glee in her words. She was enjoying the idea of his suffering.

Bastien really wished biting was still allowed; he'd give her an attitude adjustment like— But feeding was allowed in emergencies, he reminded himself. And judging by the cramps he was suffering, he was reaching an emergency point. He straightened slowly and offered the old crank a charming smile.

Terri sighed with relief as she closed the stall door behind her. Bastien had probably decided she'd sneaked out a bathroom window and run off or something by this point. If she hadn't had to go to the bathroom so badly, and feared losing her spot in line, she would have gone back out to explain what was taking so long. She would have told him to go shop, maybe have a coffee and she'd meet up with him somewhere in half an hour.

She would have been off on her time estimate, however, Terri thought as she took care of business, then left the stall. She was in such a rush, her hands were still a bit damp from washing as she hurried out of the bathroom and up the hall toward where Bastien leaned patiently against the wall.

"I'm sorry," she blurted as she reached him. "They were—"

"Cleaning the washroom and had half the stalls blocked off," Bastien finished for her soothingly. "Yes, I know. One of the other shoppers told me. It's all right. Not your fault."

"Oh." Terri relaxed, glad to know he hadn't been left wondering what on earth she could be up to all this time, and that he didn't seem angry about the wait. "Well, I was as quick as I could be."

"I'm sure you were. Shall we go?"

Nodding, Terri fell into step beside him to walk back out into the store. She glanced at Bastien curiously as they walked, wondering what was different, then she realized that he didn't look quite as unwell as he had. He didn't look 100 percent, but getting him out of the sun had already brought about some improvement.

"You're feeling a bit better?" she asked.

"A bit," he admitted. "Not back to normal yet, but I'm much improved."

"Good." Terri smiled at him. "Perhaps a little more time out of the sun will right you completely."

"That and a bit more lunch," he agreed.

She looked at him with surprise. "Did you wander off and have something to eat while I was in the ladies' room?"

"What?" He glanced sharply at her as they stepped on the down escalator.

"You said a bit *more* lunch," she pointed out.

"Oh." He relaxed again. "I meant a bit *of* lunch. I misspoke."

"Oh." She nodded. "We could do that now if you like."

"Let's shop around first," he suggested as they reached the first floor. "It isn't quite noon yet, and we *are* here at Macy's. We may as well get a bit of shopping in. Then we can break for lunch and decide where you want to go next."

"Okay." Terri agreed absently, her feet slowing as they passed the cashier who had been berated in such a humiliating manner earlier. The mean customer was still there, but her whole demeanor had changed. She was smiling apologetically and patting the girl's hand.

"I'm so sorry, dear. I don't know what I was thinking of, treating you that way. I shouldn't expect you to break the rules for me, and really—I don't even have the box for the toaster, do I? Please forgive my earlier behavior," the woman was saying.

Terri's eyebrows rose. "Wow," she whispered. "What an about-face."

"Hmmm." Bastien just shrugged. "She must have got an attitude adjustment."

"Well, no one needed it as much as she did, but it's still rather surprising. I wouldn't have believed that someone could change their attitude that swiftly if I hadn't just seen it."

"Life is full of surprises," he said mildly, then smiled at her. "So, where do you want to start? Womens wear? Jewelry? Perfume?"

"Are you getting tired?"

"No." Bastien glanced at Terri and forced a smile for her benefit. In truth, he was exhausted. The bitter old biddy he'd snacked on had eased the worst of his hunger, but not all of it, and he was still suffering. He could use another pint or so of blood, but hadn't had the opportunity to take one. And no one had seemed as appropriate a victim.

Bastien smiled to himself at the memory. He'd enjoyed changing that old woman's attitude. She'd been much more pleasant once he'd finished with her. Of course, it was just a temporary adjustment, but at least the salesclerk in the store had benefitted. Perhaps she wouldn't go home today hating her job, the public, and the world at large.

"Oh, look! Victoria's Secret." Terri stopped walking and simply stared at the storefront with pleasure.

Bastien smiled at her almost awed expression. The woman was so easily pleased. After shopping at Macy's they'd had lunch in a little deli, he picking at some sort of chicken sandwich they'd both ordered while she chattered away and devoured hers. The food actually tasted all right—pretty good, in fact—but after years of not eating, he didn't have the stomach for large quantities. After lunch they'd wandered, ducking into a music and discount DVD store. Terri had been very good about keeping to the shaded areas to keep him out of the sun. Now they stood in shadow under one of the many construction scaffolds that seemed to fill the city, and she gaped at the store across the street with its half-naked dummies in the window.

"We should go in," Bastien suggested.

"Yes," she breathed. Many women would have fussed that he, a man, would hardly have any interest in visiting a women's lingerie store. Then they would have said, "Well, all right," as if really reluctant to drag him in, despite the fact that they were dying to go. Terri didn't bother with that. She wanted to go in; he had suggested she should, and she had agreed. End of story. It was wonderful.

"Come on." Taking her elbow, he urged her to the corner as the WALK sign began to flash. They hustled across the street, reaching the opposite side and ducking into the Victoria's Secret just as the light turned red.

Terri paused inside the door, her gaze shifting quickly over everything. Perfumes and escalators were in the center, and silk and lace everywhere else. Bastien could almost imagine her mind working out where to go first. Left, right, up? She went left. A logical move, he silently approved. It allowed them to work the store in a clockwise fashion.

The first clerk they came across was friendly. She greeted them pleasantly and suggested they approach her if they had any questions, then she left them alone. Terri moved through the nighties in the area, oohing over this, ahhing over that, and at last they made their way around the store to the escalators and the second story full of panties and bras.

"Is there something I can help you with?" another woman asked.

Terri set down the pretty purple lace panties she'd been looking at and smiled. A beautiful, stick-thin model of a salesgirl was eyeing her in a condescending manner. "No, thanks," she said. "I'm just looking."

"Hmm." The woman pursed her lips and looked her over as if she were dog meat.

Bastien was off to the side, trying to stay out of the way. He had noticed that Terri seemed to flit about, looking here and there, and rarely stopping. He had found that if he followed her too closely, he ended up having to step to the side or backtrack to get out of the way as she whirled and changed direction. Such movements could be quite abrupt, as her eyes were constantly skating over the area ahead, and if she saw something that caught her eye, she beetled off toward it. If not, she veered off another way, or turned back. It was just easier to give her space to maneuver. But now Bastien moved forward, his protective instincts coming to the fore. This clerk obviously wasn't impressed with Terri's attire, her worn jeans and T-shirt.

"We'll call on you if we need any help," he spoke up, drawing the woman's eye and her full attention.

Her attitude changed in a heartbeat, her lips unpursing to become a warm smile. "Well, hello."

The clerk spoke as if stumbling across a lovely treasure in her store. Bastien tried not to grimace. He was a good-looking man, and used to women paying him attention, but he had seen the way this one's eyes had skated from his face to the expensive watch he wore, to the family signet ring with the Argeneau *A* etched in diamonds. She smelled money, and liked the smell.

Bastien glanced toward Terri to see how she was reacting, only to find that she'd moved off and was now examining a rather pretty black satin bra that would look quite lovely on her. At least, it did in his mind as he imagined it. Forgetting about the clerk, he moved after Terri.

"That's lovely."

"Yes, it is," she agreed with a grin.

"There are matching panties for it." The clerk had followed, and now she couldn't be more helpful. Moving past them she returned with several pairs. "Let's see. I'm a small. That would make you . . . what?" She glanced down to consider Terri. "An extra-large?" she suggested innocently. Then she turned to Bastien and added in a husky voice, "I can model these for you."

Bastien had to bite his lip as Terri's eyes nearly popped out of her head. She flushed, then seemed to go terribly calm. Her voice was kind when she spoke. "That won't be necessary, I'm sure. And no, I'm not an extra-large. But don't feel bad for making the error. It's the boobs," she said bluntly. "It can be terrible being so well endowed. They often give the first impression that you're large everywhere." Her gaze dropped briefly over the woman's almost flat chest, and she commented, "You're lucky you don't have any at all to cause that problem."

While the clerk choked on that, Terri added,

"Don't worry, though, a little more experience in your *career* and I'm sure you'll get the hang of sizing your customers properly."

Bastien grinned at the furious clerk over Terri's head, enjoying the woman's discomfort. Had he thought Terri needed protecting? Obviously not.

Terri turned to him and said, "I think I've had enough shopping for now. How about an ice cream?" She didn't wait for an answer, but marched off toward the escalator at a quick clip.

"You handled that beautifully," Bastien said as he caught up to her.

"I was a bitch," Terri responded. "And halfway through my ice cream I'm going to feel horrible for behaving so badly."

He stared at her blankly. This was her idea of being a bitch? And she'd feel bad after the way the clerk had treated her? If so, then it *did* seem Terri needed protecting. From herself, Bastien decided. She'd handled the woman with class and much more kindly than most would have. Others would have got huffy, or just plain freaked. Someone else might have complained to management and had the girl fired. Terri had merely given her a gentle set-down. And she felt bad for it! Incredible.

Chapter Six

Terri was stepping out of the shower when the phone started ringing. Snatching a towel off the rack, she wrapped it around herself and ran for the bedroom and the phone on the bedside table.

"Hello?" she said breathlessly, dropping to sit on the edge of the rumpled bed.

"Terri?"

"Kate!" She sat up straight, a smile curving her lips. She was pleased to hear from her cousin. She knew that Lucern had called and spoken to Bastien Friday night to assure him that they'd arrived in California safely, but Terri had been sound asleep at the time and had missed her chance to speak to Kate. Now it was Monday morning, and the first time either Kate or Lucern had called again as far as Terri knew. "How's the conference going?"

"It's going fine," her cousin assured her, adding apologetically, "I'm sorry about this. Here you flew all the way over to spend time with me and help with the wedding, and I—"

"Don't worry about it," Terri interrupted. "It's work. I understand. Besides, Bastien has been taking me around the city and showing me a good time, so it's—"

"What?" Kate said. "I'm sorry, Terri, but did you just say that Bastien has been taking you around the city and is showing you a good time?"

"Yes." Perplexed by her reaction, Terri listened as a man's voice—Lucern's, she imagined—rumbled in the distance. Then Kate must have covered the phone, because all Terri could hear were bits of a muffled conversation.

"Sorry," she apologized at last, speaking clearly into the phone again. Then she asked in nonchalant tones, "So, *how* has Bastien been showing you a good time?"

"How?" Terri dropped back to lie on the bed. She stared at the awning overhead. "Well, Saturday he took me out for breakfast, then around to the flea markets. We wandered a couple of those for a bit, then—."

"Flea markets?" Kate interrupted with disbelief. "You mean *outdoor,* open-air flea markets?"

"Yes. I take it you know about his photosensitvity, then—caused by the medication he's taking?"

There was a pause from the other end of the line. "Yes. I knew about his photosensitivity."

That was it. No explanation of what the medication was, or what it was for. Terri had briefly hoped her cousin would enlighten her. Disappointed, she

103

forced herself to continue. "Anyway, the sun started getting to him after the second flea market—well, really I think it was getting to him during the first, but he only admitted it and explained about his condition at the second. Once he did, we caught a taxi to Macy's and switched to indoor shopping. Which was fun," she added quickly. "We mostly just browsed in shops and talked and ate. It was nice and relaxing. Then we came back here, got changed, and went out for dinner. He claimed he was completely recovered by the time dinner was done, and offered to take me to a movie, but I'd noticed he still wasn't eating much and thought he might still be feeling a little rough, so I claimed I was a bit tuckered out from all that walking and probably suffering a bit of jet lag. So we stayed in."

Terri paused and cocked her head as Kate indulged in another muffled conversation with Lucern on the other end of the phone. It sounded like she was passing on the details of Terri's Saturday.

"I'm sorry." Her cousin was back, sounding a bit breathless. "What about Sunday? Did you two do anything Sunday?"

"Oh . . . er . . . well, yes," Terri admitted, then sighed and launched into the explanation. "We started a little later on Sunday. Bastien had to go down to his office and take care of some business, so we went out for brunch when he got back. There was some kind of parade going on when we came out of the restaurant, so we stood under the awning of a store to watch. Then we went to a couple of street fairs. I wasn't sure we should, what with his condition and all, but it was an overcast day and he wore a long-sleeved shirt and this hat and glasses and . . ." She laughed at the memory. He had looked pretty silly in the gear. He'd reminded her of the Invisible Man, trying to cover up every patch of his nonexistent skin to hide his state, or a celebrity playing Hide from the Public. Still, it wasn't his fault, and they'd had great fun at the street fair.

"Then we picked up some takeout Chinese and brought it back to eat with Chris," she finished, then added, "Speaking of Chris, Katie, he's not taking this broken leg thing at all well. He's terribly depressed and whiney. Or, has he always been whiney?"

"Oh, who cares about Chris!" her cousin exclaimed impatiently. "Tell me what else you and Bastien did."

"Katie!" Terri gave a laugh.

"Oh, you know what I mean. He'll be fine. And men are always whiney when they're injured or hurt. Now, tell me what else you did Sunday."

"Well, that was about it. We ate Chinese food in, and watched some rented movies. It was nice and relaxing. Bastien's a charming host."

"Yes, he can be charming." The grin in Kate's voice was obvious. "Where is he now?"

"In the Argeneau offices."

"No, he isn't," Kate said promptly. "I called there first and there was no answer. Even his secretary, Meredith, isn't in. But then, she won't arrive for another hour, I don't think."

"He must be on his way back up here," Terri decided. "He only went down to leave Meredith some instructions for the day. We're going to the museum."

"What?" Kate cried. "On a workday?"

"When I got up this morning, he said he'd had a business meeting scheduled for the day, but that the key attendee had canceled and rescheduled, so he thought he'd go to the museum. He invited me to go with him," she explained, twisting the phone cord around her finger. Her news was followed by yet another muffled conversation at the other end of the phone, but this time the hand or whatever Kate was using to cover the phone, must have slipped, because Terri heard Lucern grunt and say what sounded like ". . . he's probably the key attendee who canceled." Then the phone was covered properly, and Terri couldn't make out the rest.

Letting the cord unravel from her finger, she shifted onto her side on the bed and ran her free hand over the comforter beneath her, the same that had covered her when she'd awoken Saturday morning. Terri had recognized it from Bastien's bed in the master suite, and knew he must have carried her to bed and covered her with it. He hadn't asked for it back yet, and she hadn't thought to return it. In truth, she was rather reluctant to do so. It smelled so good.

Smiling, she buried her nose in the material and inhaled the scent clinging to it. The duvet still smelled of Bastien, a smell she liked. Terri decided she'd have to ask him what cologne he wore. Perhaps she'd buy it as a gift for someone someday.

"Terri?"

"Yes." She shifted and sat up guiltily on the bed, embarrassed despite the fact that Kate couldn't possibly see what she was doing.

"You're very lucky. Bastien is a wonderful man. Smart, hardworking, nice, and a perfect gentleman, he'll—"

"Kate," Terri interrupted. "We're going to the museum. It isn't necessarily a date. The man's just being a good host until you get back."

"Uh-huh." Her cousin didn't sound convinced. "Have fun. I know you will. And tell him hello from us. We'll call again in the next couple of days to see how the romance is progressing."

"There's no romance to progress!" Terri protested. But she was speaking to dead air. Kate had already hung up the phone. Terri stared at the receiver in her hand with dismay. Good Lord, she thought faintly, had Kate and Lucern lost their minds? She and Bastien were just going to the museum, but to those two that was apparently the equivalent of a romance. Jeez, she hoped the guy didn't ever ask her out on a real date. Kate and Lucern would consider them as good as married.

Shaking her head, Terri replaced the receiver and pushed herself off the bed. She had to get dressed and fix her hair. She was supposed to be ready to go in fifteen minutes.

"Oh, look!"

Bastien smiled as Terri rushed to the next exhibit: a work in enamel, silver, silver-gilt, and gold.

"'A Reliquary of the True Cross (Staurotheke), late eighth, early ninth century Byzantine,'" she read aloud as he caught up to her. She stepped back, tilting her head first left, then right, and squinted before

107

pronouncing, "It's really ugly, huh? Looks kind of Picasso-ish to me."

Bastien glanced at the piece and nodded. He had to agree, it did look rather Picasso-ish. Not that Terri saw him nod; she'd already noticed the next exhibit in the room and rushed off with another "Oh, look!"

Chuckling softly, Bastien followed. The next piece was a small house-shaped box seven or eight inches tall, and just about as wide.

" 'Bursa Reliquary, early 900s, North Italian, Bone, copper-gilt, wood,' " she read to him, then sighed. As she peered at it, this time she didn't step back, but leaned closer and walked slowly around its glass case. "Look at the detail," she said with awe as she came around to the front. "I can't believe they were able to do such delicate work back then. It must have taken someone forever to make this."

"Yes," Bastien agreed, stepping closer to eye the object with new interest.

"Oh, lo—"

Bastien turned with surprise when the usual refrain was cut short. She was staring at him in dismay. Before he could ask what was wrong, she blurted, "I'm sorry. I'm probably driving you crazy, dragging you around here like this. I—"

"Not at all," he assured her. "I'm enjoying myself. And your enthusiasm just makes me enjoy it more."

"Really?" She appeared uncertain.

"Really," he assured her, his hand moving of its own volition to catch hers and give a reassuring squeeze. And it was true; he couldn't think of a more delightful companion with whom to visit the museum. Terri's excitement and awe were not just a treat to watch, but were also infections. These were feelings Bastien hadn't experienced in a long while. It had been the same at the flea markets and street fair. Her delight in the simplest things, her laughter and enjoyment in each outing, had rubbed off on him, adding to his own pleasure.

Terri smiled at him, then her gaze drifted down to their entwined hands. A light blush rose to color her cheeks.

Bastien had a sudden urge to lean forward and kiss her, but they were in the middle of the Medieval Christianity section, and that just didn't seem to be the place for kisses. So he let go of her hand and glanced toward the next exhibit. "Oh, look," he teased lightly. "Another reliquary."

Terri grinned, then moved to the next glass case. Soon her shyness vanished, and she was again exclaiming over this statue or that painting.

Bastien followed her, enjoying her reactions as much as any of the exhibits. By the time they decided to stop for something to eat and drink, he had come to the conclusion that this woman was a work of art in herself. Her responses and pleasure were so unaffected and natural, it was fascinating to watch. She was just as precious as any of the items here. She was a treasure he'd been fortunate to have had cast in his path.

"It's nice outside. Why don't we take this out and eat it in the shade?" Terri suggested as the cashier handed back her change. She'd insisted on paying, and had been faster on the draw than Bastien. He suspected most women would have been content to let him foot every bill. Terri wasn't most women. It didn't matter to her that he was rich and could afford with ease what she couldn't; she wanted to contribute.

"That sounds like a plan," he agreed, and took the strawberry smoothies off the tray, leaving her to carry the sandwiches as they made their way out of the cafeteria.

"I can't believe it's past lunchtime already," she commented as they settled on the stone cornice that ran along the front of the museum. "The morning's gone so fast."

"Yes," Bastien murmured, half concentrating on the sandwich he was unwrapping, half concentrating on the older gentleman settled on the stone ledge beside them. The fellow had a bag of bread in his hand. As Bastien ate, he watched the man open the bag and take some bread out, breaking it up to toss to the birds that were quickly gathering. There was soon quite an assortment of the creatures flocking around. Small birds, large birds—Bastien didn't know the names of them all, but he did recognize the robins, grey catbirds and pigeons. The pigeons appeared to be the most aggressive birds in the bunch, and he watched them begin to flock in earnest, snapping greedily at the bits of bread the man was throwing. It became obvious that this was a regular ritual, when the more brazen birds began snatching the bread right out of his hand and even perching on him to get to it.

"I'm really enjoying the museum. Thank you for bringing me," Terri said.

Bastien glanced toward her to find that she was watching the feeding session with as much interest as he, though he suspected for a different reason. He didn't like how aggressive the creatures were getting, and was watching for one of the birds to decide that the sandwiches he and Terri held were also on offer. He worried that if they did, the pigeons might make a dive for one of them. Terri, however, seemed just innocently enjoying the spectacle, oblivious of the possible threat.

He considered warning her, but didn't want to spoil her enjoyment, so Bastien merely inched a little closer on the ledge so that he could fend off any possible threat. "I'm glad you're enjoying it. So am I."

She smiled slightly, then raised her smoothie to take a drink.

"How are your feet holding out?" he asked. They had been walking the museum for more than four hours.

"They're good," she answered quickly.

Too quickly perhaps, he thought, and he made an attempt to slip into her mind and read the truth. It was the first time he'd thought to do so since arriving home with dinner to find her sleeping, but this seemed a better excuse to try. They'd been on the go since getting up, and he didn't want to wear her out.

After spending most of the night sitting up talking and laughing, Bastien had slept until seven o'clock this morning. He and Terri never seemed to run out of things to say to one another and had stayed up later and later each evening of the past few days. Last night, they'd lingered in the living room until three in the morning. By rights, he should have been exhausted when he'd woken up after only four hours of sleep, but that hadn't been the case; Bastien had bounded out of bed full of energy and eager to meet the day—and to find Terri.

A quick tour through the main areas of the penthouse proved she wasn't yet up, so Bastien had scrawled a quick note of explanation as to where he was, in case she got up while he was gone. Then he had headed down to the Argeneau offices to be sure there was nothing to take care of before they left.

When he'd returned to the penthouse, Terri had been up and about and looking perky and cheerful and no more affected by her lack of sleep than he. She'd also been freshly showered, dressed, and obviously ready for their outing. Bastien had taken her to the Stage Deli for breakfast, and watched her eat with an enthusiasm that always surprised him before they'd walked to the museum. They'd been walking ever since, Terri flitting through exhibits, Bastien following, his attention torn between the museum offerings and his companion's unabashed enjoyment. It had all been so distracting that it hadn't occurred to him to try to read or control her mind.

"Did I mention that Kate called this morning, while you were down in your office?" Terri asked.

Bastien blinked, distracted from the effort to slip into her mind. "No. Did she?" he asked.

"Yes. She seemed surprised that we were going to the museum. I gather you don't take a lot of time off work."

"Er . . . no. I'm a bit of a workaholic," he admitted. It was probably the largest understatement ever made by man or vampire. Work, until now, had been all there was to Bastien.

Terri nodded. "I hope you don't feel you *have* to take me around. I mean, I'm enjoying this," she assured him quickly. "But I don't want to intrude on your affairs."

"My meeting was canceled," he reminded her, not mentioning that he had been the one to cancel it. He was the key attendee who was unavailable. And he had no intention of being available all week.

Her expression brightened. "It was, wasn't it?"

Seeming soothed, Terri relaxed and finished off her sandwich. Bastien watched, fascinated by her mouth as she chewed and swallowed. She had such large, full lips. He wondered briefly what it would be like to kiss them. How they would feel beneath his own. If they were as soft as they appeared.

"Is there something on my face?" Terri asked, suddenly aware that Bastien was staring at her.

Bastien blinked, apparently surprised by the question, then relaxed his posture and turned his gaze to his sandwich. It was only half eaten, while her own was finished, she noted. The man didn't seem to eat much. He'd really only picked at his breakfast that morning. Terri felt self-conscious about her own appetite in comparison, but she was always ravenous in the mornings.

She watched him lift the sandwich to his mouth. He took a bite and chewed with a perplexed expression. It fascinated her. "Is there something wrong with your sandwich?"

"What?" His gaze shifted back to her. "Oh, no, I'm just surprised at how good it tastes."

Terri laughed. Sometimes he said the oddest things. When they were touring the Renaissance section of the museum, he'd spoken with such authority and knowledge about the period that she had finally asked if he'd taken history at the university. The question had seemed to make him uncomfortable, and he'd flushed and muttered that he'd taken a course or two.

"Do you have any brothers or sisters?"

Terri gave a start. Bastien's question had seemed to come out of the blue. "No. I was an only child."

"Oh, yes. I think Kate mentioned something about that. You're the only child of a single parent."

Terri nodded. "It was tough on my mother, but she was a wonderful woman. Hardworking. We didn't have much money sometimes, but there was always lots of love." She tilted her head curiously. "You have another brother and sister besides Lucern, don't you? And you grew up with both parents? It must have been nice having siblings."

Bastien snorted. "Sometimes. Sometimes it's a pain."

"But you wouldn't give them up for the world, I'm sure," she guessed, reading the affection in his expression.

"No, I wouldn't," he admitted. "Although there was a time or two I thought I might."

"Tell me," she urged, and listened with amusement as he launched into a tale of childhood antics. Terri could tell Bastien was editing the tale as he told it—

there were small hesitations and pauses that gave him away—but she was becoming used to that. They had done a good deal of talking over the last three days, and she was quite sure that the man edited most of the stories he told her. Terri didn't really mind, though; she enjoyed listening to and talking with him just the same. She enjoyed *him*.

She watched the way his eyes sparkled with re-membered glee, then found her gaze fixing on his lips. They curved first in wry self-deprecation, then amusement. Terri watched them move as he spoke, fascinated by their contours and the plumpness of the lower lip in comparison to the upper. And as he ram-bled on, she found herself wondering what it would be like if he kissed her.

She blinked as that thought crossed her mind, then she straightened abruptly, both alarmed and startled. Terri had thought Bastien attractive from the start, and interesting to talk to. She had enjoyed the last three days immensely, and found herself waking up looking forward to what the day might bring. But she hadn't realized that she was "attracted" attracted to the man. Dear God, she was in trouble, Terri realized faintly; then she became aware that Bastien had fallen silent. Her gaze shot from his lips to his eyes, and widened slightly at the expression on his face.

"I—" she began uncertainly, but he cut her off by suddenly capturing her face in both hands and tug-ging her forward. He covered her open mouth with his own.

It had been so long since she'd been properly kissed, Terri was a little overwhelmed by the sudden invasion of his tongue into her mouth. She stilled, a plethora of responses rushing through her mind ranging from confusion to dismay. Then pleasure slid past all that to suffuse her mind, and Terri relaxed against Bastien, breathing a sigh into his mouth. It seemed to her that the moment she did, a sudden squawking set up next to them. They broke apart, and glanced at the birds now squabbling over the last of the old man's bread, then relaxed and glanced back at each other.

"I'm sorry," he said, as their gazes met.

"Are you?" she asked huskily.

"No."

"Neither am I."

They were both silent for a moment; then Bastien glanced at the birds flocking around the man who'd been feeding them. His bread bag was empty, but the birds were still hungry.

Bastien tossed the rest of his sandwich into the flock, cleared his throat, and glanced back to her. "Have you had enough of the museum today? We can come another day to finish looking around if you have."

Terri hesitated. In truth, she *had* seen enough of the museum for one day. Her feet were okay, but she didn't think they would be for much longer. More to the point, if she saw too much more, she feared it would all start to blur in her mind. Still, she was willing to risk both outcomes rather than see this interlude come to an end.

"We could do a little shopping," Bastien suggested.

Terri brightened at the suggestion. He wasn't calling an end to their outing, just switching gears, and the idea of more shopping was attractive. She hadn't really bought anything on Saturday. They had been mostly window-shopping, but she did want to make some purchases while here. Everything was terribly expensive in England. New York prices were cheap in comparison.

"That sounds like fun—if you don't mind," she added with sudden concern. Most men weren't really into shopping, and she didn't want to bore Bastien by making him take her around the shops for the second time in three days.

"I like to shop," he assured her as he got to his feet. He took her hand so naturally as he turned toward the steps, Terri hardly noticed. When she did, she bit her lip and avoided looking at him. They descended the steps to the sidewalk in front of the museum. She felt like a teenager again, nervous and awkward and suddenly tongue-tied.

They walked in companionable silence along the street, Terri glancing curiously at everything they passed. This was only her third trip to New York. She'd visited Kate before, but then they'd spent most of their time talking, shopping in the Village, and talking some more. Kate and Terri had always been particularly close, more friends than just cousins. She smiled at the oddity of her thoughts. She made it sound as if friends were more important than relatives to her, and in some ways they were. You chose your friends, but couldn't pick your relatives. Terri was fortunate in that most of her relatives were also friends. Their family was made up of some wonder-

117

ful, caring, and giving aunts, uncles, and cousins. Terri loved every one of them. It was the one thing she missed the most living in England: her family.

"How did you end up in England?" Bastien asked suddenly, holding open the door of Bloomingdale's for her to enter.

Terri considered the question in silence, and sadness overwhelmed her. "I moved there when I married. My husband was English."

"You said you aren't married, so I take it the marriage either dissolved in divorce or your husband died," Bastien said quietly. "I'm guessing he died."

Terri glanced at him in surprise. "You're right. But what made you say that?"

He shrugged. "Bad memories would have seen you move back to America. Only good memories would keep you in a foreign country when the reason for moving there was gone," he explained. "Besides, only a fool would give up a treasure like you."

Terri felt herself flush with pleasure at the compliment, but his question and words brought painful memories to the fore. She'd been young when she'd married and moved to England the year after her mother's death, not quite twenty. Ian had been only a couple of years older. It had all seemed a grand adventure at first. He'd worked at his government job; she'd attended the university. They'd bought a little cottage and played house for a couple of years . . . until he'd been diagnosed with Hodgkin's disease and begun the battle for his life, a battle he'd lost three years later.

Terri had just earned her bachelor's degree the year

the diagnosis was made. She continued her education for a while afterward, but had given it up in the last year of her husband's illness to be with him. At barely twenty-five years old, Terri had become a widow, left with little more than a cozy little cottage and a small insurance settlement.

She'd used the insurance to finish her education, graduating with a doctorate that had led to her being offered a professorship at the University of Leeds. Terri had spent the last five years working hard at a job she loved, and filling her off-hours with volunteer work with community theater. All of which had allowed her to avoid unwanted emotional entanglements. At first, she'd told herself—and all her well-meaning friends and relatives who tried to set her up on dates—that it was too early to get involved with someone else. But after a couple of years even Terri no longer believed that. The truth was, even now at the age of thirty-three, she was afraid to get involved again.

Terri had barely survived the death of her mother. Ian had been the life raft she clung to in that dark time. His brother Dave, and Dave's wife, Sandi, had been the ones to see her through his death. She had avoided emotional entanglements ever since. It was easier to just live single, untouched by feelings that would later turn to heartbreak.

Or so Terri had always thought. Yet, here she was, walking along hand in hand with Bastien, after having been kissed properly for the first time in ten years!

Without really thinking about it, Terri slid her hand free, stopping at a display to pick up a small black purse and examine it. She couldn't have stopped the physical withdrawal from Bastien any more than she could the mental one. Her guard had been down, but it was back up and in place again. It was for the best.

Terri didn't like to think of herself as a coward. She could take all the physical pain that life could dish out, but emotional pain was another thing. She felt so deeply when she loved that losing it, whether through betrayal or death, was a kind of hell she wouldn't willingly subject herself to again. And she now very much feared that if she wasn't careful, Bastien could break her heart. It would be so easy to love him. He was smart, funny, sweet, kind and terribly attractive. But Terri couldn't see someone as wildly successful and handsome as him being interested in boring-old-her for very long. Eventually, he'd move on to someone more his match. And, even if he didn't, he wasn't invincible. Just think about the medicine he took, and the IV stand in his closet. Bastien could die on her, leaving her to struggle on alone as everyone else she'd ever loved had done. It was easier not to love him in the first place. She'd have to try to keep her emotional distance from now on, Terri decided, and wished she hadn't agreed to a play and dinner tonight when he'd suggested it at breakfast.

"Dear God, you two!" Vincent Argeneau paused in the entry to gape at the bags Bastien and Terri carted into the penthouse later that day. "Do you think you bought enough?"

"I think so," Terri said with a laugh, then added, "Most of these are Bastien's."

When Vincent arched his eyebrows and turned his gaze on his cousin, Terri laughed again. A chagrined expression covered Bastien's face. The man hadn't been joking when he claimed to love shopping. She'd never seen anyone, man or woman, shop like he did. It was a good thing he was wealthy, or he'd surely go bankrupt. The man was a shopping fiend.

"I needed some more casual clothes," Bastien excused himself, unable to disguise his embarrassment. "I didn't even own a pair of jeans, and I thought it was time I got some."

"Uh-huh." Vincent walked forward to peer into the open tops of the bags. "Felt a need for some new clothes, did you?" he asked, and grinned when Bastien flushed. He added, "Well, as much as I'd like to torment you over this sudden urge you have to dress in a younger, more relaxed, not to mention more attractive manner, your secretary insisted it was important you call before quitting time. And as it's a quarter to five now—"

"She said it was important?" Bastien interrupted, setting down the bags he carried. "I better pop down to the office and see what it's about. Meredith doesn't exaggerate. If she said it was important, it's most certainly important.

"Just leave the bags here in the entry for now, Terri. I'll get them when I come back," he added as he turned to push the button for the elevator. He stepped onto the lift when the doors opened, then

121

turned back to hold them as he asked Vincent, "Did she see to the kitchen?"

"Oh yeah," his cousin assured him in dry tones. "She saw to that all right. You now have enough food—not to mention dishes—to feed a small army. I hope your guests have healthy appetites. Actually, I know C.K. does. For a skinny guy, he sure eats a lot."

"He's probably bored to tears and eating because of it," Terri suggested.

Vincent seemed to contemplate that possibility, then shook his head. "Nah. He's been editing some book in front of the television. There's some sort of marathon of old British reruns. Pretty good ones, actually."

"You might want to see if there's anything to snack on, Terri. Our dinner reservations aren't until after the play," Bastien suggested as the elevator doors began to slide closed. "I'll be back in a few minutes."

"Hmm," Terri murmured as the doors clicked shut. "I wonder what the important matter is."

Vincent shrugged. "Meredith didn't say."

"Well, I guess we'll find out soon enough," Terri said philosophically. She finally set down the bags she'd carried up for Bastien. "In the meantime, I'll see about that snack he suggested."

"I'll join you. I could use a bite myself," Vincent announced. And he followed her into the kitchen.

Chapter Seven

"I don't understand why this is such a big problem," Bastien said into the phone with forced patience. He couldn't believe that the important matter Meredith had needed his attention for was to call the florist about the arrangements for Kate and Lucern's wedding. He supposed Kate, as the bride, would think this was important, and he did understand that, but the problem in question seemed rather petty to him. Yet the florist, a fellow with an unfortunately high-pitched voice and an equally unfortunate lisp, was acting as if it were a major catastrophe.

"I've already explained, Mr. Argeneau," the florist said in exasperation. "Our grower's entire crop of Sterling roses was hit by—"

"Yes, yes. Aphids ate them."

"Not aphids, sir," the florist corrected with exaggerated patience. "It was—"

"It doesn't matter," Bastien interrupted, his own

patience beginning to slip. The man was making this more difficult than necessary. The answer to this dilemma seemed simple enough. "Your grower's roses are gone. So go to another grower."

There was a brief pause, followed by a long-suffering sigh. "Mr. Argeneau, one cannot just drop down to the local nursery and buy *several hundred* Sterling roses. These are *rare* flowers. They're snapped up before they've even finished growing."

"So substitute a different rose, then," Bastien suggested.

"The Sterling rose was the centerpiece of the whole wedding!" the man wailed. "All the arrangements and colors were chosen to offset it. One can't just—"

Bastien frowned, his ears straining as the fellow suddenly fell silent. He was sure he'd heard a catch in the florist's voice before he'd stopped talking. The guy was really upset. He must be one of those emotional artist types, Bastien decided—though he would never have thought of a florist as an artist. The guy certainly had the temperament, though. "Hello? Roger, was it?"

"Roberto," the man snapped, then cleared his throat. "I'm sorry. My assistant just handed me a fax with more bad news. This time about the urns Ms. Leever chose."

"Yes?" Bastien asked warily.

"There was a fire at the plant where they're produced. It's caused delays. The urns won't get here in time for her wedding."

"Of course they won't," Bastien muttered. He

pushed one hand through his hair and sighed. "Look, just put in roses that are as close in color to the originals as possible, and use urns as close in style and everything will be fine." That seemed a reasonable solution. He gathered by the stony silence that followed this suggestion that the florist didn't think so.

"When does Ms. Leever return to the city?" Roberto finally asked.

"I'm not really sure," Bastien admitted. Kate hadn't been too clear on the matter in her rush to get moving, and he hadn't thought to ask when Lucern called to let him know they'd arrived safely. Personally, he almost hoped the couple would be gone the whole two weeks until the wedding. Bastien was pretty sure Kate would hog Terri's time when she came back, and he had plans for doing that himself.

"I simply *must* talk to her. Either you'll have to have her call me or give me the number where she can be reached. These problems *must* be resolved now, to be sure we have the supplies we'll need on hand to have the arrangements made for the church and reception on time." It wasn't a request, but an imperious announcement.

Bastien scowled at the phone, then glanced at the clock on his desk. It would be midafternoon in California. He doubted Kate would be in her hotel room just now, but he supposed it wouldn't hurt to call and find out.

"Hold," he barked into the receiver, then put the man on hold. He next buzzed Meredith's desk, hoping she hadn't left for the night.

"Yes, sir?"

Bastien sighed in relief. "Put me through to Kate's hotel in California please, Meredith," he ordered. He added as an afterthought, "And thank you for not leaving yet."

He didn't wait to see if she knew what hotel Kate was in; Meredith knew everything. Besides, she'd told him that Kate had called the office earlier that day to leave a contact number in case they had to reach her.

"Miss Leever on line two, sir," Meredith announced a moment later.

"Thank you." Bastien pushed the button for that line, and was immediately greeted by an anxious Kate.

"Meredith gave me a quick rundown of the problem. She says you have Roberto on the other line. Can you conference-call us?"

Bastien blinked. He wasn't surprised that Meredith had given her a rundown; doing so saved him some time and trouble, which was what his secretary did best. And fortunately, to ensure that someone would call him back, Bastien knew the florist had explained the problem to Meredith when he'd called earlier that day. His surprise was at the panic apparent in Kate's voice. She had always seemed a perfectly sensible woman to him. This kind of reaction to the loss of one stupid type of flower and a silly urn seemed a bit excessive. Was the whole world going mad? Spring fever, he thought wisely. That was probably the explanation for his fascination with Terri, too.

"Bastien? Can you conference-call us?" Kate repeated impatiently.

"Er . . . yes," he said. "Hang on." He pushed the necessary series of buttons, then said, "Hello?"

"Yes," Lucern's fiancee said at the same time the florist squeaked, "Mr. Argeneau?"

"Oh, Roberto!" Kate cried with relief, apparently recognizing the man's voice.

Bastien sat back and twiddled his thumbs as the two went into crisis mode, both wailing in distress about the lost Sterling roses, then exchanging horrified exclamations over the delayed urns. It was all just *too* much, they agreed. Horrible. Ghastly. Tragic.

"Tragic," Bastien agreed, just to keep them from thinking he wasn't listening or interested. He wasn't really, though. He wished they'd hurry up and settle down to discussing what had to be done to repair the damage, rather than wasting time lamenting over how this could *positively ruin* the entire wedding.

"Good Lord!" Terri gaped at the crammed kitchen cupboards. They had gone from completely bare to overflowing in the space of two days. Anything and everything a body could want now filled the shelves. If nothing else, Bastien's secretary was certainly thorough, Terri decided as her gaze slid over the rows of neatly stacked and organized food. There was so much now, she couldn't decide what to have.

"Do you feel like anything specific, Vincent?" she asked.

"Are you on the menu?" he asked.

Terri laughed, not taking the comment seriously. Vinny was an actor. She had no doubt that flirting

127

was second nature to him. He probably wasn't even aware when he did it anymore.

She closed the first cupboard and opened another, her brow knitting as she looked over more food. It had never occurred to her that confusion would be the result of so much choice. It was, though—which was a pain, because Terri wasn't even really hungry, but knew she'd be starving halfway through the play if she didn't have a little something now. But what to have? Vincent obviously wasn't going to be any help. Perhaps C.K. would be more useful.

Closing the cupboard door, Terri smiled absently at Vincent as she stepped around him and moved back out into the living room.

"What do you feel like having to eat?" she asked Chris, who had relocated himself from his guest room. He glanced away from the television to raise a questioning eyebrow.

"Nothing. I'm stuffed," he said. "I've been eating all day, ever since the first food began to arrive."

"Oh." Terri sank down onto the edge of the couch next to him to contemplate the matter.

"How was the Met?" C.K. asked politely after a moment.

"It was fun." She perked up slightly at the memory. "They have lots of cool stuff there. We didn't get to see everything, though. It's so huge! But Bastien said we can go back another time."

Chris nodded. "It's probably better to go a couple times than to try to cram it all in one day anyway."

"Yes," Terri agreed, then asked, "How was your day?"

"Oh, you know. Long. Boring." Chris sighed, then his gaze landed on the stacked manuscript on the coffee table. "I did try to work, but the pain is distracting."

"Hmm." Terri nodded sympathetically as he rubbed his leg above the cast. She'd never had a broken bone in her life, and had no real idea how painful it must be. But it seemed best to keep him off the subject, so she asked, "What did you eat?"

She hoped that his answer might help her decide what to have, too. But the young man's answer brought a grimace to her face.

"Chips, cheese, and sausage." He shrugged.

"That's hardly a healthy diet," Terri chastised.

"Well, there was no one to cook for me. I had to fend for myself," the editor said defensively, then patted the set of crutches Terri hadn't noticed leaning against the couch. "Fortunately, Bastien's secretary brought these babies up half an hour ago. I can get around on my own now."

"Good," she said, aware that Bastien and Vincent had been helping the man get to and from his bedroom each day. She didn't know if he needed help dressing and undressing, but thought he would probably want some more fresh clothes soon, too. She'd have to mention it to Bastien, Terri decided, then allowed her mind to return to her problem.

She glanced to Vincent, who had followed her out of the kitchen. "You're sure you can't think of anything special or specific you'd like to snack on?"

The man gave a desultory shrug. "You smell good enough to eat."

Terri laughed and shook her head. His flirting was kind of nice. And she was sure he was basically harmless. Unlike his cousin, who didn't flirt but lulled a girl into a false sense of security by talking about this and that and life in general for days on end, fascinating and amusing her with tales of past antics and present life, until her jaws ached from smiling so much and laughing so often. Bastien hadn't passed a single flirtatious comment since her arrival, leaving her to simply enjoy his company until, *boom!* He took her by surprise by suddenly grabbing and kissing her with an ardor that had brought her own passions to abrupt and startling life.

Passions she hadn't even known she had, Terri admitted unhappily, moving back into the kitchen to check the contents of the fridge. Bastien was definitely the more dangerous of the two men. At least to her heart.

Bastien listened idly to the chatter on the phone, his mind wandering to Terri and their shared kiss. She'd tasted of the strawberry smoothies she'd been drinking, sweet and delicious. That kiss—while far too brief, thanks to those squawking birds—had been potent. Bastien had quite forgotten himself. He'd been right there, in front of the museum where anyone might have seen, but he didn't care. He'd have liked to continue forgetting himself, too—and would have, if not for those stupid birds.

"Damned pigeons," he muttered.

"What pigeons?" Kate asked.

"The ones who interrupted my kissing Terri."

"You kissed Terri?" Lucern asked.

"I told you he was falling for her, darling," Kate said with glee.

Bastien blinked in confusion, realizing that he had somehow joined the conversation again and flowers were no longer the topic at hand. "Luc? When did you join this phone call?"

"I picked up the other phone when you put Kate on hold. It's my wedding, too," he said by way of explanation. "Now, stop changing the subject. How was it?"

"How was what?"

"The kiss."

"I—" Bastien paused, floundering. The kiss had been wonderful. Passionate and sweet, it had made him hunger for more. But he wasn't telling them that. He was saved from trying to figure out a response by a most unlikely source: Roberto.

"Ahem. Might we get back to the issue at hand?" The florist sounded pretty prudish all of a sudden. Gone was the drama and wailing.

"Oh, yes, Roberto. Of course." Kate sighed. "I think your idea is the best. Do you have Bastien's address?"

"What does he need my address for?" Bastien asked in dismay. What had he missed while he'd been mooning over that kiss?

"To send some sample arrangements to you so that you can take pictures of them with your digital camera and send them to Kate via e-mail," Lucern said. "You weren't listening, were you? Mooning over Terri would be my guess."

"I liked you better when grunting was your communication of choice," Bastien told him grimly. He was surprised to hear a chuckle from his older brother.

"Very good," Roberto inserted, sounding as prim as an old woman. "Yes, I wrote down the address. I'll start right now and have them delivered first thing in the morning for Mr. Argeneau to take pictures. Please, please, please choose as quickly as you can, so we can be sure to get what we need in time."

"Yes, Roberto. I promise I will," Kate assured him. "Either Lucern or I will check every hour to see if he's e-mailed the pictures, and we'll choose at once."

"Good, good." Roberto took a moment to expostulate again on what a terrible tragedy this all was before saying good-bye and hanging up.

"Well," Kate murmured once he'd gone.

"Yes, well, Bastien?" Lucern queried.

"Well, I'll be sure to send those photos to you the minute the arrangements arrive," Bastien said quickly. "Now, I'd better get going if I want to be ready in time to take Terri to the theater tonight. Bye." He hung up before either Kate or Lucern could protest, and grinned at the fact that he'd managed to avoid the grilling he would surely have got.

Whistling softly, Bastien stood and crossed the room to the bar in the corner of his office. There were two fridges behind it: one unlocked and a smaller locked one. He unlocked the smaller fridge, retrieved a bag of blood, and relocked it. He then opened his mouth, extended his teeth, and slammed the bag into them as he walked back across the room.

Bastien checked the messages on his desk while ingesting the blood. None of them seemed to be urgent, which meant either he had some damned fine people working for him who were capable of taking care of matters on their own, or he wasn't as indispensable as he'd always thought.

Perhaps that was a good thing, Bastien thought as he tossed the now empty blood bag in the wastebasket under his desk and left his office. He said good night to Meredith, who was gathering her things in preparation for leaving, then walked to the elevator to the penthouse.

Bastien considered the night ahead as he rode upstairs. He had about an hour to get ready for the play, which was plenty of time. And he'd made late reservations at a nice little Italian restaurant not far from the theater. He hoped Terri liked Italian. As he recalled, it had always been one of his favorites back . . . well . . . a long time ago, when he still used to find food interesting.

He was debating whether they should take a taxi to the theater, or go by car, when the elevator opened onto the penthouse. A taxi, he thought, would be the better option; he really didn't want to be bothered with finding parking.

"Do you like cheese on your salad?" Terri asked as she finished slicing celery. She'd decided that salad was the smart choice to snack on: healthy, quick, and light enough to tide her over until the meal after the play; and it wouldn't leave her uncomfortably full.

"Whatever you like," was Vincent's answer. He

LYNSAY SANDS

was leaning back against the counter beside her, arms crossed over his chest, legs crossed at the ankles in a relaxed pose as he watched her work. They'd been chatting amicably about her stay so far. Vincent seemed curious to know where Bastien had been taking her, and if she was having a good time.

Terri had enthused about everything she'd seen and done, and how kind and amusing and smart Bastien was, and how he seemed to make everything more interesting, when she heard herself and realized she was gushing. She sounded pathetic—like a woman falling in love.

She'd quickly cut herself off and asked about the cheese to change the topic.

"I haven't seen Bastien like this in a long, long time."

Vincent's announcement drew Terri's curious gaze. "Like what?"

"Happy."

Terri felt a leap of hope and excitement, but quickly stifled it. Ducking her head, she turned her attention back to what she was doing. "Oh?"

"Yes. We were a lot younger then. Practically boys compared to now." There was an irony in his tone Terri didn't understand, but she forgot all about it when he added, "And he was in love."

Those words had the oddest effect on Terri. First she was hit by shock. That was followed by a twinge of pain in the vicinity of her heart. Stupid reactions, the both of them, she thought faintly. A man would hardly reach Bastien's age without falling in love at least once. Terri hadn't yet asked, but she was assum-

134

ing he was her age or a little older. Besides, she didn't "love" him, she assured herself, so she had no right to feel anything about his having loved before.

"That woman broke his heart," Vincent announced. "I'd hate for you to do the same."

Terri was so startled by the comment, and the assumptions it made in regard to Bastien's feelings, that she jerked her head around to gape at him in the middle of slicing the last bit of celery.

Vincent's eyes didn't meet hers; they were on the celery she was cutting. Terri saw concern flash across his face as he called, "Be careful, you're going to cut your—"

"Ouch!" Terri jumped and dropped the knife as pain radiated up from the pointer finger of her left hand. Reacting instinctively, she caught the wounded digit in her right hand and pressed it close to her body, holding it tight in an effort to end the pain, not to mention cut off the blood that was probably coursing from it.

Vincent rushed over to her. "Here, let me see it."

Terri hesitated, then raised both hands and forced herself to open her fingers and reveal the wound, then flushed with embarrassment. It had hurt like the devil, but was really just a small cut she saw with self-disgust. She'd reacted as though she'd lost a limb.

"Sometimes the smallest cuts are the most painful," Vincent commented, as if he'd read her thoughts. He was examining the wound, and the small bit of blood leaking from it, with a fascination that was a little unsettling. Especially when he suddenly inhaled, as if smelling a wildflower.

"Vincent!"

The crack of Bastien's voice made both Vinny and Terri jump in surprise. Retrieving her hand, Terri turned to smile uncertainly at her host. He didn't even notice the effort, let alone appreciate it. His eyes were focused on his cousin.

"Hello, Bastien. Rough half hour at the office?" Vincent teased lightly. Then he gestured to Terri. "She cut herself slicing celery. I was just looking at it for her."

Bastien immediately started forward, his expression softening with concern. It was a relief to know the blood he'd smelled upon entering the kitchen hadn't been from a bite. That scent, combined with the way the two had been huddled together, had led him to think Vincent had bitten Terri. He was glad he was wrong. "Is it bad?"

"Fortunately, no." Vincent stepped aside to let him take his place examining Terri's cut. "A bandage should take care of it. I'll go see if we have any."

Bastien was aware of the other man slipping from the room, but merely clasped and lifted Terri's hand to examine the injury for himself. Much to his relief, his cousin was right and it wasn't a bad cut. It was small and shallow enough that it didn't even really need a bandage, but the smell of the few drops of blood that had slipped from the wound was strong enough that Bastien was almost heady from it. He supposed it would have been worse for Vincent, who hunted at night so had yet to feed today. Which meant Bastien probably owed him an apology. He had just ingested a bag of blood, yet was hard pressed

136

not to stick Terri's finger in his mouth and suck away the small bit of blood. Yet, Vincent had been managing to resist, despite likely being ravenous.

"It should be fine, but I'll go see how Vincent is making out finding that bandage," Bastien said gruffly. He released her hand and left the kitchen quickly, fleeing the temptation in search of his cousin. He found Vincent in the office at the back of the penthouse, prowling like a hungry tiger.

"I didn't bite her," he said at once. "We were just talking about you."

"I know. I'm sorry," Bastien began; then he paused and blinked. "About me?"

Vincent relaxed and nodded. "She likes you, Bastien. I mean *really* likes you. But there's something else there. Some fear is keeping her from giving in to her feelings. She may not be an easy conquest."

"I don't want to conquer her, Vincent. She isn't a foreign country with riches I covet."

"Then what do you want from her?"

Bastien was silent. He didn't know the answer. He hadn't been this fascinated by a woman in a long time, perhaps ever. He didn't even remember feeling this drawn to Josephine. He certainly had never felt so comfortable with the woman he'd always considered the love of his life. There was something so natural about Terri. She expressed what she felt with a distinct lack of concern for what people would think; she didn't bother to try to act as if she knew something when she didn't, lest she look foolish. Terri was honest and accepting and made Bastien feel as if he could be himself around her, as if that was enough.

He wanted to be just as honest in return. That was a feeling he was constantly fighting, afraid that if he revealed the facts of his vampirism, she would shun him as Josephine had.

"That's a risk you'll have to take eventually, if you want a serious relationship with her. This is a new era, though. Vampires are 'in' right now. Terri might not react like Josephine at all." Vincent didn't bother to try to hide the fact that he'd been reading his cousin's mind. Wrought with turmoil as he was, Bastien hadn't remembered to guard his thoughts. "Can you read her mind?"

Bastien shook his head. He'd tried while shopping that afternoon and hadn't been able to read a thing.

Vincent nodded solemnly. "You'll have to tell her eventually. Perhaps Kate can help you. They're cousins. Terri might take it better from her anyway." Vincent moved to the door. "I'm going out for a snack. Enjoy your night."

Bastien watched the door close behind his cousin, then stood unmoving for several minutes. He felt restless, empty, hungry. That last thought had him crossing to the locked fridge in his desk to retrieve a bag of blood. He popped his teeth into it, ingested it quickly, then tossed the empty bag away in disgust. It didn't help what ailed him. Bastien still felt empty. Blood wasn't what he was hungry for. What he yearned for. What he really wanted was someone of his own. Someone to complete him. He wanted to belong to someone. To someone who could accept his differences and embrace him with them. He wanted unconditional love. More to the point, he wanted *Terri's* unconditional love.

"That was wonderful."

Bastien smiled at the enthusiastic smile on Terri's face and the excited color in her cheeks. Thinking she'd enjoy it, he'd taken her to see *The Phantom of the Opera*, and found he'd quite enjoyed it himself. "Are you hungry?"

"Starved," she admitted with a laugh. "That salad stopped tiding me over about an hour ago. What about you?"

"I could do with a little something," Bastien answered vaguely. He wasn't really hungry, but was looking forward to sitting across a table from Terri, watching her eyes dance and sparkle and her expressions change as she talked. "The restaurant is only a block or so away. Can you walk that far in your high heels, or should I hail a taxi?"

"Walking sounds fine," she assured him. "I'm used to wearing high heels all day at work."

"You look good in them." Bastien glanced down her short black cocktail dress to her legs in their sexy black nylons and high-heeled strapped sandals. Terri looked lovely, and somehow incredibly sexy despite the fact that the dress she wore wasn't the least bit revealing. It was sleeveless and short, but not indecently so, stopping just above the knee. And while it had a V-neckline, it wasn't cut so low as to reveal more than a hint of cleavage.

They chatted about the play as they left the theater,

discussing the scenery, the costumes, and the music. Conversation became more restrained once they reached the restaurant. They were shown to their table at once and offered menus. Terri's menu had no prices on it, while his did, and he grinned at her vexation over that fact. She would not be paying for this meal no matter what. Her pride would have to take a backseat this evening. He wanted to treat her as she deserved: to be wined and dined and waited on like a princess.

The food was delicious and the service exceptional, but about halfway through the meal, Bastien began to wish he'd taken Terri someplace a little less formal. The hushed, monied atmosphere was a bit constraining, making them both less talkative. Bastien missed Terri's enthusiasm and the tinkle of her laughter, for she had it well leashed.

The moment she was finished eating, he suggested they walk up the street to another place he knew for their after-dinner drink. The alacrity with which she agreed told him that while Terri had found the restaurant enjoyable, she too would prefer an atmosphere more conducive to their talking. Bastien suspected that trying to behave in such a subdued manner was killing her.

They walked the short block to Maison, a restaurant/bar he knew had an atmosphere that would allow them to talk more comfortably. The patio was open and filled with people enjoying the unseasonably warm night air, and Bastien was pleased when she suggested they sit outside.

Their conversation returned to the play, and Terri's

enjoyment of it was so obvious that Bastien decided they should perhaps go to a couple more while she was in town. That thought reminded him that she would eventually leave to fly home to England, an idea that he found made him grimace with displeasure. He was enjoying her company and the escape from a life that, until now, had seemed just fine—but in retrospect it seemed dull and bleak with its focus on business and little else.

How had he lived such an empty existence for so long when there was so much pleasure to be had in life?

Chapter Eight

Pausing in the middle of recounting a tale about Kate and herself when they were teenagers, Terri glanced to the side with a start as she heard a customer ask the waitress what time it was, and the waitress's answer.

"Did she just say it was four-twelve?" she asked, forgetting all about the tale she'd been telling.

"Did she? No, she couldn't have. You must have misheard. It can't be that late alread—it *is*!" Bastien exclaimed with surprise as he glanced at his watch. He lifted a stunned expression to hers, and they stared at each other for a moment then burst out laughing.

"I guess we lost track of time talking," Terri said with a grin.

"I guess we did," he agreed. "But, then, we tend to like to do that a lot. Talk, I mean. I like talking to you."

"I like talking to you, too," she admitted, then

glanced away, looking for a distraction from the wealth of feeling welling up inside her. Maison's patio wasn't as busy as it had been, but there were still half a dozen tables with customers. "I wonder why they haven't closed yet. I thought bars closed around four A.M. over here."

"I'm not sure," Bastien began, then said, "Oh. They're open twenty-four hours."

When Terri glanced back at him in question, he gestured to the writing on the awning. She smiled wryly and nodded. "I didn't notice that."

"Neither did I."

They fell silent for a moment, and Terri realized that it had grown cooler in the passing hours since they'd arrived. There was a bit of a chill in the air—not much, but enough that she felt it on her sleeveless arms.

"You're getting cold," Bastien noted when she unconsciously rubbed her arms. "I suppose we should head home."

"Yes," she agreed, but felt sad that the night was drawing to an end. Terri wouldn't have minded had it gone on forever.

Bastien stood and drew out her chair for her as she rose, then slid his suit jacket off and held it open for her. "Here, put this on. It's pretty quiet on this street, and with it being so late we'll probably have to walk up a block or so to find a taxi. Will you be all right to walk a little way in those shoes?"

"Yes, of course," Terri assured him as she slid her arms into the offered jacket. She'd been sitting for hours, and she hadn't drunk much despite the length of time they'd been there. Neither of them had; they'd been too busy talking. She paused with the suit coat halfway up her arms. "Will you be all right? You don't need this?"

"No. I'm fine," he assured her, urging the jacket up the rest of the way.

"Mmm." Terri pulled the silk material closed and hugged it to herself with a smile of pleasure. "It's warm and lovely, and it smells of you."

"Does it?" he asked with a small smile. "Is that a good thing?"

"Mmmm." She raised one lapel, turned her head to bury her nose in the material, and inhaled deeply. "Yes, *very* good. I like your cologne," Terri admitted, as she breathed in the scent of him again with pleasure.

"You don't bother with subterfuge at all, do you?"

Terri lifted her head to peer at him. "Subterfuge?"

The waitress came up to the table before he could reply. The girl thanked them and wished them both a good night as she took the money Bastien left on the table. They responded in kind, then Bastien took Terri's arm to usher her to the opening in the gate surrounding the outdoor patio. He walked her out, keeping his hand at her elbow as they started up the street.

His courtesy was one of the things Terri liked best about Bastien. The way he opened doors for her, always allowing her to enter first. His concern for her comfort and well-being, making sure she wasn't cold, or warm, or that her feet were holding up all right. She even liked the way he asked what she wanted, then placed her order for her. There were few men who would even think to do something so rich with old-world courtesy, and many women who would have perhaps been offended; but it didn't offend Terri. It made her feel special and coddled. She felt cared for. Many of the courtesies he indulged in made her feel like that. She could get used to such treatment.

Troubled by the thought, Terri glanced up at the buildings that rose like mountains around them against the lightening sky. "It's lovely here."

"Yes, it *is* nice." Bastien sounded surprised as he followed her gaze around their surroundings. "I've been here countless times on business, and never really paid attention."

Terri nodded, unsurprised. Most people became blind to their environment, no matter how glorious, and never gave it a second thought. "What did you mean when you said I don't bother with subterfuge?"

Bastien was silent for a moment as they walked; then he said, "Many women wouldn't have admitted to liking my cologne, let alone shown such pleasure in it. They would have been too busy playing it cool and acting unaffected. But you don't seem to have a subtle bone in your body, and don't bother with such games."

"Games are for children," she murmured. She glanced at him in surprise when he burst out laughing. "What?"

"You don't seem to mind acting like a child any other time. I've never seen anyone act more childlike than you at the museum," he explained as she

145

flushed. With a laugh, he added, "And shopping, and at the flea markets, and at the street fairs."

"Sorry," Terri apologized automatically.

"Don't be. It's one of the things I like best about you."

"Good. Because I'm not *really* sorry," she admitted with a grin.

Bastien chuckled and urged her to cross the street. "This is the Hilton," he explained as they walked along the building that took up most of that side. "There should be a row of taxis in front. There usually are."

"Is it far back to the penthouse?" Terri asked. It hadn't seemed like a long taxi ride to get to the theater.

"About four blocks from here," Bastien guessed.

"Why waste money on a cab? We can walk."

"Really?"

She shook her head at his surprise, wondering if he usually dated decrepit biddies who couldn't walk any distance at all. "I think you've just insulted me," Terri said, pausing to face him as they reached the corner of the hotel. "I walked around all weekend with you, and spent at least four hours walking around the museum, and another three following you on your shopping spree today. Do you really think I can't manage four blocks?"

"No. Of course not," he said, and his voice was soft with an admiration that almost embarrassed her. The way Bastien was looking at her made her positive that he was about to kiss her.

"Good," she said promptly to break the mood. "I need to sit down."

Whirling away, Terri walked under the carport, crossing the Hilton's driveway to the black marble base that surrounded the pillars fronting the street. She had meant to sit down and tighten the strap on her right shoe that seemed to have loosened throughout the night, but someone had either sprayed the marble to clean away the pollution and dirt, or splashed it unintentionally while watering the plants at either end. The wide black marble end, which had appeared so handy for sitting on, was wet. The only section that was dry, was the narrow, almost balance-beam-sized strip of marble that ran to the next wider section around the next pillar. Deciding it would have to do, Terri perched carefully on the slippery, slender rounded surface to work on her shoe.

Bastien joined her after a moment, but he sat astride the narrow marble piece, so that he was facing her side. "You had me worried when you said you had to sit down."

"This strap came undone at some point," she explained. She finished doing it back up, then Terri straightened to smile at him. "I should be all right now."

"You're more than all right," he assured her, and just as he had done at the museum, Bastien caught her face in his hands and pulled her forward for a kiss.

After the briefest of hesitations, Terri went willingly, her mouth softly parting under his, then widening farther on a cry of surprise. She arched toward him, lost her seating, and started to slide forward off her marble perch.

"Whoa." Bastien broke the kiss to catch her before

she landed on the sidewalk. They both laughed with embarrassment, and he helped her back up onto the rounded top of the strip of marble.

"I should have sat over there." She gestured toward the wider end. "But it was wet."

Bastien didn't even glance, he merely scooted forward until one knee was at her back, and the other was against the front of her knees. It was an effort to help her keep her balance. Then he again lowered his head to kiss her. This time, when Terri arched toward him and started to slide forward, she hit the knee in front of her and took him with her.

They broke apart once more, laughing as they saved themselves; then Bastien caught her hand and stood. Terri thought that would be the end of the attempted kisses, but instead of continuing on their walk, he tugged her back the way they'd come to the wider marble. He muttered something about the water, used his shirtsleeve to wipe the worst of it away, then sat and pulled her down into his arms.

Terri sighed as his mouth moved toward hers. Bastien was holding her tightly against his chest, seemingly determined she not slide off anywhere. She hardly noticed. Her concentration was focused wholly upon his mouth and what it was doing. The moment his lips touched hers, she let her own open, then gasped as his tongue met hers. The kiss was just as startling to her as it had been in front of the museum. She didn't recall ever having felt quite so overwhelmed, but then it *had* been ten years since she'd been properly kissed.

Not that she hadn't been kissed at all in that time.

There had been the rare occasion when the dreaded blind date, or setup by friends, had been impossible to avoid. But not one of those handful of men since Ian's death had done anything more than nibble eagerly at her lips, leaving her at best unmoved and at worst irritated and repulsed. If she were to be honest, however, Terri hadn't invited any of those kisses. She hadn't wanted them, hadn't been interested in those men. In Bastien, she was. She liked him; she enjoyed his company, and her body most definitely responded to his attention. Terri was plastered against him, her hands upon his chest, yet she found herself trying to get closer, pressing into him as her tongue moved tentatively forward to meet his.

The sudden squeal of tires and the angry honk of a car horn intruded and made her eyes blink open. Terri's head tilted to the side, and her gaze shot past Bastien's cheek to the street beyond. She couldn't see what had caused the noise, but what she *could* see made her stiffen and instinctively turn away from Bastien's kiss. He seemed undaunted, simply ran his mouth along her cheek until he found her ear. Terri almost moaned at this new caress, her eyes starting to droop closed again. It took a lot of effort to fight the urge.

"There is a whole row of taxi drivers here watching," she murmured, blushing as she glanced at the parked cars, their drivers out talking amongst each other while watching them.

"Let them," Bastien breathed into her ear. "The poor bastards are probably jealous."

"But . . ." Terri paused in her protest, her eyes

149

closing on a shudder as Bastien chuckled, his breath blowing against her ear.

"Besides, the taxi drivers are nothing," he said. "On my side we have the Hilton doorman, the bell-hop, the guys cleaning the lobby, the reception peo-ple, a couple of guests, and at least one street person." Bastien punctuated each witness he listed with a kiss of her neck, then caught her head, turned her face back to his, and looked her in the eye. "This is New York. I'm sure they've seen couples snogging before."

He tried to kiss her again then, but Terri pulled back. "Snogging?" she said.

Bastien blinked, then smiled. "It's a British term. It means kissing, making out."

"Yes, I know! I live in the U.K., remember?" she said, but was more interested in the fact that she now had a clue to the accent she'd been trying and failing to place. "So, that's the hint of an accent I hear. You're British."

He hesitated, then shook his head. "No. I lived there for a while, though."

"When?" You said—"

Apparently unwilling to discuss it further, Bastien cut her off with a kiss. He didn't try any other per-suasion but his lips. Terri went still at first, and after a moment realized she was waiting for something—the usual groping. But it never came. Bastien's hands shifted from her upper arms to her back, but didn't roam. All of Bastien's attention and focus was on her mouth, his lips moving over hers with hunger and passion, his tongue sliding in to dance with hers. Af-

ter a moment, his accent, the fact that they were outside, and their audience were all forgotten.

Giving another sigh, Terri allowed herself to be
swept up on his passion once more and pressed herself against him, her hands creeping up to rest on
Bastien's shoulders. There they curled in the material
of his shirt, pulling in an unconscious effort to get
closer still. Terri couldn't possibly get closer, though;
she and Bastien were as close as two people could be
without actually making love.

Time passed in a kaleidoscope of color and sensation
for Bastien. All he knew or cared about was the
woman in his arms and the lips beneath his own.
Terri was soft and sweet in his embrace, pressing her
body into his, clutching eagerly at his clothing. She
was making passionate little mewling sounds deep in
her throat, which both pleased and excited him.
Bastien hadn't felt so alive in centuries. He hadn't felt
so desperately hungry ever. But he was also very
aware of the woman he held. Terri wasn't just anyone. She might be his life mate.

His eyes opened and skated across the glass front of
the Hilton. There were three people working the
check-in desk. Only one was busy with a customer;
Bastien could have a room in minutes if they went in.
He actually considered it briefly, then let the idea slip
away. Terri wasn't the type to go for that sort of
thing. He knew it instinctively. The time he had already spent with her and his own knowledge of
women gained from four-hundred-plus years of life

told him that. If he tried, he'd scare her off so fast that he'd be wondering how the girl in his arms had turned into a dust trail.

These thoughts crossed Bastien's mind several times as he kissed Terri. And each time he came to the same result. No. It was a bad move to rush things. But eventually it got to the point where he soon *had* to stop or he *would* try to take her in and rent a room.

He kissed her gently one last time, then again, then broke off altogether to tuck her head under his chin and just hold her. For a moment Bastien smoothed his hands soothingly over her back, allowing his body the time it needed to regain control of itself. At last he said, "We should go home."

"Home," Terri echoed, and there was a sadness in her voice that made his arms tighten around her. It told him that she didn't want this to end, either. His gaze slid to the revolving doors of the Hilton, but danced away from temptation just as quickly.

"Yes." She sighed, running her fingers lightly back and forth over a small patch of his chest in an action he suspected she didn't know was rather distracting. "We should head back. It's almost daylight."

His gaze shifted to the lightening sky, then to his watch, and Bastien grimaced. It was five-thirty in the morning! It would be full daylight soon. They'd been sitting here making out like teenagers for over an hour.

"Come." Urging her backward, he caught her hand and stood, pulling her with him. "Do you still want to walk home, or should I hire a taxi?" He slipped a steadying arm around Terri as she swayed against him.

He saw her glance toward the row of watching taxi drivers. A blush immediately crept into her cheeks. "Er . . . walking would be better."

He nodded in understanding, and they began to walk, Bastien smiling slightly at the way she now had her head tucked down in embarrassment, not looking to either side. He found it charming, her discomfort at being seen kissing. After more than four hundred years on this earth, Bastien didn't much care what people thought, and until now would have guessed the same of Terri. She seemed to care so little about looking foolish, but apparently that level of comfort didn't stretch to snogging in public. He was again glad that he hadn't tried to lure her into the hotel, she probably would have been mortified at the thought of all those cabbies knowing exactly where they were going and what they would be doing.

"Something smells good." she said.

They had reached the end of the hotel carport and were standing on the corner, waiting to cross the street. Bastien glanced down to see that Terri had finally lifted her face and was sniffing the air. She turned her head, trying to find the source of the pleasing scent.

"Across the street," he said, spotting the coffee cart.

"Oh." Terri sighed the word. "Are you hungry?"

Bastien's mouth tipped at the question. Hungry? He was ravenous. But not for breakfast buns. He ran his hand up and down Terri's arm, then squeezed her into his side. When the light changed, he shifted to take her hand and lead her across the street. "Come on, I'll buy you something to tide you over until we get home."

Terri woke up after only four hours of sleep, feeling great. She felt rested, hungry, happy . . .

Happy.

She considered the word as she brushed her teeth, then got into the shower. Terri had always thought of herself as a happy person. And she had been. But that was before coming to New York. Since meeting and spending time with Bastien, she'd discovered that the happiness prior to this had been a feeling more along the lines of contentment. Terri enjoyed her job, her cottage, and her friends, but she had been just sort of coasting along in life—bobbing on the waters, so to speak. Now she was cresting the waves, diving in and splashing about. For the first time in her life, Terri was really and truly enjoying herself. She felt young, strong, and vital. She felt alive. And scared.

Having something you cared about was great, except it meant you had something that could be taken away.

Stepping out of the shower, she wrapped her long hair in a small hand towel, and used a larger bath towel to quickly dry herself off. Wrapping it around her body sarong-style, she moved to the vanity. There Terri tugged the towel off her head, picked up a brush, and set to work on her hair. At first she didn't really see her reflection, or really even think; she was just working on automatic, carrying out the morning

154

ritual of making herself presentable to the world. But after a moment, she started to notice her reflection and her hand slowed in drawing the brush through her wet brown hair, then stopped altogether.

Letting her hands drop, Terri silently stared, really looking at herself for perhaps the first in a very long time. For years, she had only ever glanced in the mirror to be sure that her hair was neat, or her nose didn't need powdering, not really seeing herself as a whole. Now she took in her reflection with new eyes, seeing what she thought Bastien must see: large green eyes, long mahogany hair, soft full lips, a slightly tipped-up nose. Individually, there was nothing really remarkable about her—or so Terri had always thought. But somehow, this morning, it all came together into a whole that was really quite lovely. Her skin glowed, her eyes twinkled, her mouth tipped up at the corners in a secret smile. This was a woman who was desired.

Terri might not have paid a lot of attention to her appearance, but she did know that she had never looked better in her life. And she looked like this now because of Bastien. Because he made her feel special, wanted, desirable. And he hadn't even tried to sleep with her.

She grinned at her reflection. The man had taken her to the museum, shopping, a play, and dinner. He'd spent all night laughing and talking with her, "snogged" her senseless for well over an hour, bought her a coffee and a sticky bun, walked back to the penthouse holding her hand, walked her to the door of her room, kissed her passionately once more, then had wished her sweet dreams in a husky passion-filled voice, and finally . . . left to go to his own room. It was the best date she'd had in her life. He'd made her feel special—not with just his courtesy, care, and concern, but by the simple fact of *not* trying to get her into bed. To Terri, it proved that Bastien wasn't just on the make. He really liked her. And she really liked him. It was wonderful and sweet and the best time she'd had in her life—and it was going to hurt so very much when it was over. The pain would be unbearable. Perhaps worse even than when Ian died, she feared. Because Terri was coming to realize that what she and Ian had experienced was puppy love. They'd been two children gamboling about until tragedy had struck in the form of Hodgkin's disease. Then everything had turned terribly serious, and she had found herself becoming almost a mother to him, caring for him in an almost maternal way and nursing him to the end.

What she was beginning to feel for Bastien was neither puppy love nor maternal in nature. He wasn't simply a friend with whom to gambol through life. He was becoming necessary to her. He made her feel complete, sated, just by his presence.

Terri wasn't a stupid woman, and she knew it was too soon to feel such things, but she felt them just the same. Perhaps her feelings were magnified because of the time limit of her stay here, but it didn't really matter. The fact was, she thought of Bastien constantly and wanted to be with him all the time. He was the first thing she thought of upon opening her eyes in the morning, and the last thing she thought of before drifting off to sleep. And she liked that. She liked this abounding joy she felt. Terri liked the way her heart sped up when Bastien walked into the room, or looked at her, or smiled at her, or complimented her, or kissed her.

Yes, she was happier than she had ever been in her life, and more scared than she had ever been. Terri really didn't want to get hurt, and yet she really, really didn't want to lose this—whatever it was—either.

Since common sense told her it couldn't be love this quickly, Terri decided to go with logic. That would be safe. This wasn't love. She just liked Bastien. A lot. And as long as she just kept liking him—and didn't love him—perhaps she could survive with her heart still intact when it ended.

"You can handle this," Terri told her reflection quietly. "Just don't go falling completely in love with the guy. Just keep *liking* him."

Feeling a little bit better and a little less scared now that she had something of a plan, Terri returned to brushing her hair. She would enjoy the time until the wedding. She'd go out with Bastien when he invited her, share talk, laughter, and kisses with him. But she wouldn't fall in love. Then, when she had to go home to England, Terri wouldn't be totally crushed; she would just be terribly sad and resigned that it—like all things—had to end.

"Good morning, Sunshine. You're looking pretty chipper for someone who only straggled in four hours ago."

Terri wrinkled her nose and smiled at Vincent's

greeting as she entered the living room. "How do you know what time we got in?"

"I heard you two talking in the hall. It was so late, I worried something had happened to delay you. I opened the door to ask if everything was all right, but you were a bit preoccupied." He waggled his eyebrows meaningfully. "I gathered everything was all right when I saw the two of you lip-locked outside your door. I didn't want to intrude, so I just closed the door and went back to bed."

Terri felt heat flush her cheeks. She hadn't realized anyone had seen them.

"*So.* Out all night, huh?" Chris said with a grin. "What *were* you doing?"

Terri was saved from having to answer that question by the elevator buzzer. Someone wanted to come up to the penthouse.

"Are you expecting anyone?" Vincent asked, raising an eyebrow.

"Yes, actually. The florists." Terri moved to the panel on the wall, grateful that she'd paid attention when Bastien had worked it. She hit the button to bring up the monitor image of the elevator's passengers, then nodded as she spotted men bearing floral arrangements. Not bothering to ask the obvious question of who they might be, Terri simply hit the button to release the elevator, then glanced at Bastien's cousin. "Will you greet them, Vincent? Just have them put the flowers in here. I want to make some coffee."

"Sure."

"Flowers?" Chris asked. Terri thought he sounded a bit odd, but then many men weren't big on flowers, she supposed.

"Yes. They're the possible floral arrangements for Kate and Lucern's wedding," she explained as she headed for the kitchen. "Bastien is going to take photos and e-mail them to Kate, so she can decide which ones she likes best."

Leaving the men to deal with the flowers and where to put them, Terri hurried into the kitchen to make coffee. It was a new coffeepot, however, with that new smell; and she knew that it needed a couple of pots of just plain water run through it.

She surveyed the kitchen for what she should, or could, have for breakfast while the first pot ran. She *could* have anything she wanted, Terri didn't think there was a single type of food that hadn't been purchased. What she *should* have was another story. She considered toast, but that sounded boring. Cereal wasn't very exciting, either. And the Pop Tarts and toaster strudels were too sweet for breakfast.

Sighing, Terri paced the kitchen briefly, then settled on an omelet. She'd make an omelet big enough for all of them to eat—though it seemed to her that she and Chris would probably eat most of it. Bastien often just picked at his food, and Vincent never ate at all. She should really ask about his digestive ailment. Surely there was *something* she could cook that he could eat.

Shrugging, Terri started to remove items from the fridge: onions, cheese, bacon, green peppers. Maybe she'd throw some potato in, too. This was going to be a yummy omelet. And she'd make toast as well. For some reason, she was starved this morning.

Bastien sniffed the air as he walked down the hall toward the living room. He'd slept late, but then they'd been out late last night. He smiled to himself at the memory of his date with Terri. It had been perfect, absolutely and completely perfect. The play, the dinner, the talking at Maison—the night had passed like minutes for him, and that hour of shared kisses in front of the Hilton had felt like mere seconds. Terri was a beauty, a joy to spend time with, and so interesting and amusing that he always felt comfortable in her company. She was perfect to be his *life mate*.

According to his mother, only someone whose mind he could not read would make a good life mate; a husband and wife should never be able to intrude on each other's thoughts. Those should be shared willingly, Marguerite said, not poached like chickens from a henhouse. Bastien couldn't read Terri's thoughts. But she did share them freely.

A pleased sigh slid from his lips, and Bastien grinned to himself. Her openness and honesty were what he liked best about Terri. Her passion for life, not to mention the passion she'd revealed in his arms, was priceless. He'd lived long enough to know that such open caring and passion were a rare find nowadays. Most people allowed fear to deaden their feelings and responses. Terri wasn't one of them. She was full of life, she was beautifully and vitally . . . dead?

He stopped short in the living room entrance and

gaped at the sight of Terri lying silent and still on the floor. Her body was splayed like a rag doll tossed to the ground, her luscious chestnut hair a pool around her head.

Two telltale red dots marked her lovely, slender throat.

Chapter Nine

"Oh, my handsome manly vampire. *Achoo!*" That high falsetto voice—not to mention the sneeze—drew Bastien's attention to the two men standing several feet away from Terri's prone body. Vincent and . . . Chris? He thought it was the editor but couldn't be sure. The man had a sheet draped over his head and caught beneath his chin in Little Red Riding Hood style. Judging from that, and from the really *bad* imitation of a female voice the editor was affecting, Bastien would guess he was supposed to be a woman. For some reason.

"How my heart beats for y—*achoo!*—you, Dracula. You stir my fire, my desire." Chris let the page he was reading drop to his side with disgust. "Who wrote this drivel?" he asked.

"A playwright," Vincent sniffed. "A *professional* playwright."

"Well, I'm a pro—*achoo!*—professional editor. And I—*achoo!*—wouldn't publish this poppycock."

"You just don't understand camp," Vincent snapped. "Haven't you ever heard of a little play—later made into a major motion picture—called the *Rocky Horror Picture Show?*"

"That was *good* camp," Chris informed him, then rubbed his nose. "This—*achoo!*—is drivel. God, I wish the drugstore guy would get here with those—*achoo!*—allergy pills."

"Believe me, so do I," Vincent said. He spotted Bastien in the entry and smiled. "Cousin! So you finally decided to join the living, did you?"

"Yes." His gaze shifted back to Terri, who blinked her eyes open, sat up to glance over at him, then scrambled to her feet.

"Good morning," she said brightly. "Did you sleep well?"

Nodding, Bastien moved purposely forward. His curiosity was killing him. Terri's eyes widened in surprise when he paused in front of her, wiped one of the red spots off her neck, and pressed it to his tongue.

"Sauce?" he asked with disbelief. A couple of drops of sauce were what had nearly caused him the vampire equivalent of a heart attack? He'd thought—

"Ketchup, actually." Terri gave a laugh as she wiped off the rest. "We were helping Vincent with his lines. I was Lucy, and Chris is Mina." She glanced toward the editor, who sneezed violently three times in a row. She then leaned forward to tell Bastien in

163

hushed tones, "He's allergic to the flowers. I suggested he go to his room until we can get the pictures done and the flowers out, but he says it won't help."

"I did when they first arrived," the editor complained. "But there are so many—*achoo!*—that the pollen is all through the apartment. *Achoo!* It wasn't much better than being out here." He removed the sheet from around his head and shoulders, and sank onto the couch with a groan.

Bastien slowly turned, only now noticing the flowers that filled the living room and made it look like a bloody flower shop . . . or a mortuary. He didn't know how he had missed them on first glance, except that the sight of Terri lying prone on the floor had so overset him, he hadn't noticed anything else.

"I made breakfast," Terri announced, drawing Bastien's attention. "Omelets. I left some of the mix in the fridge for when you got up. Would you like some?"

Bastien took in her bright eyes and hopeful smile, and found a smile of his own claiming his lips. "Lovely."

"Good. It'll just be a minute," she assured him cheerfully, then turned on her heel and left.

Bastien hesitated, then followed. He had meant *she* was lovely, not that an omelet for breakfast would be lovely. But that was okay. He'd eat the omelet if she'd gone to the trouble of making enough for him. It actually sounded good anyway. An omelet. Made with Terri's own two hands.

You got it bad. Those words drifted into his mind with a chuckle. Vincent!

164

Bastien ignored him.

"Would you like a cup of coffee?" Terri asked as he entered the kitchen. She took out of the fridge a bowl filled with a mixture of eggs and various other ingredients.

"I'll get it," Bastien said and moved to the coffee pot. He usually tried to avoid the stuff; caffeine tended to have an exaggerated effect on his kind, but it was morning now, long before he would go back to sleep. There had been a time when he would have just been lying down to sleep after having been up through the night. Some members of his family, and he supposed others of his kind, still kept their night hours, but that wasn't possible for Bastien to do and run Argeneau Enterprises efficiently. Most business was conducted during the day, and Bastien found it easier to simply consume more blood than he otherwise would need and deal with matters during the day.

"How about toast with your omelet?" Terri asked.

"No. Thank you." Moving to lean against the counter, he watched her set a frying pan on the stove and turn on the burner underneath while she whisked the contents of the bowl. "How long have you been up?"

"About an hour." She dropped a dollop of oil in the frying pan, nodding in satisfaction when it began to spit and roll around on the hot surface. "The flowers arrived just as I was starting to make the omelet. I couldn't believe how many there were when they finally finished bringing them up. I think the florist has gone nuts."

Bastien smiled and watched her pour the omelet into the pan. "I didn't know there'd be so many, either. I'll start taking pictures right after this."

Terri gave him a sympathetic smile as she set aside the now empty bowl. "That's a lot of pictures. I can help if you like."

"I'd like."

They were both silent for a moment. Terri was busy moving the omelet around in the pan to keep it from burning. He was busy watching her. The kitchen quickly started to fill with the rich aroma of onions and spice.

"I had a nice time last night," Bastien blurted suddenly, and could have kicked himself. But Terri met his gaze, a smile blossoming on her lips.

"So did I," she admitted shyly.

They fell silent again; then Bastien lifted a hand to run the knuckle of one finger down her cheek. Her eyes closed at once, and Terri tilted her face into the caress like a cat being petted. That action made it impossible for him to resist: Letting his hand slide around to catch her behind the neck, he pulled her forward and covered her mouth with his, smiling as her lips parted. Bastien immediately deepened the kiss. She tasted of herbs and spices and something sweet. Orange juice, he thought. If breakfast was as good as she tasted, it would be a pleasure to eat.

A small moan reached his ears and fanned the flames inside him. Bastien's kiss became rougher, more demanding, and Terri responded by opening further to him. Her hands crept around his neck.

She gasped, then arched nearer as Bastien let his

hands rub down and across her back. She felt right in his arms. She belonged there. He liked having her there. She felt good, smelled good, and tasted good too. And the way Terri moaned, stretched, and pressed against him was irresistible. He could go on kissing her forever.

"Your omelet," she murmured when he broke away to trail kisses down her neck.

Bastien's mouth stilled by her ear, and he almost cursed but caught it back. Heaving a sigh, he placed one last kiss on her nose, then released her.

Terri smiled sympathetically at his less than pleased expression, then turned to the stove. Fortunately, their distracting little interlude had not seen the omelet burn. It was light and fluffy and smelled heavenly when she served it up on a plate and handed it to him several moments later.

Terri sat with him while he ate, and Bastien ended up devouring the entire omelet. As good as it was, he suspected he ate it in an effort to sate another hunger that was plaguing him. The one he had for the woman who sat across from him, drinking coffee and chattering cheerfully away.

Bastien was glad he had eaten the entire omelet when Terri commented happily that this was the first time she'd seen him actually eat anything substantial since her arrival. She looked pleased as punch, and proud too that it was her cooking. Bastien assured her it was absolutely delicious, then kissed her and thanked her for the meal before heading out to the living room. He had to see about the flowers and the photos he was supposed to take.

Terri soon joined him, and she suggested they remove the flowers to the penthouse office one at a time to take the photos, then remove them from the apartment entirely to be sure there weren't any missed or double shots. At least, that was her excuse. Bastien suspected that she really hoped to alleviate some of the editor's discomfort by removing the source of his misery. He didn't mind. The office got better light in the morning anyway and the photos would work better in there because of it. After hundreds of years without daylight, he enjoyed seeing the sun and could do so, so long as his windows were treated to keep out the UV rays.

Terri was very fussy with the arrangements. Bastien would have just walked around snapping picture after picture until he was done, but she insisted on the right backdrop and lighting for each shot so that Kate could get a "true picture" of each arrangement. Between that and the process of downloading them every third or fourth photo, it took longer than expected. It was well past noon before they were what Bastien approximated was halfway through the job. He was waiting patiently as Terri fussed over the positioning of yet another arrangement, when he noted the way she absently rubbed the back of her neck as she bent to shift the urn.

"Are you getting a sore neck?" he asked, setting the camera down and approaching her.

Terri straightened and glanced over her shoulder at him. He began to lightly massage the muscles of her upper back and neck.

"A little," she admitted, relaxing under his touch.

168

She gave a small sigh. "I think I must have slept in an awkward position last night. I've had a bit of a crick all morning, but it's *really* bothering me now."

"Hmmm." Bastien's gaze moved over the top of her head as he worked, noting that her hair wasn't just brown. There were blond and red highlights in among the chestnut-colored strands. She had lovely hair.

"Thank you," Terri murmured, and Bastien froze as he realized he had made the comment aloud. But he froze only briefly; then he caught her hair in one swathe and moved it over her shoulder so that it was out of the way, revealing her neck as he continued his massage.

"You have a lovely neck," he commented as he let his hands slide down her back, beginning to include her upper shoulders in his massage.

"I . . ." Terri paused on an indrawn breath as he leaned down to kiss the tender flesh that he'd revealed.

"Bastien," she whispered. He ran his tongue in a circle over the spot he'd just kissed, and there was such a wealth of longing in her voice that he closed his eyes to savor it. His hands stopped moving, but he made them slide down her sides and back up, then again, each upward stroke taking him farther around her side and tantalizingly closer to the curves of her breasts.

A low moan slid from her lips when Bastien finally slid his hands around far enough to brush the soft curves. And when he finally gave up trying to resist and cupped the full mounds in each hand, Terri leaned back into his chest with a murmur of pleasure.

"Oh, Bastien." Her voice was dreamy and sweet. He moved his mouth over her throat, then to her ear, and concentrated there as he caressed her soft breasts through her light, pink sweater.

Her hands came up to cover his, and he paused, until Terri's fingers tightened around his, urging him to hold her more firmly, to knead her flesh. Then Bastien slid his hands downward. He heard her moan with what sounded like disappointment. That moan died abruptly, and she seemed to hold her breath as he slid his fingers beneath the hem of her sweater and allowed them to ride up over her naked flesh under the top.

Terri was warm, her skin smooth and soft. There was no impediment to his caress until he reached the bottom of her bra. There Bastien paused with indecision, then crossed his hands over her chest, allowing his right hand to find the front edge of her bra and slip beneath.

"Oh," She rose up slightly on her toes and pushed back into his chest as his hand cupped her warm, naked flesh.

"Bastien?" Uncertainty and pleading were both in that one word, and Terri said his name with an excited catch that did unbelievable things to him. *He* was having this effect on her. *He* was the reason her nipple was pebble hard beneath his fingers. *He* was why her breathing was suddenly coming in short, fast gasps.

"Terri." Bastien groaned, then withdrew his left hand to catch her under the chin and turn her head so that he could reach her mouth. Her response was gratifying if startling. This time it was *she* who slid her tongue out to run along his, and she who thrust her tongue into his mouth when his lips parted. She was kissing him with a passion that spoke eloquently of the effect he was having on her. Terri wanted him.

Slipping his other hand out from beneath her shirt, Bastien turned her to face him without breaking the kiss; then he took control, his own tongue lashing hers and thrusting with an answering passion. He had never wanted anyone as much in his life as he did Terri at that moment. He wanted to devour her. In fact, there was nothing else in the world that he thought he would rather do.

Moving her sideways and back, Bastien urged Terri down onto the sofa along the office wall. He lay down half on top of her, his elbow resting on the armrest by her head and one knee settled between her legs, helping to keep the worst of his weight supported, and the kiss turned frantic. Bastien's body was urging him to touch her everywhere at once, to rip her clothes off and explore her with the greed and want he was feeling, but he forced himself to remain in check, afraid that he would shock and terrify her with such an action.

It was hard to resist. It had been so terribly long since he had lain with a woman. It seemed forever since he had even had the urge to do so; yet now the hunger in him was worse than any he'd ever experienced. Even his need for blood had never surpassed this yearning he was currently feeling.

Terri groaned and shifted against him, arching upward when his hand found her breast again through the soft fabric of her sweater. Bastien was, at first, frustrated that it wasn't a shirt he could unbutton and open, but his brain started working again and he broke their kiss to lean slightly away. Grabbing the hem of the top, he pushed it upward to reveal the pink lace bra she wore beneath.

The words *color-coordinated* and *feminine* ran through his mind, and Bastien nearly laughed at the inane thought. Then he noticed the darker cinnamon of her nipples visible through the pink bra, and a shudder of anticipation ran through him. Before he even realized what he intended, Bastien had lowered his mouth to cover that still erect and excited nipple through the lace of the bra.

Terri cried out and trembled. Her hands caught violently in his hair, clasping him tightly to her, and urging him on. His tongue moved over the textured material of her bra, dampening it and the hard nipple beneath.

"Bastien!" She gasped his name on a cry of pure need, and began to tug at his hair. He gave in to her demand and lifted his head, allowing her to pull him back up to cover her mouth with his.

"*Ahhhhh!*"

Terri stiffened beneath him. That shout had come from outside, and reached them in the office. Both of them went still, waiting. When silence followed, Bastien relaxed and began to kiss Terri again, only to pause when a second shout followed.

Heaving a sigh, he lifted his head and met Terri's gaze.

"Maybe if we leave it alone, whatever it is will go away," she murmured hopefully.

"Maybe," he agreed, then glanced worriedly around at the sound of shattering glass. It was followed by a warning shout from Vincent, which helped Bastien identify that the first two shouts had been Chris Keyes's. It didn't look as if the situation were going away, whatever *it* was. Turning, he pressed a kiss to Terri's nose.

"I'm afraid I have to go see what the kids are doing," he said with grimace.

Terri released a sigh, but nodded and even managed a smile. She withdrew her arms from around him so they could both sit up.

Bastien helped her straighten her clothes, then stood, pulling her up with him, and led the way into the living room. What they found was like a scene from some insane, drug-induced dream. When they walked out, it was to find Chris hopping madly about the coffee table on his good leg, waving one crutch wildly in the air as he alternately sneezed and squawked. His second crutch lay forgotten on the floor between the couch and table.

As for Vincent, Bastien's cousin had removed his cape and was following the editor, snapping it in the air about the man's head in a half-crazed fashion that hit Chris in the head every second or third snap. Bastien couldn't decide if it was some new dance he was witnessing, or his cousin was attacking C.K.

He glanced at Terri uncertainly. "Is this another scene from the play?"

"I don't know," she admitted. Her expression was

torn between concern and bewilderment. "It could be, I guess."

"Hmmm." Bastien turned back to the dancing duo, wondering if he should interfere. Or if he even really wanted to. Then he stiffened. Chris had made almost a full circle around the coffee table, and was now hopping toward where his abandoned crutch lay. Unfortunately, he was too busy swinging wildly with the other crutch to notice.

Bastien opened his mouth in warning, but Terri had also seen the trouble too and beat him to it.

"Chris! Look out! Your—" She winced as he stumbled over the crutch, flailed madly for a minute in an effort to regain his balance, then cried out as an equally unobservant Vincent slammed into him from behind. The two went down, crashing to the floor in a tangle of flailing limbs.

"—crutch," Terri finished on a sigh.

"You tried," Bastien said, patting her shoulder comfortingly. Then they both rushed forward as Vincent struggled to disentangle himself from a moaning C.K.

"What were you two doing?" Bastien asked. Grasping his cousin's hand, he tugged upward, helping Vinny get to his feet and off the editor, who was definitely suffering the worse of the struggle.

"There was a bee," Vincent explained.

"A bee?" Bastien gaped at him in disbelief. "All this nonsense over a little bee?"

"*That* bee?" Terri gestured to a small insect now buzzing in circles over the editor's head.

Chris had been lying, eyes closed, trying to catch

his breath. Those eyes now popped open, round with terror. "What? Where is it?"

"It's just a bee, man," Bastien said bracingly. He was almost embarrassed for the fellow—hopping around, screaming like a girl, and all over a little insect. The editor would wet his pants at this rate. "You're a thousand times bigger than it. Get a hold of yourself."

"He's allergic to bees," Vincent explained in a hush.

"Oh." Bastien grunted, understanding a little better. "Well, hell," he added as the bee decided to settle on the editor's nose. "This can't be good."

"Oh, God," C.K. whimpered.

"How allergic are you?" Terri sounded concerned. Her expression turned to outright panic, however, when rather than answer, Chris stuck his lower lip out to blow upward at his nose in an effort to encourage the bee to leave. "Don't blow at it! I read somewhere that blowing at them annoys them and makes them—"

"Ow!" C.K. cried.

"—sting," Terri finished in horror. Apparently, the bee had decided it had finally had enough, and had done just that. She turned sharply on Vincent. "How allergic is he?"

"How should I know?"

"Well, you *knew* he was allergic!"

"Well, he *said* he was, when the bee came flying out of one of the arrangements," the actor explained. "But he was busy hopping around at the time, trying to get away from it. He didn't stop to go into detail."

"Oh, dear."

LYNSAY SANDS

When Terri turned to him, Bastien raised an eyebrow.

"I think we'd better call an ambulance," she said.

"Maybe he has one of those shot things," Vincent suggested, drawing Terri's attention back to him. "I worked with a gal once who was allergic to peanuts, and she carried a shot of adrenaline or something."

Bastien ignored the two as they continued to debate what to do. He had been watching the editor for reactions, and was alarmed at the speed with which the man's nose was swelling and his color changing. The man needed care right away, and an ambulance wouldn't do. It wouldn't be quick enough. Unless Chris had one of those shots Vincent mentioned, getting him in the car and to the hospital at once was top priority.

"Do you have a shot?" he asked, kneeling beside the editor. When C.K. shook his head, Bastien nodded and scooped him up in his arms. "Can someone grab my car keys off the coffee table?" he asked as he strode out of the living room.

There was silence for a minute, then a sudden rush of sound and movement behind Bastien. By the time he had pushed the elevator button and the doors slid open, Vincent and a breathless Terri were at his side.

"I got your keys," Vincent assured him. They all crowded onto the elevator, pushing Bastien and his bundle ahead of them.

"And I grabbed a pen," Terri added.

"A pen?" Vincent turned from pushing the button for the parking garage to peer at her.

"Yes. You know. In case we have to do one of those throat thingies," she explained.

"Throat thingies?" When Vincent glanced to Bastien in bewilderment, Bastien merely shook his head. He hadn't a clue what she was talking about.

"You know. If his throat closes up and he can't breathe, you have to slice a hole in his windpipe and stick the tube of the pen in for him to breathe through."

A stifled moan drew Bastien's gaze to the editor's now gray face. The man was looking pretty ghastly. He was almost a green color. Bastien couldn't decide if that was because he was having trouble breathing, or because Terri had just unintentionally scared the spit right out of him.

"Oh. A tracheotomy." Vincent nodded. "That could be necessary."

"Don't worry, Chris." Terri patted the editor's arm in an effort to soothe him. "We won't let you die. We'll do whatever it takes to keep you alive."

Though the man didn't say anything, Bastien got the impression that Terri's reassurance was more terrifying to Chris than the fact that he was starting to have definite difficulty breathing.

As the elevator doors opened onto the parking garage, Bastien raced to his Mercedes.

"How are you feeling?" Terri asked as Bastien set Chris back on the couch several hours later.

"Let me die in peace," he said. At least that's what Terri thought he said. It was difficult to tell with his voice as garbled as it was. The editor's face was swollen and an angry red. It looked as if he'd been in a bad fight—and lost. She simply could not believe that the hospital had released him. He looked like they should have kept him at least a week. And his labored efforts at breathing were not reassuring. Yet the doctor had pumped him full of something, made them all sit about for hours so they could "observe" C.K., then assured them he would be fine; he'd got to the hospital in time to save his life.

Well, if C.K. died, his family should sue and Terri would be willing to testify for them. She was positive the place really should have kept him at least overnight for observation. Since they hadn't, she'd keep a close eye on him herself.

"Terri?"

"Hmmm?" She straightened away from Chris to glance at Vincent, who dropped wearily into a chair.

"The next time we have an emergency and you want to drive, remind me to say no."

Terri grimaced. She had insisted on driving when they'd got down to the parking garage. Bastien had set Chris in the backseat of his car and climbed in, saying, "One of you get in on his other side in case I need help."

That had been all she'd had to hear; Terri had snatched the keys from a startled Vincent, handed him the pen, and jumped in the driver seat. Then she'd had to slide across to the other side, because she'd forgotten that the driver side was on the left in America, while it was on the right in England.

"Speaking of which," Bastien said idly, moving to

the bar to fix a drink. "Do you have an international driver's license, Terri?"

"Er . . . no." She shifted uncomfortably, knowing that she really shouldn't have driven. But when faced with the choice of driving, or possibly having to help Bastien cut open the editor's throat, driving had been her choice. Terri wasn't very good with blood and stuff. That was why she'd grabbed the keys and hopped in the car, leaving Vincent no option but to climb in the back with Bastien.

Noting the exchange of glances between the two cousins, Terri felt it behooved her to point out, "But I got us there pretty fast."

"And even in one piece," Vincent added dryly. "I feel I should point out to you that the speed limits in England are higher than here."

Terri bit her lip to keep from smiling. She would never forget glancing into the rearview mirror to see Vincent's blanching face, and the way he clutched the backseat in horror as she swerved in and out of traffic at breakneck speeds, trying to get to the hospital as quickly as possible. All while Bastien had shouted directions to her from the back seat. "Right at the next corner! Left here!" She'd been going so fast, she would swear she had taken a couple corners on two wheels.

"You did a fine job," Bastien said reassuringly, pouring whiskey into a glass. Then he ruined the effect by downing the glass in one toss.

"I could use one of those, too," Vincent decided as Bastien poured another.

"Well . . ." Terri glanced at Chris. The poor man was sound asleep, which made her hesitate. She'd been about to ask him if he needed anything to make him more comfortable. That wasn't necessary.

"I suppose I should call the publisher he and Kate work for," Bastien said, walking back from around the bar with two glasses. "I'll have to call and leave a message on the answering machine, informing them that Chris won't be in any shape to go into the office tomorrow as he'd planned."

The editor had decided yesterday that he could work just as comfortably in the office as in the penthouse, now that his leg wasn't paining him as much. He had said it would probably be better for him anyway, less distraction. Terri supposed it was out of the question for a while now.

Bastien handed Vincent the second drink he'd made, then turned slowly to contemplate the flowers on nearly every surface in the living room.

Terri glanced around, too. Miraculously, none of the remaining arrangements had been disturbed by the fracas. The breaking glass they had heard had apparently been Chris's cup of coffee smashing to the floor.

"I guess I should make that call, then get back to taking those pictures," he decided.

"And I'll clean up the broken cup while you make the phone call, then I'll help you," Terri announced.

"And I . . ." Vincent paused to down his whiskey. Setting the empty glass down, he said, "Have to go feed. I mean, find something to eat. I'm starved."

Terri glanced at her watch at the announcement.

They had wasted the better part of the afternoon and early evening at the hospital. It was now past seven. They hadn't eaten since breakfast.

"Why don't you make yourself something to eat, Terri?" Bastien suggested. "I can handle the rest of the photos on my own while you cook."

"Okay," she agreed slowly. "Is there anything in particular you'd like?"

"I'm not hungry," he said. "Just fix yourself what you want. I'll grab a . . . er . . . sandwich . . . later if I get hungry."

Terri hesitated, then said, "I'll make a *couple* of sandwiches, and bring them into the office. We can eat while we work."

Chapter Ten

"Well, that's one crisis taken care of," Bastien announced as Terri entered the office. "Kate got the e-mail last night. She and Lucern looked over the pictures and picked the arrangements they wanted, then e-mailed them to me. They were in my in-box when I got up this morning, and I just called Roberto to pass along their decision." He narrowed his eyes when he noted Terri's grim expression. She approached the desk. "You don't look happy. You should be relieved. Tragedy has been averted. We saved the wedding."

"I'm glad we've averted that problem. Now we have another one."

She laid the newspaper she'd brought with her on the desk in front of him, and Bastien glanced down. She'd folded it in half. There were three stories showing.

"I'm guessing you aren't wanting me to look at the story on New York doing a doggie census?" he asked.

"Try the story next to it," she suggested.

"'Bankrupt Caterer Commits Suicide,'" he read aloud, then glanced up blankly. "So?"

"I'm pretty sure that's Kate's caterer."

"Dear God," Bastien breathed.

"Hmm." Heaving a sigh, Terri dropped into the seat facing his desk. "I'm not positive, though."

They stared at each other for a moment, then Bastien reached for the phone.

"It's just after six A.M. in California," Terri reminded him, having guessed his intention of calling Kate and Lucern.

Bastien hesitated. "Too early?"

"From what Kate's told me about conferences, they last until late at night. She probably won't be up for another hour. And I wouldn't want to wake her up with *this* news."

"No. You're right." He set the phone back down. "I should wait another hour at least."

"I would," Terri agreed.

Bastien nodded, then began to drum his fingers on the desk. He wasn't used to inactivity in a crisis, but he also didn't have a clue what to do. And this time, even *he* could see it was a crisis.

"We could make up a list of caterers to contact in case this guy *is* her caterer," Terri suggested after a moment.

"Good thinking. At least that way, we won't just be calling with bad news. If it *is* him," Bastien added.

Sincerely hoping it wasn't, he pulled the Yellow Pages out from the drawer where it was stored. Terri stood and walked around the desk to look over his shoulder. Bastien leafed through, looking for the section with caterers. He relaxed a little when he saw that the list was several pages long.

"There are a ton of them," Terri murmured.

"Yes. That's good. Isn't it?"

"Not necessarily," she said. "Many of them will be booked up and unavailable, so we'll waste time calling those, and I haven't a clue which of those left over are good. Do you?"

"Damn," Bastien breathed. He was the detail man, the decision man, the crisis man—the one everyone looked to when a problem cropped up. But he'd never been faced with these kinds of problems. Food wasn't a big priority in Bastien's life, and therefore it wasn't a problem he had any experience dealing with. The only time he had to worry about food was during business meetings that included mortals, and then he just handed the problem over to: "Meredith!"

"Meredith?" Terri asked.

"She'll know which are the good caterers and which are the bad ones, and . . ." Not bothering to finish his explanation, Bastien picked up the phone again. This time he punched in the number to his office. Meredith picked up on the second ring.

"Argeneau Enterprises."

"Meredith, I think Kate's caterer killed himself," he blurted by way of hello. "I need a list of the best caterers in town. We have to call them all and see which are available for the date of her wedding."

184

The woman didn't exclaim in horror at this newest tragedy plaguing Kate's wedding, or bother with questions; she simply snapped, "I'm on it. Do you have her menu plan for what she wanted served?"

Bastien blinked, then glanced at Terri. "Do we have a menu plan for what she wanted served at the wedding?" he echoed.

"A menu plan?" She considered for a minute, then straightened abruptly. "I might. She e-mailed it to me. Actually, that e-mail mentioned who the caterer was, too. If I still have it, we might not have to trouble Kate with this at all. Can I use the computer?"

"Be my guest."

Phone still to his ear, Bastien stood and stepped aside for Terri to sit in the desk chair and start up the computer. He didn't bother explaining what was going on to Meredith; she had probably heard anyway. Instead, he watched as the computer warmed up and Terri logged on to the internet. It only took a moment for her to open her e-mail program and find the e-mail needed.

"It *was* her caterer," she said with a sigh. "But I *do* have the menu plan. That's something, anyway."

"Forward it to Meredith," Bastien instructed, then gave her his secretary's e-mail address before speaking into the phone again. "Terri's forwarding it to you, Meredith. Is there anything else you need?"

When she said no, and assured him that she'd get back to him directly, Bastien thanked her and said good-bye.

"She's good," he commented as he hung up. "I should give her a raise."

"Yes. You probably should," Terri agreed with a laugh. She closed the e-mail program, then the Internet itself. Once that was done, she turned off the computer. "She seems very efficient."

"Well, you aren't too shabby yourself," Bastien said softly as she stood. "Someone else might not have caught that news article, or recognized the name."

"Hmm," Terri murmured. "I need coffee."

"I'll make you one," Bastien offered.

"Actually, I have one," she said, moving around the desk toward the door. "I was drinking it while reading the paper, but forgot it in the living room when I saw that article."

"I guess we'll have to delay our outing today." Bastien's gaze dropped to Terri's behind as he followed her out of the office. He was beginning to understand Lucern's fascination with Kate's behind. Not that he found Kate's rear end fascinating, but Terri's? Well, that was another matter.

"What outing?" Terri asked. When she glanced over her shoulder at him in surprise, Bastien forced his eyes up to hers.

"I was thinking maybe I would take you around the tourist stops today. You shouldn't leave without seeing those," he said as they walked along the hall. "But we'll have to do that tomorrow, I guess. There could be a lot of places to call when Meredith finishes a list."

"I'll take half," Terri offered.

"I was hoping you would," he admitted.

She chuckled, then sighed as they entered the living room. "I wonder what else will go wrong. What's

186

next, do you think: The reception hall burns to the ground? The church floods? Or perhaps the parking garage holding the wedding limo explodes?" She dropped onto the couch and picked up her coffee, taking a sip. "I'm starting to think this wedding is doomed."

"Hmm," Bastien murmured, but his attention was on Chris. The editor's expression was making him nervous. A look of realization had crossed his face as Terri made her facetious comments.

He didn't feel much better when the editor breathed, "Oh, damn," in a sort of horror.

"What?" Bastien asked, afraid he didn't want to know.

"I just thought of something," Chris said.

"What?" Terri lowered her coffee cup to eye him anxiously.

"The flowers."

"Oh." She relaxed. "We've taken care of the flower problems, C.K. Kate's chosen the ones she wants from the arrangements Roberto sent over. It's all decided and settled."

"No. Not the *live* flowers. The tissue flowers," he explained. "For the cars."

"What about the tissue flowers?" Terri asked, her gaze shooting to Bastien. "I thought they were made and ready to go?"

"They are," Bastien assured her, quite relieved to be able to say that. He moved to sit on the couch next to her. "Lucern and Kate took care of it. He was complaining the day you arrived about it taking forever."

187

"Yes, they did make them, and it did take forever," Chris agreed, looking miserable. "But Kate's place is small. Really small. And she didn't have anywhere to store them."

"No," Terri breathed.

"What?" Bastien asked. He didn't like being the one in the dark, and her expression suggested she already had an idea of what was coming.

Chris grimaced, then nodded at Terri. "She asked me to store them."

Bastien suddenly had a thought. "*Where* did you store them, Chris?"

"My apartment."

"Where in your apartment?" he asked, knowing the editor's evasiveness was a very bad sign. And there was only one place that the flowers would have been damaged.

C.K. sighed, then seemed to decide there was no hope but to confess. However, he prefaced the confession with an excuse. "My place isn't all that big, either," he said.

"*Where?*" Terri asked wearily.

"The bathroom."

"Dear God," she moaned.

"They may still be safe."

"And the pope might be Protestant," Bastien snapped. "Why on earth would you put them in the *bathroom* of all places?"

"In case he ran out of toilet paper?" Vincent suggested. He yawned as he entered the living room.

Bastien was less than amused. "Shut up, Vinny. Don't you have a rehearsal to go to or something?"

"No. Lucky for you, I'm free today. And don't call me Vinny."

"Lucky?" Bastien snorted.

"I put them in the bathroom because that's the only place I had room," Chris explained, drawing their attention again. "It's an old building, and the bathroom is huge compared to the bathrooms they make now."

Bastien muttered something uncomplimentary under his breath regarding the editor's intelligence. Chris heard him and flushed, then said, "She brought them over in cardboard boxes. But I put those boxes in big black garbage bags to protect them from the humidity when I showered and stuff, so they might still be okay."

Bastien glanced at Terri. She was looking to him in question, a glimmer of hope in her eyes. But he had been at the apartment. From what he had seen, the chance that Kate's flowers were still okay wasn't good. He didn't want to upset Terri until he knew for sure, though. "I'll have to go check on them."

"Do you want me to come?" Terri asked.

Bastien hesitated. He really would like her to go with him. He enjoyed her company. But the landlady had given him a hard time when last he'd gone to the editor's apartment; and if he ran into her again and she caused difficulties, Bastien might have to take control of her mind again. It would be easier if Terri weren't there for that.

"No," he said at last. "Perhaps you could wait here for Meredith's call? I'll be as quick as I can."

"Okay," she agreed promptly.

189

"Thanks." He stood and started out of the room.

"Bastien?" Chris called after him, bringing him to a halt in the entry. "You need the keys," the editor said, and grabbed them off the coffee table where they had sat for the past few days. He tossed them over, then added, "Would you mind picking up some more clothes for me while you're there?"

Bastien grunted and turned to leave. Whether he would or not depended on his mood. And that would depend on the state the flowers were in.

"I tried to get a hold of Kate's catering company this morning, hoping that someone would at least be there to take calls and answer questions, but of course they aren't answering the phones. If there's even anyone there to answer the phones anymore."

"Hmm," Terri murmured into the receiver. She wasn't terribly surprised at the news. Neither was she surprised that Meredith had checked it out. The woman seemed superefficient.

"But I was able to get some information from other sources, and it would appear that any deposit Kate might have given the caterer is as good as gone. She isn't likely to see it back. Nor can she expect any service. The company is completely defunct."

"I was afraid of that."

"Yes," Bastien's secretary agreed. "So I called around to all the best caterers in town. They're all booked up, of course."

"Of course," Terri said wearily.

"However, Argeneau Enterprises does a lot of business each year in catering, and our contracts are coveted and everyone is eager to impress us, so almost all of the caterers are willing to hire extra staff and do whatever is necessary. They're no doubt hoping to make enough of an impression to get future contracts."

"Really?" Terri perked up. Perhaps all was not lost.

"They're all vying for the job. I've sent out copies of the desired menu, and each of them is working up competitive prices and arranging to send sample meals over to be tried. Bastien or you, or both of you, can decide who to go with. That probably won't be until later tomorrow, though." There was a pause, then Meredith added, "I know Kate should probably make the choice, but as she's in California, and this has to be arranged and decided at once so that the provisions can be ordered, it—"

"It will have to be us," Terri finished. She paused, biting her lip. "Meredith, I'm thinking that, since she can't make the choice, and since this news would just stress her out—"

"And at a time when she's already under a great deal of pressure," Meredith put in.

Terri felt herself relax. It sounded like the secretary had the same idea, but she said it just the same: "Do you think we should just keep this to ourselves? Bastien and I can choose the best price and meal, and Kate doesn't really even have to know about it if all goes well."

There was a pause on the other end of the line. Whether it was because Meredith was considering the question, or because she was surprised that Terri would even ask her opinion on a family matter, Terri didn't know.

"I think that—judging by how upset she was over the floral incident—keeping this from her might be the best decision," Meredith announced at last.

"Yes, I think it's best," Terri said, then hesitated before saying, "Since you're now a co-conspirator, would you care to be in on the taste testing when the sample meals show up?"

"Oh. Oh, that's so nice, but . . . no, I couldn't." The woman was obviously flustered. "But thank you."

"Are you sure?" Terri asked.

"Yes. Thank you," Meredith repeated, a hint of warmth creeping into her previously cool and efficient tone. "I'll leave that up to yourself and Mr. Argeneau."

"Well, if you change your mind, let me know," Terri said. "And thank you, Meredith. I fully expected to spend the day calling caterer after caterer to deal with this, but you've handled it all and left nothing but the eating, which is the fun part. Bastien's very lucky to have you working for him."

There was a soft expelling of breath on the other end of the phone. "Thank you, Ms. Simp—"

"Call me Terri."

"Thank you, Terri," Meredith said. "It's always nice to be appreciated."

"Well, you certainly are that," she told her, then thanked her again. Saying good-bye, she hung up.

"Was that Meredith?"

Terri glanced up from the receiver she'd just set in

the cradle to find Bastien in the doorway to the penthouse office. "Yes, it was," she admitted, getting to her feet and moving around the desk. "She's arranged for price quotes and sample meals from the best caterers in New York. We decided that, since Kate isn't here to taste them, which means you and I will have to in her place, there's no reason to even tell her about the change—unless something goes terribly wrong at the wedding." She paused and raised her eyebrows. "How did it go at C.K.'s apartment? Are any of the flowers salvageable?"

Bastien raised a bag he was holding, grasped both handles, and opened it wide for her to peer inside. Terri tipped her head and peered down at several boxes of Kleenex.

"Darn," she breathed, knowing what that meant.

"There are several more bags out in the living room," he told her dryly. "And some string."

Terri closed her eyes, then opened them again. Raising her head, she peered at him. "*None* of them were salvageable?"

"The garbage bags were ripped by the ceiling caving in, and the pipes poured water down on them, apparently turning them into tissue stew. The landlady had them carted out with the rubble when they cleared it away."

"Ah."

"The good news is, I rented several movies to watch while we make the flowers. That was the salesclerk's suggestion when I asked how much Kleenex I needed to make flowers for a wedding," he admitted, following her out of the office.

"Clever girl, suggesting that," Terri commented. In the living room, she saw the collection of bags sitting in the center of the room.

"I thought so," Bastien agreed.

Chris was no longer in the room. Terri guessed that meant Bastien had brought him back fresh clothes, and he was in his room changing. Terri rifled through the shopping bags until she found the string, then moved to claim a corner of the couch.

Bastien immediately settled next to her, and dumped the boxes of Kleenex on the coffee table. They both grabbed and ripped open a box, then paused.

"Do you know how to make these things?" she asked doubtfully.

"I was rather hoping you would," he admitted.

"Darn," she breathed.

"*I* do."

They both glanced up with surprise as Vincent walked into the room and came to join them.

"*You* do?" Bastien asked doubtfully.

"Mmmm." The actor dropped onto the chair across from them, and claimed a box for himself. "It's amazing the things you learn while working in the theater."

Terri tossed another flower into one of the large cardboard boxes Bastien had fetched. That had been Vincent's suggestion: storage that would prevent the flowers from being crushed. While Bastien was off finding the boxes, the actor had proceeded to show Terri and Chris how to make the flowers. He had re-

peated the lesson for Bastien's benefit upon his return, making Terri and Chris watch again too, since
they were still struggling somewhat with their efforts.
All of them had been working at the project almost
nonstop since. Terri was hoping that meant they
would be finished before the wedding—which
wasn't a joke. Vincent was the only one of them who
knew what he was doing; the rest of them were ruin-
ing more flowers than they were making.

They'd been at it since the morning before. It was
now late afternoon of the next day. After two days of
work, with only a pause to sleep last night, they had
watched countless movies and produced one whole
and one partial box of usable flowers. And three
boxes of rejects. They were improving, though. Two
of the boxes of rejects were from the first night, and
the third box was only about three-quarters full with
today's failures.

"How many more do you think we need?" Terri
asked, grabbing a handful of popcorn and popping it
into her mouth, her gaze fixed on the television
screen. She jumped as the actress onscreen was at-
tacked from behind, then winced as the woman's
chainsaw wielding attacker turned her into dogmeat
in a matter of seconds.

"Is it just me, or does anyone else think there is just
something so wrong about watching horror movies
while making tissue flowers for a wedding?" Chris
asked.

Terri grinned at the editor. She even managed not
to wince at his misshapened face. Some of the
swelling had gone down, but not much, and his col-

LYNSAY SANDS

oring was still an angry red. "I'd think, as a man, you'd find it totally appropriate," she said. "After all, isn't the idea of marriage itself a horror to most men?"

He paused to consider, then nodded. "You've got a point."

"I don't know," Vincent said as Terri laughed. "Some men, smart men, recognize the value of a good life mate. A partner to share life's sorrows and joys with."

"Why, Vincent," she said with surprise. "You almost sound like a romantic."

The actor recoiled. "Well, I wouldn't go that far."

Terri chuckled and picked up the ball of string to cut off a length.

"What time is it?" Bastien asked suddenly.

"Three-thirty," Chris answered, glancing at his wristwatch.

"Oh." Bastien looked perplexed for a minute, then glanced at Terri. "I don't remember you eating today."

"I had a bowl of cereal when I got up," she said absently. She finished with the string and began to fold a sheaf of Kleenex.

"But you didn't eat lunch."

Terri glanced up, surprised at the accusation in his voice. "*I* didn't eat lunch?" she echoed with surprise. "No, I didn't. But then neither did you. We were busy, so we've been snacking instead."

Bastien scowled as she gestured to the junk food on the table. "Popcorn and corn chips do not make up a healthy diet."

Terri grimaced at those stiff words. She'd said

something very similar to C.K. a day or two ago and only now realized how annoying that must have been.

"You're absolutely right, Bastien," Vincent said. "Perhaps you should make something to eat."

"Me?" He blanched at the idea, and Vincent laughed.

"Yes, you. Well, surely you weren't suggesting *Terri* cook for *you?*"

"Not for me," he said firmly. "I'm not hungry."

"Neither am I," Terri said with a shrug. "Problem solved."

She didn't miss Bastien's scowl, but merely grinned. The man hardly ever ate. And when he did, he mostly just picked at the food. He had some nerve lecturing her, when he had such poor eating habits.

"Well, *I'm* hungry," Chris announced, grabbing his crutches to get to his feet. "So I'll cook."

"Oh, I don't think that's a very good idea," Vincent said calmly and fanned out the flower he'd just finished making.

"Why not?" Bastien asked. "Terri's cooked for him, Chris can cook for her."

"Look at the man," Vincent said. "So far he's been to the hospital twice in less than a week—once for a toilet falling on him, once for a bee sting. Are you really willing to risk letting him play with fire and sharp objects?"

"Dear Lord," Bastien breathed in horror.

"Oh, for heaven's sake!" Terri set her half-finished flower down with exasperation. "I'll cook."

"No." Bastien stood abruptly. "I'll cook. How difficult can it be?"

"I'm thinking takeout would be a good idea," Vincent said as he peered down at the charred mass in the bottom of the pan. He tilted his head to get a different perspective and asked, "What was it?"

"Ha, ha," Bastien muttered, dropping the pan in the sink and turning on the tap. It would definitely need soaking to come clean. If it came clean. Perhaps he should just chuck it out, he thought, then pointed out, "It was *you* who suggested I cook."

"Well, I was trying to do you a favor," Vincent retorted. "I was afraid Terri would think you were trying to get her to cook for you. No woman wants to be a replacement housekeeper. Speaking of which, how's the hunt for a new housekeeper going, anyway? And have you found Mrs. Houlihan yet?"

"I haven't any idea," Bastien admitted. He'd given both problems to Meredith, and he hadn't been keeping up with much lately. It seemed there had been one crisis after another keeping him busy and distracted. He supposed he should check in with the office. "What time is it?"

"Almost five."

Bastien nodded as he shucked the oven mitts he'd donned to rescue the burning meal from the oven. Not that he'd managed to save it. He grimaced to himself as he recalled leafing quickly through a cookbook and choosing what had seemed simplest: Roast. Throw it in a pan and throw it in the oven. What could be easier? And Bastien had done so—but as the recipe had called for a thawed roast of beef, and he'd only had frozen, he'd upped

198

the temperature a bit. All the way, actually. Then he'd gone back to work on the tissue paper flowers. By the time he'd remembered he was cooking something, the meat was done. Past done. Black on the outside and red on the inside. Disgusting. Bastien saw there was more to cooking than he'd realized.

"How's it going?"

Both he and Vincent glanced toward the door, where Terri stood. She was glancing around curiously. "Is that dinner I smell?"

"We're having takeout," Bastien answered, walking past her to stride up the hall. "Order whatever you want. I have to check in at the office. I'll be back directly to pay."

As Bastien left, Terri raised her eyebrows and turned back to Vincent. "A problem?"

"Bastien found cooking more of a challenge than he expected," Vincent explained and gestured to the sink.

Terri crossed the room and whistled as she peered down at the mess there. A large black chunk, with several smaller black chunks, lay discarded in a pan.

"So, what are you going to order? Chinese? Or pizza?" the actor asked.

Terri shook her head and grinned. "With all the food in this place? I'll whip up something myself and have it done by the time Bastien gets back."

"That a girl! Make him feel inferior," Vincent said lightly. They both laughed, only to pause and glance around in surprise as the elevator buzzer sounded.

Terri followed Bastien's cousin curiously to a

kitchen wall panel that was an exact replica of the one in the living room.

"Hmm. Do you know who that is?" he asked, pushing the button to bring up an image of the interior of the elevator.

Terri leaned closer for a better look at the man standing by a covered trolley. She started to shake her head, then paused. "Oh, wait! It's probably one of the caterers. I'd forgotten Meredith had arranged for them to bring samples of the wedding menu for us to try."

Vincent nodded and pushed a button. "Yes?" he asked.

"Katelyn's Catering. I have a delivery."

"This is your lucky day, Terri." Vincent pushed the button to release the elevator, then flipped off the monitor. "You don't have to cook after all. It's being delivered."

Terri chuckled, but said, "I hardly think they'll be bringing anything that in any way resembles a meal. They'll just be samples—hors d'oeuvres, and bits off the menu. Nothing substantial."

Despite her comment, curiosity made Terri follow him out to await the caterer. The moment the elevator doors slid open, the deliveryman smiled at them cheerfully and wheeled out his little trolley. Stopping before them, he lifted a clipboard with a work order and read: "Terri Simpson or Bastien Argeneau?"

"I'm Terri Simpson." She stepped forward and accepted the clipboard and pen.

"Just sign on the bottom, miss," he instructed. "Where do you want this?"

"The kitchen, please." She pointed the way. "First door on the right."

Terri did a quick read-through of the paper he wanted her to sign as the men moved away up the hall, Vincent accompanying the deliveryman. Assured that it merely stated she had accepted the delivery, she signed and dated it, finishing as the men came back up the hall.

"Thanks," the delivery man said as he took his pen and clipboard back. Then he ripped off a pink copy, handed it to her, and moved back into the elevator. "Just phone the office when you've made up your mind and are ready to have the trolley taken away. Someone will come by to pick up everything."

"All right. Thanks," Terri called as the elevator doors closed. "Well." Glancing over the invoice copy she'd been given, she turned and headed to the kitchen. She was curious to see what had been sent. She expected a couple of sample dishes that were on the menu, but you never knew. "Did you look when he brought it in?" she asked Vincent as he followed her.

"No. I just watched him roll it in, then followed him out," he said. They paused by the trolley that had been left next to the small dinette set.

"Hmm." Terri glanced over the trolley. It looked rather like a chrome chest on wheels, or a chrome-colored barbecue. The top was a square lid with rounded edges and a handle. Terri grasped the handle and lifted upward, inhaling the steam released into the room.

"God," she breathed, and she gaped at half a dozen china plates of food. The caterer hadn't sent samples of different things, they'd sent two samples of *every*thing.

"He said the desserts were in the lower drawer," Vincent spoke up.

Terri hesitated, then stepped back, only then noticing that there was a lower drawer on the trolley. Grasping its handle, she pulled it out and sighed as several delicacies rolled into view. There were two of each of those, too.

"Well, as I said, you don't have to cook."

Before Terri could respond, the elevator buzzer sounded again. The actor moved to the wall panel and pushed buttons, as Terri closed the drawer and then the chest top to keep everything at the correct temperature until Bastien came back.

"Another caterer," Vincent announced. "You'll need to sign for this too, probably."

Nodding, Terri followed him back into the entry. They arrived just before the doors opened to reveal another trolley-pushing deliveryman.

"Terri Simpson?" he asked, glancing at her.

"Yes." She held her hand out for the clipboard and pen.

"Where do you want—"

"The kitchen. Follow me." Vincent turned to lead the way as Terri signed the invoice.

Chapter Eleven

Bastien tapped his foot with irritation and pressed the elevator button again. He wasn't used to waiting so long for the contraption and was becoming a bit impatient. This elevator only serviced the penthouse. It could stop on any floor when requested, but only if you had a key. Other than that, it had to be released from the penthouse suite itself for a straight ride from the ground floor up. Bastien didn't understand the present delay.

Just when he was about to go back into his office and call upstairs to see what was going on, the elevator arrived with a *ding*. Releasing a sigh of relief, Bastien stepped on board, sniffing the air as he pressed the button to take him to the penthouse. There was the faintest scent of cooked food inside. The takeout must have arrived, he realized as the doors closed and the lift started upward. He hoped the delivery guy had just ridden up and was still there. He didn't want Terri paying for the meal.

The entry was empty when Bastien stepped out of the elevator. Following the sound of voices, he headed into the living room, fully expecting to find Terri and Chris indulging in pizza or Chinese food. Instead, he found all three of his guests moving about in a sea of tissue flowers and chrome trolleys.

"This one doesn't have an invoice." Vincent opened the lid of the silver chest he stood by, waited for the steam to clear, then glanced at the contents. "There's a napkin. It has S.C. on it."

"S.C.?" Terri asked, then began to sort through a stack of papers. "S.C., S.C., S.C.," she murmured, sounding stressed. "S—Here! Sylvia's Cuisine." She crossed the room to hand Vincent one of the sheafs of paper. Bastien's cousin took the page and proceeded to extract a piece of tape from a dispenser he held, then tape the paper to the top of the chrome warmer.

"This one has B.D. on the plate covers," Chris announced, peering into another of the trolleys.

"B.D?" Terri muttered, and began the sorting exercise again. "B.D. I saw a Bella Donna or Bella Dolci or something a minute ago. That's probably it."

"I sincerely hope it isn't belladonna," Bastien said with amusement, drawing their attention to his presence.

"Oh. You're back." Terri forced a smile to her mouth, but he knew it was purely for his sake. She didn't seem to be in much of a smiling mood.

"Hmmm." Bastien moved into the room, kicking

flowers about with each step he took. "Either you overordered on the takeout, or the catering samples have arrived."

"The catering samples," she said with a sigh. Terri waved her hands at the chaos in the room and apologized, "I'm sorry about this mess. I should have been more prepared. More organized. But they came one right after the other; bang, bang, bang."

"Bang, bang, bang," Vincent agreed with a solemn nod.

"And it was so rushed. I'd barely sign for one when another was under my nose."

"Right under her nose." Chris nodded. "They were just shoving them at her left, right, and center."

"Yep." It was Terri's turn to nod. "Chris was manning the panel to release the elevator, and Vincent was showing the deliverymen where to put their carts, and the men just kept handing me clipboards and pens, then ripping off invoices and giving them to me, and there were so many of them . . ." She waved the papers helplessly. "We don't know which invoices go with what."

Bastien bit his lip to keep back the smile that threatened to stretch his lips. He didn't think she'd appreciate his amusement right now. She looked absolutely frazzled. And adorable. But he didn't think she'd appreciate his telling her that, either, so kept it to himself as well.

"I don't know how we're going to eat all of this food, Bastien. There's too much." Terri peered around with distress, then glanced back to him, held up a pen, and wailed, "And I didn't mean to, but it was all so hectic that I stole a pen!"

"Two of them," Chris said, pointing at the one dangling from her shirt collar, where she had apparently stuck it in the rush.

"Three," Vincent corrected, walking over to pluck another from where she had absently tucked it behind her ear.

Helpful as they were trying to be, their added comments just made Terri seem that much more miserable. Moving forward, Bastien urged his cousin out of the way and tugged her into his arms to pat her reassuringly. "It's okay, baby. We'll sort this out. And we don't have to eat all the food, just taste each one. And we'll do that first—that way, the ones we don't like, we don't have to match up to their invoices."

"But you weren't here, and I signed for them all. I have to make sure the trolleys get back to their proper owners."

"We'll sort it out," Bastien repeated, then urged her around and between several carts to the couch. He paused to sweep several flowers aside, frowning as he did. "How did these flowers get everywhere?" he asked as he urged her to sit.

"One of the delivery guys knocked one of the boxes off the table," Vincent explained.

"And another picked up a box to move it out of the way, tripped, and sent them flying everywhere," Chris finished. "Fortunately, they were all rejects. Terri had the good sense to have us move the usable flowers after the first mishap."

Bastien nodded. "Maybe we should put the flowers away for now. We wouldn't want them ruined by food being spilled on them, or anything of that nature. Not after all the time we've put into making them."

"I'm on it." Vincent bent to pick up the open Kleenex boxes, and started putting them away in the bags they had come in. Chris immediately started collecting the puffy flowers from the floor, and tossing them back into the boxes they'd tumbled out of. Sometimes he'd use his crutch to drag the little suckers close enough to pick up.

Bastien turned back to Terri, and found her bent double on the couch, gathering flowers from the carpet. After a moment, she gave that up and shifted onto the floor, where it was easier to reach them. Her eyes swept the room full of trolleys, and as she straightened to toss a collection of rejects into a box, dismay crossed her features. "How are we ever going to choose from all these caterers' samples, Bastien?"

"Two at a time," he said simply. He joined her on his knees on the floor. The answer seemed logical enough to him. "We put two side by side, try a bite from each, decide which is better, and put the rejects in the hall."

She nodded at his suggestion, then said, "But what if one dish is better from one caterer, but something else is better from another?"

He hadn't thought of that. After considering the matter for a moment, he said, "The main dish is the most important one. We'll go through the samples trying all the main dishes, two at a time. The rejects go in the entry, the rest go somewhere else. That will eliminate half of them right away. Then we start comparing the other dishes."

"Where shall I put these to keep them out of the way for now, cousin?" Vincent held up the shopping bags with all the unused Kleenex and string.

"The office?" Bastien suggested. He immediately decided it was a good idea. "Yes. Just put it in the closet in the office for now, Vincent."

The actor nodded and headed off. "I'll drop them in there, then I'm going out for a bite. All this talk of food is making me hungry. I won't stay out long, though. I'll make sure I'm back as quick as I can, to see if you need any help with anything else."

"Thanks, cousin," Bastien called after him. For all the nuisance the actor could be when he felt like causing trouble, Vincent was still a good man. He had always been there for Bastien when he was needed, and Bastien reminded himself they had been as close as brothers at one time. He regretted the loss of that closeness.

"Well, that's the last of it," Chris said a short time later as the last flower landed in a box. "Are we moving the rejects out of the room, too?"

"I'll take them down to the office," Bastien decided, then glanced at Terri. "Honey, why don't you go collect some plates and silverware?"

Her eyes went as round as saucers, and she stood staring at him. He felt uncertainty claim him. "What is it?"

"Nothing," she squeaked, and rushed off in the direction of the kitchen.

"What can I do to help?" Chris asked.

Bastien just about said, "In your condition? Nothing." But he caught the words back. The editor was in rough shape but had still done his best to help out, both in making the flowers and cleaning up the mess just now. Considering the streak of bad luck he had suffered—what with his apartment being ruined, a toilet falling on top of him and breaking his leg, and his face being turned into a sideshow attraction thanks to the life-threatening bee sting—C.K. had behaved pretty well, even managing to be chipper. Bastien was starting to think he might have underestimated the guy, and he was actually starting to warm up to him.

"Just relax for a minute, Chris," he said. "We could use your help tasting the meals too, if you don't mind."

"No, I don't mind," the editor assured him, and after a hesitation made his way to a chair and sat.

Bastien had caught the look of surprise on the younger man's face at the almost friendly tone he'd used, and from that realized his irritation and lack of concern for C.K. had shown from the start. He felt bad for a moment, then shrugged it aside. It wasn't like he'd been outright mean. He'd just not given the man a chance, really. Now he was giving him one. He wasn't going to kick himself over the past. Besides, he had other things to worry about. Foremost in his mind was why Terri had gaped at him when he'd asked her to grab some cutlery and plates. That had him mystified.

In the kitchen, Terri was muttering to herself as she dragged plates out of the cupboard. "He called me honey." A grin was tugging at her lips. *Honey.* And she thought Bastien might have called her baby earlier, but she'd been so upset at the time, she couldn't be sure. Honey and baby. Baby and honey. Terms of endearment. Did he mean them? It was hard to say. Some people used those sorts of affectionate terms on everyone from their dog to the cashier at the corner store.

She didn't think Bastien was one of those people.

"Honey." Terri savored the word as she collected cutlery, then placed the utensils on plates, and picked them up to rush back out to the living room. She hurried, because she didn't want to miss anything.

"It's Sylvia's Cuisine, then?" Terri glanced from Chris to Bastien, and each man nodded. Vincent had returned earlier, but, unable to eat or really help out because of that, he had found himself bored just sitting about watching them. He'd retired halfway through the selection process.

"I'd say so," Bastien said.

"Me too," Chris agreed. "They had the best overall. Though, I still say that Bella-whatever's had the nicest casserole thingy."

"I didn't like that at all. And it's not even on the menu," Terri pointed out. "Heck, it isn't even on their invoice. I'm thinking they put it on the tray by accident."

"Yeah. They must have," Bastien agreed. "I didn't care for it myself. There was something in it that I just didn't take to."

"Well, I like it." Chris moved over to Bella's trolley and peered down at the food. "So, if neither of you do, can I have the rest?"

Terri dropped onto the couch with a laugh. "Be my guest."

Bastien grinned. "Yeah. Go on. Eat it. You earned it after helping with all this nonsense."

"Well, Vincent couldn't help. Besides, this was more fun than the flowers," C.K. pointed out, taking the whole dish of casserole off the trolley. He grabbed a spoon and scooped out a bite, murmuring with pleasure as he ate.

"Ugh. How can you eat that? It was awful. I can't even *watch* you." Terri made a face of disgust, and covered her eyes with the notepad she had been using to keep track of which trolley had the best-tasting dishes.

"I'll take it to my room so you don't have to," Chris said. "My leg is bothering me anyway. I'll go lie down and watch television while I eat. Good night."

"Good night," Bastien and Terri said in unison.

A moment passed, then Bastien lifted a corner of the notepad Terri still had over her face. "He's gone. It's safe to come out now."

Smiling, she lowered the notepad and sighed. "Well, at least that's done."

"Yeah." He settled back on the couch beside her, then turned his head to the side and said, "Do me a favor?"

"Hmm?" Terri glanced at him in question.

He grinned. "Don't ask what the next calamity will be. I've had enough of them for now, thanks. And it isn't even my wedding." He shook his head. "The wedding day itself better go off without a hitch

211

after all this trouble." He laughed. "I don't know how Kate and Lucern have managed the last six months. I'm exhausted after only a week of problems."

"I know." Terri laughed, too. "It *has* been a bit stressful the last couple of days. When I booked vacation time off and flew out here, I really only expected to be holding Kate's hand and being supportive while helping with last minute details. I thought I might help out by running a few small errands or something. I did not expect to be handling the big stuff, like remaking all the Kleenex flowers for the cars and choosing new caterers."

Shaking her head, she sat up and leaned forward to peer into the Sylvia's Cuisine dessert drawer. They'd all had a bite from one of each of the three desserts that would be offered at the wedding, but that left the extra one of each untouched. Terri debated briefly, then chose the trifle. She grabbed a spoon and sank back onto the couch.

Bastien shook his head as he watched her scoop up the first spoonful. "I'm amazed that you can still eat. It seems like we've been doing nothing but that for hours."

"We have," she agreed with a laugh, taking another spoonful. "But it was just a bite of this and a bite of that, really."

"Hmm."

Terri dug deep into the dish, trying to get some of the soaked sponge cake at the bottom. She managed the task, ate the mouthful with an "Mmmm" of pleasure, then noticed she'd got some whipped cream on the back of her knuckle while digging into the dish.

Without thinking, she turned her hand over and licked it off.

"Besides," she added, "this is a dessert. There's *always* room for dessert. You should have some, too."

"Hmmm."

Bastien was simply watching her. Terri was suddenly self-conscious, but tried to ignore him and dug out another bite of sponge cake. Again, she got whipped cream on her finger. When she turned her hand over and started to raise it to her mouth, he caught it halfway, and drew her hand to his own mouth. He licked her knuckle.

Terri stilled, blinking in surprise at the tingle of awareness suddenly running through her body. When Bastien released her hand, she cleared her throat and ducked her head, forcing her attention back to the trifle. After a slight hesitation, she scooped up another spoonful. She wasn't really aware of the fact that her hands had suddenly started shaking until a dollop of custard slipped off, splashed off her chin and onto her upper chest, just below her throat.

Muttering under her breath in embarrassment, Terri set the spoon in the dessert dish and moved to wipe off first her chin and then her chest. Bastien again caught her hand, and he held it away. His eyes met hers briefly; then he leaned in to run his tongue quick and light over her chin, removing the evidence of her clumsiness. While Terri was still startled over that, he ducked his head to her chest and did the same, taking his time and running his tongue in circles over the spot to be sure he got every last drop.

When he lifted his head, Terri just stared at him.

Her heart was thumping in her chest like a bass drum, and her body was in sudden havoc. She was wishing he'd kiss her.

As if in answer to her wish, he bent his head to do so. A small sigh slid from Terri's lips as he leaned in and covered her mouth with his. He tasted of whipped cream—but somehow whipped cream tasted even better on him.

She was trembling uncontrollably when the kiss ended, the dessert dish shaking in her hand. Seeing this, Bastien rescued it; then he retrieved the spoon and eased it in and out of the dish, coming up with a scoop of cherries, custard, and whipped cream. Terri expected him to eat it, but instead he stretched it out in offer to her. Unfortunately, he did so just as she raised a nervous hand to brush a stray strand of hair away from her face. Their hands collided in midair, upsetting the spoon and sending cherries, custard, and whipped cream splattering down her chest.

"Oh." They both stared at what they'd unintentionally done. The spoonful of trifle had landed on the curve of her right breast, but was now slowly sliding down to disappear beneath the neckline of her white blouse.

"I think you're right," Bastien said suddenly.

"I am?" Terri asked, her voice shaking. "About what?"

When he responded, his voice dropped in pitch, becoming rough and sexy. "About there always being room for dessert."

His gaze lifted to her face and remained there for a moment, giving her a chance to stop him from what

214

he was about to do. But Terri just stared, her heart having gone mad and bouncing around inside her chest like a Ping-Pong ball. He couldn't mean . . . ? He wouldn't.

He did.

Bowing his head, he lowered it to her neckline and proceeded to lave away every last visible trace of the dessert. Then he undid the top button of her shirt, tugged her neckline farther apart, and continued cleaning her.

Terri couldn't stop the little moan that slipped from her lips as his tongue dipped between her breasts. She was definitely disappointed when the exercise ended. As he raised his head and straightened, her body was a great aching mass of confusion and desire. But—much to her consternation—Bastien acted as if nothing had happened. He didn't even look at her, but concentrated on the dessert in his hands. He scooped out another spoonful of cherries and custard, and slid it into his mouth.

She watched silently, her eyes flicking between her now gaping neckline and his face as he pushed the trifle around in his mouth. A considering expression filled his face. Then he swallowed, scooped up another spoonful, and held it to her lips.

Terri hesitated, then opened her mouth for him to slide it in. He waited, watching as she self-consciously chewed and swallowed; then he dipped the spoon into the trifle to scoop up more of the luscious dessert.

By rights, this should have been his spoonful if they were now going to share the sweet, so Terri was

215

LYNSAY SANDS

surprised when, instead of consuming the mouthful, Bastien started to move it toward her. She was even more surprised when he paused halfway and deliberately tipped it over her chest.

Terri gasped and sat up straighter in surprise, merely sending the sticky mixture faster on its travels down the curve of her left breast. "You did that on purpose!"

Bastien grinned. "It tastes better on you," he said simply, then leaned forward to kiss her. Terri's surprise gave way to pleasure. His tongue thrust out to slip between her lips, and within moments she had even forgotten that there was trifle dribbling down her chest.

Bastien hadn't forgotten, however. After a moment, he broke the kiss and let his lips trail down her chin to her throat. He skated quickly down to her dessert-laden cleavage, and concentrated with great effort on cleaning up the mess he'd made.

Terri slid her hands into his hair as he worked, her breath catching on a small gasp as his tongue slid along the edge of her white lace bra. Somehow, more buttons had come undone on her blouse, leaving it gaping open so that he had a path obstructed only by that lacy scrap of material. But the bra didn't stop Bastien. Again his tongue dipped into the hollow between her two breasts, following the trail of food and removing every last trace.

Once satisfied he'd not been cheated out of a single lick of trifle, he again straightened, picked up the dessert dish, and began to scrape up another spoonful. Terri lay slumped on the couch, staring at him in amazement. Surely he——? She killed the thought and tried quickly to hide her expression as he finished spooning up the dessert. He moved to press the spoon to her lips.

"What's the matter?" he asked in a perfectly normal tone of voice, seemingly unaffected by what he had been doing just moments before.

"Nothing." Aware that her voice had risen in pitch to an almost squeak, she opened her mouth to accept—and to avoid his asking any more questions.

Terri chewed and swallowed the dessert, then waited, watching as Bastien carefully scooped up bits of cherry, custard, and sponge cake. He was most dedicated, performing the task with great care and attention. But, instead of lifting it to his mouth, he again held it over her and paused to raise one eyebrow at her as if asking permission. Terri simply bit her lip and stared back, unwilling to say no, but unable to say yes.

He smiled and tipped the spoon, dropping it on her naked flesh. Terri sucked in her breath, watched the colorful mixture slide along her skin. It had not landed on her neckline. This time he had dropped it just below the lace of her bra, and it was running down her stomach toward the waistband of her jeans.

"You're going to need a shower after this," he commented apologetically, setting the dish and spoon aside. "But I appreciate the sacrifice you're making for my culinary delight," he added as he turned back.

As he glanced at her face, his gaze was arrested. Her face was as open and expressive as her nature, and he could read the conflicted feelings there: excitement, anticipation, anxiety, fear. Bastien's heart went out to her. He wanted to comfort her, to tell her it would be all right. It would be *perfect*. But he was feeling a couple of anxieties himself as he contemplated what was to come. He wasn't just eating dessert off of Terri's skin; he hoped to make love to her. The trifle had just been his gambit.

Deciding the best way to reassure them both was easier in the showing than the telling, he kissed her again. Terri was, at first, still and unresponsive under the caress—fighting her fears, he supposed. But then she opened to him, her arms creeping around his shoulders. He slid his tongue inside her mouth, and he could taste cherries and cream and her. The combination made him murmur in appreciation. The trifle really had tasted better on her than off the cold, hard spoon. It tasted better still in her mouth.

After several reassuring minutes spent kissing and rebuilding their passion, Bastien eased his mouth from hers and made a quick foray across her cheek to her ear. From there, he trailed his lips down her throat to her chest. He paused briefly in the dark warm dip between her breasts, laving until she shifted beneath him, arching and sighing in pleasure. Then he moved off the couch and settled on his knees between hers, urging her legs further apart to allow him to lean in to more comfortably reach her stomach and the sweetness that waited there.

The custard and cream were soothing to his tongue, and Bastien rasped it off of her—first licking the dessert away, then running his tongue in wider and wider circles. He was aware of the way Terri's stomach muscles jumped, and how her breathing sped up, coming in little panting breaths. He smiled against her skin, eyes closing with enjoyment at the little murmurs and groans as she arched farther, unconsciously urging him to follow the trail of food farther downward.

She was very responsive to his attention, and that natural responsiveness fanned his pleasure in what he was doing. He continued to follow the cherry path to her belly button. There, Bastien quickly dipped his tongue in and out of the small orifice—once, then twice—before continuing down to run it along the waistband of her jeans.

"Ohhh," Terri moaned, and Bastien opened his eyes to peer up the length of her twisting body. She was incredibly sexy to him, despite the fact that she still wore all of her clothes. Her top was open and gaping, but her breasts were still decently covered by her scrap of lace bra. Bastien decided it was time for that to change. She was ready. They both were.

Rising up, he moved back onto the couch and pulled her into his arms to kiss her again. He enjoyed the way she scraped her nails through his hair and clutched him closer as her mouth opened to both welcome and devour his. Then he set to work on the task he'd set himself; he slid his hands inside her blouse and around to her back to find and work the snaps of her bra. He found it difficult to concentrate on the task, and was relieved when first one, then the second snap, slid free.

Continuing to kiss Terri, he brought his hands around to her front, and slipped them up to push the white blouse she wore off her shoulders. Terri gave a murmur of protest when he forced her arms down to quickly slide the soft top off. For a moment, he feared the reaction might mean she was going to stop him, but when she shook the sleeves off her hands and quickly returned them to holding and touching him, he realized the protest had been at the interference with what she was doing, not at his undressing her.

Relieved, Bastien returned his attention to the lace bra. Rather than distract her again, he didn't try to slip the straps off her shoulders, but simply reached under her breasts to grab the bra's soft cups by their bottom hems. Bastien urged the lace material forward until her breasts dropped into his hands like ripe fruit falling from a tree. He closed his eyes in pleasure at their warmth and softness, and at the way Terri moaned deep in her throat. Her fingers clenched in his hair, tugging almost painfully as she arched into the caress, but Bastien didn't mind. *He* was having this affect on her. *He* was making her tremble and shudder and moan and cry out. He wanted to cause more of that.

Ignoring her groan of disappointment, he let go of her breasts and grabbed the straps of her bra to tug it off. He had to break their kiss to do so, and once the scrap of material was off, he tossed it carelessly aside and stared at what he had revealed. Her breasts were round and full, with cinnamon nipples that were now erect and begging for attention. Rather than return to kissing her, Bastien answered their call. He bent his head to catch one hard nub in his mouth.

His mind was filling with all the things he wished to do to her, and this was just the beginning.

Chapter Twelve

Terri moaned as Bastien bent his head to her breast and took her nipple in his warm, wet mouth. She felt his tongue rasp the erect nub then press against it firmly as he began to suckle. Her head twisted on the back of the couch, a denial of what she was feeling. Her entire body had gone stiff under the sudden assault of sensation.

It had been so long since she had felt anything even remotely like this, so long since these now aching muscles had even been utilized. She wasn't sure if she could handle it. She'd thought his kisses overwhelming at first, but this—this was a sort of torture, a pleasure pain.

Her fingers, already tangled in his hair, curled clawlike and dragged at him. A moan of pleading slipped from Terri's lips as she tugged until Bastien finally got the message and released her.

"What is it, baby?" he asked. There was concern and question in his voice.

Terri stared at him helplessly. She wanted him to stop, but she didn't want that. In truth, she really wanted him to continue. Yet it had been so long for her, she wasn't sure she knew what to do to please him—or if she ever had. And Terri *so* wanted to please him. The need to do so was almost an ache in her heart. Bastien was giving her such pleasure, she wanted to be able to do that for him, too.

"I . . . It's been a long time since Ian," she said helplessly at last. "I'm afraid—"

"Shhh." Expression softening, he drew her into his arms, his hands caressing her back in soothing motions. "There's nothing to be afraid of. I won't hurt you. I won't do anything you don't want."

Terri pulled back at his words, her eyes wide. "No. I know. That's not what—I want to please you, too," she blurted.

Surprise entered Bastien's eyes. He took her face in his hands, simply staring at her long and hard before saying solemnly, "Terri, you please me *all the time*. Just by being you."

"But—"

He covered her mouth with one finger and shook his head. "Let me please you this time. I want you to just enjoy it and do what feels right. Do what you *want* to do."

"But I want—," she tried to say around his finger, but he shook his head again.

"You're always trying to please others. Let me please you for a change. I want to."

Terri wasn't all that certain she could stand much more of his pleasing, but she didn't argue the point.

When Bastien returned to kissing her, she forced herself to relax and simply feel the softness of his lips moving over hers, the taste of him on her tongue, and the pleasure it all brought.

Soon enjoyment wiped all concerns from her mind. Moaning, Terri slid her hands to Bastien's shoulders, clutching the material there as she arched toward him. The action sent her breasts rubbing across the wool of his sweater, sending tingles racing through her body and rushing her toward the fever pitch she'd been at earlier. Liking it, Terri pressed closer and rubbed across the cloth again, chafing her sensitive nipples against the wool.

Bastien nipped at her lower lip, then slid his mouth across her cheek to her ear. Taking that plump lobe lightly between his teeth, he caught her breasts and cupped them with his hands, allowing his thumbs to flick back and forth over their sensitive tips.

She moaned into his mouth, the sound a half growl, wanting him so keenly it was a physical ache. If Terri had ever felt this particular need before, she couldn't recall it. She was pretty sure Ian had never affected her this way. It was doubtful she would have avoided sexual entanglements all these years had she known she was missing this heady, exciting, and desperate experience.

"Bastien." Terri knew her voice echoed the need she felt. She didn't care. She *did* need him. She wanted him. Now. And if asking would get, she would ask. If not, Terri felt she could be even more demanding.

"Shhh," Bastien whispered by her ear, his hands

223

gentling on her back. "It's okay. We have all night. We have all the time in the world."

Terri groaned, her body shifting restlessly in his arms. He didn't understand: She didn't care if they had all night. She wanted him now. *Now*.

On that thought, she nipped his chin with her teeth, her nails digging through the material of his sweater and into his shoulder. Neither action was meant to cause pain so much as to get his attention. And they did; he pulled back to peer at her, his expression startled.

"Terri, honey?" he asked.

"I need you," she said on a plaintive note. "Please."

Much to her relief, the desire in Bastien's eyes flared at her raw admission. Catching one hand in the hair at the back of her head, he pulled her forward for a kiss and the tables suddenly turned. Where there had been gentleness, now he was masterful, his tongue thrusting into her mouth with a passion unleashed, and the pressure of his lips forced her head back. Only then did Terri understand that he had a passion to more than match her own, but he had been holding back, perhaps not wanting to shock her.

Bastien wasn't holding back anymore, however, and a smile widened Terri's mouth beneath his at this sign that she affected him as deeply as he did her. Then she stopped thinking altogether, and simply lost herself in what was happening as he thoroughly explored every nook and cranny of her mouth.

Just as Terri thought she might drown in his kisses and be happy in the dying, his mouth left hers on a quest. She gasped and sighed, shuddered and trembled as his lips and tongue moved across her skin: first to her ear, her neck, then to the hollow of her throat. His teeth grazed her collarbone and she shivered with excitement, her hands curling in his hair again. When Bastien finally returned to her breasts, Terri didn't protest; she arched and cried out his name as he both fondled and suckled first one, then the other.

His warm hand drifted down her stomach, and Terri's muscles jumped and tightened by turn. She felt a tug on her jeans as Bastien found and worked at the button. He was shifting farther down her body as he worked and, afraid he would soon be out of reach, she gave up her hold on his hair and grabbed his sweater, tugging it upward with determined hands.

Getting the message, Bastien straightened enough to grab the hem of his sweater and tug it over his head. Terri reached for him as it hit the floor not far from her top. She placed her hands open-palmed on his beautiful, broad chest, then sighed happily as her fingers moved over the soft curls there. She caressed him lightly, pausing to run the tips of her fingers lightly over his small tight nipples.

Bastien allowed it for a moment, then caught her hands. Raising first one, then the other to his mouth, he kissed each palm, then shifted his hold to her upper arms. He turned her body and laid her down on the couch lengthwise, then came down on top of her, one knee sliding between her legs. Terri felt his thigh press against the center of her, and shifted eagerly against the unintentional caress. When he next shifted, so that his hips rested between her legs, there was no mistaking the hardness between her thighs.

Where his leg had been firm, this was rock-hard desire that ground against her, the action matching the thrust of Bastien's tongue in her mouth.

Terri didn't realize Bastien reached between them to work at her jeans until she felt cool air touching her lower stomach. The zipper worked down, and Bastien's hand followed, sliding over the skin there and across her panties.

She gasped and nearly bit down on his tongue, surprised, then caught herself and began to kiss him more desperately instead. Muscles were clenching and unclenching all over her body. Her heart beat out a tattoo as his hand moved even lower. When he finally cupped her sex through the thin white lace of her panties, she bucked violently, her legs spreading farther to accommodate him.

Bastien broke their kiss, took the time to nip and suckle lightly at her bottom lip, then lifted away from her. There was no exploring of throat or chest, no gentle teasing of her stomach. He moved himself right away to sit on the edge of the couch, his eyes on hers as he grasped her jeans and dragged them down her legs.

Suddenly aware of her naked breasts, and self-conscious, Terri raised her arms, crossing them over her chest. Bastien smiled at this sign of shyness but didn't stop. Her jeans were soon a pool on the floor next to the rest of their clothes. Her panties followed.

Terri was completely naked now, exposed and vulnerable to his view. And he did look. He simply sat for the longest time, his eyes raking over what he had already touched and, in some cases, tasted. Terri lay still, biting her lip and wishing he would stop looking. Wishing he would kiss her. Wishing he didn't still have his pants on. She didn't think it would be quite so bad if she weren't alone in her nakedness. She'd barely had that thought when he reached for her hand. Terri hesitated, then uncrossed her arms to place her right hand in his.

Bastien pulled her to a sitting position, then knelt between her legs as he had done earlier. There was no trifle on her belly now, however, and it wasn't her tummy he was interested in. Her eyes widened in shock as he urged her legs farther apart and lowered his head.

"Bas—" Her choked protest died abruptly as he buried his face between her thighs. Terri jerked and stiffened, her body arching up off the couch. Torn between embarrassment, shock, and the first slam of pleasure, she wanted to beg him to stop—but she didn't seem to have a voice to do it with. She wasn't even sure she had a tongue. Or a head. The only part of her body she *was* sure existed at that point was the part he was busily laving. Every cell of her body was suddenly focused in that area, every thought in her head on what Bastien was doing to her.

Terri became aware of a pain building in her chest, and suddenly she realized she'd been holding her breath for several moments. Letting it out in a whoosh, she gasped in another, aware of the fact that she was now panting, but not really caring. She didn't really care about much just then; the entire world could have come to an end outside the penthouse and she wouldn't have noticed. Terri was completely focused on what Bastien was doing to her and the tension he was building.

The tension was becoming almost unbearable. Bastien's ministrations were causing havoc, a pleasure-pain she wasn't sure she could stand. Terri wanted him to stop but needed him to continue, and her movements reflected her confusion. She began to twist her legs in an effort to escape, while at the same time arching herself upward into his attention.

Bastien took it all in stride, merely catching her thighs and holding them firmly in place. He continued to drive her crazy with need, making her buck against him.

"Please," Terri cried, twisting wildly, then gave an excited cry that even seemed loud to her own ears. A shaft of embarrassment slid through her, along with the fear that she might be heard by Vincent or C.K., drawing one of the two men to see what was wrong. Not wanting that, she turned her head and bit firmly into the couch cushion. It didn't stop her moans, but muffled them.

Just when she thought she could stand no more, Terri felt Bastien slip a finger inside her, adding to the pressure. She crumbled, her body convulsing as she cried out into the couch. Wave after wave of ecstasy washed through her as he continued what he was doing. Those waves slammed into her hard and fast, one after the other, again and again until she was sobbing with the release. Only then did Bastien finally lift his head. Moving onto the sofa beside her, he took her in his arms and eased them both to lie on the couch where he held her gently as she trembled and shuddered in aftermath.

Terri held him back, wonder and gratitude uppermost in her mind, but too exhausted by what she'd just experienced to offer him either. She lay still and quiescent as Bastien kissed her closed eyes, the tip of her nose, her lips. The kiss was gentle and soothing at first, then became more demanding, and despite her exhaustion Terri found herself responding.

When his hand closed over her breast, she sighed and arched against him. When it slid lower and dipped between her legs, her passion reawoke as if it had never been sated. She moaned into his mouth, her legs opening like a flower at the promise of sunlight.

Bastien groaned and broke away.

"I want you," he murmured against her cheek.

"Yes." Terri reached between them and found him through his trousers. He was hard against her fingers as she squeezed and ran her palm over his length. She slid her hand to the button of his chinos, but after fumbling with it for a moment, Bastien moved to help. Within moments, his pants were undone.

Terri caught the waistband and tugged down as far as she could, then she changed to pushing the cloth down over his hips. She gave up the effort the moment his sex sprang free of the clothing and landed, hard and heavy, on her stomach. Forgetting about removing his trousers, she caught it in her hand.

Bastien gasped, then reclaimed her mouth, kissing her almost violently as he thrust into her hold. Then he reached between them and brushed her hand away, replacing it with his own as he eased himself lower against her. She felt him probe at her entrance, then he guided himself into her a little way, stopping when she moaned at the stretching sensation.

Terri shifted; and Bastien withdrew, eased back in a little, then withdrew again. It was as if he were teasing her, taunting her with what she might have but didn't. She turned her head slightly to break their kiss, then bit at his chin in silent demand. Then Terri reached down to his behind and dug her nails in there as she arched upward, trying to force him to enter her all the way.

Bastien gave a breathless laugh at this maneuver. But he also reclaimed her lips and gave her what she wanted, thrusting his tongue deep into her mouth even as he finally, fully, thrust his body into hers.

Terri cried out as he filled her. It was what she wanted, needed, but it was almost too much. It was almost a relief when he withdrew. Almost. But the moment he did, she wanted him all the way in once more. Fortunately, Bastien had finished with his teasing and thrust forward again almost at once. Then he withdrew and thrust forward again and again.

Giving up her hold on his buttocks, Terri moved her hands to his back, her nails unconsciously digging in and scraping the skin up to his shoulders, then she grasped his upper arms and thrust against him. That need was building once more, straining, urging her to urge him on as Terri struggled toward the release he'd already given her once. She wanted it again. Needed it.

A keening started in her throat as the pressure

built. The urge to twist her head back and forth was strong, but even as she tried to do so, Bastien caught one hand in her hair to hold her in place. His kiss became more insistent as he drove into her over and over until Terri stiffened beneath him, her eyes shooting open as release slammed violently through her body. The moment it did, Bastien broke away with a groan, tossed his head back, thrust one last time, pinning her shuddering body to the couch, and spent himself in her heat.

"Are you all right?" he asked a moment later.

Terri stirred lazily, her eyes fluttering open. She lifted her head to peer at Bastien. She had been barely aware of his coming down atop her, then shifting them both so that their positions were changed. He now lay on his back on the couch, with her splayed on his chest, limp as a rag doll.

"Yes. Thank you," she said, her voice a husky rasp.

Bastien smiled at the polite words and lifted a hand to brush the hair from her face. "I wasn't too rough, then?"

Terri shook her head, aware that a blush was making its way up her face. It was rather dismaying to have to actually discuss what they'd just done. Which was silly, she supposed. They had just performed the most intimate act known to man, and she found it embarrassing to talk about it?

Bastien lifted his head slightly and pressed a kiss to her lips, then drew her head down on his chest and continued to simply hold her. His hand rubbed soothingly over her back, caressing the soft skin. She felt her eyes droop closed; then he murmured, "Thank you."

Terri blinked her eyes open and raised her head to peer at him. "What for?"

"For this," he said simply. "For giving me the greatest pleasure I've experienced in my life."

She uttered a wry, almost embarrassed chuckle. "I didn't do much. You did all the work. *I* should be— Thank *you*," Terri ended lamely.

Bastien smiled and ruffled her hair, then tugged her upward until their lips met.

Much to her embarrassment, the moment his tongue swept her mouth, Terri felt the tingling begin in her body again. There was no way to stop the moan that rose from deep in her throat. Her embarrassment died the moment she felt Bastien begin to harden again beneath her thigh, which lay draped over his hips. It seemed she wasn't the only one who still had a little more fire left.

Beneath her, Bastien felt his need for the woman in his arms stir again, and he almost groaned. He couldn't be ready again already. But he was. Just the way Terri gasped and shifted against him stirred his passion to life once more, making him immediately hard. He didn't recall ever wanting anyone this much, or ever being this hungry for a woman. Even Josephine hadn't fanned the flames of his desire like Terri could with a mere murmur of pleasure. The way she had moved against him earlier—the way she'd moaned, and cried out, and clawed at him—had all conspired to elevate his excitement to unbearable levels. Now it was happening again; his body coming alive like never before.

Catching her by the waist, Bastien shifted Terri over him so that they rested hip to hip. He kissed her, his mouth demanding what she was offering. Then he caught her by the backs of her thighs and urged her legs apart so that she half straddled him. He wanted to enter her now, let her warm wetness close tight around him and down his length, but he worried that it was too soon. It was clear from the things she'd said that Terri hadn't had a lover since her husband's death, and Bastien didn't want to leave her sore and aching from too much too quickly. Unfortunately, his body wasn't as reasonable, and his hips shifted of their own accord, pushing upward and grinding against her.

Terri immediately moaned into his mouth and ground back. She slid across his sex where it swelled between their bodies. Aware that she was as excited as he, Bastien decided it would be cruel to stop. He'd just avoid making love to her this time. He'd pleasure them both without actually entering her; and his hands found her breasts and began to gently knead.

Gasping into his mouth, Terri placed her palms on his chest. She levered herself upward so that she sat atop him. Once she had her balance, her hands covered his and she intertwined their fingers, urging him to caress her more firmly as she slid along his shaft again. Her eyes were closed, her head tilted slightly upward so that her long chestnut hair trailed down her back, and Bastien in fascination watched the play of emotions glide over her face. Pleasure, need, desperation—all crossed her features as she writhed back and forth over him. Then her eyes popped open and she speared him with a look he recognized at once. Bastien had seen it before. He'd been watching her face as he pleasured her with his mouth, and that same uncertainty and fear had claimed her just before she found release against his tongue.

"Please." It was one word with a wealth of meaning: *Please pleasure me. Please keep me safe. Please take me where my body wants to go.* Perhaps even: *Please love me.*

"Please," she repeated, then added with a sort of helpless frustration, "I can't . . ."

Unable to restrain himself anymore, Bastien rose up on the couch and shifted them so that he was seated properly, with her astride him. Then, despite his earlier intentions, he reached between them and guided himself inside her.

A small sigh of relief slid from her lips as Terri eased onto him, her arms slipping around his shoulders. Bastien caught that sigh in a kiss, and grasped her hips and began to urge her to move, controlling the rhythm as their bodies slid together, working toward the release they both wanted and needed.

Terri suddenly broke the kiss and pressed her cheek to his, gasping in his ear, "Bastien. *Please.*"

Turning his head, he caught her neck in his mouth and felt his teeth slide out. Her vein pulsed between his lips. He almost bit, almost sank his teeth into her tender flesh and drank from her. It was an automatic animal instinct, but he caught himself and tore his mouth away, forcing his fangs to retract.

"Please," she groaned once more, and Bastien again claimed her lips, this time in a violent kiss. He'd had that same biting instinct the first time they'd made love, wanting to hold her in place with his teeth like a cat, but he'd fought it then as he fought it now, the struggle turning the kiss almost into a punishment. He knew by the way Terri responded that she, too, was almost frantic with need, desperate for release, teetering on the edge, but unable to find fulfillment.

Bastien could feel his own release creeping up on him, threatening to make its arrival whether she found hers first or not. Deciding he'd best move her along, and fast, else leave her disappointed, he reached between them and found the center of her excitement. Caressing her feverishly, he urged her toward the release that would free him to find his own.

Just when Bastien thought that he couldn't stand a moment more, Terri tore her mouth from his and tossed her head back on a cry of triumph. Her body clenched in spasms around him; squeezing and releasing, then squeezing again. Relieved, Bastien immediately allowed himself to let go. His own body stiffened as he drove upward one last time and poured himself into her.

Terri lay limp against Bastien's chest as he shifted her and eased to the edge of the couch. She'd collapsed against him after finding her pleasure, and now lay with her face nestled in the curve of his neck, sound asleep. Or unconscious, he thought wryly, considering how she wasn't even stirring. He'd sat for the longest time, just holding her in his arms, their bodies still joined. But she was showing no signs of waking up. If anything, her breathing was becoming deeper and more relaxed. The woman was dead to the world.

Smiling as she murmured sleepily and shifted against

him, Bastien carefully stood, stepped out of his pants, which were bundled at his ankles, and scooped Terri into his arms. Even that didn't wake her. She merely cuddled against his chest and made lip-smacking sounds against his skin, as if she were either eating or kissing someone in her sleep. Hopefully she was kissing him if it was the latter option, he thought as he strode across the living room with her.

Bastien did consider how risky it was to be wandering naked around the apartment, with an equally naked Terri in his arms. But then, it had been even more risky to make love in the living room, where either Vincent or Chris could have come upon them at any time. Fortunately, they'd been lucky in that respect, and he could only hope his luck held out. Bastien was too exhausted to bother dressing himself, let alone her, and it didn't appear she was in any shape to dress herself. He had definitely worn the poor woman out with his demands, he thought with satisfaction, though she had been equally demanding.

He managed to make it all the way to the master suite without running across either Vinny or Chris. After setting Terri down in his bed, he made a quick trip back to the living room for their clothes. Bastien was aware that she would be terribly embarrassed should the others find that evidence scattered across the living room floor in the morning and guess what had happened. He wanted to spare her that.

Bastien heard knocking as he started back to his bedroom, and glanced up in alarm to find Chris standing at the end of the hall outside the master suite, rapping loudly. Afraid the noise might wake

Terri, Bastien picked up speed to reach the man and stop him from knocking again. At the last moment, he remembered the clothes he carried and glanced down. He'd bundled them all together, not bothering to separate them. Spying Terri's lacy bra on top, he tucked the clothes quickly behind his back to hide this indicator of what they'd been up to.

"Chris!" he hissed as the fellow raised his hand to rap on the door again. "What are you doing up?"

"Oh, Bastien." The editor turned, opened his mouth to speak, then noticed his nakedness. He let his breath out on a vexed sigh. "What is it with you and your brother? Did you guys spend your summers at nudist camps while growing up or something? Don't you guys have any decorum at all? Sheesh."

Bastien glanced down at himself, started to bring the clothes back around to cover his nudity, but at the first glimpse of white lace, quickly tucked them behind his back again.

"Never mind that," he said with a scowl. "Why are you knocking at my door at"—he glanced at his watch, the only item he still wore—"at two o'clock in the morning?"

"Oh." Reminded of his purpose for being there, Chris sighed and absently rubbed his stomach. "I'm not feeling too well, and I wondered if you had anything like an antacid or something. I don't think that casserole I ate agreed with me."

Bastien peered more closely at the man, taking in the pallor of his skin and the way he was trembling. Then he breathed in, noting the acrid scent of Chris's breath. "It more than disagreed with you, didn't it?" he asked grimly. "You've been sick."

"A couple of times," the editor admitted.

"Any stomach pains or diarrhea?"

Chris grimaced in answer, and Bastien nodded. It was just as he'd thought. "Go get dressed," he instructed, moving past him to the door of his suite.

"*I'm* not the one *un*dressed," C.K. pointed out dryly.

"In your street clothes," Bastien clarified. He glanced at the editor's boxers and T-shirt, which had obviously been pulled on to come out into the hall. "You're going to the hospital."

"I'm sure I don't need to go to the hospital," C.K. protested.

Bastien arched an eyebrow. "Chris, your symptoms suggest food poisoning. And with the streak of bad luck you've been having lately—not to mention the fact that you only ate two hours ago, yet it's already hitting you hard—I'm guessing it's going to be a serious case. *Go get dressed.*"

Grumbling under his breath, the editor turned away and moved back toward his bedroom. Bastien waited until he'd stepped inside, then opened the door to his own room and slipped through, not at all surprised to find Terri standing near the door. The sheet from the bed was wrapped around her sarong-style, and there was concern on her face. Chris had obviously woken her with his knocking. She had probably heard most of their conversation.

That was good, he decided. He didn't have to wake her up and explain.

Chapter Thirteen

"Food poisoning."

"Mmm." Bastien nodded solemnly.

"Bloody food poisoning," Vincent repeated, with a combination of disbelief and disgust. "The guy is a walking disaster. This is what? The third time he's been to the hospital in a week?"

Terri stirred in her seat and glanced at the men on either side of her. "Has it only been a week?"

Vincent frowned. "Hasn't it? Kate brought him to the penthouse last Friday. It's Friday again. *Really early* Friday," he added, scowling at the clock on the emergency room wall.

Terri followed his gaze to see that it was four a.m., definitely early. And apparently Friday morning. She pondered that information. Terri had known somewhere in the back of her mind that it was Friday morning, but it hadn't occurred to her until Bastien's cousin said it, that this meant she'd now been in New

York for a week. Only one week. She marveled over that fact for a moment. She had only met Bastien a week ago. It felt as if a lifetime had passed. It was hard to recall what her life had even been like without him. He was so ingrained in her thoughts now, it seemed as if Bastien had always been in her life, or at least had always belonged there.

"Food poisoning," Vincent muttered again with a shake of his head. "How has the guy survived to this age? He'll never make it to thirty."

"I think he *is* thirty," Terri said.

"Is he?" Bastien asked.

Terri hesitated. Kate had mentioned the editor and his age in an e-mail to her the fall before. It had been his birthday at the time. But she wasn't now sure what age her cousin had said. "I think so. Twenty-nine or thirty."

"Well then, he won't make it to thirty-five," Vincent predicted.

Terri smiled, then merely said, "Kate never mentioned him being accident-prone. I think this is just an unlucky streak."

"An unlucky streak?" The actor laughed. "Terri, sprained ankles and stubbed toes make up unlucky streaks. This guy is a walking calamity. Instead of calling him C.K. we should call him C.C.—for Calamity Chris."

Terri smiled wider, then said, "It was probably the casserole that made him sick. All three of us tried every dish that the caterers sent over, but just a bite of each. Chris is the only one who ate a lot of anything, and that was the chicken casserole."

"We ate the trifle. Or shared it, at least," Bastien reminded her, his voice dropping to an intimate tone.

Terri blushed as his words brought memories of the past evening sharply back to mind.

"But you're right—Chris is the only one who really ate the casserole. We only had a bite each," Bastien remembered with a nod. "You didn't like it."

"And you said there was something in it that you just didn't take to," she reminded him.

"Yeah, salmonella. That's what *you* didn't like, and *you* didn't take to," Vincent commented, pointing at first one then the other. Then he turned an impatient glance back to the busy E.R. waiting area. "How much longer do you suppose they're going to keep him?"

Bastien shook his head wearily. "I hope not much longer. I could use some sleep."

"Yeah, me too. I want to be well rested for the trip this weekend."

Terri turned to Vincent in surprise. "What trip?"

"I'm leaving this afternoon to go home to California for the weekend," he told her. "I'm missing my old haunts."

"Oh?" Bastien asked with interest. "What's her name?"

"I said my old haunts, not a woman," Vincent pointed out.

"Uh huh." Bastien grinned, then repeated, "What's her name?"

His cousin hesitated, his mouth twisting with displeasure. At last he gave in and muttered, "No one you know."

Bastien opened his mouth, but before he could pursue the matter further, a woman in a white coat opened the door to the waiting area and called out, "Bastien Argeneau?" She glanced around.

He was on his feet and at the woman's side at once. Terri and Vincent watched as the two spoke, then he followed her back through the door.

"Hmm." Vincent sat up a little straighter and glanced at her. "What do you suppose that's about?"

Terri shook her head. She didn't have any idea, but it didn't seem like a good thing. The good thing would have been a pale and weak but recovering Chris Keyes coming out to the waiting room ready to return to the penthouse.

They both fell silent as they waited. As the minutes ticked by, Terri found her gaze sliding around the emergency waiting area, something she'd been able to avoid while the men were talking. They'd distracted her from where she was. It was better for her to be distracted. The first trip with Chris had been easier because it had all been in panic. By the time they'd reached the hospital, the editor had almost been blue from his difficulty breathing. There had been all that rush and fuss when they'd arrived. They'd all of them been hurried through the waiting area and into one of the examination rooms to answer the questions the doctors were barking—questions Chris hadn't been able to answer in his state. Then Vincent, Bastien, and Terri had been hustled out into the hallway to wait while the professionals worked. But they hadn't had to wait long, and Terri had been so worried about

Chris she hadn't had a chance to worry much about where she was.

Tonight was different. While the editor was sick as a dog, she didn't think the ailment was life-threatening. There wasn't as much to distract her, and now there was no Bastien or Vincent holding up the conversation to distract her either.

Terri hated hospitals. Hospitals meant illness and death to her. The two most important people in her life had gasped their last breaths in hospitals: her mother and Ian. And both had been nightmares to endure. She'd stood helplessly by, watching them die long lingering deaths filled with suffering and count-less indignities. She took a deep breath in an effort to ease some of the tension building in her, but let it out quickly and closed her eyes at the scent that filled her nose. Hospitals all looked and smelled the same.

"There he is."

She glanced up at that announcement from Vin-cent, and watched with relief as Bastien walked to-ward them.

"They're keeping him overnight," he announced as Vincent and Terri got to their feet.

"Is it that bad?" she asked anxiously.

"No. I don't think so. He's very dehydrated, and they have him on an IV, but they said he should be fine. It's just that he's been through so much trauma the last week, they'd feel better keeping him here to be sure of his recovery."

"Oh," Terri said. That didn't sound so bad. It even seemed sensible.

"So? Are we out of here?" Vincent asked. "Or do we have to do something else? Sign papers, or whatever?"

"We're out of here." Catching Terri's hand in his, Bastien turned toward the door.

The three of them were silent as they walked to the car. It had been a long night and they were all exhausted. At least, Terri *suspected* the men must be; she *knew* she herself was. While she'd caught a couple minutes' nap before waking to the sound of C.K.'s knocking on the bedroom door, it hadn't been enough. Bastien had tried to convince her to stay behind and sleep, but Terri had known she wouldn't be able to until they returned; she'd simply sit up worrying until she knew that the editor would be all right. Going to the hospital and pacing about hadn't sounded like fun, but at least she'd know what was going on as it happened and wouldn't be pacing alone in the penthouse.

Terri had been surprised, however, when Vincent had insisted on coming. The man's sleep had been disturbed when Chris came out of his room after another bout of sickness, still in his boxers and T-shirt, and tried to argue that he didn't really feel well enough to be traipsing off to the hospital, but he'd probably feel better after some sleep. Bastien had lost his temper and yelled, waking his cousin up in the process. Vincent had, of course, come out to discover what was going on. He'd immediately decided to join the party heading for the hospital. Terri supposed he'd been just as concerned as the rest of them, despite his comments about the editor's misadventures.

Terri yawned and slid into the front seat of Bastien's

Mercedes, murmuring a thank-you as Bastien closed the door he'd held for her. He was so considerate, she thought on a sleepy sigh, watching as he got behind the steering wheel and started the car. And handsome, and sweet, and sexy, and smart.

Closing her eyes, she found herself nodding off as Bastien backed out of the parking spot and steered the car for the exit. When Terri blinked her eyes open again, it was to find they were pulling into the underground garage of the Argeneau building.

She tried to wake herself up as Bastien parked the car, but it seemed a terrible effort. Terri was still half asleep when she stumbled out, and was grateful when Bastien appeared at her side and drew her under his arm to steer her toward the elevator. Terri was even more grateful when, after she staggered wearily a couple of steps, he scooped her into his arms to carry her the rest of the way.

"She's exhausted," she heard Vincent comment. "What did you do to the poor girl?"

If Bastien answered, Terri didn't hear. She snuggled against his chest and nodded off to sleep again.

"Here you go, baby."

Bastien's soft voice roused Terri enough to realize he'd set her down on something soft, and that he was now working on the front of her shirt. She forced her eyelids up to see him bending over her, his face a picture of concentration. She supposed sitting up to help would be a good thing, but she felt almost drunk with exhaustion. Terri lay, eyes closed and half asleep, as he undressed her, removing first the top and bra she'd redonned to accompany them to the hospital, then moving on to her jeans and panties. He talked to her soothingly the whole while.

"There you are," he said.

Terri snuggled down into the cool crisp sheets with a little sigh as he drew the blankets up to cover her. Then she promptly tumbled back to sleep.

The awning over the bed was black.

Terri stared at it sleepily, wondering why that was. Her room was decorated in rose and blue, and the awning over the bed was a royal blue with stars on it that never failed to make her smile when she woke up. A sleepy murmur beside her, followed by an arm snaking around her waist, promptly gave Terri the answer.

Bastien. She wasn't in her room; he must have put her to bed in the master suite last night when they returned from the hospital. She had been too tired at the time to notice. She'd been rather exhausted by the evening's events.

Terri closed her eyes as memories of the night before washed over her in tingling clarity. Last night had been . . . She let her breath out on a sigh. She'd never experienced anything like it. The passion, the hunger, the need—Terri had not just *wanted* Bastien last night in the living room, she'd *craved* him. Her skin, her lips, her whole body had ached for him with a desperation that, even now, made her toes curl.

Bastien sighed in his sleep and rolled away, withdrawing his arm as he did so. Terri took advantage of the moment to ease out of bed. She needed some time alone to think. Things were moving so quickly, time rolling by so fast, her emotions were building at a frightening rate. She just needed a little breathing space, time to think over what had happened and what to do next.

If there was anything *to* do, Terri thought, collecting her clothes from the floor, then crossing the bedroom to the door to the guest bathroom. Of course, she did have a choice in this matter. Either she continued in the affair she'd started with Bastien last night—though "affair" seemed a cheap word; the man wasn't married and neither was she, and that was what "affair" usually connoted—or she stopped it now. Which wasn't really any choice at all, Terri decided. She didn't want to stop.

A little sigh slipping from her lips, she turned on the shower, adjusted the temperature, and stepped under the spray. The water beat down hot and pulsating on her head and shoulders, and Terri turned slowly, sighing with pleasure as it massaged her back, her side, her chest, and then her other side. Finally, she paused in her slow spin with her back to the spray again.

No, there wasn't any choice at all, she thought as she reached for the soap. Closing her eyes, Terri tipped her head backward and allowed moments from the night before to drift through her mind. She ran the small bar of soap over her skin. Bastien's tenderness, his passion, his kisses, his body driving into hers . . .

She wasn't at all surprised at the way her toes curled against the tile floor of the shower, or the lingering tingles that spread where her hands moved the soap. Just thinking of what she and Bastien had done, what she'd felt, made her hungry to experience it again and again. Who could willingly give up the chance at more of what she'd enjoyed last night? Or any of the laughter and sharing and pleasure that Terri had experienced since coming to New York?

She couldn't, and she was willing to admit it. But she was risking her heart and knew that, too. That was where the problem came. Every moment that Terri spent with Bastien pushed her that much closer to loving him. He was special. She'd never met anyone like him, and she knew she never would again. It was as if Bastien had been custom-made for her, and put on this earth for her to find. They talked endlessly when together, liked and disliked many of the same things, worked well together in a crisis—and as for last night, if he'd found it as pleasurable and explosive as she had . . .

Terri opened her eyes and turned in the shower to allow the water to spray away the lather on her body. *Had* Bastien found as much pleasure in last night as she? She thought he might have, but perhaps it was always like that for him. Perhaps it had only been so new and explosive for her because of her lack of general experience. She and Ian had been young, and eager, and filled with the selfishness of youth. Looking back, she could see that now. At the time, Terri had no more concerned herself with his pleasure than he had with hers.

But the answer to her question seemed simple. If the choice was to end it or to continue her enjoyment for as long as she could, then she would con-

tinue as long as she could. Even if it only lasted
the two weeks—one week, now—that she had left
here in New York. It might hurt like the very devil
when it ended and she went home, but oh, the
memories!

Deciding that, since she had only a limited time
here, she would go right away to make some more
memories, Terri turned off the taps, slid the shower
door open, and stepped out onto the fluffy rose-
colored bath mat. She snatched a small towel,
wrapped it around her wet hair, then grabbed a larger
one and wrapped it around herself. Then she started
forward, only to pause in surprise at the sight of
Bastien standing in the open bathroom door. He was
completely and unselfconsciously naked. And he was
breathtakingly beautiful.

"I woke up and you were gone," he said simply.
Stepping forward, he slid his arms around her, pulled
her against his chest, and lowered his head. Terri
thought he was going to kiss her. He didn't. Instead,
he nuzzled his nose into the crook between her
shoulder and neck, and inhaled. "You smell like
peaches." He licked her neck. "Good enough to eat."

"Peach soap," she breathed, her eyes drifting closed.
She tilted her head slightly to expose her neck to
him. Bastien took advantage of the offering, and he
nibbled a path to her ear. Terri moaned and shuddered, then lifted one hand to catch her fingers in his
hair. She held him in place as she turned her face until their lips met. Bastien accepted the offer at once,
kissing her hungrily.

She sensed him stretching past her, and vaguely

heard the sudden rush of water. Terri was even half aware of his urging her backward, but her mind was passion-clouded, and she was taken by surprise when she felt the drum of water on her back.

"What?" she asked, breaking their kiss.

"I need a shower, too. You don't mind joining me, do you?" He ran one finger lightly down her chest, caught her now soaked towel, and pulled it free. It dropped to the floor of the shower with a wet splat, leaving Terri as naked as he.

"You wash my back and I'll wash yours," he offered, stepping closer and letting one hand drift down to caress her behind. He urged her against him.

If she had doubted his intentions, the hardness pressing against her stomach cleared that doubt in a hurry. Terri felt a slow smile curve her lips, and she shifted to rub against him. "But I've already showered," she protested.

"Another won't hurt," Bastien said solemnly. "You can never be too clean. Or too wet."

One hand slid around to cup her breasts, and Terri gasped as his other hand dipped between her legs.

"No. You can never be too clean. Or too wet," she whispered, just before his mouth claimed hers again.

Bastien eased cautiously from the bed, doing his best not to wake Terri. She hadn't had much sleep the last couple of days. Last night had been especially short, thanks to the trip to the hospital. He'd still be asleep himself if a need for blood hadn't awakened him.

Kneeling next to the bed, Bastien opened the fridge hidden under it. He retrieved a bag of blood, then stood slowly and glanced at Terri to be sure she still slept. He wouldn't even have risked collecting the blood from the room if it weren't for the fact that he needed it so badly, and that the fridge in his office was empty. He should have had more brought in, but he kept forgetting. His mind seemed full of nothing but Terri of late.

Assured she still slept, Bastien grabbed the robe off the end of the bed, eased the blood bag into its pocket, and shrugged it onto his shoulders as he tiptoed to the bedroom door. He eased into the hall and pulled the door carefully closed, only then relaxing and moving at normal speed. He headed right to the kitchen. He often found it necessary to consume blood out of a bag, but it was rather like drinking milk out of the carton. A glass was always preferable. And so long as Terri was safely asleep, it was possible.

Bastien fetched a pint glass, emptied a good portion of the blood into it, and was savoring the liquid when the kitchen door opened and Vincent walked in. Startled, Bastien jerked around, slopping the liquid in his glass.

"You're awake," his cousin said in surprise.

"Yes." Bastien set the glass on the counter with a curse, grabbed a paper towel, and bent to wipe up the blood on the floor. He grabbed another towel to wipe up the bit that had slopped onto his chest.

"I didn't expect you to be up yet, and when I heard someone moving around in here . . ." His cousin shrugged. "Where's Terri?"

"Still sleeping."

"Your bed or hers?"

Bastien ignored his cousin's question and straightened to toss the bloody paper towel in the garbage under the sink. It was really none of the other man's business. Vincent already knew too much. The man had been witness to his humiliating experience with Josephine, and now he was here for the second time Bastien fell in love. Not that he had truly loved Josephine. That had been more of an infatuation. He could see that now. Coming to care for Terri as he had had shown that to Bastien. His feelings for Josephine had been mild in the extreme, compared to the passion and enjoyment he enjoyed with Terri. Which meant it was going to hurt that much more when she turned her back on him as Josephine had. And once more, Vincent would bear witness to the event.

"I wouldn't enjoy witnessing such an event now, any more than I did then, cousin," Vincent said quietly, obviously reading his thoughts. "Besides, I don't see this ending the same way. Terri isn't Josephine."

Bastien shifted with irritation. He picked up his glass of blood and drank some of the thick liquid. He really needed to remember to guard his thoughts better. He was so distracted by the uproar Terri was causing him emotionally, and all without her even trying, that he was leaving his thoughts open for just anyone to read.

"Terri's different. She won't react like Josephine," Vincent insisted.

"How do you know?" Bastien knew he sounded angry, but really his tone was to cover the hope that was trying to grow inside him. He wanted to believe his cousin was right, but he was afraid.

"This is a different era. Josephine thought you were a monster, an abomination. Terri is a modern woman, with enough intelligence to understand the science of it," Vincent argued. "And consider the benefits to her should she join us. Forever young and beautiful, and forever strong and healthy? Few would pass that up."

"She could still turn away," Bastien argued. "Not everyone wants to live forever."

"You're right, of course," the actor agreed. "She might not. So why risk it? Give her up and forget about her."

Bastien gave him a speaking glance.

"No, huh?" Vincent arched an eyebrow. "Then I guess you'll have to risk it, won't you? Every day is a risk, everything we do. Would you really give this up willingly, or bypass it altogether, to avoid possible pain later—pain that might never come?"

The answer to that was simple enough: No. Bastien couldn't willingly give her up had he wanted She was like a drug and he a drug addict; he was constantly jonesing for a Terri fix. No, he couldn't give her up. He had known that for a while. What he was experiencing now was worth any price later. But that didn't mean he wasn't going to fret about what would come.

"Well, hell," Vincent snapped, reading Bastien's thoughts. "You mean to say you didn't need me to try to talk you into this? Why did you let me ramble

253

on about it, if you already knew you were going to go for it?"

"I like talking about her," Bastien said. He shrugged. "I like being with her better, but the next best thing is talking about her. And it's always nice to have your hopes bolstered."

Vincent made a sound of disgust and turned toward the door. "I'm out of here."

"When will you be back?" Bastien asked, following him out into the entry to await the elevator.

"Late Sunday night or early Monday morning," he answered, then quirked an eyebrow as the elevator arrived and the doors slid open. "You know what that means, don't you?"

"No. What does it mean?" Bastien asked curiously.

"You have the entire penthouse—and Terri—to yourself for the whole weekend." Vincent stepped onto the elevator. "You can make love to her in any room you want, any time of the day or night, and not worry how loud she gets. She *does* get loud, cousin," he added as he turned and hit the button for the ground floor. "You must be doing something right."

Bastien grinned.

"Heck, you can even make love to her in the elevator." Vincent waggled his eyebrows as the doors started to close. "Catch it on tape, maybe, and keep it for posterity."

Bastien couldn't tell Vincent what he thought of that idea; the doors were already closed. But he'd never do that to Terri . . . unless she knew and wanted to. They could catch it on film and watch it later and . . . He shook his head at the idea. Too risky.

He didn't want personal tapes of Terri floating around. What if something happened and it got away from him? But he could make love to her in any room in the penthouse now. They'd already made love in the living room, on the couch, but they hadn't tried the bar. Or the pool table. Or the floor. Then there was the kitchen, the— A nice soak in the Jacuzzi with her would be nice, too. Of course they could have done that anyway, since the Jacuzzi was in the master suite, but . . .

Realizing that he was standing in the entryway thinking about making love to Terri, when he could be actually doing it, Bastien gave himself a shake. He started down the hall to the bedroom, realized he still carried the now empty glass, and did an about-face. He rushed back to the kitchen to give it a quick rinse before setting it in the sink. Then he headed for the bedroom to wake up Terri.

Terri tossed another acceptable flower into the appropriate box, then stretched and stood. It was late afternoon, and Bastien had yet to wake up. He had been awake already today. Twice. First, when he'd followed her into the shower, then when he'd crawled into bed at midday and woken her up in the most delicious manner she could imagine.

Bastien had kissed and caressed her awake, telling her as he slid his hands over her body that Vincent had left for the weekend, which meant they had the whole apartment to themselves. Terri had chuckled at the glee with which he'd said that, and then again as he'd told her each and every room and spot in the penthouse where he planned to make love to her. Then she'd stopped chuckling as things got serious. Seriously heated. The man was a dynamo in bed, arousing her passions like no one else could.

Despite his big plans, they hadn't made it out of bed. It hadn't mattered; they hadn't needed the extra impetus of new places to excite them—they'd done quite nicely right there in the master suite. Had they ever! Terri's body urged her to stretch again as tingles of awareness slid through her at the memory.

Afterward, she'd fallen asleep in his arms. But Terri hadn't slept long. She'd awoken an hour ago and tip-toed out of the room to take another shower before going in search of food. Getting a bowl of cereal, she'd come into the office to make a couple more flowers and eat while she waited for Bastien. The man was taking his time, however. Perhaps she should go wake him up as he had her, Terri thought with a small smile.

Deciding that was a fine idea, she stored the bag of Kleenex boxes and string back in the office closet where Vincent had put it the night before, then picked up her empty cereal bowl and carried it to the kitchen. Terri gave it a quick rinse, then dried and put it away. Then she headed to the bedroom.

Bastien was dead to the world when she entered. Terri approached the bed silently, her gaze on his face as she walked. He was a dear man—and just as adorable in sleep as he was awake, she decided, taking in the way that his hair was standing on end as if he had been running a hand through it. She wanted to smooth that hair for him. Terri also wanted to kiss his lips, which looked so soft and relaxed in sleep.

Pausing beside the bed, she hesitated, then quickly shed her clothes and climbed onto the mattress to crawl to Bastien's side. Arriving next to him, she hesitated again, unsure where to start. Terri had awoken earlier to find him kissing and caressing her. But he hadn't been kissing her lips. His mouth, as well as his hands, had been playing over her body.

Deciding to take a leaf out of his book, she carefully eased the blankets and sheets off of him until only his feet were covered. Then Terri just had to pause and stare. Dear God, the man was gorgeous, a delight to the eye. She took a moment to enjoy the view, then shook herself into action. *Kissing and caressing,* she reminded herself. But where to start? There was so much of Bastien that she would like to kiss.

After a pause, she decided his chest would be a good place to start, and Terri eased closer and began to press light little kisses across his pectoral muscles. She steadied herself with one hand, while she ran the other lightly across the flat muscles of his stomach. Bastien moaned and shifted under her touch, but didn't wake up. Terri managed to make her way down past his belly button, and was pressing light little butterfly kisses along his hipbone, before he stiffened, telling her he was awake.

Well, one part of him had grown stiff before her kisses and caresses had reached his belly button, but Terri knew he still hadn't been awake yet then. Now he was.

"Terri." Her name was a soft growl that she ignored. She also ignored the hand that landed on her shoulder and tried to urge her upward and away from where she was headed. She wanted to do this for him, and was determined not to be distracted.

Of course, that was before she reached the main target and realized she wasn't sure she would be any good. It *had* been a long while. That fact made her pause for only a moment, though; then Terri decided that there was only one way to find out: to just go for it. And since that seemed to be the motto for this relationship . . .

Besides, Terri thought, if she made a complete flub of it, she could always apologize sweetly and go read a how-to article off the Internet. They had instructions on everything else on the Web, there must be something on this as well. It was just a shame she hadn't thought to do so beforehand. But then, Terri thought, hindsight was always 20/20.

Chapter Fourteen

The woman was as skilled as a professional, Bastien thought faintly, and wasn't sure whether to be grateful, or alarmed at what it might mean. He decided to worry about it later, however, and merely twisted the sheets under his hands as he struggled not to humiliate himself by climaxing two minutes after Terri took him into her mouth.

What was she doing with her tongue? he wondered feverishly. Dear God! Where had she learned to do that? How—

"Oh," he groaned aloud, then clamped his teeth down on his lower lip to keep from issuing a second groan—one of disappointment—as Terri stopped what she was doing and raised her head to look at him.

"Am I hurting you?" she asked uncertainly.

"Hurting?" Bastien echoed, his voice unnaturally high. He was panting and finding it difficult to catch his breath. "No." He shook his head.

Looking relieved, Terri bowed her head and wrapped her lips around him once more, only to pause before she went any further. She raised her head again. "Am I doing this right?"

Bastien blinked. Didn't she know? She was driving him right around the bend! "Yes," he answered quickly, realizing that sitting thinking was only going to delay the pleasure he had interrupted with his groan.

No more groaning, he told himself, nearly sobbing with relief as she bent to take him into her mouth again. Her mouth was sweet, warm and moist. She had the sexiest damn lips—full and plump. And her tongue . . .

"Ahhhh," he cried, as she did something with her tongue that made his whole body shudder. Damn, she was—stopping again?

"You're sure I'm not hurting you?" Terri asked with concern, then explained, "You sounded like you were in pain."

Had he groaned? Bastien wondered. No. No, he was sure he hadn't groaned. But he had cried out. Apparently, that had distracted her too. No more crying out then either, he ordered himself firmly. He'd bite his own tongue off if that's what it took, but no more groaning or crying out. Better yet, he'd stick a pillow in his mouth—then he couldn't make any sound at all.

Realizing Terri was waiting for an answer, but unable to remember the question, Bastien briefly debated whether to ask her to repeat it, or to simply guess and answer yes or no. Deciding it would be faster just to guess, and that the chances were fifty-fifty either way, he blurted, "No."

"No?" She tipped her head to the side quizzically. "No, you're not sure I'm not hurting you? Or no, you aren't in pain?"

"Yes." He nodded firmly. Thinking was really quite beyond him at that point. All Bastien could think about was that he wanted Terri to wrap those sweet, luscious red lips around his—

"I'm really not doing this right, am I?" she said on a sigh. "And you're just too sweet and polite to tell me I suck at this."

"No, I'm not," he said in a panic. "I'd tell you if you sucked. Well, you are—I mean, you're doing a wonderful job. Just wonderful. Just . . . wonderful," he repeated helplessly.

"Really?" Terri perked up perceptibly, a smile tipping her lips as she stared at him, apparently eager for praise. "What am I doing right? Tell me, and I'll do more of it."

Bastien stared at her helplessly. Why was she doing this to him? Was it some sort of torture? Punishment, perhaps? Had he not pleasured her enough when he'd woken her earlier? Had he snored and kept her awake?

Realizing he was losing it, Bastien gave his head a shake. This was Terri—sweet, fun, adorable Terri. He didn't think she had a mean bone in her body, and she certainly wouldn't set out to torment him deliberately. Which meant that, despite the fact that she had his legs shaking, and his heart racing, and his body ready to explode with pleasure, she didn't have

261

a clue what she was doing. She was just following her instincts.

The woman had damned fine instincts.

"All of it," Bastien said at last. "All of it is perfect." Except for the stopping part, he thought, but didn't say it. She was only stopping out of concern for his well-being and pleasure. And her consideration and caring were sweet. Really. And he was sure he'd appreciate it. Later. Right now, he just wanted her to—

"Ahhhh." He sighed as she took him into her mouth again. Then he held his breath, terrified the sound would make her stop once more. Fortunately, it didn't. She continued to slide her lips the length of his erection, her tongue swishing across him like a cat's tail. Bastien decided not to take chances, however. He snatched up a pillow from the bed and slammed it over his mouth.

He would not make a sound now, Bastien assured himself as he sank his teeth into the pillow. He might smother to death, but he would do so silently and with a smile on his face.

Maybe. Bastien tore the pillow aside and lifted his head to peer at her with exasperation. She had stopped again and was sitting up, her head turned toward the door.

"Did you hear that?" she asked with a frown.

"No." He didn't mention he'd had the pillow over his head, making hearing as difficult as speaking.

"I thought I heard someone call out," she explained, turning back to him.

"There's no one here but us," Bastien reminded her, with what he considered the patience of a saint.

His gaze dropped to his erection. It was standing straight and tall and proud, hoping for her attention. It was also red and maybe a little angry that he wasn't getting it, at least not without constant starts and stops. Perhaps this was Terri's technique, he thought: Bring him to the brink, then stop; do it again, then stop. If so, it was brilliant. She was driving him *crazy*.

"Terri?" he said almost pleadingly.

"Oh, I'm sorry." She smiled at him and lowered her head again. Bastien saw her red lips part as her mouth opened, then . . . Terri froze again, her jaws snapped closed inches above his erection and she sat up. "Surely you heard *that?*"

He had, of course. Someone was calling his name. A woman. And as there were very few people with keys to this penthouse, Bastien knew who it must be. He would kill her.

"It's probably my mother," he said, dropping his head back on the bed with disgust.

"Your mother?" There was no mistaking the horror in Terri's voice.

Bastien raised his head to see her scrambling off the bed. He watched with regret as she climbed into her jeans, noting with interest that, in her hurry, she wasn't bothering with panties. Hmmm, he thought, then his pants slammed into his face. Terri had tossed them at him.

"Get dressed, Bastien," she hissed. "We can't let her find us like this."

Sighing, he gave up any hope of Terri finishing what she'd started and sat up on the bed. But he didn't start getting dressed right away. Instead, he watched as she fumbled with her bra. Her breasts were jiggling as she worked with the lacy material. He liked watching her jiggle.

"Terri?"

They both stilled. The voice was drawing nearer. It was also plain it wasn't his mother. Perhaps that was a good thing, Bastien thought idly; it would be a shame to kill a woman who had survived some seven-hundred-plus years.

"It's Kate!" Terri cried, but didn't seem much re-lieved. But then, Bastien supposed it wouldn't matter who was coming toward the bedroom, Terri would panic anyway. Being caught in such a compromising position might not be the scandalous thing it was in his youth, but it could still be terribly embarrassing.

"I thought you said we had the place to our-selves!" she hissed accusingly. "Why didn't you tell me they were returning?"

"It completely slipped my mind in all the chaos of the last couple of days," Bastien admitted, shifting wearily to get out of the bed. His erection had done a quick disappearing act.

"Bastien?" Kate's voice was clear as a bell now; she was nearly to the room. *They* were nearly to the room, he corrected as Lucern could be heard saying, "They've probably gone out for the day."

Bastien stilled, his mind working. Maybe if they hid in the closet or something, Kate and Lucern would think they weren't here and go away. Then he and Terri could get back to . . . His gaze found Terri as she finished with her bra. She pulled her shirt on and hurried across the room to the door leading into the guest bathroom. No. Not a chance. He couldn't see her agreeing to hiding. She'd flown all this way to help Kate with the wedding, and she wouldn't hide just to make love with him. It was one of the things he liked about her, he admitted as she slipped out of the room. Her loyalty and sense of what was right were some of the things that made her so special.

Damn shame though, Bastien thought sadly as he glanced down at himself. His erection had started to perk back up at the possibility of continuing after all. It died a quick death, however, as the door to the bedroom opened and Kate walked into the room.

"I can't believe you forgot we were coming home today," Kate said again. It was later that night.

Bastien sighed and shrugged. He couldn't believe it, either. But he *had* been rather busy of late, dealing with the various crises that had popped up around the other couple's wedding. Not to mention the added crises surrounding Kate's friend Chris. Poor bastard. The guy hadn't looked any better today when they'd gone to see him. That had been at Kate's insistence. The minute she'd heard the calamities that plagued the man, she'd insisted they all head to the hospital. Bastien had tried to get himself and Terri out of the visit, hoping to get the chance to finish what she had started, but hadn't managed. In the end, they'd all traipsed up to the hospital. C.K. was still not feeling well.

"I'm so sorry that you've had to handle so many problems while we were gone," Kate said. They'd ended up telling her everything, even about the catering. It had been hard not to, what with the apartment littered with catering trolleys. She'd taken the news pretty well, only panicking a little, and had relaxed once she heard how they had handled it. It was nice to know she trusted their taste.

"There's no reason to apologize. That's why I came early, to help with the wedding," Terri said, squeezing her cousin's hand affectionately.

Bastien noticed that the two women hugged and touched and patted a lot. It was nice in one way, warm and affectionate, but he also felt a pinch of jealousy, wishing he was the recipient of some of those hugs, pats and touches. But Terri had been keeping her distance since Kate and Lucern had arrived. She'd even been avoiding eye contact, and that troubled him. He wanted to put his arm around her and claim her as his own. She didn't seem to feel the same.

"What?"

Terri's startled exclamation drew Bastien's attention back to the conversation. Obviously, he'd missed something important. She was looking alarmed, her gaze meeting his for one of very few times since the other couple had shown up.

"Well, I want our wedding night to be special, and it won't be if we spend every night beforehand together. So, I thought staying apart for this week would be a good idea. And Lucern agreed. He'll be staying here at the penthouse until the wedding."

Bastien's lips curved with amusement as he glanced at his brother. Lucern might have agreed, but he didn't look happy about it. In fact, his brother looked pretty miserable. Bastien's amusement died at Kate's next words, however.

"So, you can stay at the apartment with me and we can have girl time. It'll be fun."

Bastien now understood Terri's expression. This must be what he'd missed; Kate announcing that Terri was to move into her little apartment for the week. He didn't like the idea at all. In fact, panic swamped him at the possibility of Terri sleeping so far away from him. He'd just moved the relationship up to the physical level, and he was damned if he was going to lose it now.

"Lucern looked pretty miserable," Terri commented.

"He did, didn't he?" Kate laughed. She moved back to the couch with a fresh bowl of popcorn and set it between them. "He wasn't exactly thrilled with the idea when I brought it up in California, but he agreed to please me."

Terri nodded and tossed another tissue-paper flower in the usable box. They had brought the Kleenex and string with them to Kate's place. It was a good project to keep them busy, and it did have to be done. Kate had claimed that she didn't trust the men to finish the job without being there to ride herd.

"Bastien wasn't looking too happy himself at dinner," Kate commented, and Terri glanced at her sharply.

They had headed out for a meal right after Kate's announcement about the new living arrangements. Once seated in the little French bistro Kate had suggested, Bastien had launched into an attempt to argue

267

that Terri should stay at the penthouse. First he'd pointed out that she was all settled in the guest room. Then he'd said the penthouse was larger and more comfortable. He'd tried countless other excuses, too—even suggesting that Kate should move in and leave Lucern in her apartment instead—but none of his arguments had gotten him anywhere.

Terri had finally pointed out that this was the reason she'd flown from England, to stay with Kate and help with the wedding. The moment she'd said that, he'd ceased trying to prevent the unstoppable and had sat quiet and grim through the rest of the meal. Terri had never seen him so silent. She missed his smiles and the talk they usually shared.

"Didn't he?" Kate prodded, drawing Terri from her thoughts.

"Did he?" she countered mildly. "Perhaps he has a touch of food poisoning, too. We all tried that casserole."

"Hmm." Kate's lips twisted with sardonic amusement. "I gather that means you aren't going to tell me how things are going between the two of you."

Terri was silent for a moment. She fanned out the petals of yet another flower, then glanced up. "He's a very nice man."

"Yes, he is," Kate agreed.

"Handsome."

"Definitely handsome. All the Argeneau men are. Of course, Lucern is the cream of the crop, but Bastien is good-looking too."

Terri had a different opinion, but she let it go. "He's so . . ." She glanced toward the ceiling, searching her mind for the word. "Special. The way he opens doors, and the way he orders for me—and he's so funny, Kate. And smart. He's definitely smart. And charming, and when he kisses me—" She stopped abruptly and blinked. "Well, he's just a lovely man."

"You love him!" Kate crowed. "I knew it! I knew you two would get along like a house on fire. Oh, this is wonderful, Terri! We can be sisters-in-law as well as cousins and best friends and—"

"Slow down," Terri gasped, cutting her off. "Jeez. I only met him a week ago."

"So?" Kate asked staunchly. "I didn't know Lucern very long before I knew he was the one. Of course, we had some things to work out before it all came together, but when you meet the right one, you know it. And you two are right together, Terri."

"Hmm," she murmured, concentrating on the flower in her hands. She wanted to believe her cousin was right, but was afraid to get her hopes up. Having to pack her things and move to Kate's had been a horrendous blow. Terri had wanted to sit down on the side of the bed and cry at the very thought. She wanted to spend time with her cousin, but she didn't want to lose out on time spent with Bastien too. Or the chance to kiss him, to make love to him, or to be held in his arms. It was as if she'd been offered a taste of heaven then had it snatched away. When she'd worried about pursuing this relationship, Terri had known it would end, but she'd thought she had the full two weeks. She hadn't been prepared for today being the end, and the wrenching of her heart was horrible.

"Really. It's plain for anyone to see that he cares for you. His eyes rarely leave you and he's terribly attentive. I'm positive he's in love with you, Terri."

When she kept her head ducked and said nothing, Kate patted her hand reassuringly. "It will all work out, cousin. Trust me. There will be things for you two to work out too before it does, but . . ."

Terri glanced up, noting the way Kate was staring off into the distance. There was a worried look in her eyes and she bit her lip. "What kind of things?"

Kate's eyes jumped back to her with a start. She'd obviously been far away. Now she got an evasive look on her face and concentrated on collecting tissue and string to make another flower. "You'll find out. It will be okay."

"Tell me," Terri insisted, but Kate shook her head. "I can't. *He* has to do it."

Terri stared, anxiety crowding in on her. What could Bastien have to tell her that "they would have to sort out"? Suddenly, she wasn't as nervous that he might love her back, as she was about the fact that there was some secret that could be a problem and come between them. She had known this relationship was too good to be true.

"Don't look so miserable," Kate said with a grin. "We'll see them both tomorrow."

"We will?" Terri forgot about Bastien's possible secret and glanced over eagerly.

"Well, of course we will. It's Sunday."

Terri blinked, not seeing the connection. "So? It's Sunday."

"The wedding rehearsal is tomorrow," Kate explained. Then she frowned. "Oh, maybe I forgot to mention that to you. Originally, I didn't think you'd be here for it. We were going to have it without you, then take you by the church the night before the wedding to get a look and have a quick run through. But now you'll be here for both the rehearsal and dinner. Lucern and I are taking everyone out to dinner afterward."

Terri nodded happily and ducked her head back to the flower she was making. She'd see Bastien tomorrow! Just the thought of seeing him caused a tingle of excitement in her. And nervousness. They hadn't really talked since the relationship had changed. First, there had been the need to take Chris to the hospital, and when they'd returned she'd collapsed from sheer exhaustion. Then, today, Bastien had woken her up in such a lovely manner, after which they'd slept again and then she'd decided to wake him up the same way—only Kate and Lucern had interrupted.

They hadn't really got a chance to talk, and Terri found herself anxious and nervous with Kate and Lucern around. She felt awkward, unsure how she was supposed to behave with Bastien in front of them. Were they boyfriend and girlfriend now? Did people even use those terms now a days, and at her age? And did she have the right to touch Bastien, kiss him, hug him in front of others?

Terri was naturally affectionate, but she found herself stifling that tendency—at least with regards to Bastien in front of Kate and Lucern— because she

271

didn't know where she stood with Bastien. And she knew she would still feel that way tomorrow unless he gave her some indicator. If Bastien greeted her with an affectionate kiss and hug, or put his arm around her, or took her hand, then she would feel free to allow her natural affection to show.

And why hadn't he done so in front of Kate and Lucern? Terri wondered as she tossed another finished flower in a box. He had held her hand and kissed her in public the day of the trip to the museum. But that had been in front of strangers. Bastien had taken her hand to lead her out of the hospital this morning, too. But that had only been in front of Vincent. He hadn't done anything of the sort in front of Kate and Lucern.

Perhaps he didn't want them to know what had happened between them. That seemed a good possibility. After Kate's reaction over the phone, when she'd learned that Bastien was taking Terri around the city those first couple of days, it was possible that if Terri and Bastien acted openly affectionate and revealed how far their "friendship" had gone, the woman might start making wedding plans. She was already leaning that way, and that was a lot of pressure. Especially from a new sister-in-law. It could make things a bit uncomfortable for Bastien. Especially if he was considering this just a casual relationship. Which was more than possible. They'd only met a week ago.

Terri picked up the string and began to measure out a length. It might be best to keep what had happened just between them. She didn't really want to, though. She'd rather be able to be herself; but she didn't want him feeling uncomfortable. Terri decided she would just play it by ear. If he greeted her tomorrow as just the cousin of his soon to be sister-in-law, she would respond accordingly. If Bastien greeted her with a kiss and hug or something like that, Terri would respond in kind. The ball was in his court.

"Thanks, brother."

Lucern grimaced. "I don't want this any more than you do."

"Yeah, but *you* agreed to it. I didn't get a vote," Bastien muttered, walking around the bar with a glass of blood in hand. That was about the only nice thing about Terri being at Kate's; he didn't have to drink out of a bag anymore, grabbing a quick fix behind closed doors. But that was the only nice thing. And he'd gladly ingest bagged blood forever to have her back. He dropped onto the couch with a sigh.

"So?" Lucern peered at him curiously. "How is it going between you two?"

Bastien frowned, then admitted, "I don't know."

Luc's eyebrows rose. "You don't know?"

He shrugged. "Yeah. I don't know." Sighing, he sat forward and set his glass on the coffee table and ran a frustrated hand through his hair. "I thought things were going great. I mean, Luc, you wouldn't believe how well we get along. Even I don't even believe it. It's all so perfect and natural and easy. We talk all the time, finish each other's sentences, we just . . . I don't know. Click. It's like she was made for me." Bastien shook his head, then added, "I'm even eating. And it tastes good. I can hardly believe now that I actually got bored with doing so in the past."

Lucern grinned. "That's pretty serious."

"Yeah." He nodded enthusiastically. "And every time we kiss? Pow!" Bastien slammed the palm of one hand against the other. "We have a sexual chemistry like I've never experienced. And it isn't just sexual. I mean, I want her all the time—but it isn't just wanting sex. I want to . . ." He paused, searching for the words to explain. "I want to give her pleasure. I want to hold her while she finds her pleasure. I want to take her inside me, my heart, and keep her there warm and safe and always a part of me."

"Yeah. That's how I feel about Kate," Luc said softly. "Have you tried to read her yet?"

"Yes, I have. And no, I can't."

"It's sounding pretty good then."

"Yeah."

"But?" Luc asked when Bastien sighed.

"But I don't know how *she* feels," he said miserably. "I just assumed that she felt the same, but then you guys showed up and she hardly looked at me after that."

"Oh, well, I wouldn't worry. She was probably just happy to see Kate. They're pretty close and—other than those few minutes last Friday when Kate dropped off Chris and grabbed me to go to that conference—they haven't seen each other in over six months." Luc clapped a reassuring hand on his shoulder. "They'll talk up a storm tonight and get all that girl stuff out of the way. Then, tomorrow at the rehearsal, she'll be all over you."

Bastien nodded, but wasn't sure he believed the prediction. He understood that Terri hadn't seen Kate in a while, but she hadn't even *looked* at him tonight. What if she regretted what they'd done? Or what if she didn't want Kate to know about it? Maybe she was thinking of this as just some vacation fling and wanted to keep it secret to avoid pressure from Kate. He really didn't think Terri was the type—he was almost positive she wasn't—but then again, he never would have predicted that once Kate and Lucern showed up, she'd avoid touching or even looking at him.

Bastien supposed he'd have to wait until the rehearsal to get a better idea of what was going on. He'd wait to see how Terri greeted him and go from there. If she acted like her normal cheerful and affectionate self, he'd know it was all going to be okay. But if she acted reserved and avoided eye contact, he'd know something wasn't as it should be.

Personally, Bastien hoped Terri would just walk up and either take his hand in hers or slip her arm through his, or even kiss him hello. He preferred the last option, though if she did walk up and kiss him, he couldn't promise he wouldn't kiss her senseless on the spot. But he didn't really expect that to happen—they'd be in a church after all. Still, Terri was naturally affectionate, and if she liked him as he hoped, she would greet him with some outward show of affection. That would free Bastien to be openly affectionate back. The ball was in her court.

Chapter Fifteen

"What is Bastien *doing?*" Kate asked. The minister had just finished giving his last-minute words of advice, wished them good evening, and moved off to speak to the wedding coordinator.

Lucern glanced down at her, then followed her gaze to where his brother stood silent and grim-faced beside Terri. "Standing there," he said.

"Well, I can *see* that. Why isn't he talking to Terri?" Kate shook her head in exasperation. "He didn't even smile at her when we arrived today, he just nodded."

"So? That's all she did, too," Luc pointed out.

"Only because that's what *he* did. Terri wasn't sure how to greet him, and she waited for his greeting to see how she should act. He was cool, so she was cool."

"You've been reading her mind," he accused. There was amusement in his tone, however.

"You're darned right I have. Terri's as close-mouthed as a clam. If I didn't read her mind, I wouldn't have a clue of what was going on between those two." Kate watched her cousin and Bastien unhappily. "I don't know why he doesn't just grab her and kiss her. That's what she wants."

"He probably wants it, too, but I think Bastien thinks Terri wouldn't welcome it because of how she acted when she was with you yesterday," Lucern explained, finding himself also watching. The couple was studiously ignoring each other.

"What?" Kate glanced at him. "How did she act with me yesterday? And what has how she acts around me to do with Bastien thinking she doesn't want him to kiss her?"

"Well, she paid a lot of attention to you the moment we arrived, and pretty much ignored him."

"And he's jealous? Of me?" Kate asked with disbelief.

"No. Not jealous. But Bastien said she hardly even looked at him. I think he's worried that maybe he was just . . . well, sort of fill-in entertainment while you were gone."

"Oh, for heaven's sake. Terri isn't like that."

"Perhaps not. But Bastien doesn't know that. Or at least, he can't be sure of it. They only met a little more than a week ago," Lucern pointed out, then his eyes narrowed. "Look. They're talking. Maybe they'll work it out now."

Across the room, Terri said, "I should thank you for allowing me to stay in the penthouse." She spoke the words almost desperately. The tension was just killing her. She and Kate had arrived at the church at the same time as the car had brought Bastien and Lucern. The men and women had met on the sidewalk, and Kate and Lucern had kissed and hugged each other as if they'd been apart forever. Terri had watched them with a small smile, then glanced to Bastien to see him watching too. Then, as if sensing her eyes on him, he'd turned her way, waited a moment as if expecting her to say something, then had nodded and murmured a polite hello.

Terri had felt disappointment drop over her, but had tried to hide it, merely nodding in return. And they had been like that ever since. All through the ceremony rehearsal, they'd been stiff and polite. Yet Terri had caught Bastien glancing at her a time or two, with a look of hunger he'd quickly veil whenever she caught his eye. Once, she'd caught him looking at her with an expression she thought might be longing, but Terri couldn't be sure. He'd cloaked that as soon as she glanced his way, too.

"There's no need to thank me. You are more than welcome in my home. And I enjoy your company."

Terri considered his words: *You are more than welcome. I enjoy your company.* Both were in the present tense, not the past tense as if whatever they had were over. She wasn't sure what to make of it, or how Bastien was feeling. And all of it made her really wish they'd had the chance to talk. The uncertainty was killing her. Terri had no patience for games, no wish to waste time guessing at what people thought or felt. She had always preferred to have the cards on the table. It was better that way and, while it could be painful at times, at least it prevented misunderstandings. Terri decided this case was no exception; she wanted to know where she stood. Last night she'd thought waiting to see what he did would be the smart move, but now that he was being so polite and she still didn't have a clue, Terri decided she was damned well going to find out.

Taking a deep breath, she turned to him and blurted, "I like you. I don't know how you feel about me, or what what we've done means to you, but I like you. If it was just good fun, and you don't want Kate and Lucern to know about it, or if it—"

Terri's opening gambit came to an abrupt halt as Bastien suddenly took her face in his hands and pulled her forward to cover her mouth with his. She sighed into his mouth with relief as he kissed her, uncaring that they were standing in the middle of the church. He snogged her senseless, actually, she decided a moment later as her arms slipped around his waist. The man wasn't just giving her a hello kiss.

"Okay, you two, cut it out. The minister's getting nervous."

Bastien ended the kiss at Lucern's words, but not quickly. He eased the kiss, then turned to nibbling Terri's lip. Once, then twice, then he straightened with a grin.

"Hi," he said with the sexiest grin Terri had ever seen.

She smiled and covered the hands still cupping her face. "Hi, back," she whispered.

"So, when's the wedding? And am I invited?" Chris Keyes asked.

Terri blushed scarlet and turned to make a face at the editor. He had been released today, just in time for the wedding rehearsal. Lucern had chosen the man as his third groomsman, to make up the numbers needed to match Kate's bridesmaids. Etienne and Thomas were the other two. Bastien was, of course, the best man, and Terri was maid of honor. And Kate's two sisters and her friend and coworker Leah made up the bridesmaids. Leah, Terri, Chris, and Bastien were the only members of the wedding party in town for the rehearsal, though. The others wouldn't show up till the end of the week.

"If you two are done, maybe we can go to the restaurant now," Lucern said, preventing any further embarrassment from the editor.

"Okay," Bastien agreed. "Lucern, you're riding with Kate. Terri's with me." He paused and eyed Chris and Leah with what might have been dread. "How did you two get here?"

"I had a car pick them up, just like with us and the girls," Lucern announced. He added, "The driver will take them to the restaurant too, then drive each of them home afterward."

Terri glanced at C.K. with surprise. "Are you back in your own apartment then?"

"Yes." C.K. grinned. "They finished the painting, which was the last of the repairs, last night. Tonight will be my first night home."

"Oh, good!" Terri exclaimed. "I'm sure it will be a relief for you to be back in your own bed."

"I'm looking forward to it," the editor admitted.

"Well, let's get this party moving," Kate said, gesturing toward the church doors.

"Good thinking." Bastien was much more relaxed now that he knew that he wouldn't have company in the car. "Come on, baby."

Terri blushed at the affectionate endearment as he steered her toward the exit. He'd called her baby! Right there in front of everyone! He wasn't trying to hide their relationship at all. Man, she was going to get so hurt if this went wrong.

Grimacing at her thoughts, Terri slid her arm around Bastien's waist and concentrated on matching her step to his. "I missed you last night," he said, quietly pulling her into his arms as soon as they were in the backseat of the chauffeured car. Then he added, "When I wasn't worrying."

"Worrying?" Terri pulled back in surprise as he tried to kiss her. "Why were you worrying?"

He hesitated. "Well, you seemed to change once Kate and Lucern arrived. I was . . ." He shrugged. "Just worried that maybe you didn't want them to know about us, or something."

"Oh," she said softly, then smiled. "I was worried *you* might feel that way."

"I'm glad we were both wrong," Bastien said. He kissed her as the driver began to back the car out of its parking spot.

Terri sighed and leaned into him. A moment later, she caught his hand with a choked laugh. It had gone wandering down her upper leg, then tried to wander back up under the skirt of her baby-blue dress.

"Be good," she muttered against his mouth, trying to sound firm.

"I'd rather be bad," he whispered, trailing his lips to her neck.

Very aware of the driver, Terri caught back the moan that threatened to slip from her lips. Excitement raced through her, brought on both by Bastien's words and what he was doing. Bastien had already managed—with just a kiss—to make desire unfurl inside her. She was so glad that she had spoken up. Silence might be golden, but good communication was priceless.

Terri was really wishing they could skip the rehearsal dinner and go back to the penthouse for a quick refresher course on Bastien and Terri 101. Or a long refresher course. Possibly a really long one. Several days would have been good. But, of course, that wasn't possible. Bastien wasn't the only one sighing with regret when they arrived at the restaurant and had to untangle from each other's arms.

"I know we aren't going to get any time alone tonight," he said as he slid out of the car. He took her hand to help her out. "But it's occurred to me that we really have to get together tomorrow for a meeting."

"A meeting, huh?" Terri asked with amusement. She straightened on the pavement beside him.

"Yes. To discuss the stag and doe."

Terri blinked. Bastien had a wicked grin that told her he wanted to do more than just discuss something. But his mention of "stag and doe" made her realize that she had forgotten all about her intention of arranging a bridal shower for Kate. Terri had intended on setting to work on that the moment she arrived, and holding it whenever was possible. She'd known it would be last-minute, but being from England made it difficult to arrange, and she'd hoped Kate's friends would understand. However, the chaos that had ensued after she arrived had driven the thought from her mind. Now she was reminded. A stag and doe party would eliminate the need for a bridal shower, which was great. It would be more fun. The guys could be there. *Bastien* could be there.

"Yes. We'll have to get together. I could come to your office and meet you for lunch," she suggested.

"Perfect." Bastien kissed her again, then they walked into the restaurant.

"Hi." Terri paused before the desk in the outer office and smiled widely. "Meredith? I'm Terri."

"Oh." The woman was on her feet at once and taking the hand Terri held out. "Miss Simpson, what a pleasure to meet you in person."

"Terri," she repeated firmly. "And it's a pleasure to meet you, too. Thanks so much for all the help you gave us with the florists and caterers. Really, you were wonderful."

"Oh." Meredith flushed and waved a hand in dismissal. She started around the desk. "It was nothing. Just doing my job."

The secretary gestured for Terri to follow as she moved toward the door to Bastien's office. "Mr. Argeneau said you were coming. The caterers haven't arrived yet, but they should be here soon. As should he," she added. Meredith opened the door and

283

stepped to the side to allow Terri to enter. "He had a meeting with lab guys from Clinical Testing on the third floor, but said he'd be back by noon. He should be along shortly. In the meantime, you're welcome to wait in his office."

"I'm a little early," Terri apologized as she stepped into the office. In truth, she was fifteen minutes early. Not that she was eager or anything, Terri thought dryly. She'd actually got out of the cab in front of the building more than half an hour ago, but, knowing it was way too early, she'd window-shopped a bit and popped into a Starbucks for one of their iced drinks before making her way back to the office building.

"Sit wherever you'd like," Meredith said. "There are magazines on the table. Books on the shelf. There's even a television and stereo in that console there if you'd like. Can I get you a drink while you wait?" the secretary offered. Then, when she got no response, she said, "Terri? Can I get you a drink?"

"Oh." Terri closed her gaping mouth. She turned to blink at the woman. "No, thank you."

"Okay." Meredith grinned. "Well, if you change your mind, there's a fridge full of them behind that bar. Of course, there's alcohol as well. Help yourself. And if you need anything else, just let me know. I'll be out here until Mr. Argeneau returns."

"Thank you," Terri called as the woman stepped out of the room and closed the door. Then she turned back to gape at the office again. Dear God, she'd never seen anything like it! Bastien's office was bigger than the whole of her little cottage in Huddersfield. Eyes wide, she peered around as she moved farther inside. A huge desk the size of a double bed sat in front of a wall of windows with an awesome view of the city. There was the bar Meredith had pointed out in the corner, a black leather overstuffed couch, two matching chairs . . .

Cripes! Half the office was a bachelor's living room, with an entertainment console and a bar, and the other half was business-related with a desk, computer, fax machine, filing cabinets, and a large table for meetings.

"Jeez," Terri murmured, then gave her head a shake. She really shouldn't be impressed. After all, the penthouse was rather impressive too. Still, to work in an office like this? Man, she wished her own was half as nice. Or even a quarter. Her office at the university wasn't much larger than a closet. There was barely room for her desk and a chair for visitors.

Terri moved to the chair in front of Bastien's desk and sat down, setting her purse on the floor as she did. After sitting there, staring for a moment, she shifted restlessly, stood, and walked to the bookshelf Meredith had pointed out. Terri scanned the book titles with interest, noting that—as in most things—Bastien's taste didn't vary much from hers. But starting a book that she was only going to have fifteen minutes to read seemed a bit silly. Turning away, she crossed the room to the coffee table in front of the couch to go through the magazines lying there. There was quite a selection: women's magazines, men's magazines, business, fashion, celebrity gossip.

Terri picked up one of the women's magazines and sank onto the couch, then recalled her purse. She carried the magazine with her to collect it, then carried her purse back to the couch, set it out of the way by her feet, and started to leaf through the magazine again. Terri had only turned a couple of pages when she became aware that she was thirsty. It must have been all that walking. Lifting her head, she glanced toward the bar and hesitated. Meredith *had* said to help herself.

Setting the magazine down on the coffee table, Terri stood and moved behind the bar. There were countless bottles of liquor on a triple set of shelves with a mirror backing on the wall. It almost looked like a professional bar. But she wasn't interested in alcohol. Turning, she surveyed the area behind the bar, noting that there were two refrigerators. One was small, and one large. Terri tried the small one first and found it locked. She tried the larger one and it opened at once. This fridge was packed with liquid refreshments of every variety. Juices, pops, even milk made up its contents. But there were also two small vials of a clear liquid.

Terri picked up the small containers curiously. She recognized the vials. She'd seen enough of them— first, when her mother had been ill, then when Ian had been dying. They were medical vials, and both had the same long incomprehensible term and medical symbol on them.

Terri set them back, confusion reigning in her. Why would Bastien have medical vials in his refrigerator? It only took her a moment to come up with the answer. Medical laboratories were one of his company's interests. Blood banks, medical research, and medical labs were specialties of Argeneau Enterprises. In fact, Meredith had said Bastien was at a meeting right now with lab guys. This was probably something to do with that.

Satisfied, Terri set the vials back in the refrigerator and surveyed the beverages. She settled on a Diet Coke, grabbed a glass from the collection under the bar and poured her drink, then carried it back to the couch. Of course, Terri forgot all about her purse, which she'd set on the floor out of the way. But not out of the way enough. She tripped over the darn thing, and stumbled forward.

She managed to save herself from falling any farther than to her knees by catching herself on the couch, but she had to let go of the pop to do it.

"Darn," she breathed, staring at the puddle of liquid on the carpet. She followed that with a stronger curse and leapt into action. Pushing herself to her feet, she whirled back the way she'd come and hurried behind the bar in search of a towel or rag. But, of course, there was nothing. Terri turned back to the room, her gaze shooting around until it landed on a door on the opposite wall.

"Please be a bathroom," Terri prayed as she hurried in that direction. She could have cried with relief when she saw that it was. And there were towels. Expensive, fluffy white ones. She'd replace them if she had to. It seemed better to ruin the towels than the carpet.

"Are the caterers here with lunch yet, Meredith?" Bastien asked as he walked into the outer office, loosening his tie. He hated wearing the bloody things, and he took them off every chance he got. He'd undo it now and not put it back on until necessary.

"No, sir, but Terr—I mean, Miss Simpson arrived a bit early. She's in your office, sir."

"Is she?" Bastien smiled at the news, then added, "If she's told you to call her Terri, then you're welcome to do so, Meredith. There's no need to call her Miss Simpson on my account."

"Yes, sir." His secretary smiled. "I'll be heading to lunch in a minute. Shall I switch the lines over to the receptionist's desk so that she can take messages?"

"Yes, please," he said. "Have a good lunch."

"You too, sir."

Bastien nodded as he walked to his office door, but waited there for Meredith to collect her purse and leave the office before he opened it and stepped inside. The sight that met his gaze made him pause in the doorway and stare. Terri was on her hands and knees, her behind barely covered by a dark blue skirt, wagging from side to side as she scrubbed a towel over the carpet. His entrance didn't faze her. She hadn't heard the door open, because she was muttering.

Bastien was so distracted by the view, it took a moment for her words to register. She was mumbling something about what an idiot she was. That was enough to make him tear his eyes away from her behind, close the door quietly, and move forward.

"Terri? What happened?"

She stiffened, her body stilling, then she glanced sharply over her shoulder at him and groaned. "Oh, Bastien, I'm sorry. I'm such a clutz. I tripped over my purse and fell and spilled my Coke all over your lovely carpet. I—"

"Shh, shh, shh. It's all right," he interrupted. Moving forward, he took her arm and urged her to her feet.

"No, it's not all right. Just look at it. I've—"

"It will clean," Bastien assured her, taking her towel away and dropping it on the stain without even really a glance. "You didn't hurt yourself when you fell, did you?"

"No. But I—I don't know if Coke stains, but if it does, I think I've ruined your rug."

"Terri, it's just a carpet. A thing. Things are replaceable. As long as you're okay, that's all that matters."

"But—"

When her gaze dropped to the stain again, he took her arm and urged her away from the couch. He moved her toward his desk to keep her from looking.

"Don't worry about it," Bastien said again, but he knew his telling her wasn't going to accomplish the task. Terri would worry; she couldn't seem to help herself. It was as much her nature to be responsible for her own actions and worry about things as it was his. If he gave her half a chance, she'd be insisting on paying for cleaning or replacing the carpet. He wasn't going to give her the chance. A distraction was needed, and Bastien decided that, if he had to sacrifice himself to the cause, he was more than willing to do so.

"Why are you grinning?" Terri asked.

"I was just thinking a distraction is the only thing that will keep you from worrying about spilling that pop."

"A distraction?" She seemed perplexed.

"Mmmm. And I decided that I would just have to sacrifice myself to the cause."

Terri blinked at that announcement, and at the cheeky way he said it; then her lips twitched with the beginnings of amusement. "You're 'willing to sacrifice yourself to the cause,' are you?"

Bastien congratulated himself. His distraction was already working. Easing closer, he raised his hands to either side of her waist. "Yeah. I'm willing to go all the way, if necessary, to accomplish the task."

"All the way?" Terri was definitely distracted now, and amused.

"All the way," he assured her, leaning in to kiss her cheek by her ear.

"That's pretty selfless of you," she breathed. He moved to kiss her other cheek.

"Mmmm," Bastien murmured. "I'm a selfless kind of guy." Then he kissed her properly, covering her mouth with his. Terri opened to him, a little sigh slipping out and rolling lightly across his lips. He loved it when she did that. Bastien loved it when she sighed, and when she moaned. He loved it when she shifted, or arched, or writhed against him. He loved how he affected her, and he loved the effect she never failed to have on him. Heck, he just plain loved her.

That thought made Bastien pause. He loved Terri. It was a wonderful thing. If she didn't turn from him as Josephine had.

Terri pulled back as Bastien suddenly stilled. She peered at him quizzically, wondering at the expression on his face. It looked pained. Beginning to worry, she raised a hand to caress his cheek. "Are you all right, Bastien? Is something wrong?"

He blinked, as if coming out of a trance or back from deep thought, but rather than answer her, Bastien kissed her again. This time it wasn't the gentle coaxing kiss of a moment before, it was desperate and a little rough. Caught by surprise, Terri fell back a step, coming up against the edge of the desk. Bastien immediately eased up slightly, but didn't stop kissing. Not that she wanted him to. After a week of having him at her side every waking moment, the last two days had been distressing. Terri had missed him—his company, his laugh, the way he gestured with one hand when emphasizing something, the way his eyes sparkled when he was teasing, the half grin he always got on his face upon first spotting her. She'd missed talking to him, and listening to him. And though it had only been two days, it felt like forever since they had been together like this, in each other's arms, bodies pressed close together, mouths meshing.

Bastien thrust his tongue into her mouth, and Terri eagerly devoured it, her arms twining around his neck. She arched into him. She felt his hands slide down her back, but was startled when he caught her behind the thighs and lifted her up to sit on the desk.

Except for those evenings in nice restaurants, jeans and casual tops had been her uniform for the majority of this trip, but today was an exception. Knowing they were eating in the office, Terri had borrowed a dark blue skirt from Kate. She hadn't wanted to look like a bum among all the Argeneau employees in

Lynsay Sands

their business clothes. She'd also borrowed a matching blue silk blouse. Bastien reached between them
and set to work on the buttons.

He was very good with them, Terri noted absently
as he undid the last reachable button and tugged the
top out of her skirt to get the remaining few. Once
that was done, he pulled the shirt open and broke
their kiss to look at what he had revealed. His fingers
immediately moved to run lightly over the upper
curve of her breast and the top of her white satin bra.

"Beautiful," he murmured, and Terri glanced
down. Her breasts rose pale and round from the
white material, framed on either side by the edges of
her blue top. Then Bastien pushed the top off of her
shoulders, and reached behind her to unsnap her bra.
It too slipped away.

Terri groaned as his hands replaced the lacy cups,
her eyes dropping half closed as he caressed her
breasts. She watched for a moment, her breath coming faster with every passing second, then she reached
for the buttons of his shirt. She wasn't as practiced as
Bastien apparently was. Terri was also slightly distracted by what he was doing to her, but she managed
to undo his shirt. She let her hands slide over his skin,
shifting them around to his back, when he suddenly
knelt to first lick and then suckle at one of her
breasts.

"Bastien," she breathed, arching into his attention.
Terri loved the things he did to her. She loved how
he made her feel. She loved the way he made her
laugh, the way he made her feel safe. She loved *him*.

The thought caught her by surprise, and Terri

292

blinked her eyes open, staring blindly at the office beyond his shoulders. Bastien continued to caress her. Her stunned mind grappled with her feelings, trying to wrap itself around them. *Did* she love Bastien?

The question was pushed from her mind as he slid one hand up along the top of her leg, pushing the skirt before it. When his hand shifted, slipping between her legs, Terri released a groan. It was cut off by Bastien's mouth as he freed the nipple he was suckling and raised his lips to claim hers. She kissed him frantically, gasping into his mouth and arching on the desktop as his fingers slid beneath the edge of her panties.

Bastien was moving so quickly it was leaving her dizzy, but dizzy with want. How had he done this to her so fast? she wondered faintly, but in the next moment she didn't care. He slid one finger into her. Terri sucked on his tongue desperately as he slid the finger out, then in again. Then he brushed the nub that was the center of her excitement with his thumb, and she nearly leapt off the desk in reaction, her body jolting under the sudden shot of pleasure that radiated from that one small spot. Tearing her mouth away, Terri leaned her head back, gasping for air. Bastien's mouth worked its way along her throat and his fingers continued to caress and excite her.

"Bastien. Please," she said at last, straightening to clutch his shoulders. "I need you."

It was all she had to say. Bastien grasped her hips and slid her to the edge of the desk, even as he reached for the zipper of his pants. In the next moment, he had them undone and was sliding into her.

"Oh!" Terri gasped as he filled her, then moaned as he withdrew.

Bastien turned his head and caught her next moan in his mouth, kissing her, his hands sliding beneath her bottom to hold her still as he drove back into her. Terri clutched her hands in his hair, her fingers curling and unintentionally tugging as her mouth became more demanding. Then she wrapped her legs around his hips, and held on for dear life.

It was fast and hard, neither of them either willing or able to go slow to drag out the pleasure. Within moments it was over, both of them crying out together as release overtook them. Then they stayed, leaning weakly against each other, trying to catch their breath.

"Well," Bastien murmured after a moment. Taking his weight off her, he caught her face in his hands and kissed her forehead. "Hello." He next kissed Terri's nose as it wrinkled with perplexity, and explained, "I might have forgotten to say that when I came in."

"Oh. I think I may have, too." Terri gave a breathless laugh. "Hello."

Bastien kissed her mouth again, not urging it open this time, but simply moving his lips over hers. Then he had a quick nibble at her plump lower lip, but was interrupted when a knock sounded at the door. He pulled back slightly and glanced over his shoulder toward the sound. When a second knock came, he turned back and smiled at her wryly. "I think our lunch is here."

Chapter Sixteen

Bastien unlocked the refrigerator in his desk and set the two small vials inside. He'd finally remembered to bring them up to the penthouse. They'd been in his office all week, since the day Terri had come for lunch, Monday. He had just been getting ready to leave for his appointed meeting with the lab guys that morning, when James came into his office to give him the new synthetic enzymes for Vincent to test. They were the latest effort to treat the condition that forced Bastien's cousin and uncle to feed from living donors. Life would be much easier for both men if they could survive off of bagged blood as most of the rest of the clan did. Vincent was usually the one who tested each new serum and, knowing that he was staying in the penthouse at the moment, James had brought the serum to Bastien.

By the time the scientist had finished explaining

295

the requirements for a true test of the enzyme—Vincent had to refrain from feeding off living donors while taking it, and he would need to be tested daily to see if it was working, as well as to be sure he wasn't suffering any damaging side effects—Bastien was running really late. He'd thanked the fellow and merely tossed the vials in the large unlocked fridge, rather than waste time on the locked one. Then he'd rushed off to his meeting.

But of course he'd forgotten the vials that night when he'd gone up to the penthouse. In fact, Bastien had forgotten them repeatedly until today, but he hadn't forgotten to bring the matter up with Vincent. His cousin had agreed to try the serum, and to switch to bagged blood, but refused to do so until the weekend following the wedding. He didn't want it to interfere with his play rehearsals, or with Lucern and Kate's wedding if there did happen to be side effects.

Bastien understood. He'd checked with James to be sure that the vials of serum wouldn't expire, but had only finally remembered to bring them upstairs with him tonight. He would keep them in the penthouse office refrigerator until Vincent was ready for them.

That chore out of the way, Bastien grabbed a bag of blood from the now restocked shelves of the fridge. Thankfully, he'd at least remembered to have that done. Although he was surprised he had even managed that. He'd been a tad distracted all week, what with finding ways and times to squeeze in visits with Terri. She wouldn't go out with him alone when Kate was free, explaining apologetically that she had come to be with her cousin before the wedding and didn't feel right about abandoning her at a time when she was so excited and nervous about the up coming nuptials.

Bastien understood. Besides, they spent time together. It was just that, in the evenings, they only managed to see each other on double dates with Lucern and Kate. The other couple didn't wish to go without seeing each other, but insisted on chaperones when they did. In an effort to make sure their wedding night was special, Kate refused to be alone with Lucern until then. And, as long as Kate and Lucern couldn't be alone together, neither could Terri and Bastien. Which meant, to spend any time on his own with Terri, Bastien had to arrange to see her while Kate was at work. While he himself should be working.

After taking off the first week of Terri's stay here in New York, Bastien was swamped trying to catch up with everything he'd neglected. But he had still managed to make time to be alone with her for at least an hour every day. He had made it a point to be sure they went places, too. After that first lunch in the office, Bastien hadn't wanted her to think that his only interest in her was sexual. But, somehow, no matter where they went or what he had planned, they always ended up making love. They'd made love in some interesting and unexpected places this week, and it wasn't always he who initiated it. Terri was turning out to be as insatiable as he had found himself becoming. She was doing a good job of making up for the years of abstinence since her husband died.

"Bastien?"

"Yeah?" He glanced up as Vincent opened the office door.

"Terri just buzzed. She's on her way up in the elevator."

Smiling, Bastien tossed the now empty blood bag into the waste basket under the desk and gave the fridge door a push to close it. He stood and hurried around the desk.

Today was the only day he hadn't managed to book a free hour to see her. And while Kate would be here soon for the stag and doe party, helping to set up for it was a perfectly legitimate reason for Terri to come early. He hadn't expected to be so lucky as to have her show up this early though.

"I thought that news would cheer you up," Vincent said. His amusement was apparent as Bastien approached the door.

"You thought right, cousin." He slapped Vinny on the shoulder and moved past him into the hall. "You thought right."

"Well then, this news might make you even happier." His cousin followed him.

"What's that?" Bastien asked with distraction.

"I have to pick up my date and take her to dinner before the party, so you'll have this place to yourself until the guests start arriving. Or at least until Aunt Marguerite, Rachel, and Etienne come back from collecting Lissianna and Greg from the airport. That should give you about two hours. You'll have to set up for the party on your own, but—"

"You're a good cousin, Vincent," Bastien said

solemnly as they reached the entry. "And a good friend."

"I'll remind you of that the next time I need a favor," his cousin said lightly.

"You do that," Bastien agreed. The elevator arrived and the doors slid open.

"Hello, beautiful," Vincent greeted Terri as he swapped places with her, taking her spot on the elevator. "Don't do anything I wouldn't do," he added as the doors started to close. "And since there isn't much that I wouldn't do, that means the two of you should have lots of fun."

Terri glanced from the closed elevator doors to Bastien with a grin. "My arrival didn't scare him off, did it?"

"No. He's gone to get his date and take her to dinner," Bastien explained. Then he stepped forward and scooped Terri into his arms.

"Bastien!" She squealed in combined surprise and alarm, her hands clutching instinctively at his shoulders.

"Have you ever had a glass of champagne in a Jacuzzi?" He started up the hall toward the master suite.

"No, I don't believe I have," Terri admitted. She unclenched her hands to slip them around his shoulders and relaxed against his chest. "I take it we're going to have champagne in the Jacuzzi before we set up for the party?"

"No," he said promptly. "*You're* going to have champagne in the Jacuzzi."

She arched her eyebrows. "What are you going to have in the Jacuzzi?"

"I'm going to have *you*."

"Mmm," Terri murmured, unable to control an excited shiver.

"Mmm," Bastien murmured back. He pressed a kiss to her lips. "God, I love it when you do that."

"What?" She asked huskily, planting a kiss by his ear.

"Shiver with excitement. Or moan, groan, writhe, or arch. I just love it when you're excited," he admitted.

Terri laughed. "You're the one who does it to me. I'm beginning to think that you're something of a magician. In fact, right this minute I'm sure of it."

"Oh? Why is that?"

"Because, we're nowhere near the Jacuzzi, yet I'm already wet."

Bastien nearly tripped over his own feet at that admission. His eyes jerked to her face and hunger immediately flared in him as he took in her wicked smile. "Damn," he muttered. "Maybe we'll leave the Jacuzzi for another time."

Terri laughed as he began to walk faster.

"Do you want me to call you a cab?"

"What!" Chris yelled over the surrounding noise.

Terri shook her head. The editor hadn't heard her over the loud throbbing music. She leaned closer until her mouth was almost touching his ear. "Do you want me to call you a car service? It can't be easy taking the subway with that cast."

C.K. hesitated, debating the matter, then nodded

and yelled, "Please. But how will you do that with all this noise?"

Terri hesitated. She hadn't thought of that. Then she knew the answer. "I'll use the phone in the office!"

"Oh!" He nodded. "Okay."

"I'll be right back," she yelled. "Just sit tight!"

Leaving him there, in the middle of Kate and Lucern's stag and doe party, Terri wove her way through the guests to the entry, then hurried down the hall to the office. She'd noticed that the editor seemed tired when he arrived. When she'd asked, C.K. explained that he'd been working overtime for the past week; trying to catch up with work. He'd managed to perk up a bit and have some fun, but it was getting late and Terri had noticed that he was starting to yawn and look exhausted. When she'd seen him take his jacket off the back of his chair and put it on, she went over to see if he wanted her to call him a car.

The office was empty when she entered; not that Terri had expected it to be otherwise. The guests at the party were all family and friends, all of them either from the city or having shown up yesterday or today for the wedding tomorrow. But it was possible that Kate and Lucern or someone else had sought out a quiet place to be alone for a bit: something she'd considered suggesting to Bastien at least half a dozen times. But, as the maid of honor and best man, they were the hosts of this party and simply hadn't been able to slip away. She was glad the room was empty. It might have been embarrassing to walk in on an amorous couple.

Closing the door behind her, Terri moved to the desk and sat down. She pulled the phone closer to her, then realized she didn't have a clue what the number would be to call for a car service in New York. Or if it was even possible. She supposed it must be, or Chris wouldn't have agreed to her calling. Biting her lip, she glanced over the desk for a phone book, but of course there was none. Terri turned her attention to the drawers. Her eyes landed on the large bottom left drawer first. It was large enough to hold a telephone book. It was also not quite closed. Reaching down, Terri pulled it open, then simply stared. What looked like a desk drawer was not a drawer at all. It didn't pull out, but swung open revealing a mini refrigerator. That was a bit startling in itself, but what was in the little refrigerator was even more so.

Terri stared at the contents: two vials similar to the ones she had found in Bastien's office on Monday morning. And there were also at least a dozen bags of blood. She stared at them uncomprehending for a moment, completely bewildered as to why these things should be in Bastien's desk drawer. She knew medical research was a part of Argeneau Industries, and she *had* heard of people bringing their work home with them, but this was a bit much.

A sound made her start with guilt, slam the refrigerator door closed and jump to her feet.

"Oh, there you," Bastien said, appearing from the hallway and crossing the room. He smiled.

"I came to call a car service for Chris, but I don't

know the number and can't find a phone book," Terri blurted.

"I know. He told me. You don't have to call, though. I arranged for several company cars to take everyone back to their homes and hotels. I already sent Chris back in one." He was around the desk by this time, and he paused before her to take her face in his hands. He smiled down into her eyes. "In fact, I sent a lot of people on their way. The rest are waiting for the cars to return, so . . . we have a few minutes before we have to go play host and hostess again."

"Oh." She smiled, but confusion was still reigning in her mind. The blood, the medical vials in both Bastien's office refrigerator and the penthouse office, the IV stand she'd found while rudely snooping her first day here, and a secret that Kate had mentioned— one Bastien would have to tell her and they would have to work out: these things were all running through her mind, round and round, like a rat on a wheel. Blood, medicine, IV stand, secrets?

Bastien's mouth covering hers was distracting, and Terri tried to force her fears from her mind. But her brain kept running. Blood, medicine, IV stand, secrets.

"Terri?" Bastien murmured, pulling back when she didn't respond. "Are you okay?"

She opened her eyes and forced a smile. "I'm just a little tired."

He caressed her cheek with one thumb. "It's late."

"Yes," she whispered.

Bastien nodded, but there was a flicker of uncertainty on his face.

Guilt immediately ran through Terri. She wasn't really tired, just confused. And she felt bad for letting it come between them when they had so little time left to enjoy each other. There was probably a simple explanation for all of what she had seen, and the easiest way to hear that explanation was to ask. She would, she decided; but first she wanted to eliminate his uncertainty. Leaning up, she pressed her lips to his and kissed him. Bastien remained still for a moment, then kissed her back gently, his mouth moving over hers with infinite care, a warm caress that slowly became warmer.

Terri moaned, her arms sliding around his neck and holding on as her body arched and stretched against his. This was Bastien, the man she loved. Did anything else matter?

The opening of the office door made them freeze, then turn toward the door.

"Sorry for interrupting." Lissianna offered them an apologetic smile. "But the first of the cars have returned, and Kate's parents and sisters are leaving. Mother thought Terri would wish to say good-bye."

"Of course!" Bastien slipped an arm around Terri as they walked the door. "We'll come say good-bye."

Chapter Seventeen

"Well, it's done. You're now a married man," Terri said lightly to Lucern as he whirled her around the dance floor. The ceremony and feast were over, and he and Kate had done the traditional bridal dance. Now Lucern was making his way through the females in the wedding party, while Kate danced with each of the males. Then they would move on to the other important guests. As maid of honor and best man, Terri and Bastien had been the first approached. "How does it feel?"

"Good." Lucern grinned, then added, "I'm just grateful the ceremony went off without a hitch. After all the calamities that plagued the arranging of this wedding, I thought for sure there would be some crisis. But it's all gone as smooth as silk."

Terri smiled at the man. She hadn't found him very talkative until tonight. Kate had explained one evening that he always got that way when he was

working on a book, but that he could occasionally
come out of his shell. It seemed tonight he had. He
seemed very happy.

"Yes, it did," she agreed, then qualified herself
with, "Well, except for C.K.'s sneezing."

They both grinned at the memory. The poor editor had been mortified: standing at the front of the
church with the other groomsmen, sneezing every
few minutes. The worst part was that he had apparently warned Kate and Lucern that he was allergic to
certain flowers when they'd asked him to stand up in
the wedding, and they had both assured him that they
would see to it that none of those flowers made it
into the wedding arrangements. They had been careful when choosing the first arrangements; but both
had forgotten all about his allergy when the tragic
floral crisis had occurred, and they had unintentionally chosen unfortunate arrangements the second
time around. The editor had been having a miserable
time of it all day.

Her gaze sought Chris out. The editor couldn't
dance with his cast, but he wasn't at the head table
where he, as a member of the wedding party, had
been seated for the meal. That table was now empty,
most of its inhabitants on the dance floor. Abandoned, Chris had chosen to join the table where his
coworkers from Roundhouse Publishing were seated.
Vincent was standing behind the editor's chair, one
hand patting his shoulder soothingly, no doubt sym-
pathizing over his floral misery.

Terri really hoped the editor's luck changed soon.
He seemed too nice a guy to suffer so.

An elegantly clad woman approached the table to speak to Chris, and Terri tilted her head to stare. The woman looked terribly familiar, and Terri was sure that Kate had introduced her at some point, but she'd met so many people today that it was hard to put names to faces.

Terri was sure the woman worked in the publishing industry somewhere, though, and judging by the way C.K. straightened in his seat as the woman addressed him, she'd guess that the lady had some influence.

"Lucern?" Terri glanced at her dance partner curiously.

"Hmm?"

"Who is that woman?"

He followed her pointing finger. "Kathryn Falk."

"Ah." Terri nodded. "Lady Barrow."

"Yes. She's a nice woman. Smart and savvy. Kathryn was very helpful to me at the first romance conference Kate dragged me to."

Terri bit her lip to keep from laughing. It was a bit of an understatement. Kate had told her all about Lucern's codpiece getting caught on the tablecloth at the medieval feast, and how Lady Barrow had climbed right under the table with Kate to help her unhook him. She'd apparently held a flashlight or something while Terri's cousin worked to free Lucern. It had sounded like a hilarious tale.

"She did more than help Kate unhook my codpiece," he announced, and Terri guessed she hadn't hidden her amusement very well. He'd obviously guessed what she was thinking. "She also gave me a ride back from the airport, and some advice, and . . ."

He shrugged. "She was a good friend to me that day, and we've kept up the friendship since. I've agreed to attend the next Romantic Times conference as a favor to her."

Terri knew that was saying something. According to Kate, Lucern refused to do any of the conferences as an attendee. Even at the one he'd gone to last week, he hadn't gone as Luke Amirault the author, but Lucern Argeneau, Kate's fiance.

Noting the man's sudden frown, she glanced back toward the table. Vincent was holding Lady Barrow's hand and carrying it to his mouth to kiss. Terri could almost hear his sexy, trademark "Enchantée," from where she stood. The man was an incorrigible flirt, she thought with vague amusement.

Lucern didn't appear amused. When Vincent led the woman onto the dance floor and buried his face in her neck, Lucern's gaze sliced to where Bastien and Kate danced. Bastien turned, as if his brother had spoken his name. Their eyes met briefly; then Lucern glanced toward Vincent and Bastien's gaze followed. Bastien murmured something to Kate, and she looked to see what Vincent was up to as well. Not one of them seemed too pleased to see Vinnie with Lady Barrow. Terri didn't understand why. He was just dancing with the woman. A little too close, perhaps; but just the same, they were only dancing.

All four of them watched the couple dance. When the music ended and Vincent began to lead the woman off the dance floor, Lucern led Terri to Bastien.

"I'll take care of it," Bastien said. "You two continue your dances. You have a lot of people to go."

The newlyweds nodded and thanked him. They moved off to find the next couple from the wedding party to dance with, and Bastien glanced at Terri.

"Go ahead, I'll be fine," she assured him, though she really didn't know what there was for him to take care of. The family all seemed to be overreacting a bit. "I'll fetch myself a drink and sit, give my feet a rest," she assured him when Bastien didn't look happy. "Go on. Kate and Lucern will obviously just worry, and they shouldn't have to worry about anything on their wedding day."

"I agree. You're a special woman, Terri." Bastien caught her by the chin and gave her a quick kiss. "I won't be long."

He straightened from kissing Terri and swung around to see where his cousin had got to. Unfortunately, the man was no longer in sight. Frowning, Bastien headed in the direction he had last seen Vincent leading Lady Barrow. His eyes scanned the people in front of him worriedly. He understood that Vincent was probably hungry about now; it was around this hour that he usually went out to hunt. But they couldn't have him running around feeding off the guests!

"Brother!"

Bastien slowed his steps and turned as Etienne hurried to join him.

"Lucern and Kate told me what was up, and asked me to help you."

LYNSAY SANDS

Bastien nodded, then glanced around. "Vincent was headed in this direction when last I saw him. I thought to search this area first, then make a sweep of the rest of the hall."

"Good thinking." Etienne fell into step as he started to walk again. After a few minutes, he said, "So, a little birdie tells me Terri is . . . important to you."

"A little birdie, huh?" Bastien asked dryly.

"Yeah." When Bastien didn't either agree or disagree, Etienne added, "I was talking to Terri at the party last night. She seems nice. Actually, she *is* nice," he said, collecting himself. He explained, "I read her mind."

"I can't do that, so it's good to know my instincts about her are correct." Bastien said.

"Well, I can read her, and I can tell you that I like her. She's like my Rachel—something special."

"Yes, she is," Bastien agreed. "She's sweet and beautiful and smart and—"

"And you can't read her," Etienne repeated. "And you love her. You've obviously found your life mate. Congratulations, brother! I'm very happy for you."

"Yes. Well, don't tell Mother that." Bastien shook his head as Etienne clapped a hand on his back. He didn't need any interference.

"Don't tell me what?"

Both brothers turned, groaning as Marguerite Argeneau joined them.

"Mother." Bastien kissed her cheek dutifully. Etienne followed suit.

"I don't know why you boys keep trying to hide

310

things from me. One would think at your age you would know better than to even waste your time trying. I am your mother. I see, hear, and know *everything*."

"Is that right?" Bastien asked.

"That's right," she said firmly. "And perhaps you will realize it in another two hundred years. It only took Lucern until he was six hundred to figure it out. Honestly. Boys are so much harder to raise than girls." Marguerite scowled at her sons for grinning at this oft-heard complaint, then sighed. "So, no doubt you don't want Etienne to tell me that you love Katie's little cousin Terri?"

Etienne burst out laughing at Bastien's grimace.

"Well, you didn't think it had slipped my notice, did you?" their mother asked with amusement. "After four hundred years, one would expect me to know and understood my boy enough to recognize when he is in love." She sighed, then nodded. "I approve, by the way. She's a lovely girl. And it will ease some of Kate's feelings of loss when she has to give up the rest of her family. Not to mention that having Katie in the family will make it easier on Terri as well. Actually, this will all work quite nicely."

"I hadn't thought of that," Bastien said with surprise. "I mean; them making it easier for each other."

"Well, that's why you have a mother." Marguerite patted his shoulder, then glanced around. "Have you tried looking out in the hallway, or the bars on the main floor?" When her two sons exchanged glances, she rolled her eyes. "Well, you didn't expect Vincent to bite her right here, did you? He'll use a nice dark corner. Come along, then. Let's find the boy before he gets himself in trouble."

"We can take care of this, Mother," Bastien said quickly. "Why don't you——?"

"Miss all the fun?" she asked. "I don't think so."

When Bastien and Etienne exchanged wry looks, she added, "Just thank me for deciding not to interfere with you and Terri."

"You won't?" Bastien eyed her with a combination of hope and wariness. He found it difficult to believe she meant that.

"I won't," Marguerite assured him. "You seem to be doing well enough on your own. Mind you, should you mess things up I may change my mind." On that note, she turned to lead the way out of the room.

Terri watched Bastien, Etienne and their mother leave the hall in search of Vincent as she listened idly to her aunt raving about this "perfectly lovely man" that she thought Terri should meet. It was sweet of the woman, really, but Terri wasn't looking for a man. She had one. Well, sort of. Her gaze slid back to the door through which Bastien had exited.

"Terri doesn't need a man, Mom. She already has one," Kate announced as Lucern led her over.

"She does?" Lydia Leever asked avidly. "You didn't say anything, dear. Who is he?"

"Lucern's brother Bastien," Kate answered.

"Oh!" Aunt Lydia was obviously pleased at the news, for she hugged Terri. "Well, that's wonderful. He's such a handsome man, and if he's half as nice as Lucern, the two of you should be very happy."

"I'm glad you think I'm nice, Mrs. Leever," Lucern interjected. "I hope that means you'll consent to dance with your new son-in-law?"

"Call me Mom, Lucern. You're family now," Aunt Lydia said. Lucern led her out onto the dance floor.

Kate smiled at Terri, as John Leever, her father, stood to take his turn on the dance floor with her as well. Terri watched them go, her thoughts drifting back to Bastien now that she was alone and no longer distracted. He had told her in the car on the way to the reception hall that he had something he wanted to discuss with her. Those solemn words had been bothering her ever since. They had immediately brought several things to mind: the vials, the blood bags, the iv stand, and Kate saying there was something that Bastien needed to tell her. Terri had been worrying over the topic ever since.

What was he going to tell her? How bad was it going to be? She hoped it wasn't too horrible, but she supposed she'd have to wait and see.

Terri shifted restlessly on her feet, then set her empty glass down on the nearest table and made her way to the ladies' room. Two ladies were leaving as she entered. Terri didn't recognize either woman, so she assumed they were either friends of Kate's from the city or relatives from the Argeneau side. She smiled and nodded politely as they passed, then walked along the stalls to the end.

Terri went in, locked the stall door behind her, pulled her skirt up and her panties down, and released a sigh of relief as she sat down. Her feet were a bit sore from her new shoes and all the standing she had done today—first at the ceremony, then on the church steps in the receiving line, and finally while posing for the endless wedding pictures. The reception had offered the first real chance she'd had to sit down, but it had been endlessly interrupted by standing as one guest or another made a toast to the bride and groom. Now the meal was over and the dancing had started. Terri wasn't too sure her feet were up to that. At least, not in these shoes. Her feet felt swollen and chafed in the satin bridesmaid slippers.

She lifted her feet, holding them straight out to examine them. The shoes were pretty enough, but damned uncomfortable. Terri briefly considered whether it would be bad form to take the darn things off and run around in stockinged feet for the rest of the night. She thought she might get away with it—the skirt was long; it might hide her bare feet—but her stockings would no doubt be ruined by night's end.

Stockings or feet? Which should she sacrifice? she pondered, staring at her raised shoes.

"Has Bastien told Terri yet?"

Terri stiffened inside her stall, her feet still straight out in the air.

"Shh, Lissianna." She recognized Kate's voice. "Someone could be in here."

"I checked first. The stalls are empty," Bastien's sister said reassuringly.

Terri glanced from her raised feet to the floor where they should have been. Having them up as she did, Lissianna had seen only what appeared to be an empty stall. Well, this was embarrassing. What should she do? Lower her feet and cough or something, to let the two women know that they weren't alone? Or should she keep her mouth shut and avoid embarrassing herself or the others? She'd also learn what they were talking about.

"Oh." Kate sighed. "No, Bastien hasn't told her yet, and I wish he would. He won't be able to keep it a secret for long. She's *bound* to find out."

Find out what? Terri wondered, prickly heat running down her neck.

"She leaves soon, though, doesn't she?" Lissianna asked.

"And do you think he won't follow? Or that she won't come back?"

"You think it's that serious?" Bastien's sister asked with interest.

"Yes. And you do, too, or you wouldn't be asking if he'd told her," Kate said dryly. "It's hardly something you tell just any gal you're dating."

Told me what? Terri repeated in her head. Damn, she wished they'd get more specific. And hurry. Her muscles were starting to burn from holding her legs up. She didn't know how much longer she could keep them raised.

"Yes, it's serious," Kate went on with a sigh. "I know Terri. She loves him with all her heart. Being just as much in love with Lucern I recognize the signs," she added dryly. "The way they feel about each other, they won't be apart for any longer than necessary. *If* she even goes home, or he doesn't just follow her back to England. Either way, he has to tell her. It wouldn't be a good thing for her to find out on her own."

"No," Lissianna agreed. "It's better he tell her than she find out by accident."

Find out what? Terri wanted to scream with frustration. Not to mention pain—her legs were now absolutely killing her.

"I don't know why he's delaying," Kate fretted.

Lissianna gave a short laugh. "That's easy enough to answer. It's because he loves her just as much as she loves him. I've never seen him like this. The man is always smiling, or whistling, or—I wasn't yet around when Josephine was in his life, but Lucern says Bastien wasn't even this happy when he thought he loved *her*."

Terri almost sighed out loud at this news. His family thought Bastien loved her. And she made him happier than Josephine—whoever that was. Her legs were suddenly forgotten. She could take a little pain.

"Well, then, why is he risking things working out with Terri by keeping quiet?" Kate asked. She sounded frustrated.

"As I said, because he loves her," Lissianna repeated. "Haven't you heard about Josephine?"

"Yes, of course. But Terri is different. She'll be more understanding. Especially after what she went through with Ian. She—"

Whatever came next was lost to Terri, for music briefly swept into the room as the door was opened, then receded to silence again as it closed. Lissianna and Kate were gone.

Chapter Eighteen

Terri's thoughts were in an uproar. *"Terri is different, she'll be more understanding, especially after what she went through with Ian."* Kate's words brought a myriad of memories floating through her mind: sobbing into her pillow at night as she listened helplessly to Ian's moans of pain, a pain that no amount of morphine would ease; the sickly sweet smell of death in the house that had seemed to cling to everything, including Terri herself, for months afterward; Ian's loss of dignity as he grew so weak he had to have every little thing done for him, down to the most personal and humiliating task.

It had been torturous for Terri. But she knew it had been a thousand times worse for him, and she'd had to carry that burden too. She'd known that Ian wished it would all just end. He'd begged her many times to finish it for him, once he was too weak to manage it himself. Terri had resented that. If he had wanted to end it, why had he waited until he couldn't do it himself? Why wait until the weight rested on her shoulders, and she had to carry the guilt of not being able to do it for him? For Terri had borne a mountain of guilt. She'd felt guilty that it was he and not she, that she was healthy while he suffered; that she couldn't save him; and ultimately, that she couldn't even end his suffering when he asked it of her.

More understanding, Kate had said? Yes, Terri understood. She knew exactly what Bastien would go through with whatever terminal illness he had, because it seemed to her that this was what they had been speaking of. The medicine, the blood, the IV stand, and the secrets all suddenly made sense. As did the medication that caused photosensitivity, and the fact that Bastien merely picked at his food most of the time, seeming to have no appetite. It was all so obvious now: Strong, handsome Bastien had a terminal illness. Terri understood. She understood how it would go, and it was always the same. Death was death, whether by Hodgkin's disease, breast cancer, or whatever Bastien was suffering. Terri knew this, and she hated the fact that he was going to suffer.

But she couldn't, she wouldn't go through it with him. It was impossible. She had thought suffering with her mother and Ian was bad. But Bastien? Watching that vital, strong, and handsome man fade to skin and bones? To see him become weak and lost to horrible pain? Having him beg her to end it for him as his body rotted away? It would kill her. Terri could not handle it. She knew she couldn't. And she was suddenly angry. So terribly angry. How dare he let her fall in love with him, knowing that he was dying? How dare he not tell her about his condition from the start, so that she might have guarded her heart and saved herself all the coming trauma? How dare he be sick on her? How dare he even consider dying? How dare he?

The bathroom filled with music and laughter as several women entered. Terri was aware of their chatter, but didn't really hear it as her mind whirled under what she had just learned. She waited where she was until they left and silence filled the room again; then she let her feet back down, straightened her clothes and let herself out of the stall. She moved to the sink and stared at her reflection as she washed her hands, but didn't really see herself at first. Her mind was caught up in memories of Ian. But now, when she recalled how Ian had lain moaning in bed at night, he had Bastien's face. When Ian begged her to end it all, it was Bastien speaking.

Movement drew her attention to her reflection, and Terri stared blankly at the tears running down her cheeks. She was crying, which seemed odd because she wasn't aware of feeling anything. In fact, her mind seemed rather numb. Yet there they were: tears leaking out of hollow eyes and coursing down her cheeks in little rivulets. She turned her attention to her face and noted that she was blanched of all color.

She couldn't go back to the wedding reception like this. She couldn't even allow anyone to see her this way. Turning the taps off, Terri contemplated the problem. She'd have to slip away. She felt bad about it, but it seemed the only option. She didn't want to ruin the day for her cousin and Lucern.

She dried her hands off, wiped the tears from her face, then moved to the door and slid out. Noise and color assaulted her at once. The reception was in full swing. No one noticed her standing by the bathroom door. Terri quickly judged the fastest and easiest route out of the hall, and then took it. Much to her amazement, she managed to escape without running into anyone who might have stopped her; and the few she passed whom she knew didn't seem to notice her.

Terri walked straight out of the reception hall and to the escalators rather than risk having to wait for the elevators. The moving stairs had been turned off for the night, but she walked down them quickly, crossed into and out of the lobby, and rushed straight out the front door of the hotel.

"Taxi, miss?" the doorman asked. Terri nodded. He blew his whistle, bringing the first waiting cab squealing into the driveway. It came to a halt in front of her, and the doorman opened the door. Terri murmured a thank you as she got in.

"Where to, miss?"

Terri gave Kate's address and sat silent in the backseat, her mind blank. It stayed that way for the entire ride. It wasn't until the taxi pulled up in front of Kate's apartment building that Terri realized she didn't have a purse. It hadn't been necessary. Transportation had all been taken care of for the wedding, the meal was paid for, so there had been no cause for her purse. Terri stared at the cabbie with a sort of horror as he turned to tell her the fare, then she suddenly went calm. "Can you drive me from here to the airport after I grab a bag?"

The cabbie looked surprised, then suspicious, then pleased at the large fare to come. He nodded. "Sure, lady."

"Wait for me. I'll just be a minute." She slipped out of the taxi before he could protest. Terri half expected him to jump out of the car and chase her to insist she pay for the fare, but some angel must have been looking out for her—the cabbie remained in his cab as she lifted her skirt and jogged lightly up the steps to the front of Kate's apartment building.

Terri didn't have the key, though. Bastien had it, because he had a pocket in his suit, whereas she didn't have a pocket anywhere on her outfit. The plan had been that, once the reception was over, they would come collect her things, and she would stay with him for this, her last night in New York. He had said they needed to talk, and that he had something to ask her once the wedding was over. Terri, in her heart of hearts, had hoped that talk had something to do with love and their future together. Now she knew it was about death and dying.

With nothing else for it, she buzzed the landlord's apartment, now grateful that Kate had introduced her to the couple. It was the wife who answered, and Terri quickly explained that she had rushed back to the apartment to get something she'd left behind, but had thoughtlessly left her key at the wedding reception. The woman said she'd be right down to let her in. Terri knew the landlady could have buzzed her in from her apartment, but she supposed the old woman wanted to be sure it was her. Whatever the case, Terri resigned herself to waiting impatiently.

"There he is."

Bastien followed his mother's gesture to a booth in the back of the bar. Vincent and Lady Barrow sat, heads together, talking.

"Hmm. I wonder if we made it in time," Bastien muttered.

"There's only one way to find out." Marguerite Argeneau strode forward, leaving her sons to follow as she wove through the crowded bar.

"Aunt Marguerite!" Vincent got to his feet at once when she stopped at the table. "What are you do . . ." His voice trailed off and his mouth tightened as he spotted Bastien and Etienne.

"I think Lady Barrow has to go to the ladies' room," Marguerite announced, focusing her penetrating silver-blue eyes on the woman.

Lady Barrow gave a laugh. "Actually, no, I don't."

Marguerite blinked in surprise, then turned a glance on her sons. "Bastien"—she gestured to the woman—"fix it."

Bastien was so surprised that his inestimable mother hadn't been able to control Lady Barrow's mind, as she had so obviously just tried to do, that it took him a minute before he tried to do so himself. And he found it impossible to even read her mind, let alone slip into it. After a moment, trying, as Lady Barrow watched them all with growing confusion, Bastien glanced to his mother and shook his head.

"Etienne?" Marguerite asked, and her youngest son tried as well, only to shake his head after a moment.

"You have an . . . interesting family, Vincent," Lady Barrow said politely, and he abruptly stood.

"Please excuse me for a moment, Kathryn. I need a word with them." He excused himself, then took his aunt's arm and led her away from the table. Bastien and Etienne followed. Once they were far enough away to not be overheard, he turned on them with irritation. "I wasn't going to bite her. God, you people act like I'm some rabid dog, likely to go gnawing on every neck that goes by."

"Well, we knew you had to feed, Vincent," Marguerite said. Her tone had changed and become soothing.

"I did that at dinnertime. I came up to the bar for a quick bite, then nipped back." He grinned evilly; then winked.

"Well, then, what are you doing up here now?" Etienne asked.

"What does it look like I'm doing?" he asked in exasperation. "I'm talking to Kathryn. She's a fascinating woman."

"You aren't going to bite her?" Bastien asked suspiciously.

"No, Bastien. I'm not going to bite her. I wouldn't go biting guests at Lucern's wedding."

"Well, how were we to know that?" Bastien snapped. "You bit my housekeeper."

323

"That was an emergency. I don't normally feed in my own home, or in the homes of relatives."

"You bit Chris, too," Bastien reminded him. "And that was *after* biting the housekeeper."

"I had barely sunk my teeth into Mrs. Houlihan when you guys interrupted. I was still weak. I couldn't hunt weak," he explained patiently. Then he added, "And, by the way, you're welcome."

"For what?" Bastien asked.

"For taking care of the housekeeper," he explained. "Meredith called upstairs one day, while you and Terri were off on one of your jaunts that first week, and I took the message. She had the address for where Houlihan was staying. I went and wiped her memory of what happened. And the memories of the two people she talked to. You won't have to worry about her anymore."

"Did you?" Bastien asked with surprise, then realized the matter had completely slipped his mind. He hadn't been worried at all; he'd been too distracted with Terri. That could have been a bad thing. Details like that had to be kept track of and taken care of. It was a good thing Vincent had been on the ball. He was sincere when he said, "Thank you."

His cousin shrugged. "I caused the problem, I took care of it. Now." He glared at them all meaningfully. "Can I get back to my guest? She really is a fascinating woman."

"She certainly seems to have a strong mind," Marguerite commented, glancing curiously over to where Lady Barrow sat.

"Yes, she does," Vincent agreed. "And now that you know the guests are all safe from ol' rabid Vincent, will you go back and enjoy Lucern's wedding?"

"I thought you came for something that little Katie left behind," the landlady said as Terri led the way into the apartment, collected her purse and already packed and waiting suitcase, then immediately turned around with them in hand.

"No." Terri paused in the hall as the woman locked the door behind them. "I'm sorry for the trouble. But I have to get to the airport, and I couldn't go back for the key."

"Oh, it's no trouble, dear. I just misunderstood," the woman assured her as they waited for the elevator. She looked Terri up and down. "Are you going to the airport dressed like that?"

Terri nodded silently.

"Are you all right?" The landlady was staring at her with concern now, and Terri was sure she must look terrible since crying her eyes out at the reception.

"I will be," she assured the woman quietly, though she wasn't at all sure it was true.

"Well, have a safe trip." The old woman said. Her concern was still obvious in her voice.

Terri thanked her, then hurried out as the elevator doors opened.

The cabby hopped from his car as soon as she came out the front door of the building. Terri could tell by his expression, as he hurried up the steps to take her suitcase, that he was relieved to see her. She guessed

325

he hadn't been at all sure she would return, and supposed the only reason for him to have taken a chance on her was how shattered she apparently looked.

Terri thanked him as he carried her case down, then slid into the backseat as he stowed her bag in the trunk.

"Which airport, miss?" he asked the moment he was back behind the wheel.

"JFK," she murmured, then leaned her head back and closed her eyes.

It was a long ride to the airport. Terri didn't sleep, though the taxi driver must have thought she was doing so. She didn't think, either—she lay quiet and still, and merely was. Her mind was blank, her heart empty. Oddly enough, that state made the long journey to JFK pass quickly.

Terri dug the money out of her purse to pay the cabbie as he pulled up to the terminal. She gave it to him as he handed over her luggage; then walked into the airport and straight to the ticket desk.

There was some difficulty getting a flight. All of those leaving New York for England were earlier in the evening. The last to leave for Manchester was departing even as Terri spoke to the ticket agent, but again her pale and shattered look helped; the woman went to herculean efforts to get her out of New York and on her way. Terri ended up with an incredibly long and circuitous route, flying to Detroit, transferring, flying to France, transferring again, then finally flying on to Manchester. Terri didn't care. She just wanted out of New York and to be on her way back home to her little cottage and her safe life.

She purchased her new tickets, canceled the old, and handed over her luggage. Terri then went to the washroom to change, only to realize she had handed over her suitcase and only had her hand luggage. It held nothing to wear. She walked right back out of the bathroom and surveyed the fashion stores available in Terminal One: Herme's, Ferragamo's, and American Clothier.

She managed to find a comfortable yet inexpensive outfit in Ferragamo's. After paying for it, she carried the bag with her through security, found her departure gate, went into the nearest washroom, and quickly changed out of her long gown. The pantsuit she'd purchased was nothing special, and Terri put her long, lavender dress in the Ferragamo's bag with relief. She'd drawn attention in the fancy gown, and she didn't really want people staring at her right now.

Stepping out of the stall, she moved to the row of sinks and set her carry-on and purse on the counter, then surveyed herself in the mirror. She looked like hell, of course. And there was very little she could do about it. Terri went through her carry on and applied some makeup, but it didn't hide the empty look in her eyes. She finally pulled out a pair of sunglasses and tried them, then decided they would draw as much attention as her hollow eyes. Taking them off, she dropped them in her bag and headed out to the waiting area.

She had a little less than two hours to wait. That seemed a long time, especially with the worry that someone at the reception might notice her missing and start looking for her. She suddenly considered that she probably should have left some message for Kate, so her cousin wouldn't waste time worrying about her on her wedding night.

Spotting a row of pay phones, she moved to them. Terri dropped fifty cents in, and dialed the hotel to leave a message with the desk. It was a cheerful, *I'm-fine-and-at-the-airport, just-waiting-for-my-flight, have-a-great-honeymoon-and-I-love-you* type of message. As if she wasn't doing something completely unexpected, leaving so abruptly and ahead of schedule. It was the best Terri could do.

She hung up, then picked up the phone again, only to pause and glance at her watch. It was the middle of the night in England. She couldn't call now; she'd wake Dave and Sandi up. Maybe she should wait and call them from France, she decided. Although that wouldn't give the couple much warning, or time, to get to the airport to meet her. Well, if they couldn't get there in time, she'd take a taxi. She couldn't really afford it, but such was life.

"Was she in there?" Bastien asked Rachel as she came back out of the ladies' room. He'd returned from taking care of Vincent, to find Kate missing. He had walked the reception hall several times in search of her, before giving up and asking Etienne's wife to step into the washroom and see if she was in there.

"No. Sorry, Bastien." His sister-in-law shook her head. "I checked every stall. There's no one in there at the moment at all."

Bastien frowned and turned to look around the

hall. She *had* to be here somewhere. She couldn't have just disappeared.

"Perhaps she stepped outside for some fresh air," Etienne suggested, joining them with the drinks he'd gone to collect from the bar. "Here you go, darling."

"Thank you." Rachel took the drink her husband held out and took a sip. "Mmmm. A Bloody Mary. My favorite."

Bastien heard the comment, but he was already walking toward the exit. Etienne's suggestion that Terri might have stepped outside for some fresh air was a possibility that he hadn't considered. That was probably where she was, he assured himself. She was no doubt sitting out in front of the Hilton on the marble base—the place where they'd snogged like teenagers the night he'd taken her to *The Phantom of the Opera.*

He smiled to himself, relaxing at the memory. It was just coincidence that the wedding reception was being held at the same place they had enjoyed such a lovely end to a wonderful date. But it was a lovely co-incidence. This was the perfect spot for him to admit his love, and to have the talk he planned to have with her. Bastien was going to tell her he loved her, and ask her to marry him, and if she admitted she loved him back, which he was pretty sure she did—at least, he hoped to God she did—then he would tell her everything. If all went as he hoped, he would take Terri back to the penthouse and turn her tonight. Then they could begin their lives together.

Of course, there was a possibility she would need

some time to adjust to what he told her. It wasn't like he was announcing he was Catholic or something. She would have to adjust her whole way of thinking, her beliefs. He reconsidered: Perhaps he should only tell her the part about his loving her and wanting to marry her here at the hotel. She was staying at the penthouse tonight, since Kate would be off on her honeymoon. He would wait until he had her there, make slow passionate love to her, *then* explain about—

No, the penthouse was no good, Bastien realized suddenly. The entire family would be staying there, and Vincent hadn't been joking when he said that Terri was loud. The woman was as uninhibited in the bedroom as she was everywhere else. Though he suspected she'd try to be quiet in the penthouse with his family there. Especially his mother. Bastien didn't want Terri feeling stifled. He *liked* her passion. Perhaps they could just stay at Kate's apartment.

By this time, Bastien had reached the exit to the Hilton. He pushed through the revolving door, then paused on the sidewalk, his eyes searching for Terri in her pale lavender dress. He frowned when he didn't see her. Where had she gone?

"Would you like a taxi, sir?"

"What?" Bastien glanced at the doorman distractedly. He started to shake his head, then paused to ask, "You haven't seen a woman out here in a long lavender gown, have you?"

The man hesitated. "Pretty? Long brown hair? Big green eyes?"

"That's her," Bastien said with relief. Finally, someone who had seen her.

"Yes, sir. I put her in a taxi about half an hour ago."

"A taxi?" Bastien echoed stupidly.

"Yes, sir."

Bastien stood for a moment, bewildered. Why would she have gone in a taxi? Why would she leave the wedding reception at all? He couldn't imagine anything that would make Terri walk out of her cousin's wedding reception. Especially without telling anyone.

Unless she'd spilled something on her dress and needed to change, he thought suddenly. That thought took hold, and Bastien found himself relaxing again. Of course, that was it. Terri had said herself that she was a bit of a clutz. She'd probably spilled something on her dress and rushed off to change.

"Did you want a taxi, too, sir?" the man asked again, lifting his whistle in preparation for calling one.

"Oh, no, thanks." Bastien pulled his cell phone from his pocket and moved to the side to call for the car he'd reserved for the night. The driver had been waiting around the corner, and pulled up within moments. Bastien slid in, ordering the man to take him home. He was at the penthouse, inserting his key in the elevator, before it occurred to him that Terri didn't have a key. And her things weren't here yet. They'd planned to pick them up after the reception. He walked to the car that still sat waiting and got back in again.

"Where to now, sir?" his driver asked. Bastien just sat there.

It was a problem, Bastien thought; he didn't know where to go. His first instinct had been the penthouse, because she'd planned to stay there. But her things were all at Kate's. However, Terri didn't have the key to Kate's place—he had it in his tuxedo pocket. She didn't have a key, didn't have a purse, and didn't have money. Of course, she might not have thought of that when she'd set out, not if she was upset about a spill on her dress or something. Terri might have ridden all the way out to Kate's, only to have to turn around and return to the reception.

That was probably it, Bastien thought. Terri was probably already back at the hotel and looking for him to fetch the key. He suddenly grinned to himself. He'd pay the taxi and have his driver take them to Kate's so she could change. Then, if he had it his way, they wouldn't bother returning to the reception. At least not for a while.

"Back to the hotel," he instructed, relaxing back into his seat. Terri was probably in a tizzy right this moment. He'd have to calm her down. Bastien could think of lots of ways to do that. Most of them didn't include clothes.

Terri settled in her seat on the plane, and immediately felt some of the tension leave her. She hadn't been at all sure she'd make it. She'd half feared that Bastien would show up looking for her. Surely, the message she'd left earlier had been given to Kate? If not, then someone would have certainly noticed her missing by now. She hoped no one was too worried.

Terri glanced at the phone set into the seat in front

of her. Just in case Kate's message had gone astray, she would call the hotel and leave a message for Vincent as well. But she wouldn't risk it until the flight was in the air.

"Cousin!"

Bastien stopped his pacing—a pacing he'd been doing for the last hour and a half—and glanced at the man rushing toward him. Vincent. Bastien had returned to the hotel to find that Terri hadn't come back. He'd decided then that her cabbie had probably had a fit when she admitted she couldn't pay, and had refused to return her to the Hilton. He'd imagined her walking the streets of New York, and had made his driver drive him back and forth along the routes she could have taken, but found no sign of her. Then Bastien had resigned himself to pacing here, every moment making him more tense as he imagined all the ways she could be hurt or killed before she made it to the hotel. A beautiful woman, dressed in a long, possibly stained maid-of-honor gown, walking alone down the street? The imaginings he'd come up with were nightmares.

He was actually grateful for the distraction Vincent offered. "Are Kate and Lucern leaving?"

"Actually, they are. But that's not why I'm here. I just got a call from Terri."

Bastien relaxed and tensed all in the same moment. A call from her meant she was all right and able to make the call, but she was probably in trouble somewhere—especially if Vincent's grim expression was anything to go by.

"Where is she?" he asked, cutting to the heart of the matter.

"On a plane on her way back to England."

"What?" Vincent couldn't have shocked him more if he'd said she was calling from jail.

His cousin nodded. "I happened to be passing the desk on my way out here to see you when I heard my name mentioned. The clerk was taking a message for me, so I took the phone. It was Terri. She was calling from the plane."

"But, what is she—Why did she—?" Bastien struggled to understand.

"It seems she overheard Kate and Lissianna talking in the ladies' room," Vincent said grimly. "They were discussing your not having told her about your 'state.'"

Bastien's shoulders slumped. She knew what he was. Now she was running from him just as Josephine had done.

"No. Terri misunderstood. She thought they meant you were terminally ill. When I said that wasn't so, she said not to bother lying to her—she'd seen the medicine and blood. She said she knew you were ill. Terri thinks you're dying, like her mother did, like her husband did, and she said she can't watch you die, too. She loves you too much to be able to bear it."

"She loves me?"

Vincent nodded, then grinned. "Well? What are you waiting for? Get in your car and get to the airport. Follow her," he said. "You have to go explain the truth. Tell her everything. She loves you, Bastien.

You need to tell her you aren't dying, and that she will never have to watch you die a long lingering death."

"Yes!" Bastien grinned as he realized that, in this instance, his state could be an advantage. Chuckling, he turned and gestured to his driver. Thinking he would need it when Terri arrived, he'd made the man stay here with the car. Now, the engine started and the car moved forward.

"Have a good trip, and give her a hug and a hello for me," Vincent said. He walked with Bastien to the curb, then added seriously, "I'm happy for you, cousin."

"Thanks, Vincent," Bastien said. He slid into the backseat of his car.

"No problem. Just don't mess up, huh? She's perfect for you. Much nicer than that holier-than-though Josephine."

Bastien paused in surprise. He'd been about to pull the door closed. "I thought you liked Josephine."

Vincent wrinkled his nose and shook his head. "None of us did. But you thought you loved her, so we would have put up with her. The good news is, none of us has to pretend to like Terri. She's a sweetheart." Then Vincent slammed the door closed and gave him a thumbs-up. The car pulled away.

Chapter Nineteen

"Ter!"

Terri glanced up and spotted Dave at once. It would be impossible not to spot her brother-in-law. Being tall, prematurely gray, and good-looking made him stand out in most crowds. Forcing a weary smile, she turned in his direction as she came through the arrivals gate. "Dave. Thank you for coming to get me."

"No problem." He gave her a hug in greeting and took the handle of her suitcase in one smooth move. "How was your flight?"

"Long," she said on a sigh.

"Isn't it always?" he asked. "A shame they got rid of the Concorde."

"Yes."

"You look . . ." Her brother-in-law hesitated to say it, but he didn't have to; Terri knew how she looked.

"Awful?" she suggested helpfully.

"Well, I wouldn't have put it quite so bluntly, but yes, you look awful," he admitted, concern now crowding his eyes.

"Wore herself out with all that partying she did in New York, no doubt. It's a good thing she's home and can rest now."

"Sandi!" Terri turned to embrace the shorter redhead, who had appeared from the crowd. "When I didn't see you, I thought perhaps you were working on a deadline or something."

"She is. But that wouldn't stop her coming to pick up her favorite sister-in-law," Dave said staunchly, slipping his free hand around his wife's shoulder to hug her close.

"No, it wouldn't," Sandi agreed, hugging him back. She smiled, then explained, "I was in the ladies' room . . . as I usually am when the important stuff happens."

Her words made Dave chuckle, and they brought the first sincere smile to Terri's lips since she'd left Kate and Lucern's wedding reception.

"Well, come on," Dave said suddenly. "Let's get you out of here and home."

He ushered the two women to the parking elevators. The couple chatted about the traffic on the ride in, and about what had happened while Terri was away, leaving her to merely listen and absorb the fact that she was home again. The funny thing was, it didn't feel like home anymore. Nothing seemed quite the same as when she'd left. Their accents—accents

337

she had lived among for ten years, and probably picked up a bit of herself over time—sounded foreign to her ears. The cars they passed as they walked through the parking garage to Dave's black Jaguar seemed oddly shaped, small and strange after two weeks among larger, sleeker North American models. Even riding on the left-hand side of the road no longer seemed normal. In truth, Terri had adjusted so quickly to being back in the States, England now felt as foreign as it had the first time she came.

"So, tell us about the wedding. Did it go off without a hitch?"

A small burst of laughter slipped from Terri's lips.

Sandi, who had asked the question and turned in the front seat to include her in the conversation, raised her eyebrows slightly at Terri's response. "Oh, now you have to explain that reaction," she said. "It sounds like quite the story."

"The wedding," Terri said with a hollow smile; then she launched into a recounting of the calamities that had befallen Kate's wedding and what she and Bastien had done to resolve them. She managed to fill the entire ride back to Huddersfield with the tale, winding down just as they turned onto the street where Dave and Sandi lived.

"We thought you'd like to stop in for tea before we take you home," Dave explained. "We knew you wouldn't have anything at home to eat, and thought this would give you the chance to unwind a bit. We'll take you to Sainsbury's to pick up groceries before we drive you home, too. Is that all right?"

"Yes, that's fine. Thank you." Terri met his gaze in

338

the rearview mirror and nodded. It was more than fine with her. She really didn't look forward to being on her own in her little cottage again. Terri knew, the moment she was alone, all those thoughts and memories she was trying so hard to forget would come crowding in.

"I'll make the tea while you girls catch up," Dave offered as he parked the car.

"You're a good man, Dave," Terri said with affection.

"He's better than good," Sandi announced. They got out. "He's a star."

"So are you, flower," her husband responded, taking her hand and dropping a quick kiss on her forehead before turning toward the house.

Terri smiled as she followed the couple inside, but her heart was aching a little at their easy affection. It reminded her of Bastien.

"Well!" Sandi led the way into the living room and dropped onto the couch with a sigh, then raised her eyebrows at Terri. "Now that we're alone, would you care to talk about this Bastien and what he did to break your heart?"

Terri stiffened, then glanced sharply at her sister-in-law.

"What makes you think he broke my heart?" she asked finally. "Or that I love him, for that matter?"

"Oh, please." Sandi gave a laugh. "Every other word out of your mouth has been 'Bastien.' And you didn't fly home early, looking like death warmed over, because things were going well. So, spill it. What did he do?"

"Actually, he didn't do anything. I'm the one who

339

left him," Terri admitted slowly. The story poured out of her. She recounted every moment of the last two weeks, without leaving anything out. She didn't even slow down or acknowledge Dave when he came back into the room to join them. It was like a purging of her soul.

The couple sat silent throughout, not saying a word until Terri finished and sat back to await their thoughts. Those thoughts weren't long in coming. Knowing the couple as she did, Terri had expected Sandi to be sympathetic and Dave to perhaps think she was an idiot, so she was taken by surprise when her sister-in-law shook her head and said, "You stupid girl."

Terri stiffened in shock, but Sandi wasn't finished. "You found true love—your perfect match—and allowed fear to make you throw it aside? You *idiot!*"

While Terri was gasping, Sandi slapped her hands on her thighs and sat back to cross her arms over her chest. "That's it, then. I suppose you'll be moving to France next."

"What?" Terri asked, confused.

"Well, I presume you love us."

"Of course, I do," Terri said. "I don't know what I would have done after Ian's death without you two to—"

"So," Sandi interrupted with a shrug, "you'd best move to France and get away from us. The more time you spend around us, the more you'll love us—and you know we'll die someday too."

"It's not the same," Terri protested.

"Certainly, it is. Love is love, and loss is loss. We all

340

love, and we all die, and everyone suffers the pain of grieving. The trick is to enjoy what you have *while you have it*. Not run like a bunny from the good things because they might be taken away sooner than you'd like."

"But—"

"Do you regret the time you had with Ian? Would you give that up, have it wiped from your memory to avoid the pain of having lost him?" she asked. "Or your mother? Do you wish she'd died giving birth to you so that you wouldn't have had to suffer losing her at nineteen? Then, as I said, there's Dave and me. If we grow sick, will you stop visiting and shun us? Or if I walk out that door and get hit by a bus, will you regret knowing me because of the pain losing me causes? Will it hurt less today than tomorrow, or next week, or next year?"

"No, of course not."

"That's because you love us, Terri. And you love this Bastien. The only difference is you gave him up before you *had* to. You're suffering *for nothing*. You're causing it yourself. You're being a fool."

"That's a bit harsh, isn't it, flower?" Dave asked mildly.

"Is it?" Sandi turned raised eyebrows on him. "How would you feel if I ran off on you, not because of something you did wrong, or because I didn't love you, but because I *did* love you and you were sick? Because I might hurt later?"

Dave's eyes widened, and Sandi nodded. "Uh huh. Well, that's about how this Bastien feels right now. Terri's punishing him because she loves him and he's

341

dared to be ill, to be human. He's probably hurting right now and not even knowing what he did to make her leave."

"But Dave loves you," Terri pointed out.

"And this Bastien loves you," Sandi said firmly. "Everything you've told me about him tells me that. And here you are, hurting both him and yourself, for no good reason other than you're a coward. It takes courage to live, Terri. To really live. To follow your dreams, to love someone, to face each day. Agoraphobics are trapped in their homes because they are terrified of what *might* happen—but as long as they stay inside, they'll never know what *could* happen. You're an emotional agoraphobic. You've been one since Ian died, avoiding emotional entanglements to avoid getting hurt. Well, it's high time you rejoined the living, my girl, and stopped acting like you're the one in the cold hard grave. I bet Ian would give anything to be alive and in love, yet here you have it and you're throwing it away." Sandi shook her head and stomped out of the room, muttering, "I'm going back to work. Sometimes people make me crazy."

Terri bit her lip and glanced at Dave, who patted her arm reassuringly. "She's just stressed out with this deadline. She loves you. We both do, and we hate to see you unhappy. You've been so unhappy for so long, Terri. And it's upsetting to see you throw something good away."

"But he's *dying,* Dave," Terri complained. "I can't watch that happen again."

"Are you sure he's dying? Do you know for sure? Perhaps it's something chronic, not terminal. Or maybe he's got five to ten good years. Do you want to miss those to avoid six months to a year of hard times? I'm not saying it would be easy at the end, but can't you enjoy the time you do have and not worry so much about what you'll lose?" He added, "You know, Sandi's right. She could walk out the door and die tomorrow. So could I. Or even, you. Even if Bastien is terminally ill, he might outlive you. We can't live on *might-be*s. Because nothing is set in stone."

Terri lowered her head, her mind running in circles. Confusion seemed to be the key word for the last day and a half. She was exhausted, and that made it difficult to think.

"You look done in," Dave commented. "Why don't you lie down on the couch and rest a bit? I'll wake you when the tea's ready."

"Yes. I think I'll do that," Terri murmured. "I've been awake for more than twenty-four hours, and more than thirteen of those were spent in airports or airplanes."

"Then you can definitely use the sleep. Have a lie-down." He urged her onto the couch, grabbed one of the fluffy pillows that sat on either end, and settled it under her head. Fetching an afghan off the chair, he laid it over her.

"Thank you," Terri murmured. "Sandi's lucky to have you. And so am I."

"Hmm." Dave cleared his throat and looked uncomfortable. Shrugging, he muttered that she should sleep, and left her alone.

Terri slept. They didn't wake her for tea, but let

343

her sleep through the night. She woke up at five o'clock the next morning, feeling like a bag of dirt. But a well-rested bag of dirt. Smiling faintly to herself, Terri got up and folded the blanket someone had put on her in the night, then folded the afghan as well. She collected fresh clothes from her suitcase and made her way up the stairs to the bathroom, managing to take a shower without waking the couple asleep just across the hall. Terri dressed, brushed her teeth, and went back downstairs. She fixed herself tea in the kitchen, took it outside, and sat on the picnic table, staring blankly at the wilderness growing there as she considered everything Sandi had said, and everything she herself knew.

In truth, Terri didn't know for sure that Bastien was terminally ill. Yet all the evidence seemed to point that way. She decided that she would go on the premise that she was right and make her decision from there, because she needed to know what she wanted if Bastien was going to die. If he wasn't, the answer was simple; she wanted to be with him. But marriage was about sickness *and* health, better *or* worse—there was no line stating *so long as ye both shall be healthy and happy.* Terri needed to know if she loved him enough to be willing to stand by him through the hard stuff, too. If she could be strong enough to do so.

She stared at the brick wall surrounding Dave and Sandi's little cottage, and imagined the days ahead without him. It seemed a pretty bleak world without Bastien. Then she imagined her time with him, and remembered how it already had been. The laughter, the talk, the working together in a crisis—Terri wanted that. She didn't want to lose it after having it. But, in effect, she already had. Sandi was right, she'd given it up already. As for suffering his illness with him, she had been through it twice before. Terri knew that she would be checking with Kate to see how Bastien was. She wouldn't be able to help herself. The updates she received, along with her past experience and her imagination, were enough for her to know exactly what he was suffering and to suffer with him, whether she was there to see it physically or not.

She *was* a coward and a fool, Terri realized. She'd passed up days, months, maybe even years of happiness by anticipating the bad that would follow. There were no guarantees in life. Even if Bastien were dying, she might—as Dave suggested—beat him to the grave. Standing abruptly, Terri walked back into the cottage and rinsed her cup. Then she wrote a quick note to her friends and picked up the phone to call a cab.

"If you can wait ten minutes while I dress, I'll drive you."

Terri glanced to the doorway where Dave stood in a pair of fleece pants and a top. She'd forgotten he was an early riser. "I could catch a cab. Then you won't have to bother."

"I want to run over to Sainbury's for a couple at things, anyway. And I know you need to stop there before going home. I'll just be a minute." He didn't give her the chance to refuse, simply turned and jogged back upstairs. Two minutes later, Sandi came down in her housecoat, yawning.

"Oh." She shook her head as the yawn ended, as if trying to shake herself awake, then glanced at Terri. "I'm sorry about what I said."

"Don't be. You were right."

Sandi shrugged. "I could have said it more diplomatically."

Terri grinned, and hugged her. "I love you."

"You're going to him," Sandi said. There was a sadness in her eyes as they parted. "You should be able to find a teaching position over there in one of the universities. I know you'll be happy. But we'll miss you."

Terri felt a thickness at the back of her throat. She'd depended on this couple as her only nearby family for a long time. She forced a smile. "Well, don't jump the gun. He might not want me."

Sandi snorted. "Yeah, right."

"And if he did, he might not now because I ran out on him."

"He'll forgive you," Sandi predicted. "You'll just have to grovel and admit you've been an idiot."

Terri chuckled, then glanced to the doorway as Dave came jogging back down the stairs. "Right! I'm ready. I'll be back shortly, flower," He gave Sandi a quick kiss, grabbed Terri's suitcase handle, then paused and turned back for another kiss before leading the way out of the cottage.

"Drive carefully," Sandi called from the doorstep.

"I will, flower. Now go back to bed—you were up late working."

"Nag," she muttered affectionately.

"I heard that."

"Of course you did," she said with a grin, then waved at Terri and went back inside.

Terri shook her head with amusement as she got into the passenger seat of the Jaguar. "You two were made for each other."

"Yes, we were," Dave agreed. He grinned as he started the car, then sent it racing down the street.

Bastien was dozing in the front seat of his rental car when the car roared up behind him. Blinking his eyes open, he saw a black Jaguar pull to a stop with two passengers inside. It took a moment for his sleep-fogged mind to recognize Terri in the passenger seat, then he spotted the man with her and he woke right up. It was seven o'clock in the morning. She hadn't been in last night when he'd arrived, and he'd sat in the car outside her little cottage waiting, until he'd dozed off. He'd slept fitfully in the car, worried sick, wondering if she'd missed a connection, or run into trouble or what. But here she was returning now . . . and with another man? Bastien thought he might pop the bastard.

Opening the door, he slid out of his car. Propping his hands on his hips, he watched the couple get out of the car behind his.

"Bastien!" Terri sounded more shocked than happy to see him, he decided; and that was irritating to his sleep-deprived mind too. And blood-deprived, he reminded himself. He wasn't sure how long it had been since he fed, but he knew it was too long. Maybe he'd bite the guy with Terri rather than pop him.

"Dave, this is Bastien," she said to the tall, silver-haired man who tugged Terri's suitcase out of the trunk of the black car. *Prematurely* silver-haired, Bastien realized as the fellow closed the trunk and moved toward him, dragging the suitcase on its wheels. He took a step forward.

"Bastien, this is David Simpson, my brother-in-law," she introduced. "Dave and his wife, Sandi, picked me up from the airport yesterday. I fell asleep on their couch last night."

Bastien felt all the hot air flow out of him. Brother-in-law. With a wife. "Oh," he said, then held out his hand in greeting. "Pleased to meet you."

"Pleased to meet you too," Dave said with a grin. He placed the handle of Terri's suitcase in Bastien's hand rather than shaking it.

Bastien stared down at the suitcase as Dave turned and hugged Terri. "I have to go. Sandi will worry. Call and let us know what happens."

Bastien lifted his head to watch the man roar off in his Jaguar. "Nice car."

"It's Dave's pride and joy," Terri said. "Would you like to come in?"

Bastien nodded, then followed her up the sidewalk, only then noticing that she was carrying a grocery bag. Obviously, her brother-in-law had taken her shopping before bringing her home, he realized. He followed Terri into her small cottage, his eyes moving curiously around the place as he closed the door. It was small but cozy and tastefully decorated, he noted; then Terri whirled to face him.

"I'm sorry," she blurted. "I'm so sorry. I shouldn't have run off like that."

"Terri—"

"No, wait. Let me speak," Terri insisted. "I made a mistake. A stupid mistake because I was scared. I . . . I love you, Bastien. I do. And the idea of your being ill and watching you go through what Ian and my mother went through scares the heck out of me, but I'm willing to do it if I can spend however much good time you have left with you. I'll take the bad with the good. I'll—"

"I'm not sick," Bastien interrupted.

Terri paused and stared, uncomprehending. "What?"

"I'm not sick," he repeated firmly.

"But the vials in your fridge."

"The vials?" he asked. Then understanding slowly dawned. "Vincent's serum?"

"*Vincent's* serum?" Terri echoed.

"Yes. You know about his digestive trouble. The lab sent those up for him to try. It's a new serum we hope will help," he answered, couching his words carefully so that he was telling the truth, but not revealing everything. Yet.

Terri sank onto the sofa with a plop. "The serum is Vincent's."

"Yes."

"But what about the blood and the IV stand?"

"The IV stand? In the closet of the master suite?" he asked with surprise.

She nodded.

"That's been there a long time. Lissianna needed it at one time, and we've just never gotten rid of it."

"Lissianna?" Terri's voice was a squeak.

"Yes. Lissianna."

"And the blood?" she asked hopefully.

Bastien hesitated. This was where it got tricky.

Terri went on, "And Kate said you had something to tell me that we would have to work out if *we* were going to work out."

"That's true," he admitted, glad to avoid the blood for the time being. "There *is* something that I'll need to discuss with you if you agree to marry me, but it isn't that I'm terminally ill. I'm not ill at all."

"You want to marry me?" Terri asked with pleasure.

Bastien rolled his eyes. "Terri, honey. I just flew two thousand three hundred miles chasing after you. It wasn't to ask you on a date."

"Oh, Bastien!" She launched herself off the couch. Bastien caught her with an, "oomph," then found his face peppered with little butterfly kisses.

"Terri, honey, hang on. We do have to talk."

"Later," she murmured. "I've been so miserable since hearing Lissianna and Kate in the bathroom, I—" She paused and peered at him with question. "What were they talking about—that I should understand, because of Ian? I thought they were saying that you were ill, and I should be able to understand and deal with it because of my experiences with Ian."

"We have to talk," Bastien repeated with a sigh.

"Just tell me," she said.

"It's not something you just blurt out, Terri."

"Now you're making me nervous again."

"I'm sorry, but it's . . ." Taking her hands, he drew her back to the sofa and settled beside her. "It's not bad," he started, hoping she would agree.

"It isn't?"

"No." He glanced around the living room of her cottage, absently noting the comfortable charm as he tried to think of the best way to tell her. "Well," he said finally, "have you ever seen the movie *An American Werewolf in London*?"

She gave a perplexed laugh. "Yes. Hasn't everyone?"

He nodded. "Well, I'm not American, or a werewolf, and we aren't in London."

She blinked several times at his comment. Then she said slowly, "No, this is Huddersfield."

"And I'm Canadian and a vampire," he finished brightly.

"Uh . . . huh," she said slowly. "Bastien, are you feeling well?"

"Terri—"

"Is this your idea of a joke?"

She was getting annoyed, he thought with alarm. How the heck had Etienne and Lucern told Rachel and Kate that they were vampires? "Terri, honey," he began. "It's not a joke. I really am a vampire."

"Oh. I see." She was getting snippy. That was interesting. He'd never seen her snippy before. Well, perhaps with the cashier at Victoria's Secret. No, Bastien decided, Terri had put the clerk in her place, but she had not got snippy with the girl.

"You're a vampire." Her voice was disbelieving, and she was nodding her head up and down in a way that didn't look promising. "Fine. Bite me."

Terri held her arm out in challenge, and Bastien frowned. "Terri, I don't want to bite you," he said. Then he paused and said more honestly, "Well, actu-

351

ally, I am a pit peckish right at the moment, but I'd rather not—"

"Uh-huh. Bite me!" she snapped. "If you're a vampire, bite me."

Bastien peered at her arm for a minute, then took it in hand, lifted it up, and bit her.

"Ouch!" Terri leapt off the couch, retrieving her arm as she went. Bastien had to snap his teeth back double quick to keep from ripping her vein and flesh. "You bit me! You've got fangs!"

"Now do you believe me?"

Clutching her arm to her chest, she began to back away.

"Please don't be afraid of me, Terri. I love you," he said softly, taking a step after her and holding out his hand in pleading. He was relieved when she hesitated. "Honey, this is a good thing. Really. You'll never have to worry about my dying a horrible, lingering death," he offered. "I won't die like your mother and Ian. I can't."

She stared at him. "Your father is dead. Was he staked?"

"No. He burned to death. We can burn to death." Then he added quickly, "But that wouldn't be a long lingering illness. None of the ways we can die are long and lingering."

"So, the blood in your fridge . . ."

"Was to feed. We don't bite humans anymore, not unless absolutely necessary."

"You aren't human."

"Yes, of course we are. Sort of. We're just a different nationality, really. We're almost immortal, as opposed to mortal. Atlantean rather than British. Well, we're Canadian now. At least my family is." He paused and frowned; he was really making a flub of this. "Look, honey, sit down and I'll explain everything. Our vampirism is scientific in basis, not a curse or something. We aren't soulless. That night-walking demon thing everyone thinks vampires are—well, it was all just a big misunderstanding."

Terri didn't sit down; instead she narrowed her eyes. "So vampires can walk in daylight?"

"Yes." He frowned. "Well, the sun does a lot of damage, of course. And going out in it means we have to consume a lot more blood to make up for it, but we can go out in it without bursting into flames or anything."

She seemed to accept that, but then, she had seen him in sunlight. She asked, "How old are you?"

Bastien sighed. "Four hundred and twelve."

"Four hundred and—jeez." She sat, then stiffened. "So, all that stuff you knew when we visited the museum . . ."

"I was there for the stuff I was telling you," he admitted. "Not the medieval stuff, just from the 1600s through now."

"Is that all?" she asked dryly. Then shook her head and muttered, "This is nuts."

"No, it's science," Bastien explained. "See, our Atlantean scientists made nanos that would repair and regenerate the body, but they use blood at an acceler ated rate to do so, a rate the body can't keep up with. Thus, we need to ingest more blood to feed them and stay healthy. We drink blood to survive, like diabetics need insulin injected because they don't produce enough of their own."

"Atlanteans," Terri muttered. "I went and fell in love with the man from Atlantis." She glanced up sharply. "You don't have webbed fingers and toes, too, or something, do you?"

Bastien sighed, trying to remain patient. There was so much myth around both Atlantis and vampires. None of it ever tied together, however, thank goodness. "Honey, you've seen me naked. All of me. You know I don't have gills and fins."

"Oh, yes." She was silent, then cleared her throat. "Bastien?"

"Yes?" he asked hopefully.

"I think I'd like you to leave. I need some time to . . . er . . . digest this."

He felt his stomach drop. "How much time?"

"I'm not sure," she admitted.

Bastien stared at her for a minute, then stood and moved to the door. He paused, then glanced back to ask, "You won't tell anyone, will you?"

"No, of course not. They'd think I was nuts, anyway."

He nodded. "Good. Because you'd threaten my whole family—including Kate."

"Kate?" Terri's head snapped up.

Bastien nodded. "Lucern turned her. She's his life mate."

"Was she willing?"

"Of course she was," he snapped. "We don't go turning people without their permission. Well, we did Rachel," he admitted. "But she was an exception. She was dying, and we had to save her."

"Rachel is a vampire, but wasn't one before?" she asked.

"No."

"And Greg?"

"Your garden variety Canadian psychologist—until he and Lissianna fell in love and she turned him."

Terri nodded slowly. "So, for me to be your mate, you'd have to turn me?"

"Yes. If you were willing."

"And if I wasn't?"

"Then I'd have to watch you age and weaken and die, just as you did Ian and your mother—only over a much longer period of time, of course. I'd do that for you, Terri. And I'd love you till the end. It would kill me, but . . . we mate for life in our family." He opened the door, took a step out, then turned. "I'll be staying at the George Hotel for two nights, then I fly back to America."

Terri nodded slowly, and he nodded back; then he pulled the door closed and walked to his rental car. Bastien didn't know if he'd done the right thing leaving her with this knowledge. He might be risking his entire family. But love was about trust, and he trusted Terri. She loved him, and while she might not be able to accept what he was in the end, she would never set out to hurt him.

Terri unwrapped her prawn sandwich, took a bite, then set it down with a sigh and glanced out her office window. Prawn was her favorite, but it didn't taste very good at the moment. Nothing did since she'd left New York. Since leaving Bastien.

Terri grimaced and picked up her sandwich again. It had been almost a week since Bastien had left her cottage. And while she had said she needed time to digest what he'd told her . . . well, she had indigestion. She couldn't quite seem to get a grip on what he was. Terri understood what he had said, and while she knew there was probably a lot more explanation, she could mostly comprehend the nanos and blood bit. But understanding and believing and accepting were vastly different things. Terri *understood* what he claimed to be, she *believed* it was possible, but she was having trouble *accepting* it. Her wonderful, sweet, perfect, fairy-tale romance had turned out to have a twist. Prince Charming was a bloodsucker.

"That looks tasty."

Terri glanced up at that dry comment, then leapt to her feet. "Kate!"

"Hi." Grinning, the other woman removed her sunglasses and started forward, walking around the desk with every intention of hugging her.

Fear shooting through her, Terri instinctively held her hand out to stop her cousin, then blinked at the sandwich she was holding up like some Victorian wench holding up a cross.

"Bite?" she offered lamely.

Kate stared at the sandwich, burst out laughing and took it. She tossed it in the garbage bin under Terri's desk, snatched her hand, and drew her towards the door. "Come on, we're going to Harvey Nichols for lunch."

"Oh, but Harvey Nichols is so expensive," Terri protested, dragging her feet.

Much to her amazement, it didn't even slow Kate down. Terri had to wonder if the added-strength bit in vampire movies was true.

"It is," Kate answered, as if she'd spoken the thought aloud. She grabbed Terri's light spring coat off the rack as she dragged her cousin past it.

"You can read my mind?" Terri asked, shocked.

"Yes. That's true, too," Kate said mildly.

"So, all that time, Bastien could read my mind?" she asked in horror. "He knew what I was thinking?"

"Nope. He couldn't read your mind. Which is why you two are perfect together."

"It is?"

"Uh-huh."

"Kate, I don't think . . ." Terri paused abruptly as her cousin stopped walking and turned to face her, eyes narrowed.

"Terri, I am Kate. The same Kate you've always known. The cousin you love, who loves you. The girl you used to hunt tadpoles with. Nothing has changed. And it upsets me that you would be afraid of me because of a change in my medical condition." She paused, then added, "Especially since I took time out of my *honeymoon* to come here and straighten out what Bastien messed up."

"Your honeymoon?" Terri whispered.

"Yes. My honeymoon," Kate repeated. "The

minute Marguerite called and told me what happened, I insisted Lucern and I change our original plans to include Huddersfield, England, as part of our tour. Then I left Lucern all alone and lonely in the George Hotel and caught the train here to Leeds to see you, all because I love you. I want you happy. I would never hurt you. If I'd wanted to bite you, I could have done so countless times while you were staying with me in New York, but I didn't. I don't bite. Now, please just come to lunch and let me maybe make more sense of this for you. That way, you can at least make an informed decision."

Terri hesitated then nodded. "All right."

Chapter Twenty

"Bastien, you aren't listening to me," Marguerite Argeneau accused.

"Yes, I am, mother," Bastien said, a tad impatiently. He didn't bother to lift his eyes from the file he was reading.

"Then what did I say?"

Bastien set down the papers he'd been going through, and sat back in his chair to give her his undivided attention. Not that she noticed; she wasn't looking at him at all, but was pacing back and forth in front of his desk with agitation. Sighing wearily, he recounted, "You said that you received a letter from someone this morn—"

"From Vincent," she cut in.

"Fine, from Vincent," he repeated dutifully, then paused to frown. "Why would Vincent send you a letter? He's staying in the penthouse with us. Why didn't he just—"

"Good lord, you really are out of it," Marguerite interrupted. Pausing in front of his desk, she scowled at him over her crossed arms, then heaved a sigh and reminded him, "Vincent is back in California."

"Is he?"

"Yes. He is. He flew home a week ago."

"What about his play?" Bastien asked with a frown. "*Dracula,* the musical?"

She gave a discounting wave and began to pace again. "The production closed down two weeks ago."

"Already?" His eyes widened. "I should have gone to see it on opening night, but I didn't know it had opened. Did I?" he asked, not at all sure that he hadn't been told and either not paid attention or just let it slip his mind. Many things had slipped his mind since Terri left.

Marguerite stopped her pacing to say with exaggerated patience, "It never made it to opening night, Bastien,"

His eyebrows rose. "Why?"

"They had to close down. Too many of the cast and crew dropped out due to illness."

"What kind of illness?" Bastien asked, his eyes narrowing.

Marguerite hesitated. "They weren't sure."

He couldn't help noticing that his mother was suddenly avoiding his gaze. "Mother," he said in warning tones.

Sighing, she admitted, "They weren't sure, but apparently it was some sort of contagious anemia."

"Contagious anemia," Bastien echoed with disgust. There was no such thing as contagious anemia. Now he knew where Vincent had been doing his feeding since arriving in New York. He shook his head in wonder. "The man ate himself out of his first lead role in a play. Dear Lord! How did he manage that? What was he thinking?"

"I don't think he was," Marguerite said with a sigh. "Thinking, that is. I suspect he was so nervous about his lead role that he just—"

"He didn't seem nervous," Bastien snapped. He had known the man for four hundred years; nothing made him nervous.

"That's true," his mother allowed reluctantly, then her expression cleared. "Well, of course!"

"Of course, what?" Bastien asked, suspecting he didn't want to know.

"Well, it was probably comfort eating."

"Comfort eating?" he repeated incredulously.

"Mmm." Marguerite nodded. "Well, there were Etienne and Lissianna, happy with their life mates, and Lucern marrying his, and you with Terri . . . He was probably lonely, suddenly aware of his solitary status, and overfeeding because of it."

"Dear Lord." Bastien sank back in his seat and shook his head.

"The poor boy," Marguerite murmured.

"Yes, poor boy," Bastien said dryly. He rolled his eyes. His mother had always had a soft spot for Vincent; he was her favorite nephew.

"Perhaps I should go visit him," she murmured thoughtfully.

Bastien perked up at this suggestion. "Perhaps you should. Understanding as you are, you might be able to help him."

"Yes." Marguerite picked up her purse off his desk. "A trip to California would be nice this time of year."

"I hear it's lovely," he agreed encouragingly.

"Yes. I think I will." She slung her purse strap over her shoulder, then paused to peer at him. "You know I love you and wouldn't run off to California to tend Vincent if I didn't already know your little problem was taken care of, don't you?"

Bastien's head jerked slightly. Her comment caught him by surprise. "I don't have a problem," he growled, then added, "And what do you mean it's been taken care of?"

Marguerite ignored the question. Whirling away from the desk, she headed for the door. "Well, I'm off to California. Vincent will no doubt insist I stay with him, so ring me there if you have any . . . news."

"Wait! Mother!" Bastien half rose, then paused and simply sank down in his seat again when the door closed. For a minute, he stared blindly at the closed door, wondering what she had been talking about. Bastien suspected she had meant his broken heart when she spoke of his problem, but he had no idea what she meant when she'd said it was taken care of. The possibilities were endless. No doubt a half-dozen New York psychologists were going to call him over the next couple of days—pretty, single *female* psychologists—all claiming a need to talk to him about his mother.

Bastien scrubbed his hands through his hair with agitation. Marguerite Argeneau had to be the most annoying, interfering . . . And she was now Vincent's problem. For a while, at least.

"Sorry, Vinny," he muttered under his breath. A small smile plucked at his lips at the idea of the chaos his cousin was about to suffer, but it died quickly. As annoying and persistent as she could be, Marguerite Argeneau often got what she wanted. She had managed to get Kate back for Lucern when the woman had fled him for New York. And she had arranged for Thomas to get Etienne and Rachel back together when they had fallen out. It was just a shame she hadn't set her mind to getting Terri back for him.

Not that he wanted her interference, he assured himself.

Meredith was talking on the phone when Terri walked into her office. The woman stopped dead in the middle of her conversation and gaped at her; then she hung up the phone without a word of good-bye or an explanation to whomever she had been talking to. "Am I glad to see you."

Terri smiled. "Well, it's nice to see you too, Meredith."

"Trust me, not as nice as it is for me to see you, Terri." The secretary stood, collected her purse and jacket, and walked around the desk. "He's been a miserable grouch ever since returning from England. He loves you, you know."

"Yes." Terri smiled. "He told me that in Huddersfield. The problem was whether I could handle what you all are." One of the things that Kate had explained was that most of the employees at the upper level were vampires as well. There were many employees at Argeneau Enterprises who weren't, but those in important positions were. It eliminated the possibility of a disgruntled employee blabbing about what they were to the rest of the world.

Meredith paused in front of her and nodded. "And now?"

"And now, I'm unemployed, homeless, and here," Terri said wryly. She'd quit her job, and even managed to sell the cottage before leaving. She intended to look for a position in America, or Toronto, or wherever it was that she and Bastien ended up. If he still wanted her.

Smiling, the secretary leaned forward and hugged her. "Welcome to the family," she said. Then turned to gesture to Bastien's office door. "It's not locked. He'll be happy to see you. I'm going to an early lunch."

"Thank you," Terri said quietly. She waited for the older woman to leave the office before she knocked, waited for his "Enter"—which *was* rather snappish, she noticed—then walked in.

"Meredith, where the hell did I put—" His harassed tones died abruptly as he glanced up and spotted her. "Terri."

"You didn't put me anywhere, but you left me in Huddersfield." She closed the door and crossed the room, suddenly unsure that Kate and Meredith were right, and that he would really be happy to see her. He didn't look too happy.

Bastien was confused for a minute; then he reran his last words to himself—"*Meredith, where the hell did I put . . . Terri.*" Understanding dawned. "I waited the two days."

"I'm a slow thinker," Terri said apologetically. "And thick sometimes. Kate had to come see me before I got over old presumptions."

"Old presumptions?"

"Well, you know. Thirty-three years of vampire movies can leave an impression," Terri explained with a shrug. "I was stuck on the word, not seeing the man. Or the woman, for that matter." She paused in front of his desk. "I was even afraid of Kate when she first showed up at my office in Leeds."

"Kate came to the University?" Bastien asked.

Terri nodded, a small smile tugging at her lips. "She said she just knew that you'd mess up the explaining part."

"I didn't mess up the explaining part," he snapped.

" 'Have you seen the movie *An American Werewolf in London?*' " she quoted back to him. She shook her head and laughed.

Bastien flushed. So, okay—maybe that hadn't been the smoothest opening. Since then, he'd thought of at least a dozen better ways to start.

"I was under a bit of pressure," he excused himself. He gave a weary shrug, then sat back in his seat and eyed her. "Are you going to tell me why you're here? Or are you enjoying torturing me?"

"I'm here because I love you."

That sounded hopeful, he thought, his body tensing.

"And because I hope you still love me."

Bastien stared at her for a minute, part of him wanting to leap over the desk and take her in his arms and show her how much he still loved her. The other part urged caution. "And what about"—he gestured to his body—"my medical condition?"

Terri gave a laugh. "Medical condition?"

Bastien sighed wearily. "You know what I mean."

She hesitated, then asked, "Do you still love me, Bastien? Or are you so hurt that I needed time to think about this that you aren't sure you want anything to do with me anymore?"

"I still love you," he admitted. "I'll love you forever. Or at least for the next four or five hundred years. After that, we might have to work at it."

Terri grinned and walked around the desk.

Bastien watched her, unable to move, still wary, then gave an "oomph" as she dropped into his lap.

"I can accept your 'medical condition,'" she told him. "And I'd like to spend my life, however long it is, with you. Now, if you wouldn't mind, would you make love to me please?" She slid her arms around his shoulders. "I know we still have talking to do, but I really need to feel close to you again. I've felt so cold and scared inside since you left."

Bastien felt some of the numbness that had claimed him for the last three weeks slip away, and compassion took its place. That was how he'd felt; cold and scared, alone inside. It was like all happiness had gone out of his life along with her. Bastien let his arms slide around her waist, and he dipped his head to kiss her.

She was warm in his arms, and sweet on his lips,

but it wasn't until she sighed into his mouth that Bastien felt passion begin to creep warily into him. He'd missed her. He'd missed touching her, talking to her, just being with her. And he'd missed her sighs, her moans, and the way her body moved against his.

Bastien let a hand slide from her waist up to her breast, and he squeezed gently, a small sigh sliding out as she arched her body and moaned in response. He could almost feel the protective ice that had formed around his heart three weeks ago cracking and crumbling away. It left his chest aching. He now understood the phrase "I love you so much it hurts." His heart did hurt, and only Terri could soothe it.

"Terri," he murmured, breaking their kiss and trailing his lips over her cheek. "I need you."

"I need you, too." There was a catch in her voice as she admitted it, an excited breathless sound. Then she caught her fingers in his hair and forced his mouth to hers, kissing him with the passion he remembered and yearned for. The ache in his heart eased, but now the rest of his body ached in its place.

Bastien wanted her badly, and didn't think he could be gentle and caring and considerate about it. His instincts urged him to rip at her clothes and bury himself deep inside her. The hand at her breast shifted to the buttons down the front of her blouse, working them carelessly and popping several in his impatience to feel her skin. It was a relief to get the top open. Then he found himself frustrated by the black satin bra she wore underneath. Terri immediately reached between them and unsnapped the front hook, allowing the material to gape open. Bastien was on those breasts at once, his hands covering and then squeezing the warm soft skin. He broke away and closed his mouth over one erect nipple.

"We should move to the couch," he muttered against her skin.

"No," Terri murmured—and he felt disappointment shift through him as she suddenly slid away and out of his reach. But it seemed Terri wasn't in the mood for much foreplay, either. Before he could suffer disappointment for long, or even move, she settled back onto his lap, this time straddling him.

"You wore a skirt again," he breathed against her breast, then licked at the erect nipple in his face. He ran one hand lightly up her stockinged thigh. "But these will get in the way."

"No, they won't," she assured him. Terri took his hand and guided it up under her skirt to her hip.

Bastien's eyes widened. Those weren't panty hose, but true stockings. And she wasn't wearing any panties. He groaned against her breast, then caught her nipple in his mouth and slid his hands over her bare bottom, wondering how soon would be too soon to enter her.

Terri answered that question by shifting and reaching between them to undo his pants. "I need you *now*, Bastien."

"Thank God," he muttered, sliding one hand between her legs to caress her. He found that she was indeed warm and wet and ready for him.

The moment Terri freed him from his trousers, she brushed his hand away from between her legs and moved, repositioning herself so that she could guide herself onto him.

"Terri . . ." Bastien groaned as she sank slowly down to take him into her. Her wet heat closed around him.

"Yes," she breathed, lifting herself off and sliding back down.

"Damn." His mouth fastened on her neck and he sucked urgently; then he felt his teeth try to slip out to bite her. He forced them back and turned his mouth to her lips instead. Terri kissed back just as hungrily, her body sliding against his as she raised and lowered herself. Her languid rhythm was driving him crazy. He needed fast and hard after so long without her.

Pushing her skirt farther upward and out of the way, he fastened his hands on her hips and urged her on.

Astride him, Terri broke the kiss on a gasp and caught her hand at the back of Bastien's head, urging his mouth against her skin. The tension inside her was building to unbearable levels.

"Bastien, please!" she gasped, begging for release. He almost had her there. Then she felt his teeth sink into her, and she stiffened in surprise.

Terri stopped moving, her body gone taut as she trembled on the knife edge of excitement, but he continued to pump into her as he sucked at her neck. Suddenly, pleasure exploded through her. Wondrous, ecstatic pleasure. Terri cried out, her arms clenching around his neck and shoulders, and her whole body jerking in his arms. Wave after wave of release rode her until Terri didn't think she could stand it anymore, then darkness crowded in.

"You fainted."

Terri blinked her eyes open at those words and stared up at Bastien, then glanced around. He'd moved her to the couch. She was lying on it, her clothing in disarray, while he sat on the edge brushing the hair back from her face with his gentle fingers.

"You bit me," she said with disbelief.

He grimaced. "I'm sorry, I tried not to, but you forced my head back to your neck and I——"

"It's okay," she said quickly to stop his apology. Then she sighed. "Jeez. Kate said it was something, but that was an understatement."

"Are you all right?" he asked with concern.

Terri nodded slowly. She felt all right. She felt better than all right. She felt excellent. Her eyes sought his. "I love you, Bastien. I'm sorry for the last three weeks, but I needed time to accept. It was all so easy, so natural from the start. Like some sort of fairy-tale romance."

"Then it turned into a horror," he said.

"No. Not a horror," Terri said, then admitted, "Well, okay, maybe a little horrorish, but that was only because your explanation——"

"I'm sorry," he interrupted. He gave a slight laugh and ran one hand through his hair. "Can you believe I had to explain it to Rachel for Etienne, because he was flubbing it? Then I turned around and flubbed it with you. I guess it's harder to be smart when it really matters. And it did—*does*—matter to me."

"I know. I understand," Terri assured him. She eased up into a sitting position. She was surprisingly light-headed.

"In my excitement, I got a little carried away," Bastien told her apologetically. "It won't happen again."

"Are you kidding?" she cried. "I sincerely hope it does. That was . . ." Terri shook her head. It was mind-blowing.

Bastien smiled slightly, but said, "Terri, I do love you. But I'm not perfect, and I've made mistakes, and will make lots more over the years. I'm sorry I—"

"Shh." She hushed him and took his face between her hands. "No one's perfect, I'm not perfect, and you're not perfect, Bastien. But you're perfect for me."

They kissed gently, and Bastien pulled back and eyed her. "So, what are you doing for the next forty to fifty years?"

"Hmm." Terri smiled. "Actually, I don't have any plans at the moment. I just quit my job and sold my cottage, so I'm rather at loose ends."

"Yeah?" He grinned. "Would you care to spend them with me?"

"I thought you'd never ask," Terri said with a smile.

"Hmm." His expression turned solemn, telling her what was coming was important to him. Bastien brushed one finger down her cheek, then asked, "Would you care to make it four to five hundred years or more? There's a lot to do in this world, and it would be nice to do it all together."

Terri raised a hand to caress his cheek in return, and nodded. "I think I'd like that."

Bastien let his breath out on a sigh and hugged her tight. "Damn, woman. I love you."

Terri laughed as tears pooled in her eyes. "And I love you."

"Come on." Jumping up, he tugged her to her feet and began straightening her clothes.

"Where are we going?" Terri asked as he pulled her out of his office.

"To the penthouse," he explained, pausing at the elevator to push the button. The doors opened at once and he tugged her inside. "There's champagne and the Jacuzzi, and . . . I want to turn you now and start our lives together."

He pushed the button for the penthouse, then leaned back against the wall and pulled her into his arms. The doors closed, sealing them in. "I can't wait. I suspect that, with you, life is going to be one hell of an adventure."

Bastien bent to kiss her, and Terri sighed into his mouth. She somehow knew he was right. There would be good times and bad, but life together would always be an adventure.

And speaking of adventures; now *she and Bastien* had a wedding to plan.

Turn the page for a sneak peak at the
fourth novel in The Argeneau Vampire series,
A Quick Bite

Prologue

'It's just a *little* dinner party.'

'Uh huh,' Greg Hewitt murmured. Standing, he caught the receiver in the crook between his shoulder and neck, holding it in place with his chin as he began to clean up his desk in preparation of leaving the office. His sister's voice had taken on a wheedling tone which was always a bad sign. Sighing inwardly, he shook his head as she continued rattling on, telling him what she had planned for the meal and so on, all in an effort to convince him to attend. He noticed she wasn't mentioning who else was to be at this little dinner, but suspected he already knew. Greg had no doubt that Jackie had meant for it to be herself, her long suffering husband John, and yet another single

1

female friend she hoped to hook up with her still single older brother.

'So?'

Greg paused and caught the phone in hand. He'd obviously missed something. 'I'm sorry, what was that?'

'So, what time can you get here tomorrow?'

'I won't be coming.' Before she could whine, he added quickly, 'I can't. I'll be out of the country tomorrow.'

'What?' There was a pause, then a suspicious, 'Why? Where are you going?'

'Mexico. I'm going on vacation. That's why I called you in the first place. I fly out first thing in the morning for Cancun.' Knowing he'd just set his sister aback, Greg allowed a smile to tug at his lips as he juggled the phone around to don the suit jacket he'd discarded earlier in the day.

'Mexico?' Jackie said after a long pause. 'A vacation?'

Greg couldn't decide if her bewilderment was amusing or just a sad commentary on his life to date. This was the first vacation he'd taken since starting his psychology practice eight years ago. Actually, he hadn't gone on vacation since starting University. He was a typical workaholic; driven to succeed and willing to put the hours in to do so. It didn't leave much time for a social life. This vacation was long overdue.

2

'Listen, I have to get going. I'll send you a postcard from Mexico. Bye.' He hung up before she could say anything to stop him, then grabbed his briefcase and quickly escaped the office. Greg wasn't surprised to hear the phone start ringing as he locked the office door, Jackie was the persistent sort, but he ignored it. Smiling faintly, he pocketed his keys and started down the hall for the bank of elevators that serviced the whole floor.

Dr. Gregory Hewitt was now officially on vacation and the knowledge made him relax more with every step away from his office. He was actually whistling softly as he boarded the elevator and turned to push the button marked P3. The whistle died, however, and Greg reached instinctively toward the panel, his eyes searching for the hold button to keep the doors open when he realized a woman was hurrying toward the closing doors. He needn't have bothered; the woman was quick on her feet and managed to slip through just before the doors closed.

Greg let the hand he'd half-raised to the panel drop away and stepped politely out of the way so she could select the floor she wanted. He gave her a curious once over as she moved in front of the panel, idly wondering where the woman had come from. The hall had been empty when he'd traversed it and he hadn't heard a door open or close, but then he'd been distracted with thoughts of his coming vacation. There were several offices on this floor besides his own, and she could be from any of them, but he was sure he'd never seen her before. She was not the sort of woman a man forgot in a hurry with her long legs, curvaceous figure and long dark wavy hair.

Greg had only got a glimpse of her face as she'd boarded the elevator and most of her features were a vague blur in his memory, but her eyes had been attention grabbing, a silver-blue he'd never seen before. They were beautiful, but unusual. He now decided they were the result of colored contacts and immediately lost any interest in her. Greg could appreciate a beautiful woman, and had no problem with them making the best of their appearance, but when they moved on to this level of artifice to try to attract attention, he tended to be turned off.

Shrugging her out of his thoughts, he relaxed back against the wall as the elevator began to move. His mind immediately began to fill with his coming trip. Greg had planned a lot of outings, he'd never been anywhere like Mexico before and wanted to enjoy all there was to do. Along with the usual lounging on the beach, he hoped to get in some parasailing, snorkeling and maybe go on one of those boat rides where you got to feed the dolphins.

Greg was also interested in going to the Museo Arqueológico de Cancún to see relics from digs, he

4

definitely wanted to go to the Museum Casa Maya, an ecological park with walking paths where you could see the local animals and a reproduction of how the Mayans lived centuries ago. And he might even give the bullfights a chance, though that idea wasn't really very interesting to him, he hated to see animals suffer. Then there was the night life. Greg had looked into it on the web and thought he might like to have dinner on the Cancun Queen, a paddle wheeler that served dinner as it cruised a lagoon. If he had any energy after that, he might just hit Coco Bongo or the Bulldog café, dance bars full of half-naked people gyrating to deafening music.

The elevator's cheerful ding drew Greg's thoughts from half-naked dancing women to the panel above the doors. P3 was lit up; parking level 3. His floor.

Nodding politely in the general direction of his companion, he stepped off the elevator and started walking through the large, nearly empty parking garage. Half-naked women still dancing on the periphery of his mind, it took Greg a minute or two to notice the sound of footsteps behind him. He almost glanced over his shoulder to see who it was when it did infiltrate his thoughts, and then let the matter go. The sound was the hollow '*tap tap*' of high heels on concrete; sharp and quick and echoing loudly in the nearly empty space. The brunette was obviously also parked on this floor.

His gaze moved absently over the open space toward where his car should be, but got caught on one of the supporting beams as he passed. The large black P1 painted on the concrete beam made him slow in confusion. Parking levels 1 and 2 were reserved for visitors to the various offices and businesses in the building. He was parked on P3 and had been sure the elevator panel light had been on P3 when he'd looked . . . but it appeared he'd misread the sign. Stopping, he started to turn back the way he'd come.

This is the right floor. There is the car ahead.

'Yes, of course,' he murmured under his breath and continued forward. He strode up to the lone vehicle.

It wasn't until he stopped at the back of the car and found himself opening the trunk that the thought broke through his mind that this wasn't his car. His was a dark blue BMW, not this small red sports car. But as quickly as that thought – with its accompanying alarm – claimed him, it blew away like fog under the influence of a breeze.

Relaxing, Greg set his briefcase inside the trunk, climbed in after it, arranged himself in the small space, then pulled the trunk closed, trapping himself inside.

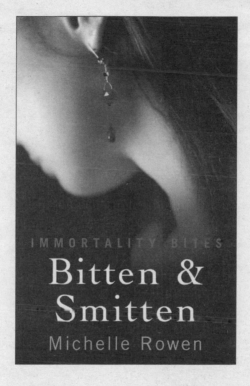

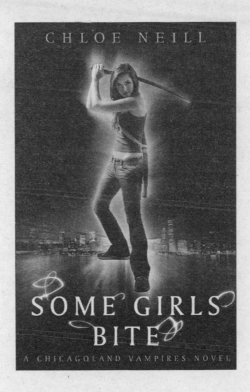

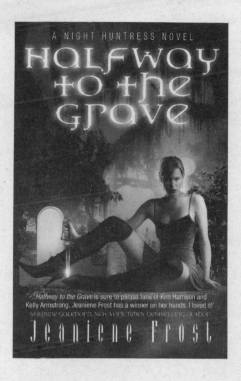

Lynsay Sands was born in Canada and is an award-winning author of over thirty books, which have made the Barnes & Noble and New York Times bestseller lists. She is best known for her Argeneau series, about a modern-day family of vampires.

Learn more about her and her novels at:
www.lynsaysands.net